Michael Collins was born in Limerick in 1964 and educated in Ireland and in the US. His fiction has received international critical acclaim and his work has been translated into numerous languages: his first book was a *New York Times* Notable Book of the Year in 1993, his short story 'The End of the World' was awarded the Pushcart Prize for Best American Short Story and the *Toronto Globe & Mail* selected *The Feminists Go Swimming* as 'one of the must read books of the year'. Michael Collins received his PhD from the University of Illinois in Chicago and he currently lives in Seattle.

BY THE SAME AUTHOR

The Life and Times of a Teaboy
The Feminists Go Swimming (stories)
Emerald Underground

The Meat Eaters

MICHAEL COLLINS

PHŒNIX

A PHŒNIX PAPERBACK

First published in Great Britain by
Jonathan Cape in 1992
This paperback edition published in 1993 by Phoenix,
an imprint of Orion Books Ltd,
Orion House, 5 Upper St Martin's Lane,
London WC2H 9EA

Reissued 1999

A CIP catalogue record for this book
is available from the British Library

ISBN 0 75380 756 4

Printed and bound in Great Britain by
The Guernsey Press Co. Ltd, Guernsey, Channel Islands

Dedicated to my parents and my wife

Thanks to William O'Rourke
Richard Napora
Richard M. Elman

CONTENTS

THE MEAT EATERS

RORY CARRIED AN inordinate amount of dead meat in a suitcase with him when he left for America: racks of hacked spare ribs, dozens of translucent sausages, stuffed rolls of blood pudding mixed with bones, sour-smelling kidneys, dark-lobed livers, and sundry other sanguinary organs. He also had twenty-four pints of Guinness piled in an old orange crate.

His mother kept crying. His father fumbled with a pocket watch on a gold looping chain.

Rory stared at his father's callused hands. He could identify his father by those swollen appendages alone, if the time came, if the night came when he had to go to the police station to identify an assortment of bloody limbs. And that was not an impossibility. He had an eye like a butcher, a conscience like a cleaver, and he knew it.

In the corner of the bar his young brother played video games.

'You'll write every day, won't you?' his mother sniffled.

Rory began to rewrap some dripping meat, sprinkling a curious seasoning like sawdust on each strip to prevent it from spoiling. It was a tradition of sorts. People from the homeland were always wanting relatives and friends to bring them meat from Ireland. Of course, they also requested non-perishables like jams and hawthorn sticks.

His father bellowed in exasperation, pacing back and forth. 'Jasus! There's only one thing certain in this fuckin place, and that's that there is nothin certain.' His belly swelled in agitation. 'It won't be like that in America.' He shook his fist. 'By God, them boyos live by a clock. They punch in in the mornin, and they punch out at night.' He seemed lost for words, flicking the dirty gold-faced cover on the watch open. 'And that's the way it should be. That's what keeps idlers off the street.'

The young boy came darting out from between two stools like a rat, his face twisted with toffee. 'Da! Giv'us ten pence for the Pacman.'

His father kicked out at him stubbornly. 'Jasus! The history of civilization, isn't it just? We only got rid of one load of tyrants, and now these young ones are payin fuckin tithes to machinery.'

'Ah, come on, Da. Don't start tellin me about when you were a boy. All I want ya to do is to give me ten pence. I swear it's the last one.'

The father rummaged through his pockets, his handkerchief billowing into a prodigious rag, blowing his nose. He wanted to create a scene. 'Let me see now. When I was young I didn't even know what a penny looked like.'

'The money, Da?'

Rory threw his brother fifty pence, and the boy disappeared between the flannel trousers of two old farmers in muddy boots.

His mother raised her head in disgust. 'Wouldn't you think that them farmers would wear somethin besides them manure-covered boots into an airport?'

The farmers heard her. 'I hope you're travelling on the flight with us, Ma'am, because we'll be wearing these boots on the plane to America.'

'Will you shut up for awhile,' scowled the father. 'I don't fuckin care if they ride a donkey on to the plane.'

His mother rambled on. 'Now listen to me, Rory. You'll need to keep showering in America. Them Americans have noses like bloodhounds. Only last year . . . ' Her voice rose.

'One of these slick bastards said I smelled like . . . '

'For shit's sake, Mother, will you shut your face for awhile.' The father steered Rory over to the edge of the bar. 'You hold back there, Mother, and get a nice sup of tea and a sandwich off the trolley. And keep an eye to that black guard yonder, or he'll hijack some plane or other contraption.'

The barman adjusted his black dicky bow in the dead light of the small bar alcove and then turned with a smile. 'What'll it be, men?' he said in an upbeat tone, rubbing the counter with the flick of a wrist.

'I'll tell ya what, sunshine. Giv'us two whiskeys on the rocks.'

'On the rocks?' The barman stopped smiling.

Rory's father nudged him. 'I'm only coddin.'

The barman winked almost imperceptibly, wheeling about on his heels.

'Americans like it on the rocks. Ya know? With the ice thrown in.'

'I'll remember that.'

'On the rocks. That's what ya say to them boyos.'

Rory looked over his shoulder at his mother. She supped away at the cup of tea.

'Don't bother with her.' His father poked him in the ribs. 'Well now, boy.'

The tension mounted for a few moments. His father put a pinch of snuff on his thumb, inhaling the brown powder into each of his hairy nostrils.

'I'll . . . ' began Rory.

'Relax and listen to me, boy.' His father was stern and passionate. He shot his haggard face toward his son, his luminous eyes huge and wet. 'The police won't catch on for a few weeks yet. Norris down at the pub was talkin about how they haven't even a clue where the body could be. There's no fear for ya now. You'll get away, all right.' His father edged closer, his thighs spilling off the stool. He touched his son's smooth chin with his flaccid hand, his penetrating eyes beaming. 'Tell us what you did with it?'

Rory fumbled his hands in his pockets for a few moments. Slowly he shook his head, raising his fist to the table, allowing a small trickle of seasoned salts to pass through his hollow fist. 'It's a secret,' Rory whispered, accenting his clandestine remarks with a hunch of his shoulders. His father opened his mouth wide.

The suitcase bulged by the leg of the stool.

Rory listened to the gasping breath of his father. This man had said the rosary for fifty years of his life, every night. How many Hail Marys was that? Millions?

'I never thought I'd . . . ' He shot the whiskey into his parted lips, grimacing, 'Ah . . . ' He looked eminently incomplete, with his face beet-red and tears rimming his eyes. 'Ah . . . ' he said again.

He waited a few moments, pointed to the empty glass, and the barman went to the shelf once more.

'When you get to the Bronx, go to this address. There are other names there, too. I got them off the schoolteacher. He knows who's who over there.' Again he let his thoughts linger. 'He's disappointed in you, boy.'

His father handed him a piece of folded paper. 'But he'll say nothin to no one.'

Rory felt the whiskey in his stomach. His face was a river of sweat.

'Wipe yourself with this, for God's sake.'

Rory refused the soiled handkerchief.

The barman banged two more shots of whiskey on the counter. 'It's on the house.' He winked again.

Someone blew wreaths of smoke into the dimly lit bar alcove as two policemen walked by, slowly and deliberately, like two crows.

His father sneezed violently into his handkerchief, swivelling on the stool. A button popped on his waistcoat. He raked his fingers through his iron-grey hair.

'Ah . . . ' He sighed. 'Memorize them names, and make sure you tear that thing up before you land.'

Rory felt uncomfortable and hot. The swig of whiskey compounded the warmth in his body. Beads of sweat ran down his neck.

'There is no need to worry now, boy,' he whispered furtively, rubbing his nose on his strained white knuckles.

His father poured the contents of the glass into the pit of his ulcerated belly. He worked his thumb and index finger between his nostrils. 'Your mother's in complete ignorance. She knows nothin.' He banged the table with a sudden fear. 'And I'll keep her that way.' His father looked at his watch again. 'Another one for the road, boy.'

His mother moved closer, protesting, seeing his head rising. 'He'll need a head on his shoulders when he gets to America!'

'Mother, Jasus! Another foot forward and I'll slay you here in the airport.'

His father nodded and then turned back to Rory. His pouched eyes were weary and bloodshot. 'Why?'

Rory soured.

'But you're young. I'm blamin that fuckin telly. That's what does it, ya know?' He admonished unknown forces before implicating himself. 'That fuckin telly!'

'Please, Da,' began Rory. 'We better be off.'

The father nudged Rory. 'See that fuckin saint there?' He pointed to his wife. 'I've never even seen her knickers.' His eyes grew huge. 'Her knees, less times than I have toes on me feet.' His father gave him an irreverent stare. He shot the whiskey into the pink corridor of his windpipe.

'Let's be rid of this thing,' he scowled, shuffling away from the bar. He stopped suddenly, pulling Rory close to him. 'You were all that I had.'

The mother moved in from the periphery with a paper cup of tea in her hand, her four young children straggling behind. Fifty years of life, and pregnant again . . . He shut his eyes.

This life of drudgery, savagery . . . Babies for a Catholic army, filling heaven and limbo with souls, filling graveyards with small white boxes and tiny feet.

'Your father says this Mick Night will see by ya in New York.'

The speakers echoed through the glass corridors.

His father pushed his hand to his face again, burying his flat nose. Rory felt a depressed intoxication, aware that this ritual masking was some subtlety of disgust on his father's part. He saw his mother's face disappear in a wad of tissue paper. She was crying. She must have known, he thought.

He inhaled the cool, clinical air of the airport. Airports somehow reminded him of hospitals, their long sour echoing corridors, the muffled speakers crackling, the gleaming polish of the marbled floors, the strained hush of a waiting room, families hovering in despair. He could feel the distance already mounting. All around him he saw last embraces held for too long. The world was not quite real under the fluorescent lights, the suitcases waiting ponderously in the distance. It was like the horror of a mother holding a dead child in her arms in the aftermath of an accident, the past and the present fluxing. He had felt that way when he held that limp throat, the melancholy of impotency after masturbation.

'Maybe you shouldn't write for a while. I mean . . . ' She stopped dead.

His father surveyed him closely.

Rory saw his father's face nodding to his wife in some sort of conspiracy.

Did she know? Maybe she was worried about the postmark on the letter. The police would be able to track him down.

She began talking foolishness about sausages again, and Rory breathed easily once more.

His mother moved with sublime maternalism. She neither denied nor accepted anything. She knew all things, but she thought about nothing. It was easier that way. She could feed a family on a few pounds a week. She had nurtured a generation of pain and suffering. Her breasts bled from years of raw budding gnashing teeth. He knew his father would have her flesh in his teeth this night.

The line of emigrants pushed slowly forward, penitently, like souls departing for limbo.

As a parting gift the father put his pocket watch into his son's damp palm. 'Keep that safe. It's kept the time for two generations. Your grandfather left that to me on his deathbed.'

Rory walked through the narrow tunnel to the plane. He didn't want to look back. All he heard was his father slapping his young brother. 'That fuckin Pacman will break me ... ' Rory heard the shrill scream. A presentiment of horror stopped his progress for an instant. He turned for one glimpse, then turned once more and left that concourse of wet smiling Irish eyes and wept.

He drank twenty-four bottles of Guinness in transit. He left a legacy of broken bottles and half-eaten bags of crisps and filled four sick bags in the rear of the plane. 'It was a record of some kind,' one of the stewardesses commented. He didn't know which quantity was a record. He wanted to use the toilet outside. He went for the emergency latch numerous times. He smoked in the non-smoking section, much to everyone's annoyance. Finally he slept with an inflated yellow life jacket at his head in the rear of the plane.

He arrived in a snaking gangway of corridors like commissioned misery. He visited every official office unannounced. 'Frrriends! I'll have it on the rrrocks.' He was finally steered toward customs by a menacing Mexican. 'Are you a nigger, or do you just have a tan?' he howled away. At customs he declared only the black pudding as a perishable item.

'Made from the blood that spills from a sheep's throat.' He kept saying this to the four fat American officials. They screwed up their faces in disbelief. Finally he left with the black pudding next to his breast. He dragged the suitcase of meat behind him.

In the vast glass cube of the customs hall he moved about like some aquatic fish, slow and meandering, staring at the quiet screams of those land-breathers above.

He was a picture of Irish debauchery, the tail of his shirt half tucked into his trousers, his bootlaces undone, his hair like a plundered bird's nest. He wavered forward, the meat tailing him in the bursting suitcase.

His breath alone parted the throngs of American-Irish who spilled over the police barricades in exuberance. His eyes swam in their sockets. He saw the blurred aspect of floating billboards, impatient hands fighting for space as they held up what seemed to be the entire phone directory of Ireland.

He threw up the last of the brown, frothed Guinness on a young American girl, a champion Irish traditional dancer in a tasselled jumper.

'Send the bill to Saint Patrick!' he spluttered, falling unconscious, hopping his head off the polished floor.

He didn't remember the journey.

He awoke in a small, sweltering bedroom. He still felt groggy. He scanned the immediate blackness. It faded to grey as his eyes adjusted to the light. A small clock read 11:30 p.m. The pipes clanked and hissed.

He felt the urge to vomit once more, heaving over to the side of the bed. A pancake of pink vomit reeked.

He raised his head again with great effort. The room resolved with that same mystique of a developing film. He felt this slow palpable resolution into life, hearing the faint sound of a television and the soft rumbling of some appliance. He became aware of the textured carpet beneath his feet. He was used to linoleum in bedrooms. His head still throbbed. When he turned his neck a sharp pain shot from the base of his skull to his temples. He sat still by the bed, listening to the sounds of this new world. He knew the sound of television, but nobody watched television at this hour of the night at home. Things were different.

Suddenly, he remembered the suitcase of meat. It stood obediently by the bed. A trickle of juice oozed from the lining. He breathed easily.

A frigid night air blew in a window just beyond his bed. He sprawled over the quilt. Before him a vast twinkling world glimmered, the light piercing his wounded head. He ventured further into the cool façade of eddying air. The street seemed to be miles below. He saw the swan-necked streetlamps casting saucers of light for miles. He took a deep breath. Even the air seemed to glow, alive with some distinct energy. The light never faded; it existed as a constant, its freedom exhausting. There were no stars in the skies. There didn't need to be. This was the brilliant light, the luminous city of hope, and yet, as he stared, he sensed its omniscience, its cool scrutiny encroaching. He drew his head back into the warmth of the bedroom, like some nocturnal creature returning to its burrow, perplexed. He needed anonymity, above all else, but he knew that this life would demand that he always be a foreigner, that he flaunt his foreignness.

The door swung open, and the light poured in, exposing his naked white body. He recoiled, covering his genitals.

'You're awake?'

All he saw were yellow shapes drifting before his eyes. 'Mick Night?' he asked. Something moved into the room.

'I'll get you some aspirin.'

He listened to the trenchant voice, swallowing saliva in his mouth. The dry heat had him parched. 'Could I have a drink of water?'

A dark cat with gas-blue eyes gingerly approached the case of meat.

Rory frantically shot a foot at the creature. The cat swaggered away, hissing, its corpulent stomach dragging against the carpet.

Rory heard the distant sound of gunfire from the television in the background. He searched for his underwear, saw them at the end of the bed, and stepped into them. He wondered how the man had found him. He thought he should ask that at least. From there the conversation could progress. Was this fellow angry with him?

A glass of water was pushed into his face, and then the two aspirin were dispensed into his other hand.

Rory nodded thanks and swallowed the aspirin, taking a long gulping drink of the water. Standing in the doorway, he could see into the adjacent room. The blue shifting light of the television throbbed against the small enclosure. It was no bigger than the bedroom. A halo of flies circled a naked bulb in what appeared to be the only other compartment of space. The cat purred contentedly in the far corner of the outer room.

After he ate the tablets, Rory felt he should speak, as the man apparently felt no need to explain.

'I'm sorry about the ... incident at the airport. It's not that I can't hold my drink...' He stopped, waiting for a response. There was none. The heavy-set man just stood there fingering the ridge of his concave brow. His head was completely bald.

Did he understand? Rory began to feel the sweat building on his neck. 'Listen,' he pleaded. 'You know how it is. I've never been on a plane before. It must have been the altitude that done me in. Listen, man. I've drank double that in an evening and could walk a tightrope blindfolded.'

It seemed pointless. The man turned his rotund body and went back to the television. He flicked through the channels with a small remote control. He stopped at the cartoons, giggling occasionally.

The cat curled in on itself, and still its pale blue eyes burned softly. It stared at the case of meat in the small bedroom.

Rory cursed to himself. He couldn't understand a country that showed cartoons at eleven-thirty o'clock at night. But

maybe that was what accounted for this fellow's behaviour.
Rory paced back and forth. He resolved not to speak either.
He'd wait until morning.

A seam of light under the doorway opened into a wash of
light. Rory stepped back, almost falling.

'Is it yourself? Well, fuck me! Come out and give us a
hand . . . For Jasus sake, let me see ya, boy!'

Rory turned his eyes up at the sound of the drawling
brogue.

The man bustled through the door, bags of food under his
arms. 'Take hold a this,' he beckoned, releasing pressure on
the bag sandwiched between his arm and his ribs.

Rory complied, taking the weight of the bag.

'The name's Mick, Mick Night. And by Jasus . . . You're
the spittin image of . . . ' Night's massive hand shot forward.
He shook Rory like a thief shaking change from a beggar. Rory
smiled. At least this fellow was civil. Immediately, Rory made
light of his incident at the airport. He wanted to test the
waters.

'Were you there when I gave that young girl a real Irish
welcome?' He laughed as he spoke, forcing the issue.

Night laughed, then coughed, then laughed again, slapping Rory on the back. 'Jasus. But you're a queer boyo.'

Mick smiled, and Rory saw his blackened teeth.

This was a voice of authority, of judicial equanimity. Rory
knew that Night was gauging him with his handshakes and
slaps, a kind of rudimentary prowling, a jocular forerunner of
things to come. Rory liked this animal. He had the eye of a
butcher about him again, slowly beginning to size Night up.

'Did you meet Murphy? And yer man?' Night was
fingering the grinning cat. 'Black and tan! Call him Cromwell!'

Murphy screamed laughing.

Rory shivered and smiled feebly, following Night as he
opened the refrigerator.

'He doesn't say much,' Rory said.

'Cromwell?' shouted Night.

11

'No! Murphy . . . ' Rory took a deep breath. The cat slinked out of the window-frame.

'Murphy's gone in the head. Deaf as well.'

Rory's eyes lacerated Night's bent back. He brought a stiff cleaver-like hand down on Night's back. He wanted to force the point, to establish a covenant of power. His face grew twisted and black.

Murphy turned and saw Rory's look.

Rory went and sat down by the table. The cat purred softly near Night's hand.

Rory rapped the table with his knuckles in private rebellion. His aspect signified languid poise. He was a killer, and he wanted them to know it. The cat ignored him, pawing at Night's shirt-sleeve.

Rory pictured a different scene from this stark pair and their cat, seeing fat, mottled faces, serene and plump, nursing pints of stout in an absurd bar like 'The Shamrock Arms', or 'The Emerald Isle', or 'The Queen's Knickers'. He would be brash, yet self-contained, if he could get out of this place. A personification of good Irish humour, laughing with an eye turned backward, always wary of some imperceptible enemy. He would shake hands in the most congenial manner, massaging his trigger finger in their warm palms, pumping a few rounds of salutations into his 'nearest and dearest friends'. The room would be suffused with an easy air of brotherhood, the lingering taste of acrid stout on all their throats. They hated the damned stuff, each of them secretly wishing for a Budweiser. He'd walk shotgun through this massive emerald underground, carrying a legacy of eight soldiers with him. When he would sit they'd leave him room for the dead to sit by his side. At night he would tell them how he could feel the cold mist of these ghosts upon him. And they would believe him, because they wanted to be Irish. They would believe in pots of gold at the ends of rainbows, because it was romantic to believe in fables. This would be his world, his face masking a thousand subtleties, demanding attention and respect.

Night shut the fridge and offered Rory a corned beef sandwich. Rory nearly fell to the floor. 'Corned beef, my arse,' he thought to himself. The cat opened its mouth, and its tongue seemed like a small, pink wound.

Night held the cat at bay, waiting patiently with a tin opener in his hand. 'Well?'

The deaf man giggled in the living room, his head bobbing up and down. 'I'll have a corned beef sandwich, too,' he shouted.

'Uncanny,' smiled Night in a soothing manner. 'A nose like a hound.'

'I'd love one,' Rory said, licking his lips in feigned relish. 'What's his Christian name?'

'He's Sean. The poor fellow was shot in the head with a rubber bullet in the troubles in '69. I think maybe he was a little gone before the bullet, but nevertheless they love that fella here in the Bronx.'

Rory bit his lip. 'Yeah, '69. That was before they got tough up there,' he said severely.

'That's right, boy. Before things got tough ... ' Night moved dexterously about the kitchen, opening and closing presses, peeling away the jelly slime about the meat. The cat whined softly by Night's sleeve. Rory decided to put his trousers on. He felt a sudden embarrassment; underwear wasn't the attire of a killer. He walked back into the bedroom and shut the door. He flicked on the light. A pool of blood circled the case, the zipper bleeding. He threw a towel down around the case and went through his coat and trousers searching for the piece of paper his father had given him. He remembered that he was supposed to have memorized the phone numbers and then to have thrown away the note. Frantically, he tossed his rucksack onto the bed and fumbled away, looking for the piece of paper. Where was it?

'Is everything all right?' Night inquired.

'Grand,' Rory shouted out. 'I'll be there in a second.'

Night tuned in an Irish music station on the AM dial. 'My

Wild Colonial Boy . . . ' he bellowed in discordance with the wheezing singer.

Rory sat on the bed's edge, shaking. He could see Night moving about, smiling and singing. He slowly searched through his pockets again, looking between Night and his belongings. His hands were hot and moist. He pulled out sweet wrappers and a few pounds, but there was no sign of the note. He poured the contents of his duffel bag out on to the bed, rummaging through socks and shirts. 'Oh Jesus,' he groaned, letting his head drop forward into his hands.

'Are ya okay, boy?' Night called out.

'Fine, fine.' Rory took short breaths, rubbing his fingers into his eyes. 'Christ. A fuckin simple thing like tearin up a slip of paper, and I couldn't even do that much. Imagine fuckin yerself like that!' Rory wiped his face. Just as long as Night hadn't found it. He could see himself answering that face. Rory kept muttering to himself. 'Come on, relax.' He decided it must have dropped out on the plane somewhere. But sure, who would be the wiser, even if someone found the thing? Did the CIA look at every bit of fuckin rubbish on a plane? It was only a list of names. Nobody knew he had the note except his da. 'All right now.' Rory raised himself, pressing his hands into his thighs, shaking off the bewildering fear, trying to smile as he looked at Night tapping along with his foot to 'It's a Long Way to Tipperary'.

He emerged into the adjoining room with a smile on his face. The blood was slowing in his veins.

'Well,' sighed Night, displaying an array of corned beef sandwiches on a shamrock-crested plate.

'Let's eat,' joined Rory, his cynicism brimming at the sight of shamrock plates. He forgot the lost note. 'I suppose you have green toilet roll to boot.' He laughed out loud.

Cromwell the cat ate in reverent silence.

Night snorted, his face filled with a corned beef sandwich. 'This fellow's a funny one,' he said, pushing the mass of meat and bread to one side of his cheek with his tongue.

The deaf fellow stared at the television. 'I got *The Quiet Man* on video for you,' Night announced, tapping Murphy on the shoulder.

'What?' Murphy looked up into Night's face. 'What?' he repeated like some hideous bird of prey.

Night held out the video. '*The Quiet Man*.'

Murphy nodded his head, mauling another sandwich.

The cat curled its tail around Rory's leg. Rory flinched and brushed the cat aside with a soft lick of his stockinged feet.

Rory surveyed the apartment with a critical eye, appalled by the general squalor of the place. He wondered why his father had sent him to these fellows. The room was a shambles, papers and cans of beer scattered everywhere. The only sign of opulence was the new fridge. He took note of its huge freezer compartment.

Cromwell hissed instinctively, his eyes flaring in cold blue bulbs.

'It's a beauty, that fridge, isn't it just? The freezer holds close to forty pounds of meat alone. And there's another one down below, not just the rival, but the superior of this fellow.'

Rory flinched. Why was Night elaborating on the fridge, and the freezer? He wondered if he had been staring at it for a long time. 'Yes, it's a fantastic luxury,' he answered laconically.

'Oh, it's a necessity, not a luxury. Yer man here eats nothing but meat. Won't look at a salad. I'm inclined to his thinking myself. We're what you'd call in the "Jack Sprat" syndrome. He'll eat no lean, and I'll eat no fat. We're not into that American health scene at all. "Fuckin rabbits" is what Murphy calls them. I'm inclined to his way of things. A leg of mutton does me dandy.'

Rory ate another sandwich in silence. He took a deep breath.

'I suppose you're feeling the jet lag,' Night interrupted, unbuttoning the white shirt cradling his cannonball belly. He gave a belch of contentment. Cromwell sprang up, nuzzling his whiskered face into Night's chest. 'By Jasus! Dere's happiness for you,' Night said with supreme satisfaction, gently rubbing his pastured belly.

Night surveyed Rory. Rory ate his sandwich self-consciously.

Night's jaws seemed to breathe like gills as he chewed his sandwich. Night drank in all of his fears.

'I'll toss you for the last one,' Night grinned.

Rory shook his head, 'No.'

The coin curled in the darkened room, its shadow arching downward.

'Heads,' shouted Murphy before the coin landed.

'Deaf in one ear, and can't hear out of the other,' Night whispered with awe. 'He's a bastard, dat boyo! By Jasus! I'll tell you.'

Murphy kept his head forward, extending his hand over his shoulder, pawing for the meat.

Rory knew they'd played this game before. Night threw the sandwich over to Murphy.

When Night smiled, there was corned beef stuck to his black teeth. He could see the horrible expression in Rory's face. He acquiesced with a slight tip of his head, offering another sandwich and a beer.

'Where do you sleep?' Rory asked.

'Me and yer man there sleep downstairs in our own boudoir.'

Night picked the meat from his teeth with a small tooth-pick. 'You'll have the place to yourself, except for ... ' He waited. Murphy chuckled. Night shouted, 'Wait for it!' Rory looked quickly between the two men. Neither attended to the other, and suddenly Night dropped his hand, and Murphy shouted in perfect synchronization, 'The girl.'

Rory waited for Night to explain. Night was in no great hurry. He worked the toothpick diligently in between the rotting crevices of his teeth, dislodging the salty meat. 'That poor bitch.'

Rory inched his head forward. 'What girl?'

Night pushed his chair backward, re-establishing the exact distance that Rory had gained.

'Go on,' Rory stammered. He felt a tremor of excitement.

Murphy asked for the tape.

'We'll watch it down below.' Night pointed his finger downward. 'I have to think out loud with this fellow,' he said, rising from the table.

'But what . . . '

'Give it up boy,' Night said frankly, patting his potted belly. Night sat for a long time in the living room, kneading the cat's soft belly. He even smiled at Murphy who never turned his head from the television.

An hour of quiet passed in the small room. The cat slept soundly, dreaming of mice. Night let his tongue roll out of his mouth, snoring and swallowing occasionally, slowly digesting his belly of meat.

When a siren screamed in the distance, Night awoke in a splutter of coughs, grabbing the languid cat.

'Come on now, boy!' Night began, his new meal crawling to the very ends of his toes until he could feel his nails pushing through his black boots. He put a head of cabbage into a huge iron pot and took some meat from the freezer. 'A man's got to plan his next meal, Rory. That's what makes us different from other beasts. We make the future, creating and destroying. Ah yes, destruction is the God of progress.' He smiled softly.

Murphy plodded toward the door like a docile animal herded out of a barn. He raised his fat hand. He seemed to speak in gestures.

Mick Night kept patting Murphy on the back. 'Good man, move on there. We'll see you in the morning then.' When Murphy had been successfully pushed into the hallway, Night tucked his head into the room and whispered. 'I smelt meat in your room.'

'I smelt meat in your room,' Rory repeated to himself. It was thoroughly ludicrous.

'It's been a tradition. When the boys come over they always give us a few pounds of the pudding and the sausages. If you would be good enough to put that meat into the fridge. Murphy loves a good Irish breakfast when he can get his hands on it.' With that he withdrew his body from the doorway and vanished.

Rory shut the door with a beaming smile. Cromwell stopped purring and crawled under Murphy's chair. Rory went into his own bedroom and looked at the clock. The small red digits shone 1:45 a.m. He felt tired again. He picked up the suitcase and filled the freezer and fridge with the warm, fragrant cuts of meat. He sat for a few moments. The heat in the apartment was stifling. When he rubbed his feet on the carpet, sparks flashed, the colour of the cat's sapphire eyes.

It was eight o'clock in the morning in Ireland. He felt he should try and sleep some more. But he kept thinking of how the police would be out searching for the body in the misty hills. He lay on the bed, stripped naked, the framed window casting grey bars across his body. He began to drift off to sleep in the warm hiss of the heater.

Outside it began to rain lightly, the droplets hitting the window in soft splats. His eyes gleamed in the fractured light of the otherworld.

He seemed to sleep for hours.

When he opened his eyes, the rain had turned to snow. He yawned and stretched his limbs. He heard the same distant sounds of the television. The cat scratched the door with its claws. Rory hadn't been to the bathroom since the flight, and now he felt the urge. As he rose, he heard another human voice. It came from the living room. The girl must have come back when he was asleep. He heard another whispering voice, or rather a grunt, a deep guttural grunt.

All he could smell was the watery odour of stale cabbage that Night had left to boil overnight on the cooker.

He slipped into his trousers and tiptoed to the door. The voices were quiet. He peeped through a crack in the door. The television throbbed its murky light, but he saw nothing. The cat shied backward, its eyes squinted.

Rory opened the door further, leaning forward.

In panic, he withdrew his head. In the furthest corner of the room he saw two bodies. One of the shapes lay prostrate, the other, the girl, moved like a sea nymph in the light of the television. He felt a sudden shock in his body. Above the creatures, he'd seen the framed picture of Jesus. The image came as an effigy from across the waters. He took a slow breath. He didn't remember seeing it when he sat with Night a few hours ago. Beads of sweat streamed down the insides of his thighs. He felt a sudden gorging of blood in his veins.

He crept on all fours into the kitchen, straining not to rustle the crumpled rubbish strewn about the floor.

The cat arched its back, hissing quietly. The young girl stood in the unreal light, her lucent body like a saintly apparition. The eyes of Jesus seemed to follow her.

Rory snaked into the kitchen. He stared at the girl again. She was frail and beautiful, her long limbs moving slowly in the shifting candlelight.

'Well, let's begin,' grumbled the man. He was naked already, save for a white tank top.

The girl seemed unnerved. She lit a circle of small candles about her. The oval of faint light danced on her body. Her shadow shimmered on the wall.

Cromwell knocked the milk off the counter. It smashed into fragments.

The man rose up.

'Cromwell.' The girl shivered. He saw her body flex with fear.

The man sat inert against the head of the bed once more. The man didn't seem afraid of the picture of Jesus. Rory saw that the man had a small penis, like a child's, which contrasted with the huge aspect of his outstretched hands. He wondered why bodies were proportioned that way. Was that evolution? Survival of the fittest? You needed big hands like an ape to grab what you wanted; the other extremities could live on the prowess of that stranglehold.

The girl turned her head away, an oblique grimace passing for both pain and sorrow forming on her face. She moved in a halo of yellow light.

'Begin,' grunted the heavy man, slapping his fat, clawed hands in agitation.

The girl began like some delicate machine, a kind of doll on a music box. She curved her hips in a soothing gyration. Her spine arched gently like a bow, her pubic hair glistening with a clear lubricant like melted butter.

'Sweet Molly Malone, you're all alone,' he whispered.

Rory stared at her. She kneaded her own buttocks with her long fingernails.

He strained to see her, the transformation from machine to whore slowly enveloping his mind. The cheeks of her bottom moved gently in silken underwear. Slowly, she slipped her hands beneath the torn silken panties, finally stepping out of a lavender circle of silk.

Rory held his breath. The lavender-shedded skin made him shudder.

With a click of her bra she let her small breasts fall forward.

Rory shut his eyes for a brief moment.

She began to pirouette before her audience of one, her lean body stretching upward, her hair gently wavering in the stillness of the air.

The man beckoned for her to come close. She did not venture forward. She raised her arms above her head, the nape of her neck exposed, her hands cupping her hair into a careless bun.

The man seemed impatient. He raised his voice. 'Come here, or there'll be no money.'

The girl complied. Rory could no longer see the delicate outline of her ribs. A small pouch of fat rippled about her waist. She looked like one of those eighteen-year-old girls at home on the strand who had just had a baby, or a late abortion. Suddenly the girl vanished out of sight. Rory propped himself up instinctively.

The bodies aroused Rory. He tucked himself back behind the barricade of the kitchen table and listened.

The man kept repeating something. Rory heard the slurping of their union and suddenly he felt the ebb of passion, the alienation of a prisoner who must watch from a distance. He was once more drawn to that contorted face of Jesus above the shaking bed. A ruby-coloured bulb burned softly within a rich cavern of human organs. He stared at the ripe heart in the centre of the chest. They ate this kind of heart at his house; they called it religion. He hated eating these bloody organs, tasting the bitter piss of the kidneys, remembering how his mother turned his potatoes to an orange hue, mixing the heart juice with them.

He was breathing hard. As a boy he saw these bleeding stigmas in every house. The hideous hearts thumped everywhere. He was always aware of his own heart when he passed them, thinking of its spongy aspect. One day at communion he chewed the host and then became frightened, thinking he had punctured the heart of Jesus and had a pint of thick blood in his mouth.

He shut his eyes, and still he could not keep the image of the ruby light from flickering penitently in his brain.

The girl coughed violently. Slowly he crept back toward his room and closed the door.

Later he heard the girl vomiting in the bathroom, and he cried into his pillow.

At breakfast, Murphy was in great form. He had a face like an intelligent ox. He whistled away through a prodigious snout, the grease from the pan spitting furiously back in his face.

Night came up to the apartment in an old flannel robe, sniffing the air with satisfaction. Rory sat by the kitchen table, saying nothing. The girl lay curled on the bed settee with the ease of a slumbering cat about her, a sheet drawn across her waist. He could see the outline of breasts. She had dark red hair.

'How did you sleep?' Night inquired, buttering a slice of bread at the table with his index finger. He had fingers like knives, Rory noticed, disconcerted. He knew he would never trust this man; he would never turn his back in his presence.

'Fine,' Rory answered laconically.

Cromwell sat on his hind legs like a porcelain figurine watching Murphy prepare a meal of tripe and ribs with left-over mashed potato and the boiled cabbage. Its bleached head steamed in a massive colander.

The fragrant, savoury whiff of the pan filled Murphy's pink nostrils. He giggled away to himself, a primitive creature refining his culinary skills.

'By Jasus, it smells a treat,' shouted Night, his lips moist with saliva.

They ate their breakfasts in silent ravishment, save for Murphy's constant slurping of tea. Rory shunned the meal, complaining of stomach cramps. The rich burgundy bouquet of organs was piled in a formidable heap.

The cat approached with tail erect and tore a piece of liver off the plate and ran to the sanctuary of the window-sill.

Kathleen said in a soft voice from the adjacent room. 'May I have some?'

'Look at that fuckin face as long as Lent!' Night shouted, punching Murphy on the back, and Murphy kept half-choking, grunting replies, and fitfully nodding his head.

Night pulled the bacon-like slices apart with his fingers, peeling away the white line of fat in long delicate ribboned strips. 'I didn't see any money on the table,' he said between slobbers.

'He didn't give me anything. He said he'd fix it up with

22

you,' Kathleen replied in a weak voice. 'He said you said it was okay.'

'When did I ever give any of my property away for free?' he roared. 'He'll tell me that he gave it to you.'

'I swear ... I swear on my mother's life that he said he fixed it up with you.' Kathleen began to sob under her breath, but she didn't let Night see her crying.

Rory felt a great pity for her. He'd heard Night calling her 'his property'. He wanted to fall down beside her and gently rub her head and tell her he would take her away from that pig. But he said nothing, surveying his two captors.

Night smiled, and Murphy eyed the pile of meat with unconcealed zeal, juice squirting from his open mouth.

'Help yourself, boyo. And I'll try some o' those ribs you're not touchin.' Their dark hands writhed like octopus tentacles, weaving dexterously through the carbuncled kidneys, the slick copper-coloured liver lobes. Rory reached for his tea, the saucer trembling as he touched the cup. He was nervous. Night sensed the tension, stabbing at Rory's hairless hands. 'What doesn't move, I'll eat,' he laughed.

Rory smiled, withdrawing the china teacup with his stiff trigger finger. Night grinned, and Murphy belched. Night prowled with his eyes, protecting his kill as a savage dog protects its bone.

Rory held his cup before his face.

Night continued, orchestrating the entire frenzy with his fork and knife, his grizzled face flecked with spots of bacon grease.

Finally Kathleen appeared, wrapped in a sheet like a sculptor's model. She was tall and supple, the white sheet tucked between her narrow cleavage, accentuating the shape of her breasts. Rory looked at her in astonishment.

'Don't stare,' she said brashly.

Rory nearly choked on his tea, spitting a horrible poultice of bread into Murphy's vacant face. Murphy kicked the table over, falling backwards. Night toppled sideways, a chop firmly clenched between his teeth. He brought the tablecloth down with his sharp fingers, grabbing Rory with his other hand. He was no fool. If he was going to die, he would kill others. He believed that death was not a solitary event. He growled in pain, but the chop remained steadfast between his teeth.

The girl moved off into the bathroom, not caring to see the outcome of the fall.

'Jasus Christ.' Night frowned as he heaved Murphy's flaccid body off the floor. 'That's two nails in your coffin, girl!' he roared.

Murphy aligned himself again at the table and began sucking a bone meditatively, staring openly into Rory's face. A large bruise grew on his left temple.

Rory turned crimson.

Night fanned the tablecloth. It fluttered like a phantom moth in the luxuriant heat of the small room. 'What do you do with a girl like that?' he said directly to Rory.

Rory shrugged his shoulders. 'I don't know.' He listened with his eyes closed, hearing the slow trickle of urine. There was no door in the bathroom. And when she farted, Night snorted tea through his nostrils, and Murphy banged the table. The meats quivered.

'Oh! What do you do with a girl like that?' Murphy shouted.

Rory said nothing and left the table. Flies circled the unattended meat. Night flashed his knife over the plate, appropriating a small strip of meat for the girl, placing it on to a small plate. 'Here you are,' he grumbled. 'Don't say I'm not a fair man. The likes of you living here under my roof and robbing me blind . . . I'll have that money before I go downstairs, if you please, girl.' He nudged Rory. 'Nothin like scarin the knickers off her, hey boyo?'

Rory paced back and forth. He wondered why Night put himself in such a bad light.

The two men began eating once more. Kathleen ate at her

assigned place, on her bed settee. She nibbled her food in a mouse-like manner, turning bread in her small delicate fingers. She kept staring at Rory as she swallowed small bites.

'When can I leave the apartment, to get fresh air and the like?' Rory asked, trying to look away from the girl.

'You'll stay put awhile. We don't want any of the neighbours knowing you're here,' Night answered. 'You see, there are spies always and everywhere. It goes with a democracy. If there's money to be made, it's going to be made out of another's mistake, so everyone watches everyone else.'

Kathleen turned her dark head and smiled. 'So, what is your name?'

'Rory.'

She seemed as innocent and harassed as she had been the night before. 'Was it ... Was it you who was out here last night?'

She seemed to ask it for fear that Rory had seen her naked.

He didn't answer. He began pacing the floor once more. No one talked for a few moments. The flies clotted the pale light above the sink.

Night dabbed grease on his shirt-sleeve, nodding solemnly to himself, blotting the grease on his lips with the edge of the tablecloth. He rose and took Murphy by the shoulder and steered him toward the door. 'We're off for now! Don't let a soul in, or think of going out today. I'll try to arrange a meeting for you at one of the bars so you can get a chance to meet people later on,' Night said, as he fumbled for a key to lock the door.

Kathleen nodded and began collecting the dirty dishes.

Rory remained in the bedroom all day. Night rang on the phone some hours later. Kathleen called Rory out of his room. She was still wrapped in the sheet. Rory wondered if she had any clothes, since there were no cupboards anywhere in the house, and he saw none of her clothing around the place, except for the pale, silky underwear near the television.

'What is it?' he said. He saw that her blanched shoulders were covered in small, purple welts; her slender neck, marked by fresh bites. She showed her white teeth and smiled a hapless smile of friendship. 'That was Night. He says you're to meet under the Pleasure Emporium at nine o'clock.'

'And where is that?'

Kathleen came back a few moments later. He'd seen her looking through the keyhole like a child. He saw her eye in the socket, watching him. 'Come in!' he shouted.

She came in and stood motionless. 'Where are you from, Rory?'

Her voice was sweet. He liked how she said his name.

'Originally from Limerick, but I spent most of my years in Belfast.'

'You don't have a Northern accent,' she replied, smiling faintly. 'I'm . . . I'm sorry about last . . . '

'Shoo . . . ' whispered Rory. He gave her a weary look, trying to convey an abject quietness, the kind of penitent demeanor that he felt patriots would adopt in moments of self-reflection and humility.

She seemed to understand, but she blushed all the same. She brushed her gentle fingers along her scarred neck. He felt her wounds in his own mind. 'Myself, I'm from the Falls Road.'

He nodded his head. Belfast or Derry? He couldn't decide.

She shifted her weight to one hip, her hair falling to the side. He only imagined her lips moving as she whispered, 'Would you like a cup of tea, Rory?'

His own name lapped in the soft solitude of the moment. She was a creature of beauty, not something for sale.

He eased into conversation once more. 'How long have you been here, Kathleen?'

She smiled self-consciously. 'Too long.' She ran her fingers through her hair.

Her scent remained when she left the room.

Rory shut his eyes and grimaced. He could hear the muted

sounds of the taxi horns in the distance. What would it be like when he actually moved out? He thought of stories of men left to die in the streets of New York and nobody coming to save them until it was too late. That was a kind of horror that he could not endure. At night, under the invisible sun of his homeland, in the midst of a bar, in the pitch of an argument, maybe then he could have killed; indeed he did kill and walk away, but, in the daylight of some cold city, could a whole nation have the courage to keep walking by a dying man?

Rory stepped out of bed and moved toward the kitchen. Kathleen moved quietly, the sheet falling in cool pleats about her body. He watched her attentively, wondering what held her prisoner in this slum.

The silence fell for a few more seconds. Rory stared out of the small rattling window in the front room. The night was settled again. Snow drifted by and by, the world burning in the icy lights of Manhattan.

'How many spoons?' she shouted.

'Two,' he said absently.

Rory felt himself humming in an affectless tone that tripe that Night had tuned in, 'The Wild Colonial Boy'. He stopped himself abruptly, but he knew he was slowly becoming infected.

Kathleen laid two piping cups of tea on the small table in the sitting room. Her hair flared in flaming, orange tongues as the strobed light of a passing ambulance flashed into the room.

'Do you know that way more people are killed here in a year than have been killed since the Troubles began?'

He didn't answer her. Her hair turned dark once more in the greyness. She crossed her legs, the sheet billowing, falling away in two halves at her hip, exposing one of her thin legs. He caught a glimpse of her bottom, covered with small goose-pimples.

He drank the tea, scanning the pathetic aspect of the small room.

'How long have you been here?' he asked again.

She took a sip of her tea. 'It doesn't matter, Rory.'

He smiled feebly. In a sudden anxiety he saw that image again from the previous night, her flickering tongue licking the night air. He shook his head. 'I have money,' he said softly. 'You could get away.'

'It's a long way down, Rory,' Kathleen smiled.

Rory felt she had heard this kind of pleading before. How many other fellas had there been before him? He looked to the wall, taking a soft breath. He noticed that the picture of Jesus was gone. He didn't want to say anything about it, though.

'Are you religious?' he said at last.

She stopped smiling. 'You better not tell them.' She clutched the sheet about her breasts, her bottom still raised with goose-pimples.

He thought again of that throbbing heart and of her, naked in the yellow light of the candles. He could still see small rings of the opaque wax on the floor.

She let the sheet fall from her shoulders. 'Don't tell.' She had her back turned to him. He turned his head away. 'Please, you don't have to ... ' He grew sullen. The night air flowed into the room. He kept staring at the city high-rises.

Kathleen took another sip of her tea, her head bent in repose, as though in prayer. Another siren wailed through the city. Rory stared at her stooped spine, curved like a pathetic question-mark. The light and sound came in pulses. He reached to pull the sheet around her shoulders. She shivered, and he let the sheet fall.

He rolled his eyes in despair, his hands sweating on her pale bottom ...

The snow fell in a rich blanket beyond.

'I'm sorry for you ... ' Kathleen whispered.

Rory gently put his lips to her neck, kissed her and went to his room once more.

When he came out, the picture was on the wall again.

Kathleen squatted before the image, her eyes like green gems. The cat stared, mesmerized by the shifting red glow of the light. Kathleen had removed the sheet. The city had grown darker, a serene silence consecrating her nakedness. She put her hands together as though in prayer, raising them above her head. He edged back. He did not want to intrude. Her eyes were closed now. She sensed his movements. She remained stiff, her body a cathedral, her thin arms extended as a spire. She turned her gaze at the ceiling. His eyes migrated from her dark form to the bleeding eyes of the enigmatic face upon the wall. The room shimmered in a nebula of pain.

The ruby light poured from the plum-coloured heart. Kathleen didn't move, the wind breathing gently through a half-open window, quenching the candles. She shuddered.

Again, Rory closed his door. He kept anticipating this other life that he had been promised. There was a future beyond these weeks of gloomed captivity. They were whispering his name in the emerald underground, even now. He was sure of it. 'The man who killed eight soldiers ... '

'I'm not a whore, Rory,' Kathleen whispered from beyond the door.

Rory said nothing, the image of the bar washed away by her soft voice.

'No,' the voice whispered once more.

Still Rory persisted. He buried his head in the pillow. The slayer of eight soldiers! That would hold stock among the emerald underground. They would take care of him. There was work off the books on construction sites, work in bars all over the Bronx. His accent alone would draw a crowd. He would be set free from this bondage. But he had to believe in what he needed to be if he were to stay alive, and that was what scared him. In his heart he knew that was what the girl had done. She had, in her most intimate moments, believed that she was a whore.

He kept checking himself. He had to stop thinking of her.

They'd understand him in his new dominion. They'd tip him well. Civilizations survived on myths; why couldn't he?

He slept until it was dark outside. He heard a tapping on the front door and then some noises. In another few moments, Kathleen came into his room. 'You have to meet Night at nine o'clock,' she told him.

He looked at the clock. 'Will I get there in time?' he asked, yawning, sitting up by the edge of the bed.

She was wearing her torn silken underwear again. The sheet was gone. She wore a small, laced bra.

Rory stretched out his fingers, letting them writhe in the strobed, orange light of yet another siren. He saw her breasts heave under the stretched polyester.

'Which is your trigger finger?' Kathleen asked. 'These are the kinds of things you will have to know. They ask questions at the beginning and at the end of the night, week in and week out. They find out the lies from the truth, and then they start to tell you new things all over again, and then one day . . . '

Rory closed his fist. Then he started counting slowly. 'When one gets tired, I just start on the next fellow till there's none left.' He was transformed by the lurking monstrous city beyond.

Kathleen nodded. 'It's the only way.'

They heard the sirens and looked at one another. How many died tonight? The Negroes up in Harlem were singing the blues in the dark like they did in the movies he'd seen on television.

'Look at us shivering. The whore and murderer.' Kathleen smiled haplessly. 'How long will it be before we don't shiver?'

Rory shut his eyes and kept trying to see those eight bodies, as she had to keep seeing those fat-bellied men groping.

'Let me tell how it is,' he began. 'The black hearse comes hauntingly by. There is always a black hearse pulling up in the smouldering rubble. But we know it is really the man from the glue factory. He's painted the stable boxcar black. He's nervous as hell. He has a £100 bet on a horse in the fourth at the Curragh. He carries a bag like a doctor, a big black bag. He has lots of saws and hammers and chisels. He pays great attention to detail, separating the bone from the flesh. He keeps the teeth for himself, puts them under his children's pillows at night. "They still believe in the Tooth Fairy," he says affectionately. Down in the lanes the word buzzes. "Eight plucked turkeys . . . A smouldering armoured car . . . " Everyone's laughing, clinking their glasses. "Guinness: the only drink dark enough to toast death," an old man sighs. "They'll be eating well tonight at Paddy O'Driscoll's The Great Wall of China," someone whispers. You'd be a fool to eat Chinese in Belfast. By Jesus! Paddy buys that stuff at a steal, a real capitalist, and he knows it. There is great celebration, drinks all round. Paddy O'Driscoll is buying. "How many can that feed, Paddy?" But he won't tell . . . '

Rory turned his head slowly.

'That won't do at all,' she smiled.

Rory held her hand.

'Did you have a piece of paper from your father?' Kathleen asked.

Rory seemed stunned, his face contorting at her touch. 'What paper?'

Kathleen sighed. 'They know about the note, Rory. An informer down at customs told them about it.'

Rory kept pressing his face into Kathleen's long white hands. 'I . . . I . . . '

Kathleen pulled her hands away. 'Don't say anything.' She loitered in the perpetual gloom of her small prison, weaving in and out of the night light.

He wondered if the picture of Jesus was glowing outside. He smelt the faint odour of sulphur. She had lit the ring of candles. They burned in the drowsy slumber of the heaters.

'Will you run?' she whispered quietly.

'Did you ever run?' he whispered.

31

She didn't answer and left the room.

When he came back out he saw that the picture was gone. Kathleen had left a sandwich made from his cold cuts on the table. He didn't feel like eating.

'I made a sandwich,' she began.

She turned her head and took another bite of her own sandwich.

Rory said nothing. He just stared into her face, into her innocent white face. He knew that in time, when he was gone, she would swallow this memory. How many fellas had come here, he asked himself. And she had lived through it all. He let her eat the meat; he wanted her to continue, because he felt there would be someone to liberate her someday. But for now he would let her digest the living and the dead, semen and flesh.

He dressed in the circle of candles, the wax congealing on the small saucers. As he left he saw her turning the television on. She waved goodbye, and then the ludicrous colours of cartoon fantasy washed away the greyness, and she disappeared into Murphy's chair.

In the slush of the street he shivered, tugging his coat tight around his body. He felt strangely foreign, moving conspicuously in a flimsy raincoat. He had hoped to assimilate. To exist he would have to lead a dual existence: the docile domestic in buttoned-down shirts by day, the raucous amiable Gael by night. He would have to live as an alien in this vast island jungle. He couldn't drive a car or get a credit card. He couldn't be a true American. He would have to pretend, drink cold Budweiser by day, and call people assholes. It seemed so elemental. He could say asshole, and one of these days he felt he might even drink Budweiser.

The buildings loomed about him, the snow falling hard. Cars swished by in yellow blurs, the confusion of horns drowned in the powdered snow. Small poodles snapped at his heels. Old ladies tapping the pavement with their walking-canes cried adamantly, 'Stop it, stop,' their little, wizened faces hidden in bonnets and earmuffs.

These ladies were afraid of Negroes. An ambulance cried like a wounded animal. He saw the domed ruby, the spiralling heart whining. He shut his eyes, and he thought of Jesus and Kathleen.

Black garlands of hair fell about Rory's face as the snow melted on his warm skull, his breath condensing in white puffs before his face. He stopped for a moment, surveying the entire street. Cars came streaming forward. He felt as though he were looking through a shattered window, the refracting light splintering in a million halos of green and blurred red.

The Pleasure Emporium glimmered. A cocktail glass tipped back and forth in flashing lights, the cherry winking intermittently on a stalk of blue light. Four blacks stood near by, shackled to the night in chains of gold. Prostitutes moved like cats, prowling in the shadows. 'Hey you, sweetness.' Rory stopped in the bleeding snow, flashing lights racing off a billboard. A woman opened her coat, exposing the dark flesh of her polished nipples.

A man with a small face like a rat sat alert in a glass booth. He pointed to Rory. Rory drew nearer. More prostitutes called to him. Rory turned away.

A car glided to a halt outside the pornography house. Three 'X's' wobbled in the black sheen of its opening door. The door opened further.

Rory dove in. 'Jasus Christ! I thought I was done for.' He pressed forward. 'I'm a friend of Mick Night. Is it me you're looking for?'

A head nodded.

He crouched down and fell into the warm chamber. The car pulled away quietly. Rory sat dumbfounded, and yet not scared. He had his own myth, a story streaked not in the red haze of Manhattan light, but in the thick blood of British soldiers.

He looked back, seeing the city recede into the distance.

33

The Empire State Building stood like a syringe sucking down the blackness of the sky. In the front seat, he saw the eyes of the driver darting back and forth.

The car turned down an unlit road. Patches of light blotted the blackness occasionally, and then less and less until he saw nothing.

The car ground to an abrupt halt.

A cube of light opened up in the blackness. The car door clicked.

'Hello,' Rory called out, blocking the steely light with his arm.

'Turn it down!' a voice shouted. The door shut the night out.

'Rory! Isn't it?' He heard a huskiness revealing decrepit age. A surge of power coursed through his body. 'Yes,' he answered civilly.

'Give him a chair!' someone whispered.

His body trembled. He heard the grating noise of a chair being dragged across the concrete floor. A hand pressured him to sit. He put his hand on the hand. 'Brother!' he whispered, smiling broadly. Fear reigned in his heart.

'Relax! Would you like a cigarette?'

He strained to see the face. 'I would.' He kept trying to smile.

A crooked hand ran down the back of his head. Someone moved close from behind. He could smell the liquor-stenched breath, the rasping throat wheezing. Rory held the cigarette in his hand, pressing it to his lips. A hand manacled itself to his shaking wrist. A match flamed. He pulled hard, puffing smoke into his eyes.

'Could you turn some of the lights down?,' he whispered. The smoke remained, shrouding his face. There were no currents of cool air. He saw the earthen bricks rising to an unseen roof. Snow was falling again outside.

'It's great to be among friends,' he said finally. 'So tell me, is Pat O'Donnell among you?'

He heard the bodies shuffle. The light faded to black, then a small lamp spilt a trickle of light between himself and the group.

'I'm Pat.' A hand shook his.

Rory remained in his sedentary position, smoking casually with a languid authority now mounting. 'You've done a service to Ireland. Your name is a household word to all of us at home.'

The man kept pumping Rory's arm, like a man priming an old water pump.

'How was the trip?' someone shouted. A fist landed on his crown. He felt dazed. Was it jest or vengeance? A diminutive creature moved unhesitatingly forward. Rory stared into his mahogany face. The dwarf circled him. 'So how are you liking our city?'

'It's a blaze of lights,' Rory answered deftly.

'You didn't have trouble finding the place to meet?'

Rory answered, 'No.'

'Because in a city a man can lose himself when he's not accustomed to the way things are.'

'You become forgetful,' added another voice. He saw the head shaped like a heart, the chin dimpled like pinched dough.

He smelt cologne amid the smokiness.

'Why didn't you tear it up?' someone asked from the far corner of the room.

Rory was in his own trance of emotion. Three bleak figures walked back and forth in the darkness of the warehouse.

'My father sends his regards.'

'Where's the note?'

To say, 'What note?' would be suicide. Rory whispered, 'Sorry.' He sounded pathetic, as though this act was of some venial consequence.

A hand slid a rope around his wrists. He didn't resist.

'The police followed me here,' he said in a mad fit of laughter. 'I'm not some thick fuckin idiot.'

'You have been found guilty.' The callous voice bore a grievous malice.

'My defence!' he shouted. They shook their heads. He could see seven dark phantoms before him in this emerald underground. A pregnant tension held them at bay, their verdict undermined in the dismal surroundings of this untenanted warehouse. They killed by proxy in normal circumstances. They were the men who packaged gelignite into the arses of porcelain statues of Uncle Sam and Mickey Mouse sent to Ireland. This night was their nightmarish invocation of ideology and murder. It hadn't been that way before. But they were scared. The note was out. The police were knocking on doors.

'Who'll ever care about that note anyway?' Rory cried in his most trenchant voice.

The executioner stood idly behind Rory, showing no apprehension.

'You know how much money we stand to lose?' said a man in a blue pin-striped suit.

'Shoo,' they whispered. 'What about Murphy?'

Murphy kept his eyes to the ground. He knew they were talking about him.

Rory looked forward. 'So that's the game!' he shouted.

Rory turned his head. Murphy squatted there beside him. The veins throbbed in his fingers.

'So you bastards brought me here as some kind of evangelist for your own cause.'

'You Irish have a way with words. Evangelize.' The man in the pin-striped suit blew a wreath of smoke into Rory's watering eyes. Rory's body twitched like a stricken animal.

'Written off as a bad credit!' he shouted. His composure waned.

'Bad credit . . . I like that.' A small squat man jiggled his belly as he moved forward. Another gaunt man, the antithesis of the other, rubbed his lean, clay-like hands together, whispering, 'Let's get on with it.'

'Shut up!' shouted a hollow voice. 'Don't think that we don't know what you did over there. You killed no soldiers. We know what you did.'

'What did I do?' scoffed Rory. He took a stifling breath. His eyes burned with fatigue. 'What do you know?' he shouted out. His voice echoed through the warehouse. 'I saw you last night.' A faint sense of recognition surfaced in his mind. 'Yeah, you were with Kathleen last night . . . '

'Let's get on with it!' the small squat man shouted.

'You fuckin bastards. They'll be wanting to be hearing from me. You can't just kill me. I swear to God, you'll all fuckin die.'

Murphy began his ritual with a solemn sign of the cross. He rolled a trolley of golden receptacles into view, a penchant for severity about him. The gibbering voices receded. Murphy breathed his decaying meat breath into Rory's vapid face. Their eyes did not meet.

'We'll leave it to you,' one of the men said.

Murphy felt their bodies press about him. But he would not be rushed. He had a certain fidelity to his own discipline, as a mule had to its own stubbornness.

The others withdrew still further, unnerved by Murphy's invocation of faith.

Rory watched them change once more into impalpable shapes.

Murphy worked diligently. He sprinkled holy water over Rory's body. Rory felt the tepid water trickling down his hairless chest. He was nineteen years old.

Murphy did not look into the dazed eyes of his victim when he put a hood over Rory's head.

Rory took one last breath. He smelt the warm grease of his hair under the sack.

Murphy continued with tedious detail, lumbering about the chair. Rory could still hear the laughter of the mob.

Murphy mixed cement in a small basin, meticulously adding ladles of water.

37

'It's a marvel to see a master at work,' one of the men laughed, touching Murphy.

Murphy brushed the hand away, and set a small crucifix and the holy water down beside him. He had the faith of a saint.

Rory felt Murphy's steady fingers unlacing his boots. He could smell the odour of his damp socks. Murphy never steered from his work; the smell was an occupational hazard. He slowly began pushing Rory's wiggling toes into the soft, suctioning quagmire of cement.

'Just like in the movies,' the plump man joked. He hopped forward like a satisfied toad. He had swindled over a million dollars from the borough's Belfast Relief Program. He referred to the children that came over as 'snotty-nosed bomb-chucking motherfuckers'.

The sack was drawn tighter around his throat. Murphy's fingers looped the knot tighter, like an industrious boy scout. The panic began to set in. His eyes stared beyond the illusory pitch-blackness of the coarse-textured sack. Murphy began a low, mumbling prayer. In a perplexed schizophrenia Rory saw his father punch the blackness with his huge fists. Night cut throats with his razored fingers. Kathleen prayed to Jesus. He fought for air, his head sweating profusely.

Murphy held the chair as it began to quiver. He could feel the fear trembling in the fibre of the wood. Salt burned Rory's eyes, a red, searing ring circling his bobbing Adam's apple.

Night appeared out of thin air. 'Let me see that face again!' he shouted in mirth.

Murphy eyed Night like a dog not wanting to give up a bone. 'Take it off, I said, Murphy.' Murphy obeyed. Night's face was hideously red, the pendulous fat of his chin rippling as he shook his head back and forth. 'I thought maybe you would like a final meal. Something to take with you. Like the Egyptian pharaohs of ancient times . . . '

The others looked at one another in exaggerated stares, their ears erect.

Rory wrestled furiously on the chair. Murphy brought his hammer of a fist down on Rory's face.

'This boyo has done us in,' Night began. Slowly he unwrapped the meat, seasoning it with pinches of pepper he had in the breast pocket of his suit coat. 'You sick cunt.' He drove his fist into Rory's kidneys. 'You hear me, you fuckin bastard?'

The diminutive man clenched his fists. 'Night, you motherfucker, keep out of this. We're handling this one. If you don't watch it, you'll be joining him.'

Night let the meat hang between his fingers. 'I've been the front man in this for you all these years. It's me that the police wake up at night. Don't think I don't control this game. I'm the one who has made you rich. Who bought that house in Queens for you?' He shot the accusation like an assassin. 'And you, Riordon? That pub of yours, Forty Shades of Fuckin Green, who bought it for you? I did with the bodies of boys and girls. I was the one at the masses collecting for the Belfast funds. I was the one followed by the police. Do you hear me? I own this game.'

Riordon spat into the darkness. 'We don't need you, Night! We have Murphy.'

'That stupid thick queer ol' bastard?'

Murphy eyed Night. Night consoled him with an easy eye. 'Rest up a while, man.'

'Even a dog will bite its master,' the tall emaciated man said.

'Murphy's the man they want to see,' shouted the man in the pin-striped suit. 'He says nothing and says everything. He's deaf, and so nobody is worried to say what they want. The women call him "hero", and "son". And what do you think they say about you, with your prostitute in the Bronx?'

The group nodded attentively, forcing Night to acquiesce. He did his part, casting glances between them and Rory's soaking head. 'I'll tell you what, then. The meat that our friend brought over on the plane will be given to you fine gentlemen.'

'What did he bring?' The fat man waddled over. He smelt the ripe heart. 'Wasn't it the deal that we always got what they brought?'

Night grinned. 'Yes.'

The fat man pulled the meat from Night's fingers. The others asked for their cuts to be delivered that night.

'Murphy will take care of it all.' Night smiled. He walked over to Rory. 'Jasus, I think I could love you like a son.' He winked. 'First thing tomorrow, gentlemen.'

Hands passed over Rory, groping for a leg, an arm, his chest. He writhed in their struggling arms, his muffled curses lost in the scuffling of feet, drowned in the trundling roll of the wheelbarrow.

The monstrous galvanized sliding doors in the warehouse parted. The vaulted night came crashing in, the air sucking Murphy's long black coat tails. He was dressed for a funeral. He wore a bowler hat with a black forked ribbon like a serpent's tongue. Rory's knee-caps strained from the dangling pendulums of cement. He felt a giddy terror, his breath becoming weak. He thought he heard Kathleen in the distance, calling to him. Meat crawled in her belly. The heart of Jesus spiralled in his mind, pounding in its viscous bloody juice, thumping, thumping. In moments his body would tremble in shock, the icy Hudson River lapping his tense body in the freezing blackness, the silver glimmering moon moving in the sterile night above. He'd turn blue and black, the bubbles rising slowly as he fell deeper and deeper in that alien aquatic universe.

'Hurry up,' he heard one of the men insist in a shrouded whisper.

He heard the slushing ice breaking against the steel pylons, the night air wrapping him in a cocoon of misty spray. Birds squawked. A tug boat sounded its lugubrious horn somewhere on the black water. Feet slapped the cement.

Night kept laughing in a ludicrous manner, tears in his eyes, patting Murphy on the back. He could do no more.

Rory didn't struggle. He felt his body swaying. He heard a warbled, infamous one, two, three. It sounded comic, and yet sinister. This was his life they were throwing away. Murphy was saying another prayer, moving constantly to keep warm. The rock of Manhattan with its shimmering effigy to freedom shone brilliantly, a crystal palace, an oasis of liberty. A convoluted history of myths chiselled its tunnelling architecture. Rory had misunderstood the myth of the leprechaun; he was the docile simpleton, the Guinness guzzler. He felt the slow release, the intoxicating enlightenment. Night turned, blessing himself.

The sack was empty of air, his brain swooned. His blood surged one last time. Gravity pulled him down, down. The cement plunged into the unknown, his body following in the cool, streamlined foam, his cradled head vanishing for evermore in one last quiet splash.

FIRST LOVE

HENNESSEY FELT HIS heart racing as he stood panting, ferreting the cold air. He stared at the talisman of the severed rabbit paw bleeding in the mud. His tongue hung out of his mouth. 'She has it.' His fist punched the sky, his scream echoing in the cool autumn air. He spat triumphantly upon the grassy field, wiping his sleeve across his face. 'First blood, by Jasus. That's the Pink Angel for you. Did ya see that speed? Two points for that alone, one for a kill. Oh, Mother of God, she got this one!' Hennessey's face was mottled with the cool air, crimson with effort, the brown meadow of his waistcoat billowing before him. The sun shone brilliantly overhead, yet it contained only a faint heat, shining through the skeletal trees. Again, Hennessey ran on in a teetering wobble through dark smears of manure, his small notebook fanning in the wind, his pencil aimed like a dart at his dog in the distance. He held up three fingers. 'Three points for the bitch.' His other fanning arm helped balance his prodigious bulk. There was spit on his lips. He could see the pack of greyhounds flaying their limbs about, smashing their heads into one another, descending on the writhing rabbit. His girl had been there first.

The Pink Angel coveted the trembling rabbit, the white of her eyes lost in her head. Her body convulsed as she sucked the neck wound, chewing the hot flesh, clawing the ground with her long curled nails.

For a whole year, the Pink Angel had eaten nothing but

42

brown bread, egg yolks, and porridge. Now a torrent of juice and instinct coursed in her long pink tongue. Her sinewy body arched, cut in curved ribs. Her heart pounded in her breast, the pelt shining in the cold sunlight. She growled uneasily.

A scrum of locked dog heads tore and gnawed at her face and tensed hind paws. Her jaw was frozen, the teeth deep in the silky meat of the rabbit's neck. The Pink Angel could not move, inebriated, her eyes seeing nothing, lost behind a translucent skin of protection and ecstasy.

'She'll be killed,' Lovelace screamed. 'Get her free, for fuck's sake!'

The air reeked with the smell of liniment and sweat. The men beat the dogs away from the Pink Angel, kicking at their painted heads. The dogs snapped at the fragrant air of blood and their masters' sweat.

When Hennessey unhooked the Pink Angel's jaws from the limp bloody rabbit, her head collapsed into his fat fingers. The jaw muscle was ripped in a clean laceration. Skin on her muzzle was torn away, leaving the pearly nose cartilage exposed. Hennessey cradled the head, spat into a handkerchief and dabbed the wounds, streaking the blood behind the ears. 'My Jasus, ya won it girl.'

'Will she live, Hennessey?' Lovelace tipped his hat back on his forehead. Flies clotted the body of the dead rabbit. 'I don't know about that one, Freddy. No, sir.' Lovelace sucked his cheek, oiling the polished knob of stick with his sweating palm.

'Go on, will ya? A few scratches, nothin that this girl won't see herself through ... What a fuckin girl!' Hennessey kissed the bleeding face of the dog. A froth of ruby bubbles formed around the Pink Angel's mouth as she took fitful breaths. Her eyes slowly lost their white-skinned film. Her tongue curled out and licked his hand. Hennessey wiped tears from his eyes. The cold noon sun fell on the vapid dog, shining upon

Hennessey's hairy hand as he stroked the dog's bleeding face. Lovelace turned away, leaving Hennessey to stare into her dark shining eyes, kissing her deep wounds with his own lips, whispering, 'You'll be okay, my girl.'

When Hennessey left, his car was packed with three children, one midget, two fat men (not counting himself), two greyhounds, the maimed Pink Angel, and two terrified hares. The springs groaned as he swerved on to the muddy lane, spraying up mud from the rear wheels. 'Hold on now!' He kept beeping his horn, butting dogs and men out of his way, the gear lever cocked like a pistol on the dashboard, himself working it with his strong gloved fist, elbowing Mr Long in the dead centre of his chest. Mr Long had suffered a heart attack a few months past, and he begged, 'Will ya lay off with that elbow, for fuck's sake? Do ya want me to die right here, Freddy?'

Hennessey smiled away to himself, feeling the sweat and ointment in his black gloved hand making his fist swell with blood. He shouted curses out the window and, with a sudden movement, repositioned himself like a jockey over the steering wheel, squatting, riding out every hole in the road with great feats of balance.

The children and the dogs in the back were sandwiched together so tightly that they could feel only their insides moving from side to side. From the neck up, their heads moved in a limited orbit, their eyes swimming in their heads.

'Da, I don't feel well,' Bridget whispered, trying to lean forward toward her father's ear.

'Yer okay there, Bridget.' Another series of sustained beeps made members of the congregation hop like frightened hares out of Hennessey's way. People spat indignantly as the car jolted onward. A flurry of pounding fists hit the roof. The young boy in the back seat began to cry at the faces looking in at him all so red and cold.

'Da, will ya pull over for a bit? I'll be sick.'

'Throw up on me and yer dead!' Lovelace shouted.

Hennessey ignored all caution, driving the car like a rabid dog among lambs. The greyhounds trotted along, stone-faced, sniffing the air with regal poise. The dogs in the back of the car put their hot noses to the windows, clawing with their curling yellow nails. The men kept screaming, 'Slow it down, fer the love o' Jasus, Hennessey!'

Hennessey was full of his own indignation. 'Come on, Johnny. If ya can't be master of a dog, what the hell good are ya?' or 'I'll do ya the favour, Mick, and run the mutt down now, so ya won't lose more on him!' Every word and sentence was delivered with laughter, full of coughs and curses, bangs on the dashboard, and pumps of the accelerator pedal, as his elbow drove its way into Long's weak chest with the ten stitches resembling a dog bite. The disconsolate men moved in slow procession, led by their sleek hounds. When there were but a few men left in front of him, Hennessey cocked back the gear lever like a trigger and shot himself on to the Ballybunion road with a 'Hi, ho, Silver, away!'

A ribbon of soft browning sky tainted the wet mountains in the distance. Everyone breathed easier. The rains were coming from the northwest, bringing down the cold freezing rains from the strange white islands beyond Mullen Head in the north. The hedges dreeped in tiny pearls from the cold sea-blown winds. The car snaked through the twisting road, cutting two deep scars into the mud. Hennessey took a deep breath and looked behind himself, winking. 'How's the Pink Angel lookin now, Bridget?'

'She'll be fine,' Lovelace whispered, absorbing the tranquillity of the mountainside. He opened his coat, letting the heat of his body escape in a sticky odour. The houses looked like leviathans to him, darkened in the distance, with small trails of smoke rising into the sky. He could smell the peat burning in the fires.

Hennessey repositioned his magnetic St Joseph statue to the centre of the dashboard and blessed himself. 'That was a close one, boys. All I'm worried for is that the girl gets over that shock of meat.' Hennessey looked straight ahead. His head was like a tossed salad, full of leaves and straw. He kept brushing flecks of dandruff on to Mr Long out of nervous habit.

'I've seen that sort of thing happen before,' Lovelace replied. 'Couple o' years ago, a dog got a fierce scare in her, but it did her no harm.'

Hennessey felt an ease in the day's tension. An awareness of the vastness of the mountains filled with living things came over him. His eyes focused on the tunnelling road, his mind wandering. He envisioned the Pink Angel beside his wife's grave, howling, the creature's honed face in that lonesome field. He took a breath, hearing a murmur of conversation in the back of the car. 'I'll tell ya something for nothin, boys.' Hennessey faced Long with an earnest frown. 'I don't know if it isn't best to feed em blood in trainin at least once or not. I heard fellas sayin it spoils a dog, but I don't know after this. I think the dog didn't know what she was about when she bit into that neck. I mean, Jasus, isn't experience the brother of reason?'

'Well, sixty pounds for an evening's work isn't all bad. What do you think, Lovelace?' Jackie asked.

'Yer right on one account, Hennessey; that girl won not on speed alone, but on brains. But as sure as God is my witness, I've never seen a hound run after it's been bled at home.'

Jackie shook his head, jiggling on the dead legs of Mr Long in the front seat. 'Believe you me, Hennessey. Your girl got a life of experience in those few seconds out there today that are worth a hundred scratches.' Jackie looked like a doll. He was all of five feet tall, with tiny hands of a soft buttery colour like a child's. He wouldn't work to warm himself. He professed he'd been a famous jockey in Newcastle for years. 'Jackie the Jockey,' he said. He had a battery of old trophies which were rumoured to have been purchased in a pawn shop in Limerick. Now he made his living as a journeyman, advising men at markets as to what looked authentic and what was 'mutton dressed up as lamb'.

Lovelace stretched his broad shoulders, pressing Bridget's face into the backdoor window. 'Dem dogs of yers are somethin else, Freddy. By Jasus, did ya see the face on her when she cut between dem other fuckin idiots, dipped her head, and nosed that hare over on its belly, before it knew what hit im? She's a natural player. A killer is nothin. She plays the game by instinct. She racks up the points. She knows murder is a game.' Lovelace rubbed his hands together. He was a fisherman who had retired early on a small fortune left to him by an aunt whom he used to stuff with kippers, mackerels, and sour lobsters on Fridays.

'Stop still,' Mr Long wailed. 'My legs have no feelin left in em!'

'What do ya want me to do, Mr Long? Stick Jackie here into the glove box?'

Mr Long kicked out his legs, disrupting the cage beneath. The small hares twitched, rustling the old newspapers with their soft clawed paws. One of the famished dogs lunged forward, smacking his muzzle into Bridget's face.

'Stop it, will ya?' The other dog shook its head and hit her in the face with its jaw.

Lovelace gave the animal a sudden fist on its wet black nose, and it yelped and retreated, whining and growling. 'I think those fellas are hungry,' Jackie suggested with a frowning of his brow, leaning around at Lovelace, reaching into his pockets for a bit of brown bread.

Hennessey brooded alone, staring down that unfathomable enigma of his wife's death, with that vision of his Pink Angel lying on the soft mound of the wet grave, hearing that haunting cry which came from the grave, not the animal. 'How is she?' he cried.

Bridget looked out her window and said nothing.

'Give em nothin, for Jasus' sake.' Lovelace brushed

Jackie's hand aside. 'A dog's got to work for his keep. If ya feed em now, after dey caught nothin, yer just trainin dem to expect somethin for nothin. Starvation is the greatest medicine in life for creatures like dem good-for-nothin idiots.'

The young boy laughed, and Hennessey hit him across the face with the back of his hand, then wiped more dandruff on Mr Long. 'You watch it there, young fella.'

'There's no call for that now, Freddy.' Mr Long rubbed his chin sanctimoniously.

The air in the car was stiflingly oppressive. Everyone took short breaths, feeling the warmth of human flesh.

Mr Long wiped a handkerchief across his face and neck. His face was red with the suffocation. He was a strange man who had never married. He was the only man the men had ever known who carried an abacus everywhere. If the odds were good, he was there for the deal, calculating risk to the last decimal. Secretly, they nicknamed him 'Long Division'.

'How about a pint for the sake of celebration, Hennessey?' Lovelace shouted out. His fat neck spilled over his unbuttoned shirt as he nodded his head up and down, answering his own questions.

Jackie rubbed his small hands together, 'Now yer talkin.'

'My legs, fer the love o' God, Jackie!'

'Da, I'm not well at all. Please, will you leave us home?'

'Check dem dogs, Bridget, and stop awhile wit that stuff.' Hennessey felt the dream-sensation of the moment embalming him in warm sweat and greasiness, the dying vibrations of that terrible howling rolling further and further away from his ears, the image of that brutalized face and the white mist on the mossy cross rising in his mind. Everything magnified itself until he could see his own footprints by that grave, staring at the silken trails of invisible worms. He could taste the earth's humus. He kept steering the car along the jagged precipices, seeing that iron cross. It stood out in such detail, with the fresh coat of white paint. He smelt it on his hands, feeling the rhythm of his hand as he etched her name and year of death, with the capital 'A.D.' at the end, as the sea inched toward him. 'Nearly there!' he shouted.

Bridget squeezed free of Lovelace's massive arm and wedged her body over the back seat. She had her face in the window, unable to turn completely, yet her hands moved knowingly over the animals. She stroked the two dogs' chests, touched their warm fur and hearts beating faintly. She felt the animals' muzzles. They wore leather muzzles strapped behind their ears with a metal buckle which often cut into the backs of their necks. Bridget ran her thin fingers over each neck, feeling for any blood or scabs. 'They're okay, Da.' The girl shut her eyes in another bout of pain. Her hand gripped Lovelace's leg for an instant. He squirmed at her touch, looking at the back of Hennessey's balding head.

Bridget's face was flushed, almost raw, dotted with small pimples on her forehead. She had two dark crescents beneath her hard green eyes. Quickly she retracted her hand, discretion vanquishing the pain for an instant. She took a deep breath, feeling the gentle throb of the engine in her soft nipples as Lovelace pressed her body into the window, shaking slightly, keeping his eye on Hennessey.

Lovelace breathed on her neck.

Outside, a front of clouds descended, low and ubiquitous, letting the skies pour. Bridget held her breath, staring out the window, watching the rain running down the warm glass. She had a certain resignation in her face. The rain had a musky smell. Her hand touched the Pink Angel. She remembered the terrible image of the poor Pink Angel when it came in, trembling in the arms of her father. She kept looking at the cataracts of water on the window.

Again Lovelace breathed on Bridget's neck. His breath was stale, yet all she smelt was the odour of the alcoholic rub her father had kneaded into the hounds' thighs and chests.

Jackie passed a squashed package of sandwiches to Hennessey. 'Nothin like a bit o' cheese and bread.' He put a small blue bottle to his lips and drank with his head tilted back on Mr Long's stiff neck. 'Ah, Jasus . . . A sup there, Lovelace?' The bottle left his tiny fingers.

'Are you okay, Bridget?' Lovelace whispered into her ear. His mouth was stuffed with the white bread. The bottle glimmered before her, Lovelace's face full of composed languor, rounded without a chin. He had small eyes like a Chinaman.

Bridget had lived within this dominion of oblique submission for over a year. Her mother had died the previous autumn while giving birth to the small child. The burden of the child fell upon Bridget. Hennessey fed Bridget like a fatted calf, stealing her childhood from her, ushering her into womanhood, stuffing her with extra cuts of bacon and boiled eggs, skimming the cream off the milk for her before bedtime, feeding her liver and cow's tongue for Sunday dinners, and salmon and lamb on Fridays. 'Oh, that was their secret,' her father smiled. 'You don't have to confess that.' Bridget had grown plump from the food, from the responsibility of this surrogate motherhood. The child lived, cradled on her pelvis, making feeble attempts to suckle at her breasts. She needed every morsel to endure the terrible nocturnal life of the motherless child. And on those dark cold nights of winter there were the awful screams of her father sitting by his fire in drunkenness. 'I loved her, Jesus,' he shouted over and over again until the baby wept into Bridget's breast.

Lovelace put his hands on Bridget's knee, like he was inspecting some creature, and smiled. He could see the soft angles of her body beginning to form under her dirty clothing. Her legs were lean and strong, coated with light ginger hair that reminded him of his animals.

In the back of the car, a crimson wound opened on the hind leg of the Pink Angel. Her tongue shone between her teeth as she gasped for some clean air. Her eyes moved slowly in her head, staring at the envelope of blue sky peeking out from the dark clouds swirling on the horizon.

'Dirty day,' Mr Long commented, rubbing the condensation off the window.

Hennessey bit into his fat lower lip, letting his massive head bob up and down as he drove along. His eyes stared into the rear-view mirror with vexed solicitude. He could see his daughter trying to push Lovelace's hand away. He kept chewing the sandwich in his mouth, moving his eyes severely between the St Joseph statue and Lovelace's image in the back seat. He could see Bridget's face breathing into the wet glass. 'We'll be there in a bit, now.' Hennessey's voice was full of phlegm and bread. Everyone was quiet. They concentrated on the soft squeak of the wipers on the windshield. The dogs circled each other in the back of the car, letting their sleek bodies rub against one another.

Hennessey coughed in sudden agitation. 'Bridget, leave dem . . . Jasus.' He took a deep breath, swallowing, 'Leave the dogs alone.'

'She's a good one, Freddy,' Lovelace laughed.

'Shut up.' Hennessey pressed the accelerator pedal to the floor, and the car shook, the tail end weaving in the mud, toppling the dogs upon one another. The Pink Angel closed her eyes and let her head absorb the rumble of the wheels.

Lovelace let his fingers creep off the girl's knee, seeing Hennessey's eyes on him. 'So tell us, Jackie, it was yourself that picked this champion, is that right?'

'It was,' shouted Hennessey, feeling a tension ease in his back, rubbing Jackie on the head as if he were a child prodigy.

The weighed-down car slowed on a steep slope, moving like a dark slug around a cragged precipice that dropped to the dark green waters of the Atlantic hundreds of feet below.

Bridget stared at the margin of gleaming sand and the small trawlers bobbing on the inrushing tide. Puffs of smoke boiled away in grey vapours. She remembered the cold saltiness when she had gone there, wrapped in a towel and rubber swimming-cap, with her mother the year before last, seeing all the children turning blue with red shovels and painted buckets in their hands. Her mother had told her how the sand was the dust of all living creatures. Bridget felt that sudden chilliness now as then, breathing in death. She knew she had still been a child on that day. Her mother had smiled and whispered, 'There are things which must be believed to be seen,' pointing out into the vast sea. She looked away. 'From ashes to ashes and dust to dust, and to dust thou shalt return ...' the priest had whispered, and she knew her mother was telling her something even then.

Hennessey worked his gear lever in and out on the dashboard, toggling the brake and clutch. Beads of sweat ran down his wrist. The black glove was sopping wet. 'Five minutes will see us in, boys.'

Everyone felt the rumble of the engine in their organs, smelling the sweet scent of petrol and the taste of salt. All their heads seemed to rock with a certain cadence. Bridget felt a strange uneasiness, her packed white breast visible before Lovelace's knowing eyes. The car continued to rock away. The sky faded above the hillside to the east, the west brooding to itself. As the car continued to crawl and groan along the gravel road, Jackie pulled out a tin box, struck a match on his zipper, and lit three cigarettes, putting one in his outstretched lips, passing one back to Lovelace, and placing the last remaining one into Hennessey's pursed lips.

Hennessey blessed himself when they went by his wife's grave.

'God rest her soul,' Jackie whispered, blessing himself in a benediction of smokiness.

Bridget thought of that wet iron-cast gate with the huge rusting padlock which kept the dead from the living. They had placed an iron cross over her mother's grave. Below, the sea was mute, but for her it carried with it an eternal whisper. The cold statue of Mary of the Sorrows seemed to levitate on the bend in the road. The figure's back was turned to the road.

Below her feet there was a little mossy cement bowl into which she had wept when Irish boys were killed at Gallipoli. Bridget went to the statue after her mother's death. She wept at the sight of brown scabs of rust speckling the statue's arms and abdomen. The face was eaten. She remembered the voice of her radio telling her of Hiroshima, of a bomb that left shadows and people without faces and skin.

Mr Long scowled away to himself. 'Will ya open a window at least? Do ya want me to die right here in the car for want of a breath of air?'

Lovelace took a drag of his cigarette and smiled, blowing a wreath of smoke above Hennessey's head.

Mr Long frowned, opening the window and letting a small tail of smoke stream out the passenger window.

The parking field was a quagmire of mud and deep trenches, lined with sunken cars, cattle wagons, horse trailers, old milk vans, two tractors, and littered here and there with tilting bicycles, braying donkeys, dazed horses, snorting pigs, and pecking chickens. The Autumn Market was in full swing. Hennessey drove around the outskirts of the scene, searching for a free space, cursing away. 'Where elephants come to die, for Jasus' sake . . .'

'Over there, Freddy.' Lovelace brushed his finger across the girl's breasts. 'Do ya see it?' He smiled to himself, drawing his lips into a bud of satisfaction. 'Over there!'

Hennessey knocked over two bicycles when he threw the car into reverse. The last rev of his car sent him coasting into the churning mud. A young man leapt in fright, dropping into the mud.

Jackie tipped his cap out the window.

'Ya bastard, Hennessey!'

Hennessey was already squeezing himself out of the car, stepping into the sinking mire, swaggering forward, butting his massive belly into the young man. 'Do ya want ta make somethin of it?'

'Four to one is some odds, Hennessey.'

Mr Long fingered his abacus in his pocket, whispering, 'If you get a reputation as an early riser, you can sleep till noon.' His smug face was a darkish brown as though it had been cooked by a fireside for too long.

The young man walked away ignominiously.

Mud oozed over Hennessey's shoes, soaking his socks. He could feel the sawdust aggravating his hairy ankle.

Bridget swung her door open and touched her father's arm. When she stood upright, the soft fattiness of her face faded into a long white neck. She reached her father's chest. 'Da, I'm not stayin here again.' Her face was taut with defiance and innocence, her eyes wide open. 'You said I could go home before you went out. You swore this time.' Her face quivered. 'Are you goin to leave the dog out here into the night? She needs blankets and food.' Bridget bit her lips.

Hennessey threw his hands in his pocket, fumbling about. 'Come on now, Bridget, love. Just a few drops, I swear to ya. We'll be on the road before ya know it.' His lips wrinkled with a smirk. 'Come on now. I'll give ya a coat here to put over her.'

'You're a liar.' The girl turned her back on Hennessey. The three men looked on. Mr Long sucked his tooth, shaking his head. 'Ten to one he hits her.'

The sting in Hennessey's hand made him wince more than it hurt Bridget's face. She remained stoic. The cooling breeze of the evening air blew her hair about her face. 'Don't think Mam can't see what ya did to me.'

'Go on, will ya?' Hennessey shouted to Lovelace who took a heavy puff of his cigarette, nudging Jackie who stepped aside, lowering his eyes. Mr Long grinned in smug satisfaction.

Hennessey took hold of Bridget. 'I'm sorry. If I didn't . . .' His hairy hands trembled on her shoulders. 'If I didn't have you . . .'

Bridget suppressed the tears in her eyes. 'She'll die. Ya know that, don't ya?'

Hennessey coughed and swallowed his spit, touching Bridget's taut face. 'Come on now, my love. I swear to ya.' His lips touched her hot cheek. He could taste the salt on his own lips. 'Will ya cover the Pink Angel for me?'

Jackie waded through the mud and green manure, each pull of his leg giving a soft sucking sound. 'We'll send out minerals and crisps to ye in a few minutes, Bridget. Come on now, girl. This was a good win for us all.' His small hand rubbed the red imprint on Bridget's face. 'There now, girl.' He put a silver coin into the small boy's hand. 'There ya are, winnin's for all,' he laughed, smiling at Hennessey.

'Spare the rod, spoil the child,' Lovelace said in a severe tone, his toes twiddling in his shoes. He had his cap askance on his head, like a school bully. 'Leave her be, for fuck's sake.'

The sky was purple overhead. Streaks of weak light from the cars circling the lot washed the faces of the four men. Everyone seemed to be converging on the pub.

'We'd best be gettin in if we're to get a seat at all,' Long grumbled under his breath. He already had a deck of cards in the palm of his hand.

'Rain will be coming down in a bit I'm figurin, Freddy,' Mr Long said with a sigh of agitation.

'Jasus, there'll be no chance of a seat at this fuckin rate.' Lovelace took another pull from his Sweet Afton, blowing smoke through his mouth.

Hennessey kissed his daughter. 'Okay, love?'

Bridget nodded amidst sniffles, 'Ya,' smiling behind her long auburn hair. She could still feel the sting of his hand.

'I'm countin on ya, Bridget. Mind yerself awhile. This is the last time, I swear.' Slowly, Hennessey began to unscrew the window levers from two doors and whispered, 'Get dem ones over there, will ya, Bridget.' She leaned over her small sister and twirled the handle off the door and gave it to her father. Lovelace had the passenger handle in his pocket already.

'We're off then,' Jackie sang as he turned and made an

earnest dash for the dry gravel path leading up to the pub door.

Hennessey put the handles in a brown paper bag and put it under the rear wheel. One last time, Hennessey stuck his head into the hound's den of coarse hair and piss, petting their warm heads, letting them nose and lick his gloved hand. He could see the Pink Angel's eyes staring at him from the corner. 'I'll send out a bit of brown bread and a bucket of gruel in a while for her, okay?' Hennessey shut the door and turned the key. His eyes shut tight for a moment. The mud smelt of animal waste and human piss. He let a shudder pass through him, thinking of that dog and his daughter, but he could not bring himself to go back. He assigned the animal's fate to providence for no better reason than that he was a coward among the clamour of other males.

Lovelace put his menacing head to the window, his neck bulging like a frog, smiling at Bridget. 'Ya have yer hands full there, Freddy,' Lovelace began in disgust.

Hennessey shook off Lovelace's touch. 'Come on, will ya?' The vision of the soft reddening evening and the abject spectacle of the cars and animals sunk into his head.

Bridget smiled at the two young children.

'Da says we's getting crisps and minerals, Bridget.' The young boy's nose was running in two lines of green snot.

Bridget pulled his shirt down below his belly-button. 'Martin, yer a good fella.'

He smiled, and his lips wrinkled. 'We's gettin cheese and onion, Da says.'

Bridget looked after her father and the men as they sauntered toward the bar, the diminutive Jackie holding her father's hand like a child. Lovelace had his long black coat under his arm, smoke pouring from his head. Mr Long was waving his fanned-out cards like a Spanish Señorita, the beads of his abacus clacking faintly in his coat.

Bridget sat quietly in the car, running her fingers through the boy's hair. 'We'll let her sleep, okay?' The small baby girl rested her back against the car door. A garland of blonde curls touched her elbow. She breathed like an old man, snoring with her chin resting on her chest, her fat little legs stretched out on the seat.

The young boy stroked the dogs in the back. They moved their heads from side to side, rubbing their faces into one another, their pink eyes watching the front seats. They could smell the hares' fur and urine on the newspaper. They whined interminably, shrugging off the young boy's groping hands, their teeth shining under their gums.

'Leave them alone, Martin,' Bridget smiled. 'They haven't eaten today.'

'Are they hungry?' The boy pulled his hand away, hearing the animals growling.

Bridget could see the stricken shape of the Pink Angel huddled against the arched wheel column. The creature's face was buried in her palpitating stomach. Bridget pushed the other dogs aside. The Pink Angel cowered, flicking her ears, and stiffened her limbs at the girl's touch. Her body was cold, the pelt soaked. 'There now, girl, shoo.' Bridget kept stroking the Pink Angel between the ears. She could feel the deep cut along the jaw muscle, feel the black spider-like thread her father had used to sew up the wound. The soft brown fur was blotted with dry maroon spots. Hennessey had not put the muzzle back over her face for fear of agitating the wound.

'Will she be okay, Bridget?' The boy looked earnestly at the twitching body.

'She'll need rest and food.' Bridget nodded her head silently, holding the boy's hand. She took off her own cardigan and tucked it gently around the Pink Angel's body. The other dogs whimpered around her, letting their long pink tongues lap at her hand. Bridget took a deep breath, inhaling the pungent odour of the menthol ointment and alcoholic rub. She felt that sudden queasiness again, cramping her stomach and swooning her head. The dogs passed by her face, their pelts rubbing against her cheek. She could not move, feeling their fur teeming. Their legs were beginning to knot with fatigue.

A cold rain washed away the dead insects on the windshield. The young boy cried when he could see nothing at all, the loose rain hitting the windows, drumming on the roof. 'Da said we was gettin crisps and minerals,' Martin sniffled, clutching his sister's arm. 'Why won't he come out to us?' His red face was buried in his sister's warm lap.

The cold wind tugged at the car, letting it sway gently. The baby girl awoke and began to scream. Bridget took her in her arms and rocked her back and forth, putting a bottle in her mouth.

'You'll be okay, my little baby.' Bridget could see nothing in the window. She knew her father would not come out in this downpour. There was to be no food or milk or brown bread for them or the dogs. The Pink Angel licked her lips. She was on fire. Bridget ran her fingers on the cold window. The beads of moisture dropped into the animal's mouth. The dog closed its eyes, its tongue curling on the wet fingers. The wounds had not been cleaned properly around the face. The crude stitchwork of her father's hand cut a series of small deep wounds into the dog's jaw that were already swelling in rings of white infection. Bridget stared at the teary windows, gathering water for the animal. She thought of her father inside the warmth of the pub, his face cooking in the heat. Mr Hines always had stew and potatoes simmering, with lots of brown bread and melted butter.

The child in her arms cried. The rain drifted in a cold iciness, teeming on the windows in a fine mist. The young boy curled into his sister's arms, feeling the sudden stiffness in his sister's cold body, trying to rub the baby with his own small hand. 'I want my Da,' he sobbed, 'I want my Da.' His small fingers ran across the baby's swollen cheeks.

Bridget rubbed his head, fighting the pain. 'Come on, Martin, he'll be back with crisps for you when the rain dies.'

In some other car some maddened children danced on the car horn, shouting curses at the top of their voices. 'Da, fuckin come out to us!'

Martin turned his flushed face up at Bridget, smiling, hearing the other children. 'Their da is goin to beat dem ones, right, Bridget?' Then he felt his own hunger. 'Will he come soon, Bridget?'

'Yes, pet, shoosh a while.'

The boy nodded his head, laughing as the children kept screaming, 'Ya fuckin gombhean, Da. I'll fuckin break the window, do ya hear me? I'll fuck up these chickens.' Feathers floated in one of the cars. 'Look, look, Bridget! Dem fellas killed a chicken over there. Look!'

The wind blew in from the sea, filling the rain with the aroma of seaweed.

Bridget looked down at the child in her arms. The small baby's face was soft and pudgy, the chin shining with dribbles. Slowly, she placed the child on the seat. She put her finger to her mouth and went, 'Shoosh,' and the young boy nodded his head, trying to peep through the wet window. 'They killed a chicken. I seen em do it.'

Outside, the clouds came down low, thick as fog, bringing with them a cold ubiquity. A brooding copper poured into the sky. A light went on in the pub. Bridget smelt the peat burning. A sudden shudder went through her body. She was stunned by the proximity of this concealed life of food and warmth.

'I'm hungry,' the boy whined in Bridget's face. He saw the light go on, instinct filling in the scent of honey pork and baking apples.

Bridget rubbed his forehead. She could see the shapes of men bobbing their heads about in the small square windows. She braced her body, feeling the cold bodies of her father's two children against her waist. She imagined her father and all those men enveloped in the warmth of the roasting fire, the warm gestation of their fattening flesh growing big with heat and potatoes. Slowly, she stroked the baby's hair, curling it behind the ears. The baby sucked air through a rubber teat, her blue lips and tongue working instinctively in her sleep. Bridget knew the child's stomach would be filled with air, but she could not bring herself to wake the baby. The baby turned her head, and Bridget took her hand away. She could see the contrast of the baby's alabaster skin against the old stained seat. The brown cloth covering had frayed and come apart along the edges. A few wayward springs pressed through the bleached threaded cloth in the ribbed stitching. Her father had stuffed straw and old clothing into some of the tears where the dogs had eaten the soft mustard sponge cushioning. Scabs of blackness were dotted here and there from errant cigarette butts.

Outside, everything was cold and wet, desolate. On her radio at night, the soothing English ghost spoke to her of the miles upon miles of trenches and the dead bodies of boys being carried back from nomansland. She named this sea of mud between her father and these children Nomansland.

The late evening sun was lost in the sky behind the clouds, only breaking through in chinks. Bridget knew the sea would be a dark copper colour now as this wind blew the sand on the shore up on to the graves. She'd once found a seashell with a snail curled into it near her mother's grave. She wondered if a bird had dropped it there, or was the wind so fierce that it could do such things?

A young boy's face in the window next to her car stared at her. He looked straight at her without smiling. Behind him she could see three small boys with tears in their eyes. Bridget smiled softly at the boy. He looked about him, wondering if he was the one that she was smiling at. He saw no other faces.

He blushed and pushed a fringe of hair out of his face, smiling back feebly. Their eyes locked on one another. The boy pointed to the pub and Bridget rolled her eyes in her head, shrugging her shoulders. She felt the dampness creeping into her bones. They both smiled and then turned their eyes away for an instant. Bridget could see the whitewashed pub beyond. Bridget felt a word in her throat, her lips wanting to say something. She took a deep breath. The closeness of the car wrapped itself around her oppressively. She smelt again the odour of the dogs, the liniment ointment, the stale wounds and blood of the Pink Angel. She could see strands of the dog's hair stuck to the cold windows. There was a sourness from the small baby's empty bottle. Again, she looked at the boy. She held back screams. Her knuckles were white with the coldness and hunger.

The youth nodded toward his brothers who clambered around the front seat window and stuck their tongue out at Bridget and her small brother. Martin put his thumbs in his ears and wiggled his fingers. Everyone burst out laughing, Bridget and the boy imagining the soft laughter of each other. Again, they turned their eyes away. Bridget looked back at the curled, slumped body of the Pink Angel. She was panting, beads of sweat running into her eyes. Bridget rubbed the tears of sweat away with her index finger. 'You'll be okay, my girl.' She tucked the stray edges of her cardigan around the creature's freezing body, looking away toward the warm throb of the snug publican cottage. She thought of all those words her father spoke to her about grief and pain, and how he fed her until she felt she would be sick because he needed her to be strong. 'I love ya,' he screamed all those nights. 'You have to be the mother now.' Over pleas and hot whiskeys, he whispered, 'Bridget, I want ya to name the child. She belongs to you.'

The wind outside brought with it the lovely smell of the late autumn apples. It whistled through the rusty exhaust pipes of the cars, rattling the horse trailers. The wet scented air curled around each car.

The children could taste the raindrops before they began falling again. Bridget looked at the beautiful face of the boy in the window. He seemed to huddle low. The rainy clouds dragged their soft dark bellies over the sharp crosses needling heaven up on the hill. The children all dipped their heads below their windows, even the boys who broke the chicken's neck. The clouds burst in a torrent of hailing rain. All the children closed their eyes. Their faces turned white with the cold shock of the wind. They could hear the lone donkey braying. Bridget thought of that boy in the car beside her. His face burned in her heart. She felt the stab of pain again in her stomach. She cried faintly. Her small brother clutched her arm. The two dogs sat very still, staring at the Pink Angel. She didn't move, her black eyes frozen stiff. A thread of blood hung from her mouth.

'I want my da,' Martin sobbed, his face hidden from the grey clouds. 'He said we was getting somethin to eat, Bridget. I heard him tell us. He promised.' Martin kept sniffling on to Bridget's arm, wetting it with sobs. His small fingers were nearly frozen.

Bridget sat rigid, cradling her brother, whispering, 'Shoosh,' minding the small nursing face of her little baby. Her eyes kept seeing that boy. She would tell him she had named her father's baby. She would let him share that secret, and whisper to him about the poor Pink Angel and how her father left her there in his car even though she had won him sixty-five pounds. 'Bastard,' she sobbed.

The rain continued to pour out of the sky, drumming down on the roof. Huge droplets splatted on the windows. She kept praying her child would not wake up. Martin had eased his sobs. The rain mesmerized him. The light had grown so dim that Bridget could barely see his face. She saw his thumb in his mouth.

On the dashboard the small figurine of St Joseph weathered the rain with stoic humility and patience.

Bridget let out a small animal cry, feeling a long slow unfurling of something inside her body. She suppressed low groans. She put her hand down the waist of her skirt. Her stomach was drenched with cold moisture. Then the pain eased. Her eyes were weary with effort, her face fagged with exhaustion. She had not eaten her breakfast that morning. Her father had been in too much of a hurry to get this new dog out for her warm-up.

In the back of the car the two dogs licked each other's face. Bridget could hear their coarse tongues. They would start howling soon when the hunger became too much. A child had been eaten the past spring by two starving creatures.

Slowly, the evening began to brighten again. The sky cleared to a deep viscous red. Droplets of rain glowed in coloured beads. The sun was visible as a huge red eye. Bridget peeked above the door, trying to look through the misty window. She saw a shimmer of light on the hillside. She rubbed the mist away from her window with the cuff of her shirt. She could see the rain had flooded the field. The cars were marooned like small islands in the red water. All about the still pool of reddish water, children stared out at one another. A static quietness prevailed. The cold suck of the wind rippled the glassiness of the lake. Bridget could see small fingers cutting the thin film of mist away, exposing the new world. She felt the chilling dampness of the car slowly seeping into her bones, feeling that same twinge of pain in her stomach. She swallowed softly, putting her hand on her small sister, feeling the soft hair of her baby's eyelashes. The baby's tiny fingers gripped her empty milk bottle.

The boy was already clearing his window, his eyes fixed on Bridget's car. She could see his face gawking through the red evening. Bridget put her lips to the window, tasting the icy glass. The boy put up three fingers, then pointed downward, cradling his head on the palm of his hands. Bridget nodded her head and pointed to her two invisible bodies. In the distance they could see that the boys who had killed the chicken were still hidden away beneath the glass. Their windows were frosted.

Everything shone with a new gleam, all wet and glossy. Bridget stared at that face in the other car. She had not even heard him talk. What must he have been like? Did he talk like a boy or a man? 'A boy,' she whispered to herself, but it did not matter, as it did not matter in dreams where the mind filled in abstraction with the colours of necessity. A rich black smoke rose from the chimney, carrying with it a hive of floating soot and red needles. That was another world of which she knew nothing. That was a strange man's world so inviting and warm, a place neither she nor any woman could be a part of. Her mother died when her father was away at this place. When Bridget had finally come to get him, they would not let her in. She had to tell a strange man to tell her father that his wife was dead.

Bridget kept staring at the face of this boy in the window. Her fingers were white and trembling. How many men had whispered that terrible secret of her mother's death? Was this soft face to be numbered with those beyond? She used to dream about that mad confusion of her mother's death, the horrible buzzing rumour of death, like a virus, turning smiling faces black. A chant of voices whispering, 'Your wife is dead.' She knew she would have said it differently, in woman's words, but they made her stand there in the night, outside, alone.

The boy pointed at her window, moving his hand in a slow circle. Bridget took a breath, instinctively trying to breathe in the freshness of the afterrain. The small car teemed with a film of water.

The boy put his hand to the glass, smiling. Bridget pointed downward and shook her head, turning her hand in slow motion. They both raised their eyebrows, and showed their teeth with laughter. When she stopped smiling she could hear the faint squeal of the hares in the front seat of the car. She looked toward the cage. Polished eyes looked at her. In the back, the two dogs flicked their tails back and forth, resigned to the long evening. They seemed to understand that the girl could do nothing for them. Bridget smiled at them, stroking their muzzled faces. Their wet eyes looked at her for an instant and then left her face for the solace of each other's blank stare. In the other corner, the Pink Angel was perfectly still. Her eyes remained open, drifting in her head. There was a dribble of blood in her right nostril. Bridget shut her eyes and felt the burn of sorrow. The Pink Angel moved its head toward her outstretched hand. It wanted more water. She felt the creature's cold nose against the tips of her fingers. It seemed to want to know its crime. It would not submit in ignorance.

In the other car, the young boy was not looking at her any more. His head was bent. Bridget sat slumped against the window, looking at him. Her two children were fast asleep. She knew it was the kind of sleep that vanquished hunger and poured in dreams that would last until morning. It was the kind of sleep that was more of a drug than anything else, it was some innate response within the body to give up for periods of time, relying on time to change circumstances, like some hibernation of sorts. Bridget kept thinking of how the men would come tumbling out and wrench these babies from their sleep and breathe on them and make them weep. She thought of the cold fingers of Lovelace when he touched her knee. Her father must have seen it. Oh yes, and must have done what he could, which was nothing. She was not his to own, just to abuse.

Bridget's face was knotted with the pain in her abdomen. She kept looking at the nameless boy in the glass. She thought of her mother in that shaking bed at home, how she screamed when her man was not there, with such pain bleeding down her legs. The mother held a picture of Jesus in a frame against her face. The brutalized wounds in his hands seemed to flow from her mother. She screamed, a stigma there between those legs. Her mother's flesh was so withered and rough on her face and hands and arms, but it was not like that there. Everything was white and fatty. She saw everything. She never told her father how her mother had torn at her hair when she went crying into her arms, not knowing what was wrong. Did he ask when he saw that pink bald spot on the back of her head or the cuts on her arm and neck? He must have known, and why didn't he say anything, just one word so she would have understood that what she was thinking was right? But he said nothing, drinking, miles away from his dying wife and shaking daughter. She blamed herself all this time. She should have known. Only a fool wouldn't have known where babies came from. But nobody had told her the truth. Under a head of cabbage. Holy Jesus, she believed that, up until she saw that thing down there between her mother's legs, with eyes – yes eyes – and, Jesus, then she knew. A baby! And one mile to the next house, the door left wide open. Running through those fields, the cows looking at her with their heads cocked sideways, eating dandelions, as ignorant as what she had been before those moments.

The boy saw her face. He put his brother down, shouting, banging his hand on the glass.

Bridget let her face fall from the window until her body was out of sight. She curled against her children, shaking with the pain stabbing through her body. The baby girl began to cry as Bridget pressed herself too hard against the child's head. Young Martin gripped her arm, crying, 'What's wrong, Bridget, what wrong? I want my da . . .'

The dogs growled and sat up erect, thrashing their heads into one another. They could smell the hares again in the front seat.

Martin tried to put his hand out to touch the dogs, but Bridget snapped it away. 'Don't touch them, Martin. Do you hear me?'

The dogs butted the Pink Angel, tearing away the cardigan around her body. Her eyes were adrift in her head.

Bridget let her body slump down in the back seat. She had her eyes shut, her body rigid, her hands groping at her small baby. Her mouth was half open, panting. 'Oh Jesus, no! Martin, leave them dogs alone.'

Martin stood on the seat, crying.

The boy could see his contorted face. Martin began screaming.

The dogs lunged at him, smacking their hard muzzles into his face.

The boys in the next car saw the dogs and began dancing on their father's horn. All over the field, horns blared. A flock of birds rose out of the thatched cottage roof, squalling. 'The dogs are killin em over there! Get help!'

Bridget shook. 'Martin, oh please, come here to me.' She was screaming, the pain in her abdomen racing through her neck and back, paralysing her. Only her mouth opened and closed. 'Mammy!'

Martin fell on top of her, crying and shaking. 'Bridget, get Daddy. Please, get Daddy!' The dogs kept snapping fitfully over the seat, biting at Martin. Their eyes were drifting back into their heads. He hit one of them on the snout. The dog wheeled about, jumping forward at Martin. Again, he hit the dog. The creature desisted, growling, with water streaming out of its eyes.

Bridget drifted near unconsciousness, her face white. She heard the smash of glass. The three tinkers had broken their father's windshield. 'Martin . . .' She reached out toward him. 'Give them the hares now.' She swallowed and turned her head to the baby.

'Look at them out there, Bridget!' Martin was trembling with excitement.

One of the dogs took a bite at the Pink Angel and she groaned softly, scraping her nails against the thin metal of the door frame.

'Do it,' Bridget whined. 'Don't let them kill her, Martin.'

Martin looked at the dogs and they glared at him, defying him. Slowly, he reached into the front of the car and took hold of the old mesh cage and looked at Bridget, and then at the silent children outside. He raised the cage before them all. The dogs whined, their heads moving imperceptibly.

Bridget could hear the dogs growling and tensing their

necks.

Martin was crying, the tears were in his eyes and then the cage tipped over and the hares scraped the mesh, thumping their legs in the air. One of the dogs tore a paw away, and blood sprayed all over Martin's face.

The children outside roared, breaking windows, kicking away shards of glass. The boy screamed inside his car. His brothers sat on the horn.

Martin wailed, the blood streaming down his face.

The throb of music in the pub stopped abruptly. Bridget imagined the dark semaphore of the faces with upturned eyebrows passing on the message of the rebellion in the sea of the parking field. A hundred faces piled out the doors. They would beat sense into these creatures.

There were windows smashed everywhere, legions of children splashing in the mud, painting with the reddish-brown slime like newborn creatures with twisted faces and sharp teeth, screaming curses at one another, kicking at the greyhounds, spilling ducks and geese and hares and rabbits out of mesh hutches, throwing away everything in sight.

Other sombre-faced children sat quietly holding one another.

Hennessey and his three companions scrambled through the mud. The pub door swung on a broken hinge. Hennessey could see Martin crying in the front seat, beating the horn. None of the men said a word, their eyes fixed on their children. Hennessey dropped his keys in the mud. They were swallowed immediately. He kept running, slipping and sliding in the slick mud, his fingers clawing into the wet clay.

'Oh Jasus, what is it, boy?'

Martin began screaming, 'Da . . . Da . . . Why did ya do this to us?'

Hennessey drove his fist through the back-door window. He could see Bridget twisted on the back seat with the baby in her arms. 'Nooo . . .' The dogs worked intently, licking the bleeding hares.

Lovelace came panting behind Hennessey and put a set of keys into his hands. 'Loo ... loo ...' He tried to catch his breath. 'Look at this place.' There were chicken feathers and dead geese all over the muddy sea. Young children scurried about, tarred and feathered, spitting at the grown men, swinging animals and sticks in their hands.

Hennessey's hands trembled as he tried to open the door. Martin's face was white with shock, his tiny fingers reaching for his father's arms. 'We had to give em the hares. They was goin ta eat us all, Da.'

'Yer okay now, boy.'

Hennessey roared at the top of his lungs. His son wrapped himself in his arms. Hennessey pushed him aside. Jackie held the child around the shoulders, rubbing his head, feeling the timid pressure of the boy's hands. 'Easy, boy.' The wind pulled at Jackie's small grey beard.

The sky grew dark behind Hennessey's back. The children were still screaming, tearing away at each other's faces, jumping on top of cars, kicking the stubborn braying donkey. Inside, Hennessey saw his girl lying curled around her sobbing infant. Blood seeped through her skirt. She had her scapula pressed to her bosom.

Bridget felt her father's cold hands on her breasts, covering her body.

'Gimme somethin for her, quick, for Christ's sake.'

She shut her eyes when he carried her in his arms. She felt the slow maturation, the metamorphosis of adolescence throbbing inside her, uncoiling itself in a hidden darkness under her clothing. There seemed to be so much flesh inside her body, slowly padding her breasts and hips. All those rashers and eggs and brown bread had brought her to this flood of womanhood. She felt her mother's legacy in the inheritance of this blood. If only this nature had come a year earlier, all these secrets would have unfolded themselves to her then. She would have known what to do for her mother. A year in limbo, a child posing as a woman, touching her own breasts at night, massaging them, trying to mould them into something they could only become with time. She could feel her father's hot kisses on her head. He smelt of whiskey and stew. She did not resist. Her eyes moved under her eyelids. She was far away, thinking of that graveyard with the wet mossy headstones and the smell of that freshly dug earth, herself in a black dress holding that small white infant when they poured the first shovel of dirt into the hole. Her mother would spend another night there alone with the roaring sea. The black print of her name would be peeling away with the winter's storms.

Bridget shivered at the touch of her father. His swollen lips kissed her on the forehead one more time. 'I'm sorry, I'm sorry . . .'

All about the car, faces poured over her slumped body. 'Is she dead?'

Long superintended everything, his face pickled with the cold rush of the night air. Every pore was open, sweating from the warmth of the fire and the money he had left back at the pub.

The world had a strange deformity. There were no shadows, only the inchoate emotions of trembling boys looking at their fathers, whining, 'Da . . .'

The cool evening wind rippled the water. It stirred with some organic intent, feeling these hidden feet sunk in its body. The cars and the people and dead animals and the hounds were all castaways in this sea. Everything had an eerie silence like midnight as Lovelace coughed, standing solemnly before the crowd, holding the stiff corpse of the Pink Angel in his arms.

THE BUTCHER'S DAUGHTER

I KEEP TELLIN myself to relax, but I can't. I want to tell em all. If I can just stop myself from tellin em . . . Ya get scared, ya know? That's all. When I was young I used to tell the other children there was no such thing as Christmas, because I just couldn't keep the secret. I was a right wee bitch. It had been spoiled for me. I had to tell em all on the street, 'Listen ya thick fools, yer dad and yer mam buys yer toys, not Santa Claus.' I got a doll named Sweet Colleen that year. I was still very young. That was just when the Troubles started. I was too young to remember things like Bloody Sunday. But I remembered that doll all right. I've never slept a night without her since.

I'm not a child. Children don't have babies. I have a baby. It's in my womb. That's what the doctor calls it. He has icy white hands like a woman. I can feel my baby at night when I'm lyin down. It's like a small sweet in my pocket, or a plum. We share the same blood, my baby and me. It's a wee boy. I just know it. That's 'mother's intuition' for ya, or that's what the nurse at the clinic says. She knows. She's delivered most of the babies on our street, and she says, 'Mothers! Yeah, they know stuff that others don't. They know what they got inside em.' I think I fed it too much smoke and gin and tonics for it to be any good. No! I'm not a very good mother. I don't eat right or nothin. But it doesn't matter. I would have been. But I knew from the beginning it wouldn't matter. Mother's intuition, ya know what I'm sayin, like? Mothers know that

71

kind of stuff. My child will have a different life, a life in death. Doesn't that sound strange? Well, ya haven't lived here. He'll be another unborn hero of Ireland in fifteen minutes or less.

When you're pregnant ya get seats on buses, and people say, 'after you,' and they smile at ya, and they carry your messages up the street for ya. This ol one from across the road comes over of an evenin sometimes when her ol fella's out, and she rubs my ankles. She says, 'Ya don't want to get toxaemia.' She says, 'Lay off the salt and vinegar crisps if ya know what's good for ya.' I tell her, 'Sure, sure,' just as long as she rubs my ankles. Ah, people are funny all right when you're havin a wee baby. They want to make sure nothin happens until it's out. It's like when you're in somebody's house and they keep sayin, 'Don't make a noise or bang a door. We've a cake in the oven. It has to rise.' And ya just nod your head and say, 'Oh, I see now. A cake in the oven . . .' And then what do they do when it comes out? They eat it in big crumblin bites.

No . . . No, I'm savin my baby from all this. I know a mountain of things now, like mother's intuition and . . . and toxaemia. I've grown up quickly here. They'll be sayin all sorts o' tripe, like how it was really the boyfriend come back for revenge in the body of the girl he loved. Oh, love is a very potent thing! Don't think they won't believe it. On the bus they used to hear me talkin to the baby. I was so beside myself with grief and the pain. I could never love another. Of course a man could. A widow like me is a saint. Ya don't touch a saint. Ya just nod your head reverently like when ya go to Mass and bow your head when ya light a candle. And when ya have a baby and your man is dead, people want to give old clothes. 'Franky doesn't need these shirts. He's outgrown this long ago.' I saw her polishin the floor with that shirt the week before. Charity is a queer thing. Do ya think I would dress a wee baby up like a rag doll?

It'll be over soon, though. And then the talk will start when they start seein the empty milk bottles pilin up by the front porch. They'll build a shrine of graffiti to me and my little one, ya can count on that. I'm goin to be famous all right. There's a hero in every family I know here. Ah yea, pictures in the papers and all . . . Oh God, it's so hard to stop from sayin somethin. All these weeks I've been keepin it a secret, just tellin my baby. He says he understands. He's seen with my eyes and heard with my ears, so don't ya make me cry. Do ya hear me? Tellin me I didn't give him a chance . . . I did. I did! And there is no limbo. You're wrong. The Pope done away with that. That baby of mine, he knows what it's been like all these months within me. Yeah, yeah . . . Standin in line at the clinic for hours, and him twistin about in pain . . . Easy to point a finger, isn't it? I stood for that bus every Tuesday and Friday for an hour in the rain, with only a slip of a coat around my belly. And why shouldn't I have drank to keep warm? Well, tell me. Tell me. I never meant to hurt anybody. I swear . . .

That bartender looks like a basset hound over there. Jasus! I'm strong. Just don't ask me questions or tell me not to do what I must do . . . Look at him, just will ya? He's nervous as hell. He keeps lookin at my purse. He has a bald spot like a wet eye. There are cameras everywhere. Ya see em over there? Don't look! What is he thinkin?

He knows they starve themselves up there in the alphabet prison. But a girl with a wee baby and a pram and a bomb? They do that kind of thing in Palestine or whatever it is, but not here. It's amazin how people will just look into a pram and say yer baby has a lovely smile even when it's only a doll. Ya just have to say it's tired. People don't expect anythin from a baby.

But Christ! He's nervous. His eyes are gettin redder and redder. I know he's afraid. Jesus, have mercy on my soul! I shouldn't shake so. I think it's the pneumonia. 'Walkin pneumonia' is what that nurse down at the clinic says it was. Jasus, I nearly laughed, or I mean I would have if I could have, but I couldn't. Jasus! 'Walkin pneumonia', funny name that. All these names of things ya never knew were out there: mother's intuition, toxaemia, walkin pneumonia. I suppose I would have learned a lot more of em if I was goin to be here longer.

There's really nothin to be afraid of in here. I have escaped from out there. This is my universe in here. I have chosen the living from the dead.

Those whores over there just won't stop! They don't believe in babies. Laugh, laugh, laugh! Over on the weekend boat from Loverpool ... Three hundred pound for a good weekend of it ... Christ! Ya could live great durin the week. That's the way it is with big countries. Ya can do what ya want. Alienation has its freedom.

'Can I get ya a drink, luv?'

'No! I'm waitin on someone. Maybe later, okay?'

'All rightie, luv. Ya shouldn't smoke with a baby.'

Must have been checkin the accent. Cute as foxes, these boys. I saw him peekin down me blouse, don't tell me I'm imaginin it. I saw him right enough.

'How old?'

'Ten months and a day, thank you very much.' Big smile from me to him, and from him to me again ... That same ol smile goes round and round. I know the world now. Just in time for what? Ya well may ask, my baby ...

I'll have to say an act of contrition or somethin before it's all over. 'Bless me father, for I will sin.'

Well, there's no turnin back now. Goodbye to nailbombs and all that stuff. Who says the crucifixion happened only once? Last year this young fella comes home with a bit of his ear in his school bag. Can you imagine that?

I shouldn't have wasted the money on them drinks, though. Two pound ten a drink! But it's not every day ya die. I shouldn't be worried about money. But still, some things will follow ya to the grave. I was worried for so long about it that now I can't forget. All them bus trips in that slip of a coat from

Marks and Spencer's Spring Collection, all through the whole bloody winter . . . My belly turned blue. I was like that wee bitch in *The Exorcist*. Oh Jasus, drink and be merry. Ya can't take it with you! But the Egyptians thought otherwise. That's what they said in school. I don't really care, though. I'll just sit here with the bomb in my pram, sippin rum and coke at two pound ten a glass and thinkin about nothin at all.

There is sweat runnin down the barman's back. What girl buys her own drinks at two pound ten a go? Either suicide or martyrdom . . . He can't decide. He doesn't even know he's askin himself the question. He's just sweatin, loosenin his collar. He'll never approach me. He's too civilized to save his own life. And I'm too ignorant to save my own. Two sides of the same coin, I suppose . . .

Did I tell ya that my father has only two fingers on his hand? I didn't. Well, he does. Yes, and that there's always meat under his nails. He's a butcher, a man as tender as his meats. When he rubs my head at night, I turn into the pillow and shiver. But ya can't tell your father to 'piss off', now, can ya? I don't mind any more. I've been smellin the sour meat on his clothes for all my life. He's got fat fingers that crawl up my back at night. He loves his wee girl. That's just what I'll tell them up in heaven.

His hands smelled of a different meat in the mornin, though. Jasus! I grew up too young.

Did I tell ya my father's been livin on one joke for years? I don't begrudge him anythin. People live on one hope for all their lives, so why not a joke? He says I'm a fine 'cut' of a girl to all our patrons. They think that is the funniest thing in the world, because they want cheap meat. I don't blame em, either. Who doesn't want a cheap Sunday roast for a nod and a wink?

I used to look up their knickers. I could tell ya who they were, without seein their faces, by the age of three. And all that talcum powder . . . They used to shake their fat arses in my face. Jasus!

'We are descended from apes,' I told the nuns at school long before I had ever heard of evolution. I was five years old then, 'advanced for my years', everyone said.

Maybe I'll break this fiver and get a few more heads of the Queen into my pocket before the grand finale.

He sees my orange shirt. I look like a fuckin bumblebee, for Christ's sake. I scared the shite out of him. Would he believe me if I told him Eamon had a cat named Ian Paisley? Christ! He'd burst out in tears, for Jesus' sake. He must know now that I'm goin to kill him. 'A rum and coke, Charlie!' And he just obliges with a smile, without showin his teeth. He has that kind of typical English face that burns when things don't go his way. He's still smilin though. Always a gentleman . . . Always a silly bitch . . . Me and him, two sides of the same coin . . . Who knows or cares? We'll be on the same side of the grave in minutes.

When I was young, I crept into my father's room because I heard moanin, and there was my father turnin the light on and his fingers covered in blood. Can ya imagine that? I know I was a butcher's daughter, but it's one thing to have a lip for blood on the choppin block, and it's entirely another to have your father's fingers covered with blood in the bed. 'Red Hand' of Ulster, I'll tell you . . . I could smell different kinds of blood even back then. I always thought it was strange, though. Ya know? I think it's strange that Catholics have to do it durin that time for it to be safe. Don't you? But then life is full of compromises when you're a Catholic.

My father was a better man than to eat what he served his customers. For breakfast we ate lumpy porridge ladled by my mother into our bowls – I hated the shite – and slices of pink salmon on brown bread, washed down with tea and milk. That was for him, 'not for little rats like me', said my mother. My dad used to gimme some of his, with a grin on his face, when my ma would have her back turned. I bet she knew all the time, though. I wonder if I would have been that kind of a mother.

Those were the good times, though. Nine years of age and nothin to worry about, the news cracklin away, the pale mornin floodin into our shop, warmin my father's meats, all the flies swimmin in the blue light of my father's window . . . I loved my father and mother. I hope this business doesn't hurt Da's trade. There'll be jokes. You'll be damn sure Ma won't be there. She'll be havin one of her fits.

Rain or sunshine, my father lit a gorgeous fire in the back of the shop. The mornin fire was as dependable as sunrise. All day my father laughed away in the distance, and I would be doin my homework on the floor smellin supper. I used to toast the soft cuts of bread on a fork for all of us and butter my father's toast with the back of a glowin knife we kept by the grate, with its handle wrapped in a towel. My mother was always sayin, 'Ya let that tinker away with too much. Spare the rod and spoil the child, John!' I don't think I would have said that to my baby. No, I wouldn't have. But my mother used to eat Valium for breakfast, dinner, and tea.

Vincent was my father's helper. He used to give me chickens' feet and show me how the knuckles in the chickens' and the pigs' feet could be moved about. Ya had to squeeze the skin just so. It took the mystery out of life. He told me not to tell my father, and I didn't. He taught me all about the inside of a cow, of a pig, of a sheep. I put my hand into a chicken. I sat down in the carcass of a cow. He slapped stomachs and kidneys and livers onto my father's choppin block, cuttin away fringed fat and silky tissue.

They arrested Vincent when I was ten. My father said he was a 'poor bastard'. We never saw him again. And I stopped mentionin the 'poor bastard' in my prayers shortly afterwards, because I thought it was vaguely a sin to curse durin prayers.

People said I was advanced for my age when I told em that a cow had four stomachs, and that a liver produced bile, and that the kidney stored piss. I could have said urine, but who in the hell says urine? But that was years ago.

I said I wouldn't cry, and I won't. I'll be quiet for a while. A real mother would rock the pram. I know that because that's what mothers do with prams at the clinics. They also beat their kids when they're cryin. I never liked to see that.

The night Eamon died we slept together in his granny's house. It was better that way. We were alone. We used to laugh about how I got nettles on my bottom out in McKenna's field. I suppose I should have known it would turn out like it did. When we first met, he said that black puddin came from black sheep. I nearly laughed into his face. But I set him right. I pointed out the different organs in the body to him, and he was fascinated. He lived on the other side of the city. Jasus! I should have let him go then. But five years later and he was still by my side.

I remember when he first came to the shop, and he was standin there with his confirmation jacket on him, and Jasus, such a fool with the pin of the confirmation rosette still there and all. There was no accountin for him, but I loved him from the moment he looked into my eyes. I believe in stupid things like love at first sight. He was poorer than we were. He'd worn that jacket for two years every day without ever washin it. But he was beautiful. I knew beauty when I saw it. He was beautiful. He asked me to hold a turkey for his granny for Christmas. He picked one out himself in the back of our garden. He used to come by on a Friday with some crumbs and seasonin meal that his granny used to say was to be fed to the turkey, because it kept the turkey flavour in the bird. He said that his granny said that my dad fed the turkeys sawdust. That was a bloody lie. I told him to tell his granny to stuff the special meal up her arse. He said he would, and we both laughed. He had a lovely smile. His lips used to kind of wrinkle, and then you'd see his teeth, and he'd turn his eyes up at ya . . .

But there were other times as well. Why? I don't know why. Before the baby and all . . . The Hunger Strike and all . . .

This friend of Eamon's used to come to the granny's some nights drunk, and he used to be singin 'A Nation Once Again', and then he'd start shoutin and cursin and goin on and on, and he'd start up with 'Starvation Once Again', and Jasus, ya didn't know whether to laugh or cry. And Eamon used to tell me to 'fuckin shut my face' when that racket started up, and he used to never say that kind of stuff to me, but that was because of Joker Murphy and his stupid fuckin singin. People would ask him to step outside when we were together at the pubs other times. They didn't care if they left me alone for the rest of the night.

Christ! I remember one night. We were there and all, with some of the girls from my school, and we were havin great crack messin about sayin that we were goin to leave and move off to a rich uncle in Boston who was this and that in politics, and in walks Bertie McCance from Derry, and he's furious as hell, and he starts in with this story about this man that comes up to a barracks and says to a soldier, 'My family's been held hostage by the IRA, and they've a bomb in this car, and they want me to park it down the road there.' Well, the barracks come alive, and the next thing ya know they won't let yer man out of the car, and they make him drive to this dump, and he keeps shoutin to em that he wants someone to get his wife and children freed before the IRA realize that he's pulled a fast one on em, and the soldiers wouldn't listen to him, and they told him to stay where he was, and he tried to get out of the car, but they kept aimin their guns at him, and he started screamin and shoutin about his family and askin em to give him back his watch, and Jasus, he was screamin because he didn't know how long there was to go, and this solider says that he could get out when the bomb robot arrived, and then all of a sudden the car blew to pieces with him just cryin with his head on the steering wheel . . .

Jasus! All this murder from boys who wanted a free nation and yet knew nothin of what this country had been in some far distant past . . . So bloody stupid . . . Fools with bits of Irish words in their heads . . . Oh God! To imagine a father trapped in a car like that . . . Why, Why? And those poor fellas who only years ago laughed at the old Prod joke, 'What is a Gaelic?' 'Somethin that queers do to each other.' But nobody laughed in secondary school. Oh no, ya wouldn't dare. That night I didn't ever think I'd see Eamon again. Things just grew worse, though. He was always sorry for cursin at me. I used to tell him I understood, and he used to bring me Toblerone bars and After Eights, and I used to shrug my shoulders and tell him that he didn't need to feel sorry for me and . . .

On the night he died he seemed agitated. But he never forced the issue. He kept talking about children, the babies we would have, and his dog . . . Ya know they poisoned his dog? Those bastards. He said he must have gone missin. His mother told us in secret that he buried it in the back garden alongside the cat, Ian Paisley. Christ! I loved that boy. Would ya call me a baby if I broke down and cried now, even though there are only minutes left for me to live?

All those deaths and it was the dog that got to him. He kept sayin that night that he didn't want the dog to be put to sleep or feel left out when we had children. I couldn't keep myself from sobbin. I kept whisperin, 'Shoo, shoo,' into his gentle face, and he kept bendin over me, kissin me, tellin me, 'Sorry, sorry.' And that stupid bar of chocolate that he brought me . . . I still have it in my room at home with that card on it. 'To my girlfriend.' I loved him, Jasus! I want em all to know what they done to me and my lovely boyfriend and my wee baby. It's gettin dark outside, I can feel the cold wind when the door opens. The smoke is all red and orange in here. people are driftin in front of me. They're mostly drunk. Even the whores from Loverpool are easin up now. They might as well enjoy themselves. For the first time in months I feel that my belly is warm. I feel like I have a little hot-water bottle under my shirt. It's a very soft warm feelin. Oh that lovely baby. He'll be with me there to the end. Oh Christ! It's the pains. He is in there. Don't tell me he's not. I know, I have 'mother's intuition'.

On the night he died, Eamon asked me if I could love again. I was cryin in his arms. I kissed his hands ever so softly. This boy of mine loved many creatures. He asked me very quietly if I would follow him to heaven or hell, when he unzipped my skirt. We were both lyin naked by the fireplace before I would look at him. His face was so beautiful and innocent. He wasn't a man; he was a boy. I'm sorry for cryin. They can't see me in this haze of red smoke, though. They can't see the tears, can they? No, they can't because I have no tears and no blood left in my body.

God, I loved him. He kissed my hands. They were swollen and white from dicin meat and potatoes and turnips and parsnips in a hand basin all day long thinking about that night with him. I wish they could have been soft and warm. His face was full of orange and red light. He did love me, that poor boy. His tongue was a soft flame on my stomach. I nodded with a gentle smile to his soft kisses. He kept starin at my body in the soft light. He was always patient. He kept askin me if I would follow him to heaven or hell? I told him with a smile to 'go to hell', and he smiled faintly. There were tears in his eyes. My stomach was wet with his tears. He said he was cryin because he was so in love with me. I saw his lips turnin in a soft smile as he rose from beneath the covers, draped like a druid. We didn't talk for hours. The fire smouldered, wheezin in puffs of smoke. We saw the same fleetin images in the amber fire. I saw the Red Hand of Ulster in the flames and shut my eyes, and he felt me tense in his arms and asked me what I saw. We hugged each other tightly when we heard his grandmother flushin the toilet above our heads. And then we heard her feedin tenpence coins into the gas meter, and suddenly the sitting room shone in a dirty light. We seemed too real in the light. And there was a tea cloth draped over his granny's parrot. He turned the light off, tiptoein to the switch. I laughed into the pillow. He was the only boy I had ever seen naked. We slept for a while. I nestled my head in against his damp armpit.

When he went out on nights like this he used to tell me to give him my engagement ring, and he used to put it in his pocket, and he used to take his ring and place it on the mantlepiece and tell me that when he left the room I could take it, or leave it where it was, and he said he would understand if I left it there. I used to always take it and put it on a chain around my neck and pray with it in my grasp. He needed those prayers. Oh God! We could have escaped. There were worlds beyond this place.

He told me once that life depended upon not so much makin the right friends as makin the right enemies. He was right and all. Could ya trust a man who'd murdered? I don't know, but I loved a boy who'd murdered. He told me to go to the railway-crossing shed the next day near Williams Street if he did not come to my house. We agreed to leave for Australia if he made it through this night. He wanted our baby to be conceived in Ireland. I agreed, and he pulled me close, and his breath was filled with the sweet smoke of the burnin wood, and he asked me once again, 'Would you follow me to heaven or hell?' I didn't want to cry, and so I concentrated on the soft burnin sensation and felt him slip beneath my skin, and I began to sob into his chest.

We slept for hours, and then we dressed, and he rattled the parrot's cage, and it squawked 'Brits Out', and oh Jasus, we nearly wet our knickers, and it wasn't really funny. My beautiful boy ... We went slowly into the hallway, and he gave me a flower from beneath a cracked porcelain statue of the Madonna on the hall table, and we crept outside and walked about the streets under the soft dribblin lights. And we kept each other warm, wrapped up in the same quilted anorak, gigglin because we felt like a centipede, watchin our hurryin feet. And I could feel everythin tinglin in my body, and it was as though we were one creature. We ate fish and chips and sprinkled vinegar and salt on em. I didn't know about toxaemia then, or mother's intuition or walkin pneumonia. We were babies together.

'A feast for kings!' I shouted down the lonely black road. And the sound echoed away into the blackness. He whispered, 'Shoo, ya Loyalist,' into my ear, and we doubled over, intoxicated with our damp sweat. He said he was a big spender, pullin me close. I told him to 'shag off'. He had fifty pence in his pocket. He was tellin me about boomerangs and kangaroos as though he'd been to Australia himself. He'd only been to the library, but he had all the big cities in his head: 'Sydney, Melbourne, New Hampshire.' I giggled at him but didn't want to tell him he was wrong about New Hampshire. Maybe there was a New Hampshire in Australia. I would let him lead the way. All things were compromises. I knew that more than most. I was a woman. I had a broodin devotion to him. And yet he was always the martyr.

'I want a city where the streets have no names. I want to walk down a First Avenue, stop at Third and Fifth. Who the hell wants to fight for ghosts?'

I didn't tell him they had Park and Lexington in New York City . . .

'We'll go Down Under,' he whispered.

I tensed my body, a tear in my eye. 'Down Under,' I repeated.

He was shiverin frantically by the time the chips were gone. I looked into his shadowy face. His eyes glimmered in the fallin misty rain. 'Would you follow me to heaven or hell?' he whispered. He pushed away from me for a moment, his arms outstretched in the blue dark light. He put no stock in his own mind. He was afraid to go away. 'I only know this life,' he whispered.

'We're goin to Australia,' I whispered. I could feel my womb absorbin his life. 'Australia,' I said again.

'Down Under!' he shouted at the top of his voice. He gripped my waist tightly. 'Down Under,' he sobbed.

This pain is too much. This smoke is burnin my . . . oh, my eyes. I have to keep breathin just a little longer. 'Come on, girl. You can do it.' I know, I know. I'll try and smile. I can feel somethin happenin on my face. That's it. Those pills of my mother's are workin, but that pain's still down there. But that beautiful water bottle is becomin so hot. I have so many stories to tell ya, and so little time.

I nodded to my man. 'Australia,' I whispered. I had to be strong. We stood under a tall unlit lamppost with its wires torn out. I stared down at the empty box. Had he pulled that timin device out for his own work? There was always this terrible economy . . .

The mornin after, I knew he wouldn't be comin over to our house for breakfast like he said he would. My father was up unusually early. I could see the sky was still filled with stars. There was no moon. I wept thinkin of nettles in my bottom and how he had kept slappin my bottom all the way home. And that mysterious parrot of his granny's kept lookin at me in my mind with his black seed eyes. My father crept rather than plodded. He'd answered the door over an hour ago for the first time. Someone had come on a bicycle. I could hear its squeaky saddle from up the street. That was trouble. I tried to sleep again, but I couldn't. When a car coasted down the streets with its lights off, I wept into my hands. I could hear the shiftin footsteps, the muffled voices. I could see a sliver of light from our hall porch cuttin across the cold grey wet road. On my wall I looked to the grainy image of a poster he won for me at a fair in Dublin. 'I Will Follow', read the caption in black ink. Did it mean to the end? The door opened slowly to my room. My mother was shakin. I could hear the jingle of pills in a bottle outside my door. She peeked in, checkin to see if I was asleep. She closed the door ever so gently and went to the hot press.

I could hear the gentle putter of my father's machinery below in the back of the shop. The car moved off slowly into the distance. I ate no breakfast. My mother, that lifelong inmate of the kitchen, was dressed in a heavy black pullover and a thick tweed skirt. She was boilin a rabbit in a large transparent pot. Jasus Christ, I hate those pots! Just like a television, the grey image of a rabbit shrivellin away, the splutterin foam dribblin down the sides into the blue gas flame ... We all stared at the poor rabbit and watched the cabbage on the other burner like a tremblin brain. It hid the smell, and that was all. My mother cradled a mug of coffee in her cupped hands.

'Add more salt and water to that before the meat falls off the bones, for Christ's sake,' my father shouted. He was sweatin, smokin a cigarette. His head was pink and spotty like his meats. He leaned over a cup of pipin hot tea, dejected. He had lost that predatory sneer that he used to frighten the old ladies into nervous titters and sell em more expensive chops than they had asked for. He kept starin at my mother, and she kept starin at him. They wouldn't look at me. I saw my ring forlorn in the middle of the table and took it quietly, without cryin. As I walked away I could see my father, drummin his fingers on the oaken table. 'Will ya work up front for a while?' he whispered.

Eamon's mother came into the shop. We said nothin, and she said nothin. She was an innocent woman. He went Down Under, or at least that is what she told the soldiers when they came to her house that mornin. She complained about her lumbago. She said the parrot wasn't eatin; maybe he was sick. It was hard to tell. I nodded my head. I could hear that terrible squawk, 'Brits Out. Brits Out.' That horrible humour.

I worked quietly behind the counter in my white pinafore uniform. Ma's face was blotched, and her eyes were huge and glossy like binoculars. I looked to my father with hapless eyes. In my head I kept hearin his question, 'Would you follow me to heaven or hell?' And the wall upstairs kept scribblin, 'I Will Follow. I Will Follow.' I shut my eyes and excused myself, and all I could think of was the pink worms of mince oozin through the sputterin machine in the back of the shop. My father shut the door when he saw me standin there in the cold corridor. The blood was fallin in thick splats into the mesh grate on the floor. I kept very still. My father worked diligently with his two-fingered hand, wrappin up six chops in the morning paper. The headline read, 'Botched Car Bomb on Falls Road!'

And now there are twenty-five seconds to go in this butcher's daughter's life. My father's mutilated hands are bleedin again tonight. I can smell it in the air. The women said I had a nose like a rabbit when I sniffled as a child. And here in this room everythin is really dead, but it pretends to be alive. The music throbs my womb with its energy, with the boomin bass of mammoth speakers. Does this child not want to be a corpse? I run my hand over my white stomach as though it's a pearly egg. Can foetuses feel fear? I feel it kick. I would have called it Eamon. There's a soldier kissin one of the whores, and she's cryin, and she's lookin at me and thinkin that I should be some other place, playin bingo. Two little ducks, twenty-two ... Legs eleven ... But still I endure. I sit here all alone with my belly swellin bigger and bigger. Thank God she can't see my heart under my fat milky vulnerable breasts. And the barman is wipin the counter frantically with his ear cocked like an alert fox to the Army radio. 'Finish up now, gents, finish up.'

Ten seconds to go ... It'll all be over, all this life. The rain patters fitfully on the corrugated roof. Everythin slows to a crawl. The last seconds pour in upon themselves. The explosive cough of a fat captain tremblin with fear ... He sees the timer in my hands and the sweatin sticks of dynamite in the gouged-out plastic belly of my childhood doll.

He can't catch his breath. The splinterin mirror is on the verge of explodin into needles of piercin glass. Three seconds ... I brace my womb. The doll's eyelids open and close. People see that and scream. They are turnin and puttin their hands to their mouths. The captain is sayin somethin. It's drowned in the music. Suddenly everyone hears the clock tick-tockin in Sweet Colleen's belly. Her eyes are wide open, her tiny plastic fingers outstretched like our wee Jesus.

THE WHORE MOTHER

THE WORD WAS that no man had ever died a happier death than Paddy Sheedy. He fell into one of the vats in the Guinness brewery. Everyone down at Jack Quigley's place thought it was the funniest thing they'd heard in a great while. It was a fellow worker raking the brown froth from the stout who had seen the body bobbing on the surface two days later. He said, he 'knew right away.' Everyone nodded. 'It must have been a sobering experience.' The brewery dedicated a plaque in Sheedy's honour right on vat number four and sent eight barrels of Guinness to the funeral. The old women said it was a sacrilege to have the 'spirits of his demise' on hand at his own funeral. Other men became suspicious of such an enormous amount of stout being donated by the brewery and circulated rumours concerning its origin. It soon became part of the myth. Quigley was said to have bought one of the coveted barrels, having it nailed to the floor in his pub. There were lots of nods and winks. People took their cues as the weeks passed, things developing into a sort of pantomime before the month was out. 'Good night, Sheedy,' they shouted, tapping the barrel of stout. 'He was a barrel of laughs,' said Quigley, gloating over the barrel, polishing it with a damp rag. He set it in a kind of tabernacle in the middle of the pub. Everyone had signed their names to the barrel by the end of the month. Politicians, priests, and businessmen were seen shaking on deals over the lip of the barrel. The regulars dared one another to drink from it. 'For free,' Quigley whispered. Nobody took up the offer.

The widow knew it was a bloody lie that her husband had died the happiest death in Ireland. When they had finally dredged for all his belongings and laid them alongside his corpse, they knocked at her door. The rain poured outside. The priest had a prayer book in his hands. Someone took her children by the hand and left. She said she didn't want a coat. When she saw her husband's body, it was bloated to twice its size. It was the colour of a greenish cheese. She held her man's dead fingers. They were massively udder-like. The nails were missing. His wedding-ring had cut a blackish-blue circle into his finger. It oozed with a brownish froth. She said she wanted the ring. She did not cry, even when she saw his toes had split through his shoes. She was given his belongings and a fifty-pound note and told not to worry about the funeral arrangements. 'You'll be goin back to the country, I suppose,' the accounting clerk, Mr Greeves, asked and answered himself with a nod of his head.

The widow shook her head. 'My children are Dublin Jackeens, Mr Greeves.' She allowed a faint smile to sift through her rigid face. She wore the ring around her neck on a silver necklace.

'But what'll you do for money and ... ' Suddenly, Mr Greeves saw the windfall of the fifty pounds as a paltry sum figured against a lifetime to come. He could see a certain resignation which he could not estimate as mourning or obstinateness set in her face. 'If I could give you a word in the know, Mrs Sheedy,' he began. 'Well now, how should I begin without sounding ... ' Mr Greeves took a cigarette from his pocket and drew hard until little puffs of smoke rose through his cupped hands. 'Obligations. Well, you understand the necessity of obligations between parties, I presume? There can be no more ... well, the company has done by your family.'

The widow held her purse close to her chest, groping at the handle in a demeanour of embarrassment. 'I must be going. Thank you for your kindness.'

Mr Greeves blocked her passage with his shoulder. 'I'm not good at this sort of thing. I'm in charge of ... money matters and the like, and, please, Mrs Sheedy, this is a most ... a highly unusual circumstance. Could I get you a cup of tea, or ... '

'No, thank you.'

On his wall, a series of black and white photos of men sipping stout seemed to toast his good health, urging him to put this woman in her place. This brewery had a history that outweighed the mortal grief of any one person. 'Well, let's be frank then. Fifty pounds is ... is not going to feed you and clothe your children and keep coal in your fire until the end of November. I mean, there you have it.' Mr Greeves squinted his face, drawing his sleeve across his rotund cheeks. Smoke trailed from his fingers. 'I'm sorry. A man of business always talks like a fool. Forgive me, forgive me. But life is a business, is it not? Let me put this by you, if you will. You are a religious woman, no doubt ... Yes ... Yes ... If I may proceed.' Mr Greeves took a deep breath and filled his lungs to their fullest capacity. The widow could see that his waistcoat was about to separate at the seams. 'When a man is called by his Maker, he must go, and those behind must abide by that divine will and not interfere with whatever plan God has put in those remaining souls. It is not the will of man which we must obey. You're followin me, Ma'am?'

'I will have to leave, Mr Greeves.' The widow stared at the grainy portraits of dozens of old men perched on bikes and leaning against rickety gates, toasting every living thing in sight.

Mr Greeves tipped his balding head. 'Madam! Let me put it this way. It is financially not prudent to stay in this city.' His face puckered into utter indignation as he looked straight into the widow's face. 'It will bring hardship upon yourself.' He wagged his finger. The widow thought for a moment how fat it was, browned and cracked by years of smoking, the nails blackened and yellowish. It brought back that terrible image of her husband's wedding finger. 'Ma'am, are you listening? To test friendship beyond its bounds is not a Christian thing.' With a quick shudder he broke off, stubbing his cigarette out in a black ashtray on his neatly arranged desk. 'Good day.'

The widow felt a flush of blood in her breast. She stared at Mr Greeves' massive back, placed the fifty pounds on his desk, and, sidestepping his obstructing body, walked out without a word.

In the subsequent weeks the butcher often gave the widow extra slices of corned beef, and the breadman sold her today's bread at yesterday's price. The milkman said, 'Not to worry. Better you than the wife's good-for-nothin cat.' The widow's general thrift and good-natured smile served her well. She asked for nothing but got everything. The men were always willing to carry her bags up the street or bring her coal into the back shed. She always made it a point to resist emphatically, but she offered the men tea and biscuits for their troubles. The men always accepted. Everything moved in a sort of panorama of procedures, without words. The men called it their Christian duty. That was what worried the women. Soon the street began to whisper secrets about the widow, behind her back and then to her face.

'Do you know that my Jack nearly broke his back mendin that shed of yours? He can't hang a picture for the life of him back in our place without makin a shambles of the place, but he's bloody Leonardo da Vinci when he's off somewhere else.'

'I told him he shouldn't have,' the widow pleaded.

'Jasus Christ. Do you think that my man would let you freeze to death? Do you think we don't take stock of our prayers?'

'Tell us, are you considerin goin to the country for the winter?'

'Sure, I've been here eight years. Why would I be thinkin of the country,' the widow smiled. 'Aren't my children . . . '

A chorus of women bellowed, 'Ah yes, Dublin Jackeens.'

A lady in slippers with rollers in her red hair put her fat arm on the wooden counter at the butcher's and let it wobble. 'You know, Mr Sullivan, it must be hard to be about your business when . . . well, when your business is just plain charity. You know?'

The butcher nodded his head severely. 'To be sure, ladies. This is a land of feast or famine. What you have, you share. But when there's nothin there, what can you give? And the sin lies not in the withholder, but in the beggar.' The butcher's eyes looked straight between the scales at the widow as he wiped the meat shavings off his steel blade on to the floor.

'Some would have you give them a pound of your own flesh, to be sure.'

The widow looked at the old woman's flaccid arm like a red piece of meat on the block. The widow excused herself, 'Well, good day to you,' noticing that her small pile of corned beef was not as generous as she had expected.

Michael rubbed his hands vigorously together after dropping the bits of wood near the hearth of the fire. 'Jasus! Ma, it's freezin cold. I got a couple of ol crates from the shops on the street, but they're hard to come by these days, ya know, Ma. Mr Malloy says dem things cost money . . . but he said okay this time. He told me to tell ya; he was askin after you.'

The widow pretended not to listen. 'I've the supper on. Michael, are ya hungry?'

The boy smiled, watching the blue tips of his fingers turn red. He could feel their faint stinging sensation, like when he got a leathering at the school and his hands throbbed with pain. The pain seemed to be the same that had made him cry at school, but somehow it didn't carry that vengeful hurt that was always felt by blameless souls being beaten for no good reason.

The widow gave the children a supper of toast, eggs and tea. The boy ate in silence, groping at the powder-coated loaf of brown bread, swabbing his bread in the bright yellow of the runny yoke. The girl watched him and sniggered, and he snarled at her and winked. 'Is there any milk for the tea, Ma?'

'Too big for his britches, right, Catherine?' The widow smiled and petted the small girl. She smiled back and held her mother's hand. 'Ya, too big for his . . . '

'Ah, shut yer face.' The boy brooded and then stuck out his tongue, grinning.

The widow mixed a drop of milk with water, brought the opaque liquid to the table, and unwrapped a wafer of beeswax. 'There ya are, and somethin to sweeten it.'

The boy smiled, his half-open mouth filled with mushy bread and egg. 'Ma, yer great.'

Nursing her baby, Paddy, the widow turned, letting the purple ring of her gnawed nipple pop out of the child's spluttering lips. 'Michael, will ya go down by the coal yard after and see if there's any coal about on the streets?'

The boy nodded, 'Sure, Ma.'

The widow felt a redness in her cheeks. 'I think I'm catchin somethin or other.'

'Ma?'

'Michael, shoo.'

'I don't know if I'll be able to get coal, Ma. These fellas keep on at me.'

'Michael, let me get Paddy to sleep.'

'I think he's too big for his britches,' Catherine giggled.

'Shut yer face.' The boy peered over his steaming tea. His face was wet with moisture. 'Ma,' he whispered, 'what's a whore?'

*

When the children had gone to bed, a knock came at the door. The widow was washing her children's stockings and underwear in a tin basin. A taut string of wire held some of her own bleached underwear. She looked at the clock on the mantelpiece and buttoned her shirt to the collar. When she opened the door, a tall man tipped his hat. 'How are you, Niamh?' A hot kiss passed from his lips. He began coughing.

The widow smelt the liquor. She tried to obstruct the dark man's entry, but he pushed his way inside.

'Jesus! Don't wake the children, for God's sake.' The widow curled her long hair around her ear, turning her eyes toward the underwear. 'Would ya mind not gawkin?'

The dark man stared at the pearly suds dripping from a limp pair of stockings. The amber fire bled the underwear to a soft burgundy.

For a terrible moment, the widow felt the nakedness of her body underneath her skirt. She was wearing no underwear. She could feel the moistness of her flesh teeming with sweat, her thighs hot in a gorge of blood. 'I haven't seen you in so long. Jesus, I was worried to death that you left me.' Her feet curled in apprehension.

'How's Michael keepin?' The dark man struck a match, let the flame flare in his face, and began pacing. He took careful stock of the small room from its grey stone floor to the dark reeking wood of its roof beams. Everything was grey, save for the fire and the dripping underwear.

'Michael's fine.' The fire crackled behind the widow's back. She looked down at her fingers withered with pinkness from the cold soapy water. 'Where have you been?'

'So you got a bit of coal, then, I see. And did you get the bread and rashers I told you to get for Michael?'

'I did . . . Jesus! What are lookin at me like that for?'

The dark man wandered around the room, running his hand over the shredded thread of an old rocking chair, feeling the greasy imprint of the dead husband's head. He stopped in the kitchen and viewed the cracked china cups in the bare press lined with waxed paper to catch flies and other creatures. Then he moved off, scanning the bedroom door, finally looking out the window again. 'Do you have a saucer for the ashes?' He held a grey finger of ash outward.

The widow gave him a glass off the table. When she put it in his hand, he grabbed her wrist. 'How many sausages did he get at tea tonight? Well, tell me?'

The widow's eyes shone with gleaming tears. Soft soapy splats sizzled on the fire and went hiss. The walls shifted in the throbbing light of the fire.

'He got none, then, is that it?' The dark man's mouth breathed hot vapours into the widow's face. His tongue glistened with every formed word. 'Are you going to starve him to death?'

'Will you leave me alone, for Christ's sake.' The widow's fingers gripped the dark man's coat. She began shivering in his arms, letting her fingers grope toward his smooth face. 'I thought you left me. Oh Jesus, protect me. You know these people here keep whisperin that there must be some reason for me stayin here and not goin home. Oh Jesus.'

The dark man let his cigarette burn itself out in the glass, staring at the bedroom door. 'Don't wake your man, all right?'

He let his body cradle the dead weight of the widow.

The widow put the kettle on the boil, brushed away the flies in the press, and unwrapped a half loaf of bread. She cut away a fringe of green mold around the edge of the crust and began cutting thin slices of bread. She kept smiling at the dark man through the grey light of the kitchen. The moon was full in the sky. She could feel its coldness spying her. Near the back door, she uncovered her raw nipple and squeezed the tender flesh between her thumb and index finger, letting some milk dribble into a small bottle.

The dark man stared at her soft black hair.

'Any sugar?' she whispered, turning around again, placing the warm bottle on the table.

'A spoonful or so.' The dark man scraped the bottom of the

coal box. He threw a layer of slack on to the shifting flames, bedding the heat for the night. 'Do you have any papers and sticks for the morning?'

'Some waxed paper over there. Do you want a rasher with the bread?'

'Give us a couple there, any chance of a sausage?'

The widow smiled, and her blue eyes looked straight at the dark man for a long time.

They ate at the table without saying a word. The dark man stirred the milk into his tea and began supping away at it. 'Somethin to sweeten it?' The widow gave him a sliver of the beeswax. The dark man broke the yellowish wafer over the tea in silence. He dipped the soft flesh of his bread into the tea occasionally, wedging the spongy crusts of the slices into his mouth. The widow watched him peeling away the rind of fat from the rashers and then putting the meat into a sandwich. 'Whoever it was that invented the sandwich was, by Jasus, a genius.' The dark man dabbed his lips with a handkerchief, pushing his body away from the table, his eyes locked on the widow. She moved away. The dark man put his hands on the table and stared at the widow's slim body. 'Let me say it straight. I won't be comin around again for awhile.'

'But ... what about Michael, and Catherine and Patrick? You told me you wouldn't let us down.' The widow felt faint, her body drifting through the damp palpable air in the small room.

'I'll be goin to sea again.' The fire wheezed quietly, and the underwear steamed in the light.

'You told me that was over. You swore you'd stay with me.'

'It makes no difference now. What's done is done.' The dark man waved his hand. 'Don't start with me.'

The widow huddled herself in her own embrace, pulling her legs against her chest. She could feel the coldness of the night around her naked thighs. 'Do you want, em ... another cup of tea, or bread ... I'll ... '

A whistle from the brewery pierced the darkness, calling another shift of men to its dark studded doors. The dark man and the widow listened to the shuffle of feet, coughs and curses of men dodging the dampness of the evening rain. They could see the glass streaked with the white faces and dark clothes of all the outer world's inhabitants.

'Nobody saw you comin in, did they?' The widow tucked her skirt between her thin thighs.

'Stop still, will you?' The dark man licked a piece of rolling paper with his tongue, compressed the sheet on the table and let a pinch of tobacco drop in a small heap. 'I'm goin over to England for a spell.' Then he smoothed the dark weed and knotted the cigarette, licking the entire bud when he had it rolled, sealing it tight. He held a small candle under the cigarette and let it partially dry in the flickering heat.

The widow attended to his every move, staring at her milky cup of tea. The clock ticked quietly on the mantelpiece.

The dark man let his eyes wander over its sombre face. He caught sight of the widow's soft thighs, sagging down toward the floor. He traced them to her bony knees, slipping his glance to her small dirty toenails. She had legs like a child. 'Did you hear about the storms up north and in England? The whole fuckin countryside's covered in a blizzard. They say it's comin down here.'

'No.'

The dark man loosened his collar and rubbed his neck. 'Remember what I said to you this while back? Well, do you?'

'Please.' The widow bit her lips.

The dark man moved his face forward, his heart pounding. The bedroom door creaked open. A small face peeped out. 'Uncle, is that you?'

'How are you, Michael? Come here, boy.' The dark man's fingers moved in the dusk.

The small child crept over the cold stone and stood still beside the dark man. 'Did you bring me that liquorice you promised me, Uncle?'

The dark man pulled out a black ribbon of liquorice and patted the boy on the head. 'It's too late for a boy like you to be up and about.'

The boy kissed his mother goodnight and crept back to bed. His face was already black from the liquorice. He looked like a small dark man.

The chimneys were like grey organ pipes in the vault of blackness that enveloped them. The dark man stood up and saw a pale blue fire burning in the chimneys at the brewery. He traced the dark shadow of the rounded brick wall laced with barbed wire and glass cuttings. Beyond the wall, everything on the small street was segmented with a solid red façade of brick. There was a certain hospitality that ended in paganism beyond each wall. Everyone had an implicit understanding of home, of escape, of refuge, but they believed in strange things as well, like banshees. These homes were places of comfort and foraging. There were things left unsaid beyond these walls, strange Catholic rituals. All those children coming out of those small homes, those one-bedroom homes and that secret life where a mother of ten began the rosary with beads in one hand and a hairy penis in the other, the children silent, with their eyes shut tight . . .

The dark man kept looking at the brewery walls. He had come from these same streets, falling about as a boy, growing up to understand the day from the night but somehow never understanding the twilight of the city. Again, he looked at the massive brewery, a place where they fermented water and hops and other ingredients in vats to brew a mad dark liquid that made everyone who drank it blind with either lust or brooding, love or hate . . . the darkness did not discriminate, it only knew that it must implicate everything except itself.

The dark man turned from the brewery and the grey walls. 'I have a young fellow I want to come and visit you.'

'Come on, will ya . . . ' The widow put her hand to her face. 'Do you know what yer precious Michael says to me tonight? He says, "What's a whore?" Lord Jesus, is this what it has come to? They're talkin about me out there in those streets as though I did somethin wrong. Well, I didn't. Jesus Christ! It was you who came to me all those nights, tellin me how you loved me . . . '

'Keep it quiet.'

'"You'd kill im for beatin me," is what you said. And all those tears that you wept for me. And now?' The widow lowered her head, her long black hair falling to one side.

The dark man's hand hung in the air like a great marauding paw. It hit the widow on the exposed neck. 'Have respect for the dead.'

The widow clung to the leg of her husband's old chair, smelling the odour of his body still ingrained into the damp cloth. 'Jesus Christ . . . And to think I believed you when you said you loved only me.'

'Niamh, he just wants to come around and see you. Is there shame in that?' The dark man stared at the widow's veiny breasts under her tattered shirt. He could see the crescent-shaped scars about her thin neck where his brother used to bite her flesh and grit his teeth with his head lost in her hair and mouth.

The widow stood at the doorway, the cold wind rattling the door. 'Why don't you mention Paddy? Is it that bad? Do you hate me that much?'

'Well, by Jesus, for you to think that a man doesn't have enough animal in him to smell his own bed, like a horse that wouldn't know its own stable, and know what has happened to him, or that someone has been there before him. A house with one pair of sheets, my fuckin God, aired with nothin but the cold wind blowing through the doors. He must have choked on that smell at night, layin in that filthy spot in his ol shirt, lookin at the walls and prayin to Jesus . . . '

The widow narrowed her eyes. 'You dropped the pennies and the tenpences at my door, bird crumbs to a bedroom. And it was you who came when he was out and toasted the bread and melted the butter for me with those brown eyes. Do you remember puttin the iodine on my shins and my back? And your lips, like a woman's, so soft and the words you told me so gentle. "If only he was away for ever and ever." Fairy tales that made me cry in your arms. You saw the bruises all over, didn't you, and you cried . . . and you fed my boy with sweets while you took me away.'

'Did you tell me he hadn't been with you in months? Ah no, that was a rare bit of trickery, I'll tell you. A baby on the way, and he says to me, his eyes filled with tears, "Did ya ever hear of the Immaculate Conception?" Wasn't that a good one. My brother tellin me about his wife. Do you know what they say on the streets? They say secretly that Paddy Sheedy didn't die the happiest death in Ireland at all, but that he threw himself into that vat. Imagine that, will ya? The story goes that there was this young one who wanted to get rid of her man so bad that she gets the better of another poor bastard, and, well, there ya have it, a child on the way, and the husband can't fathom what's what. He says, "That's no child of mine!" and, well, Jasus, he's shakin his head, and then his wife confesses and swears that it wasn't her fault, and then off goes your man and kills himself, and there is she at home just waitin for her other man to come and be her husband. There you have it, in all its contrived plottin.'

'You're a liar! But I see now. Your sin is my downfall. Oh don't you start. I swear to Jesus, I'll tell them you killed my man.' The widow bit her lip gently, cradling the heavy weight of her breasts.

The dark man searched long in his pocket and came up with a few coins. 'Isn't that just lovely. You do what you see fit to do, girl.'

'These coppers won't see us through the week, for God's sake. Ya told me not to worry, and now look at me.' The widow flung the coins on the ground. 'He was your brother, not mine. Don't think I'll die for the dead.'

The dark man edged his way past the widow into the night air. 'Sweet Jesus, a poet and a whore. I'll send you more when

I'm settled, but for now I'm goin to be sendin this fellow your
way for a bit of company. Do you hear me?'

'Get out, ya bastard.'

'You'll not kill that boy in there, do you hear me, woman?'

It had never snowed in November in anyone's memory, but it
snowed in November that year. The Liffey had a thin skin of
ice on its black undersurface. The county council had to make
signs to warn people, 'Keep off. Danger!' But the signs only
served to inspire mischief. When the widow was about her
business, she could hear all the women. 'Jasus! Ah, leave em
alone, I says to Franky, sure them kids in Norsways and
Scansylvania do be skiddin around all the time, and nothin
comes of it. Sure, it only snows once in a lifetime, for God's
sake. Leave em alone.' And other ones, too, with big faces like
juicy red apples and throaty voices full of phlegm like women
on Moore's Street bantered away. 'Ah, for the love of God.
Isn't it wonderful and all, them ones down there at Fitz-
william's Park on the pond lookin like figurines on a weddin
cake?'

The widow moved like a ghost between these women
now. The secret of the dark man was slowly circulating on the
street, but nobody confronted the widow. Charity had
become as scarce for the widow as it had for the pigeons
begging for crumbs in the snow. People needed all that they
had themselves 'and more'. The widow was an unwelcome
sight dawdling down their street in a pale blue dress, with a
necklace of small-faced children dragged alongside her. 'Yes,
yes, and them young ones are always watchin the shop
windows with a certain sinful relish, like thieves,' Mrs Bacon
whispered through blackish teeth, peeping through her lace
curtain, sipping tea. Mrs Mallon concurred, 'It's a bad thing to
have a young woman like that in the midst of our street, as if
this place isn't bad enough already.' 'What I'd like to know is
where she got that dress. I've never seen the likes of it in this
town before.' Mrs Conroy had a face like a small bird.

The widow's girl, Catherine, nearly died of pneumonia in November. She was lucky, though. Two boys in Mrs Boyce's house did die. Their father screamed the whole night long. He raved outside the widow's door, crying for her to leave. Everyone heard the furious banging. 'Whore' rang out. Michael saw the man's face in the window. He had no shirt on his body.

'I'll smash your door down, you whore, if you don't come out.'

The child Catherine was asleep. The small boy cried in front of the widow, 'Leave my ma alone.'

'Michael! Jesus, get away from that window.' The widow never opened her door. Someone pulled Mr Boyce away, kicking and screaming, 'She's a whore, a devil that stole my children!'

The widow's son whispered under the covers, holding the cold body of his sister, 'Ma, what's a whore?'

Throughout that night and for a fortnight the whole city was covered in a blanket of snow. There was nobody out at the pubs at night. Everyone was around their own meagre fires. The convergence of the snow and its dire consequences on the consumption of stout in the pubs led to a twofold disaster hitting the street. The coal yard gave warning that it was nearly depleted of its coal reserve, and at the same time the brewery, having its worst fortnight in modern history, laid off forty men 'until further notice'. Nobody would believe it, but the names of the men were posted on a tiny white piece of paper on the huge vault door at the brewery. In the ensuing days nobody came out to explain the situation, the door remaining sealed.

Suddenly, not only the widow's children but all the children were sent out to get bits of wood and scour the coal yard gates for bits of coal and briquettes to keep the fires burning in the small houses. The night air was clean and dry and frozen. There was no haze from the vacant chimneys.

'Father, ya can hear the chatter of teeth, this place is so quiet,' someone whispered on the streets. The priest had no answers. All the doors shook in the cold air, the whitish dust of the snow swirling about the bleak homes of the street.

The widow went without fire for three days while it snowed at her doorstep. On the fourth day, she got Michael to carry the dresser from her room to the living room. She burnt it all, except for a drawer in which she put the baby, Paddy, wrapping him with her old jumpers and skirts. Catherine was covered with not only all the blankets but also with all the curtains in the house, as the cold was so bitter.

'Will you come to bed, Michael?'

Some men at the brewery took the terrible weather and the redundancies as an omen and contrived all sorts of stories about meeting Paddy Sheedy down by the Liffey at night, himself always following behind them with this terrible squelching sound coming from his shoes. In the height of the coldness, the smell of spoiling hops reeked from the warm granaries with an odour never known to them before. Only managers were asked to report to work through a small gate at the rear of the brewery. The blue flame of its chimney burned in the night sky, shining on the falling sheets of snow. The men stomped their numb feet, the flame accentuating the barren concrete squares of their fireless homes. A group of men resolved to go and break into the brewery. They found that a guard with two dour Alsatians had been hired to obstruct the entrance. They also saw one of the managers, standing next to an old barrel packed with flaming coals, watching them. He had with him a small pencil and paper. They could see as they adjusted to the light that he was wrapped in a fur-collared coat. The coat steamed with warmth. 'There is nothing here,' the sentry called out. The manager ducked away from the sizzling warmth of the fire and the men could see him writing down the names of those who had approached the brewery and the dogs.

In frustration, the men went away. They marshalled a

band together to go to Paddy Sheedy's grave and plead for mercy, fearing that their irreverence to his death had brought ill-fortune on the street. They threw a lump of ice through the widow's window, 'Fuckin Whore,' then went off toward the graveyard. The parish priest drove them away with a stick, shouting, 'Sacrilege,' standing sentry over the bleak snow-covered graveyard.

The following morning, the world was encrusted with a hoary snowfall. All the houses along the street had small mounds of snow at their doorsteps and loaves of white snow on their window-sills. The sky glowed faintly behind a low front of clouds in the early morning sky. The sentry still stood in the cold with his dogs, crunching the icy snow with his feet, yet he had retreated to the warm drum of coal.

Before the birds were awake, someone shouted. 'Has anyone seen Deirdre O'Mahony?'

'What's that? Who? Where, ah . . . When's this now?'

The widow stared through her smashed window and saw the street filling with the refractory images of crooked men and women. A cold light dribbled over her stone floor, the splintered glass shining on the floor. Small splinters of wood from the dresser glowed in the fire. The cold wind wafted about the house a pungent odour of glue which had originally been used to stick the dresser together.

'Let's just wait a minute here. There's no need for alarm now.' The men's coats flew up in black forked tails as they stomped their feet and rubbed their hands together briskly. 'We'll find her about. Will you relax, for the love of Jesus, and tell us what happened.' A brood of blue-faced bawlers gripped at Mrs O'Mahony's shins.

'Get them brats in for Jesus' sake, will you, before they die of cold.'

The sentry and the dogs remained silent by the smoking drum.

Mrs O'Mahony was given a sup of whiskey for medicinal

purposes, and then she began. 'She was off skatin about, the last we heard, and then she was goin over to Therese Maguire's place, and with the snow and everythin we didn't bother goin out. Ah, Christ, where could she be?' The woman let her body sag on her neighbour's arms. 'Oh Jesus.'

A cold burst of air enveloped the widow when she tugged open her door and shouted, 'I saw her down by the quays at about half-six last night, on the ice patch there.'

Everyone looked at her and said nothing. The widow shut her door again and soberly broke up the last splinters of wood on the floor and tended to the weak embers of her fire. She knew she had made a terrible mistake. In the distance, she could see small ant-like creatures with brushes scrubbing away the soot from the black-fingered chimneys at the brewery, the dark chimneys pointing toward the heavens in a sort of grim mockery. The image of her husband's wedding finger rose in her mind. She shut her eyes.

'Give us back the girl,' one of the children squealed through the broken window.

The widow's alabaster face looked mournfully into the tunnelling iciness of the street as it stretched off into the horizon.

When they found the child, she was covered in ice, her jacket spread open, sheeted in ice like two wings upon her back. 'She looked like an angel of God,' the priest told the family over a hot cup of tea, warming his hands by their fire, the snow melting on his long black coat. He said he would take care of the arrangements.

Everyone heard the dogs howling that night, the bitterest night of the cold spell. And everyone, too, heard the whistling roar of the flames, and saw the dark beasts at the brewery gate, and they dared not speak. Early in the morning, someone broke another window at the widow's house.

In early December the snow stopped. Everything was polished with a sheen of ice. The widow stood in her bare feet at her door, watching an occasional child skidding on the ice. Somehow the novelty of the snow had hardened into bitter understanding. A crust of ice around her door reminded her of the fish eggs she used to scoop up when she was a child. The dark soot of the roofs speckled the snow just so. She reached out and touched a glazed drainpipe by her doorway, letting her tongue skim over the rigid coldness of the object. It was something thrillingly cold and pure, the taste of the ice, not like water but like something ethereal, nourishing. She had not eaten in three days. She felt a certain light-headedness. Again, she let her tongue and lips slurp at the sheening wetness of the ice. She could feel her stomach filling with the coldness, and she felt like laughing, but when she went to take her kiss away, she felt her lips stuck to the pipe. Slowly she teased her flesh away with her hands, still feeling a terrible urge to start screaming laughing. When she finally got her lips and tongue free, she could see the white skin of her flesh stuck to the icy pipe. For one strange instant, she thought that she had no mouth or tongue left.

When she went inside, she could feel the cold ice in her belly. Nobody had worked in over a fortnight. The widow saw that the brewery with its black chimney stacks was barren, its formidable grey brick walls gleaming in the sun. Even its dark studded iron gate was frosted with tentacles of ice. There were now more dogs, and more sentries. Hot wounds of coal bled away in the iciness of the street. People didn't even walk on the same side of the street as the brewery for fear of the animals, or for fear that they would throw themselves upon the coals for want of heat. The priest said that, according to church records, there had never been a time when smoke had not been seen coming out of the brewery's chimneys. It was alarming beyond all measure, this terrible stalemate. The priest had records on the brewery, because it had slowly become the custom after many years of service by the brewery, that it would mimic the smoke of Rome, burning dark smoke until the heralding of a new pope sent white smoke up the chimneys. These allusions to the history of the brewery were not lost on the workers, and they did not complain about the hostile sentries and dogs before the priest. All they could say was that they could not remember when they had not seen a stream of animals and wagons coming and going with the barrels of Guinness and Harp.

It was the tinkers' horses that first brought music to the streets, offering a reprieve from the fathomless iciness of the city. Their horses went by with tentative clip-clopping shoes. The tinkers were wrapped in burlap sacks and scarves that blew in every direction. A swarm of tinker children and mothers came through the street in a huge iron-wheeled cart, flanked on both sides by robust men with heavy sticks and black caps. The men began rapping on all the doors. They could see the vacant aspect of the smokeless chimneys set against the clear blue sky. They had sixty bags of coal mounted on their flatbed wagon. A militia of children guarded the coal with sundry weapons, sticks, pitchforks, brushes, and sling shots. The children's red faces contrasted with the whiteness of the snow. 'Come out here, Missus. I've got somethin to warm yer hearth, indeed I do.' Suddenly, the street was alive with the commotion of the tinkers and squabbling women.

The widow held her children close to her and cried. She pushed the small drawer with her dead baby into the corner of the room. She sold an old clock to one of the devilish faces covered in soot. 'You can just leave it there,' she smiled, running her fingers through her matted black hair. The young tinker saw that she had pale blue eyes. He saw the ring around her neck on a chain.

'You've nothin else to sell?' he grunted, as he unmounted a sack of coal from his stooped back.

'Nothin.' Her delicate fingers fumbled with the chain.

'Did you burn everythin, or what?' There was a sudden consternation in his voice. He caught sight of the blue baby child swaddled in jumpers and skirts. He said nothing and blessed himself.

The widow shook her head fitfully. She left her face unseen in a wall of hair. 'I have somethin else ... ' She held the ring before the black face of the tinker.

He spat on the ground in defiance. 'Dat?'

The widow dared not look him in the face, she just felt his hot body and fingers creeping over her hand.

When he shut the door she saw that he had left a fistful of silver coins on the mantelpiece. He left the ring there besides.

That same night, when the fire burned for the first time in a fortnight with any aspect of heat, the widow and her son cut into the hard soil, making a dark solid hole in the back garden and buried the baby in the drawer. She dressed the child in one of her own cardigans and put heavy-knit stockings on the baby's tiny feet. She sprinkled holy water into the pit, crying.

'I'll cover the grave, okay, Ma?' Michael stood still by his mother.

The widow began to hear women at the shops gossiping and telling tales of strange occurrences at the brewery. It seemed that vat number four produced 'a flat stout that wasn't worth talkin about'. Jack Quigley foresaw the circumspective glances of his ill-clad customers and knew they were in search of answers. The coldness was still persisting, and the brewery had given no word as to when it would rehire its workers. One evening when he opened for tea, the infamous barrel of stout was gone, all that remained was a ring of nails hammered into the floor. With this last effigy gone from their midst, they all had exonerated themselves from wronging a dead man. Suddenly, everything became inextricably bound up in the secret life of the widow woman. A young man had been commissioned to go to Kilkenny and find out the terrible tale, but the parish priest met him off the Limerick train and made him swear on his knees in the station not to reveal a word of what he had discovered, 'or perish in the miasmic fires of hell'.

The boy looked at the priest strangely, 'They could tell me nothing down there, though, father.'

Near Christmas, the widow asked one morning for a side of bacon, a stone of potatoes, six parsnips, a package of marrowfat peas, a loaf of white and currant bread, a custard pudding mix, and two pounds of tealeaves. Three women and the proprietor, a Mr Finch, all swore she paid cash and held the twenty-pound note as evidence, as though they were going to dust for prints, when the other women came ambling in for their bits and pieces. They all swore they had seen at least three other twenty-pound notes in her possession, as she had the brazenness to unfurl her stocking right there in front of them, and in the company of Mr Finch, and hand over the warm note without as much as a 'How-do-you-do?' from her.

Down at the coal yard, the same fever was raised when the widow unfurled her by now infamous stocking, baring her ankle to all who dared to look, and handed another damp wad of bills to the black crow-like hand of Mr Sutton, the coal yard manager. By the time she arrived at Mrs Dawson's Drapery Store, the news was searing the white fluffy snow on the path and filling old women huddling about from the cold in dirty anoraks and tattered skirts trying to calculate where the next victim of the widow's infamous 'stocking shedding' would be found. It was likened to a snake shedding its skin, a black devil incarnate, the serpent that Mary crushed with her ivory foot.

The priest was summoned from a lovely breakfast by the time Mrs Dawson threw four saucepans out her doorway at the hopping widow who was trying desperately to get her stocking back on her left foot. 'She's a whore, father,' an old woman hissed. 'The dark man it is that goes there like Satan to his bride. We've seen it with our own eyes for months.'

The priest dismissed the cackle of women after performing

a kind of exorcism on the evil stocking which the widow had left outside Mrs Dawson's doorway. Someone gave him matches, and the whole affair lasted only a few minutes but satisfied the women immensely. They all shuffled away with their fat bottoms wagging their entire torsos from side to side, their small fat hands reddened with efforts of precarious balancing.

One night while the widow was washing dishes in the back of the house, she heard a delicate tapping noise on the window. She could see nothing, as a small dirty bulb glowed above her face and made the window reflect her own image. Again she continued to rub the plates and cups in the cold soapy water.

'Whisht! Widow, let me in.'

The widow stood with her hips pressed against the wooden sideboard. Her soft eyes moved slowly in her head. 'Who's that?' she whispered. She could see her child, Michael, in the other room, sleeping quietly by the fire on an old blanket. 'Will you leave me alone?' she cried.

'Come out here, Widow.'

When the widow opened the door, the rain fell like a mist on her face. She could still see nothing. The wind tugged the door from her. 'Who is it?' she asked again.

A shape moved near the coal shed. 'Widow! It is the dark man.'

The widow held a broom in her hands, bracing herself for any advance. 'There is no dark man.'

'Tell me, Widow. Is it lonely at night?' The voice was raspy.

'Leave me alone.'

Suddenly, a flame lit up an oval of light. She saw the face of the man. She did not know his name, but knew he was one of the men from the brewery.

'You're a beautiful woman, did you know that?' The face smiled. 'Oh, yes, so very, very pretty.' The match died and the face became invisible. 'Tell me, is it easier for you this way, I mean, in the dark, out here in the coal shed, or do you make the boy stand and watch you?'

'Get away, or I'll scream.'

The unseen face laughed gently. 'I suppose your whole body gets black layin there in the dead of night. But it must be nice, though, all that coal draped in a blanket, with the dark man inside you.'

The widow let out a faint cry and bolted her door. Suddenly, another match lit up the darkness. The man had a penis like a small radish.

The month of February continued to be a bitter month. The widow always blessed herself when she passed her child's grave on the way to hanging clothes on the line. Her boy had put a small fence of lollipop sticks around the perimeter of the grave and stuck a whitewashed cross at the head of the grave. The priest at school had told him that children were to be buried in white coffins and to have white crosses for headstones.

The widow stared at the brownish scab of earth. It had not taken root with the seeds she had planted. She knew it was too early, yet she kept an eye for a sprig of greenery or a shock of purple lilies. All she could see were the strewn bulbs like pearly eggs on the soil. As she began hanging the dripping clothes she could see the heads of some men down at the fence of her backyard. They said nothing, but watched her hang every item of clothing on the line. She ignored their stares, glancing back at the drenched glistening clothes, seeing the men move away.

'Don't think you'll get away with this!'

The widow stood defiantly clutching her shirt collar in one hand while balancing the basin on her hip. The wind blew her skirt about her knees.

'What have I done to you?' she asked. She raked her black hair out of her face. The cold westerly wind brought the smell of hops.

'Don't speak to a whore.'

'That's right. Didn't you kill children with your sins, you whore?'

'And what of the brewery and the winter that fell upon us? Didn't you do all that and more?'

'Because I wouldn't leave my home?'

'And what of the men that come to you in the evenings?'

The heads waved in an excitable fashion, an aggregate of faces popping up and down over the fence to shout abuse.

When the widow was indoors, she put the latch on the door and cried into her damp hands. She prayed in front of a small statue of Mary in the hallway, kissing the cold white feet with the serpent beneath them.

That night she washed her daughter in a tin tub before the fire. She made her son sit at the table and swear not to look at his sister. He smiled and said, 'Ah, come on, Ma.' Then the widow got out a bowl and placed it on the girl's head and snipped an even fringe around the forehead. 'Will ya stop still?' The girl whined, and the boy kept laughing as he sat on his seat staring out at the drenched street.

'I'll give ye a sup of tea, and a bit of potato, and then off with the both of you.'

The children ate their fried potato beside the fire. The widow held an onion on the end of a poker. The boy's eyes twinkled as clear as a star in the firelight. The door rattled at his back. The three peeled the onion apart and ate the fragrant skin with their hands moving slowly from their laps to their mouths. 'Well, off with ya now,' the widow said finally. The girl was already nodding her head with tiredness when the widow carried her body into the back room. The boy already had the hot stones in the bed, and was curled against the wall when the widow laid the girl down beside the boy for the night. 'Ma, are ya not comin in?'

'You go to sleep, Michael, do ya hear me?'

The boy buried his head in his sister's back. His muffled voice whispered, 'Good night, Ma.'

'Good night, Michael.'

She knew the dark man's impatient rap upon the door. He entered without a word, pointing toward a shadow that watched from the blackness. 'What's this?' The widow drew back from the freezing rain.

The youth had a narrow head, with long black hair. He seemed agitated in the doorway. The widow saw his face was soft and white. It seemed to crane toward the warmth like some strange flower. 'Come in,' the dark man said in a hoarse voice.

When the young man smiled, she could see he was no older than seventeen. He had a feminine face, the cheek-bones standing out and the lips full, engorged with blood. His body was lost in a heavy coat.

The widow wore a white linen slip that let the light pass through her body. The young man could see the outline of her breasts and protruding stomach. He glanced at the dark man, but did not advance.

'It's been cold these last few weeks I hear.' The dark man took a smug surveillance of the room.

The blackish stalk of a rosebush in the back-garden touched the back window in the cold blowing wind. 'Yes, and snow all through November.' The widow smiled softly. 'I'm afraid I've nothin but tea.'

The dark man lowered his shoulders and let the widow take his drenched coat and hang it over a chair by the fire. 'There, now it'll dry nicely.' She smiled again.

The young man said something in a strange tongue. His voice was full of softness and easy sounds. The widow withdrew herself, though, and moved toward the fire.

The dark man stared, steadfast, at the widow in solemn expectation. His massive eyes blinked at her. He turned spit in his mouth. 'You sit over there, boy.' He motioned to the youth to sit in a chair by the kitchen.

'Would you like a cup of tea?' The widow could see a dark curling snake-like tattoo on the youth's thin forearm when he took off his coat.

The dark man held the widow's arm. She gave off a low moan. 'Please, the children will wake up.' Her soft legs trembled under her slip.

'You got that money in December?'

The widow nodded silently.

'I want you to be nice to this fellow over there. He's been after me this while to meet someone special, you know?'

The widow shook her head slowly. 'Please, you can't make me . . . '

The dark man poured three cups of whiskey and raised his arm in the air. 'Slàinte.'

The youth swallowed his cup and the dark man refilled it. 'Easy does it,' the dark man said with a scowl. He winked and grinned, taking the cracked cup of ginger whiskey to the widow. 'Here.'

He put it to her lips. 'The boy is a foreigner, from over beyond England.'

'Please,' the widow whispered. Her eyes burned.

'Looks like a girl, doesn't he, with those big black eyes, and that long black hair?'

'He's only a boy.'

The dark man took another swig of whiskey. 'Will you stop? Did Michael get something proper to eat tonight?' The dark man's breath reeked of the whiskey.

The widow gave her cup back to the dark man. 'Just let him go, please. Not him, he's too . . . '

'Beautiful?' The dark man laughed out loud.

The young man swallowed another cup of whiskey. He turned his face away, speaking his foreign words. His head shook on his slender neck.

'The darkness knows not beauty, knows not age,' the dark man smiled. 'He's a good fellow. He promised me he wouldn't look at you. He has imagination all right.'

'Please, leave me alone.'

'You won't kill that boy in there.'

The widow took quick breaths, her small breasts heaving, 'Will you stay?'

The dark man shook his head.

The widow looked at the young man. He was sitting erect at the table, looking toward the fire with another cup of whiskey in his trembling hands.

'Maybe I should . . . ' She could see a small patch of red on the youth's forearm. She moved toward him, seeing red and black rings around a series of prick marks. The trembles of his body were not fear but something else that she could not understand. 'Is he sick?'

'Will you hold back awhile, for Jasus' sake?' The dark man lowered his voice and turned his face. 'Do you think I'd bring somethin to hurt you, my love?'

The widow clenched the dark man's arm. 'Please . . . I'm beggin you.' Her eyebrows curled in supplication and fear. 'Don't you love me any more?'

Michael stood in the doorway, rubbing his eyes. 'Hello, Uncle, did you bring me the liquorice?'

'Don't I always?' The dark man held out his arms, and the boy gave his body up.

'Where have ya been? Did ya see any creatures when ya was away, like the other times?'

'I'll tell ya in bed, okay?'

The small boy giggled. 'I love ya.' He was silent for a few moments. 'Do ya want to know a secret?'

'What?' The dark man hugged the small boy's warm body.

'Ma cries sometimes for you,' he whispered.

'Will you stop with that, Michael.'

The boy laid his head innocently against the dark man's shoulder. 'Well, she does. Did you see whales on the ships this time?' There was a black streak of liquorice on the side of his face.

The young man stood up and went for his coat. Again his words were strange, only his gestures showing intent.

'Leave it alone,' the dark man shouted. The child gripped the dark man's arm. 'Who's that, Uncle?'

'Shoo. It's a friend, Michael. You'll have to go to bed now. Maybe I'll follow you in and tell you a story if you're good.' The child slouched again in the dark man's arms. 'He looks like a girl.'

'He's a nice enough fellow, and my friend.' The dark man tickled the child, and he laughed.

'Will he be mad at me sayin that?' Michael whispered.

'Go on, will ya.' The dark man stood with his back to the door, staring at the widow and the youth. The youth was shaking with his coat in his hand.

'Michael, go on in with you,' the widow finally said in a soft voice.

The boy crept off. 'Will ya tell me that story, Uncle?'

The dark man smiled and nodded, 'A minute, son.'

The widow shut the child's door. 'Stay where you are, Michael.'

'Good night, Ma,' the boy whispered.

'Good night, son.'

The dark man rubbed his hands together. 'Great fellow. Well, now. I'll go in with your man and chat away, and, well . . . There's more drink there.'

The widow turned the lock in the child's door and clenched it in her fist. 'You stay here. Can't you see the boy's scared of your friend? He'll come out if you go in to see that I'm comin to no harm.'

The youth sat very still at the table. He pulled out a spoon from his pocket and a small candle. Slowly, he poured a brown powder into the spoon and let the candle burn the metal to a greenish copper colour.

'What's he doin?'

'Shoo . . . ' The dark man held the widow by the wrists.

The youth was enveloped in an aura of yellow light. His

head seemed in a halo. The widow could see his face twitching softly. She could smell the bitter taste of the spluttering substance. Then the youth took a small strip of cloth from his pocket. His body shook with nervousness. He began speaking in his strange way again.

The widow began to cry. 'What is he doin? Jesus help me.'

The dark man let the widow go and gave the youth a penknife. He took it in one hand and turned the gleaming blade slowly over the yellow flame. Then he poured the steaming hot liquid into a small blue bottle, and ran a stream of the substance down the hot blade. The entire room smelt of a queer syrup. The widow could taste it on her tongue, staring at a clear drop on the tip of the knife.

'What is that, Ma?' the small boy whispered through the keyhole.

'Go to bed, Michael,' the widow screamed. She could hear her son crying. 'I'm sorry, Ma.'

The youth at the table seemed to sink. He raised his eyes softly, groaning. He placed his forearm bare on the table. It quivered. Slowly, he turned a piece of twine, tighter and tighter about the wrist. There were more words, not foreign, animal moans.

The widow felt a numbness in her wrists. 'Oh Christ!' The dark man held her tightly. 'Easy, will you?'

The young man stuck the reddening tip of the knife into the tender flesh of his bluish veins. 'Ah ... ' There was an instant trickle of purple blood.

The widow closed her eyes for a moment. 'Jesus ... '

The young man smiled faintly at the dark. His face was very pale. Then he emptied the blue bottle on to the strip of cloth and placed it over his bleeding wounds, grimacing from the sudden sting. His eyes stared at the widow. They were red and watering. His lips were glazed with his own spit. He was speaking again to her, his arm trembling, outstretched, streaming with lines of dark blood.

The dark man gripped the youth's arm and squeezed it, drawing himself into a huddle. 'Come now, boy.'

The young man leaned on his arms, his face dazed for an instant. He said something again.

The dark man sat the youth down again and poured another drink into his cup. 'Ische Baith, hey now. Water of the soul.'

The youth pumped his arm back and forth. His trembling seemed to leave his body. '*Merci!*'

'Jesus, what did he say?'

They all sat very still for a long time.

The widow poured more coal on to the fire, poking away at the glowing embers. The two men could see the curve of her buttocks and the gentle points of her nipples in the light.

'But you'll have to stay in the room,' the widow whispered finally. The dark man tried to muscle himself free. 'Don't touch me.' His face scowled under his dark eyebrows. 'Do you hear me? Don't touch me.'

The youth stared blankly at the fire. His face was flushed, and his eyes were bulging in their sockets. He kept singing some strange song, shrugging his shoulders and then smiling like a fool at the widow. The foreign words poured from his lips once more.

The dark man sat again and shot another cup of gingery brew into his belly. Then he rose again and walked to the widow as though he was going to strike her. 'Okay, then, if that's the way you want it, Widow.'

'I want nothin,' the widow whispered. She saw the dark man's teeth exposed.

'Ma, let me see ya!' the small boy in the bedroom cried. 'I'm afraid, Ma!'

'Shoo, boy.' The dark man shook his head, banging on the door. 'Do you know what happened to the boy who left his bed when he was told not to,' began the dark man. 'Do you?'

The boy whimpered and sniffled. 'I'm sorry, Uncle. Good night, Ma.'

'That poor boy.' The dark man turned away from the door and pushed his face into the widow's face, his breath full of spirits. 'You won't get away with this.' He had a terrible spluttering half smile on his face. 'So help me God.'

The widow felt faint. 'You must stay in the room.'

The dark man withdrew to the table. With the turn of a wrist he had another whiskey down his stomach.

The widow saw the two of them sitting very still, like docile creatures, both dressed in black, brooding over cups of whiskey. The dark man seemed a figure of failing strength. His eyes were weak in his head, the widow could see the small threads of wrinkles, his hair was thinning at the top. There was a small polished circle under the scant hair. The young man was no less demoralized a sight with his emaciated arm baring the elongated mark of a curling snake. The fresh wounds looked like fang marks.

The widow squinted her eyes and teetered, feeling the warm flush of the whiskey moving through her body in a sudden rush.

The dark man stood in the kitchen. He could see the bodies of the youth and the widow.

The young man moved over near the fire on to a blanket. The widow placed the key to her children's room on a hook above the doorway.

The young man had a hairless chest with another tattoo, a heart, below the left nipple. That was where the widow started to run her tongue. She kept swallowing hard.

The dark man could hear the sounds. 'Keep it quiet, for fuck's sake.'

The widow was beneath the youth's arched body. His flesh was warm and red, teeming with sweat. The widow felt his weight upon her groin. His pants were about his ankles. He grunted with effort. She could see the youth's arms flexed, and the serpent head seemed to twitch and turn and look at her. The small fang wounds bled drops of blood on to her neck. The linen felt like a layer of dead skin about her, clinging to her arms and breasts and legs. His body had saturated her. He bent his head and began running his soft face over the smooth surface of the slip. Then he undressed her, moving her arm slowly in a kind of swimmer's crawl, finally edging the slip over her head. He held the article in his bony fist, kissing it. She could see the black glossiness of his eyes, his face without a wrinkle, so foreign and clean.

The widow looked away, wanting to scream, staring over toward the dark man, moaning, 'Why . . . ' He was staring at her face. He put his finger to his lip. She winced and shut her eyes. Then she felt the youth's cold fingers sinking into the soft pith of her opening legs. Each finger was like a shard of ice. She arched her back against his dead weight. His shiftless eyes remained open as he tensed his body. His teeth grated in his head. The widow could hear the brewery outside screaming once more. She imagined those insipid-fingered chimneys out in that blackness prodding the darkness, filling it with warm grey pouring smoke, and she saw the blackish green finger of her husband, and him on her, that strange pain, those horrible juvenile nail-bitten fingers, ringed with dirt, tearing away at the soft fringe of skin deep within her body. Her organs burned with a scraping penetration. She could see her child's hair in a small heap near the green chipped chair. She stared at the moonlight filtering through the wet locks. She clutched the hair in her hands, bringing it to her lips, kissing it, smelling the odour of soap. 'My baby,' she sobbed quietly. The dark man had his back turned. The widow shut her eyes, feeling that same flood of soft effulgence spilling down her thighs, running between her bottom. The tears trickled down her face. She could hear the dark man filling the kettle. 'You'll have an appetite on ya when this is over, I'll tell you.' The dark man was nodding his head. 'Yes, sir.' The widow heard him spit and heard the rhythmic sawing of the bread knife through a stale heel of bread. Then the youth groaned and slumped and cried out, and the widow opened her mouth, and the dark man turned, and they saw the youth with his head in the air, gasping for air like a fish in the greyish light, his beautiful face covered in tears of effort, his eyes as black as obsidian, his shadow falling on the door of the bedroom where the small child had his eye locked in the keyhole, crying, 'Ma.'

The following morning the widow dabbed iodine on to her neck. Her son tugged at the door, crying. She let him out, and he would not look at her. The widow did not look at him. He saw the glint of some silver money on the table. His face was smeared with the liquorice.

'Are you goin to school?'

The boy held his sister's hand and nodded, 'Can we have a bit of bread, Ma?'

The widow set the butter before the dead fire and let it slowly melt while she took away the half-empty whiskey cups and rinsed them in a tub of freezing water.

The boy kissed her on her lips and squeezed his sister's hand. 'We'll be killed if we don't go, Ma, okay?' He smiled and looked at the money again.

The widow held a cup of tea to her mouth as she stared out the window, breathing a hot mist on the window-pane. She wondered if the men would come and taunt her again this morning. She kept looking at light pouring through the chinks in the fence. There was a roar of life in the street when she eased the window open a crack to see the small boy taking his sister off with him. The brewery was enveloped in a cloud of vapour, stacks pouring ribbons of smoke into the sky. She remembered Mr Greeves' office with his old photographs and green velvet walls and mahogany desk. Her neck stung with the coldness of the air. It was hard to believe that a company could grow so rich and offend so little. The establishment had the blessing of both Church and State. It kept both parties happy, for the brewery and its produce relegated the men to a nation of wall-pissers and, importantly in the eyes of the Church, a nation of Catholic-breeders.

The widow knew it was Greeves at her door all that time ago, but she dared not tell anyone. As she ventured toward the back of the house, she could see her clothes blowing in the icy wind. She set up the clothes-peg around the fire, coralling the heat as it were for the freezing clothes outside.

Suddenly, she let the cup drop from her hooked fingers. She saw a little mound of clay dug by her child's grave. She held her breath, seeing the lollipop sticks smashed to pieces, the bulbs of her flowers sliced and strewn around the garden.

When she leaned forward inside the hole, there was only the dark drawer. The child had been stolen. The widow dug with her small hands into the black earth, covering the gleam of her ring with the brown earth. She kept sobbing gently, 'Where is my child? Oh Jesus! Who would steal my child?' She threw the drawer aside, dipping her head and breasts forward, filling the empty hole with her tears and face. Fat earthworms squirmed before her face, tunnelling away with their blunt wet heads.

All the neighbours peeked out of their windows, stealing glances toward the widow's house. The thick smoke from the brewery brought with it the smell of fermenting stout. Behind her back three chimneys puffed billowing black ash. Nobody could see the widow until she stood up. She was very silent, the clothes dancing on the line like fairies before her face. She walked forward, following a trail of footprints. Her breasts and stomach were wet with the black humus of the grave. She could feel the grainy soil and wetness all about her body. She clung to a lone strip of stocking she had put on her baby's foot. She tried not to cry, standing still finally, watching the sun blaze and conceal hundreds of faces beyond windows. Slowly, she began to unpeg the clothes on the line, her dirty nails leaving a faint animal print on each article. She felt her legs weakening under her.

'The dark man came and took that baby to hell,' someone

whispered beyond the fence. 'An angel took him from limbo to heaven.'

The widow walked slowly back into her house again. Her face was black with the soil. Two tributaries of tears coursed down each cheek.

A small note fell through the letter-box. The widow moved toward the door, feeling the coldness of her floor against her feet. Her pale mottled legs were set with goose-bumps. Her blackened fingers trembled as she read:

'The child will be waiting at the station when you leave.'

If she refused, would her child be for ever in an ice vault, at perhaps the brewery or in some merchant's ice room, like some small doll martyr she had seen in churches down in the country? She remembered seeing the blackened head of Blessed Oliver Plunkett in a church once. Three hundred years it had been preserved by the priests so that everyone could come and see what a true saint looked like. She shivered more and more.

She went to the hot press beside her fireplace and took out her pale yellow dress, the one her husband had bought for her that summer when it had been so hot that people put ice in their Guinness. She smiled faintly, but it was a futile rebellion. Yet, she persisted. She set her children's pants and shirts on the clothes-horse. Then she put four moulds of clay on a tray over the fire. The day was brutally cold once more. The children would need the stones to hold when their fingers froze as they carried their cases to the station. The widow gathered her own belongings, waiting until her children came home for their dinner at twelve o'clock.

The boy held his sister's hand, linking himself to her. 'Hello, Ma.' His face was swollen with the coldness. He moved his jaw about, holding back something.

'Do ya know what a whore is, Ma?'

The widow shook her head. 'Will you eat?' The widow gave them porridge and potatoes with salt and glasses of milk. They ate in silence. The money was piled in the middle of the table. The boy glared at the coins, his small fingers clenched tight on his knees.

'There's my man.' The boy stood with his sister by his side, holding two brown suitcases that went up to his waist. The widow straightened his hat upon his head. He turned his head slightly. The coins still gleamed on the table. 'A whore, Ma, takes money.'

The widow turned the key in her door, nodding her head. Her face was red with tears.

At the station, the priest pointed in the distance. In between the vast echoes of screams and running children, the rain overhead drummed on the plastic roof. 'The station was covered in a series of grey footprints from the rain, and yet there were few people about. It was as though spirits moved invisibly. The widow and the small boy stared at a small basket. The boy let the cases down easy. The priest did not approach. He stood very still. The widow ran her gentle fingers through the boy's wet hair, holding her daughter's hand gently with her other hand. She could feel the boy's body convulsing, feel his shoulder-blades tensing. When the boy Michael lifted the basket on to his shoulder, the widow could see the small parcelled infant covered in wax-paper, the kind of wax-paper she had used to catch flies and other creatures on her shelf in her abandoned home.

THE GARDEN OF EDEN

THE RED HEAT of the sitting room gave it all away. The heat blew the curtains in gentle waves of velvet, the windows teary and fogged. Upstairs, curled in her bed, Reilly's wife was crying. Of course she woke the boy with her carry-on.

Reilly's boy crouched between the bars on the landing, watching his father. His small hands were white with the cold. Ever so softly he breathed, smelling the roasting air of the dining room. He could hear the delicate snip, snip of his father at work.

'Are ya okay, Da?' His voice was weak with the coldness.

Reilly stood very still.

The boy whispered in the background. 'Please, Da?'

A candle dripped its wax on to a saucer in the kitchen. Reilly raised his head slowly. 'Go to bed.' He could feel the mechanics of the metal band around his head preventing the stalk of his neck from pivoting. Only the cool softness of the gauze about his face gave him any comfort.

The boy stared at his father's figure, seeing the gleam of the two solid strips of metal riveted to a band ringing his father's head, running down to a shoulder harness.

'Ma says they're watchin ya, Da.'

'You should be in bed.' Reilly's head gleamed in the dining room. 'Is she awake?'

The boy stood invisible in the cold darkness.

'Why won't ya go up, Da?' He saw his father's phantom head wrapped in the greyish bandages.

Reilly let his fingers fumble in the wet soil in a long tray of plants. The air was thick with an aroma of minty heat from a small bedding of cress which he had pulled out of several trays. He had a series of parallel lines of trays arranged in a massive mahogany box which ran on tracks down an incline into a hole. Slowly, he set the entire contraption into motion and the box glided soundlessly into the depths of the padded grave.

'Da?'

'Stay away,' Reilly whispered. He kept his eye on the stairs while he drew down the trap-door on the hole. From the seams in the floorboards he could see the blazing bulbs of light. He manoeuvred the rolled-up carpet with the leg of his boot, covering everything into a concealed oblivion. Then he emerged stoically from the dining room, leaving the heaters burning. Sweat ran down his trouser legs. He put a cigarette toward his mouth in sudden relief, pressing it through a membrane of gauze.

'Ma says they're goin to see the lights, Da.' Again, he whispered, 'Why won't ya go to bed, Da?'

Reilly lit his cigarette in slow animated style. 'I'm smokin. Do ya want me to set the street on fire?' Reilly's voice was filled with a hoarse smokiness. He took a shallow breath, illuminating the shadow of his invisible face with a pull on his cigarette. 'Fuckin inquisition in me own house. Jasus!' He was trying to smile. It was okay for now. The secret was kept. He was just going to talk himself out of this near disaster. Still, he found the sweat was sopping his legs. The thrill of excitement lingered in each shaky drag on the cigarette. He felt a sudden pinch, the buckles of the shoulder harness digging into the nape of his neck. 'Jasus, ah, now you've done it. I'm fuckin banjaxed.'

Reilly's boy bit his lip. He ferreted the night with his small face, nosing the odour of minty cress and a strange rich tropical odour of some unknown thing. 'Can I get meself a drink of milk, Da?' The boy's face drew itself away from the landing railings.

'Okay. Be quick now.' Reilly followed the boy into the kitchen. His walk was inhibited by the metal contraption about his torso and head. He proceeded toward the softness of his solitary candle on the kitchen table.

Reilly's house was a small two-storey construct with shared walls adjoined to neighbouring houses on the left and right. Only the redbricked façade of the house faced on to Eden Street. Reilly thought it fostered all the discomforting aspects of acute claustrophobia. Things seemed to have a triple resonance. Reilly heard toilets flushed three times as much every day; the breakfast, dinner and tea were prepared all of nine times a day, thus inducing in Reilly the odd disposition of always feeling full. He existed in a kind of frenzied world, each lobe of his brain attending to the trials of his neighbours. He was oft telling people that he had three wives. If the truth be known, he actually did sleep in closer proximity to his neighbour's wife than to his own. A mere nine inches of plaster wall separated their most intimate experiences.

On the landing, the boy held on to the varnished wooden railing and crept down the stairs. He stopped in the ebbing warmth of the sitting room. The heater burned the musky dampness of the room. As his eyes adjusted, he could see the charcoal whiteness of his father's immobile head negotiating a path toward the kitchen.

He stood motionless behind his father. The coldness of the lino numbed his feet. The muted softness of the candle-lit room seemed to lack any dimension. 'Did ya write dat note for me, Da?'

'I did.' Reilly was a self-professed man of letters, un-educated but thoroughly knowledgeable on all subjects. He had honed a queer style for teachers' notes in his time.

'What did ya say for it?'

Reilly put his finger to his lips, making a horrible face, pointing with either hand to the neighbouring walls. The street had developed a language all its own which constituted a dialogue of low guttural snorts with an emphasis on pantomime.

'Da, what does it say?'

Reilly looked at the vague imprinted whiteness of a religious picture of Jesus he had removed over five years ago when he had banned all such articles from the house. That had caused a holy war in his parish. He won out in the end. Jasus, it was his fuckin house, but the outlines still defied him. It was that kind of irony which gave him philosophy. He knew there was no such thing as freedom even from one's own self when all was said and done.

The boy moved by his father. 'What does it say?'

Reilly unfolded the piece of paper and gave his perfunctory theatrical cough. 'It says: "Please excuse our Billy's absence yesterday. His mother was in bed with the doctor. Signed, Your friend in Christ, Billy's Da"'

'Could ya say somethin else, Da?'

'I couldn't.' Reilly let a long invisible grin ripple across his face. His eyes wrinkled instinctively under the gauze.

The rectangular kitchen table sat in the middle of the sitting room serving as a boundary between the true kitchen and the fireplace. Space in the house was neatly arranged in partitions which were shifted to suit the mood and circumstances of a situation. For now the kitchen table was firmly entrenched in the limbo of inanimate things waiting to serve the morning breakfast.

The boy edged forward through the dining room and could see his father had set the makings for the morning fire in the fireplace. He could feel the intensity of his father's silence. A coldness seemed to come from where his father sat. He gave a sudden shudder, yet he still felt the hotness in his thighs from squatting. 'Ma is cryin, Da.'

Reilly felt the slow resolution of life intoxicating him. He could hear footsteps in the house next door, and then someone shouting. It must have been Rebecca coming back home. Oh Jasus. Paddy Nolan had a time with that one. On the street, everyone's perception of everyone else was a series of half-truths and conjecture, complete with nods and winks. It made for great fights. Everything was a terrible struggle, some mad architect's romantic vision, inflicting a seamless brick existence on a fragmented, clandestine populace. Between the rows of houses, looping clothes-lines fluttered and billowed in the wind. There was a smell of starch in the air in the mornings. Reilly knew the bra size of every woman on his street. And that wasn't the half of it. Hundreds of sheets charted the mating lives of his neighbours. Wasn't Biddy Maguire still using the pink nightgown that her Granny Burke died in last Easter? Granny Burke had worn it like skin for four long infirm years. Reilly was none too familiar with politics, but he knew this street of his was some experiment of sorts. For him, the street life was the kind of fraternity that only intellectuals could have endured out of some Marxist arse-ology. On wet days the clothes bled in dark droplets. The thing was a ballocks, all the road filled with strange rainbow puddles of detergent and suds. He'd lost count of how many white shirts had been ruined by that cursed rain.

'Da, can I get a drink?'

'Didn't I say yes? Now go on with it, quick.' Reilly's finger and eyes averted upward. 'She'll ate the head off ya for bein down at this hour.' Reilly dismissed the figure of his son with a wave of his hand. His taut face grimaced slightly within the nest of wires. He could feel the intense pinch of the broken vertebrae in his spine. He had been having dreams at night where that old monkey tailbone down by his arse broke off and vertebra, disk, vertebra, disk, vertebra, disk ran down his spinal cord like pegs off an abacus. It was a whore of a dream.

'Da?'

Reilly looked past his son to the oval photograph of his

wedding day nailed to his neighbour's shared wall. There was an unbroken chain of events unfolding beyond the fixed stare in his eyes. He could hear the taunting idiocy of childish rhymes, little girls with fat faces and little dresses with white socks and buckled shoes singing, 'First comes love, then comes marriage, then comes baby in a carriage.' It was more sublime than that, and yet that was the baseness of his species. The sense of estrangement and animalism was all there, even in the minds of children. A consciousness of history and tragedy seemed to come quickly when children saw their clothes inherited on to the backs of the next child and so on and so on.

'Why don't ya go to bed, Da?'

Reilly let his cigarette burn itself in a warm smoulder on a china saucer. He conjured a smile despite his bugger of a son. 'She doesn't let me smoke in bed. She thinks', his words were perfectly formed by his lips, 'that I'll burn the place to the ground.'

'Why do ya smoke, Da?'

'Jasus!' Reilly let his eyes roll in his head.

The boy remained unconscious to the full melancholy of his father. He turned away with a vague filial happiness which his father understood but found wholly ineffectual.

Yet Reilly found himself saying, 'So how was that match the other day?'

The fridge hummed in the solitude, filled with its insulated world of dark frosted milk, dishes packed with eggs, sausages, cheese and wild mushrooms. The boy's head was invisible.

A scab of ash moved through the beige aura of the still flame. The back of Reilly's head glowed in a sullen halo of softness. The cotton gauze smouldered in a soft orange. The light of the fridge dribbled out to the edge of his feet.

The boy moved his head out of the iciness of the fridge.

'Did ya score, son?'

'What?'

'The match. Did ya score?'

'I was sent off . . .'

'Ya were what? For what?'

The boy smiled and turned, 'Dirty play inside the penalty box.'

Reilly looked straight at his son with all the bewilderment that flesh and blood ties could elicit and implicate. There was a definite cruelty in unimpeded procreation. He wondered if Hitler's mother had known what she was rearing. Mass murdering began in the home, as did all other nasties, like taking the name of God in vain, not flushing the jacks, and dipping bread in tea.

In the next house Murphy was already lighting his fire. He worked at a bakery in the city. He was a bastard for noise, flinging blocks around in the fireplace, bashing bits of turf against the walls to break them. Reilly felt like shouting, but he refrained.

'Dirty play,' he found himself whispering. Ah yes, he had to admit sex was a dodgy business. Imagine having a boy who got sent off for 'dirty play'. Things were out of his hands, he had to grant now. 'Sent off for dirty play.' Jasus Christ, he'd put a fiver – win, place or show – for all the arsehole scientists to show him where that gene resided.

Of course, like all middle-aged men, he had a philosophy on his penis. Rather, the truth of it all was that the bugger had the discomforting aspect of looking like him. That was the damnedest spectacle for Reilly. People could identify the bugger as his own by those big ears and short snout.

The boy did not face his father but whispered, 'Are ya still scared, Da?'

'For the love and honour of Jasus, can a man smoke in peace?' The words trailed in a benediction of smoking curses. Reilly remained still in his chair, feeling the pressure of his elbows against the table. The walls of his neighbours seemed to close around him. His knees rocked unconsciously beneath him, making the candle tremble and shimmer on the bare table. In the darkness his voice had the resonance of an eternity of submission. In his neighbour's house to the right, the young girl Mary with the small hunch on her back coughed through the night. It was driving Reilly demented. Slowly, he leaned his torso forward, folding another cigarette of knotted tobacco. He pivoted on his hips, moving the encased mechanics of his torso toward the flame, his lips pursed. The pain in his neck was excruciating. The extent of his movement limited his perspective to a narrowed stare, or rather squint. At times he was reduced to walking backward since, for some reason, it caused less strain on his back. Not that it wasn't awkward, adjusting his mind to the perspective of seeing things recede as opposed to confront him as he walked along. It reminded him of journeying in a train carriage.

'The priests won't hurt you any more, Da.' The features on the boy's face were huge and cherub-like, the soft babyish hair in loose curls on his forehead. 'Okay, Da?' The boy turned away and stared into the coldness of the fridge.

Reilly shook his head. 'Will ya stop with . . . The priests! What are ya on about?' He mouthed the word 'neighbours' like a fish in water, raising his hand to slap the face of the boy.

'The fellas at school was sayin . . .'

Reilly broke in. 'I fell down off the bike the other night in that frost, and that's the way it was. Do ya hear me? March is a whore for the frost.'

'But the priests . . .'

Reilly tried to kick his leg outward but grimaced instead. 'Black frost, son. It's a whore in March, right?'

The boy lowered his head in submission. 'Yes, Da.'

'Is it so hard to shut yer face and do what yer told?' Reilly stubbed the remnants of the old cigarette out in a cracked china saucer, grinding the butt until the flaking tobacco crumbled beneath his fingers. The aroma of the Virginia weed filled his nostrils. He thought for a lingering moment of those

Blue Mountains of Virginia, that strange land of azure hills filled with dark people singing songs under the blazing sun of the Americas. He rubbed the weed nervously in his nicotine-bronzed fingers. He still felt the coarse spidery stitches in his index finger when he pinched his thumb against the tobacco. The stitched finger was a darkish plum colour, still half-separated with a deep slit of rawness. It was horribly crooked. Reilly was thinking to himself, thanks be to Jasus he didn't play the piano or flute with a finger like that now. At the bottom he was a queer sort of optimist.

The boy drank straight from a bottle of milk. He closed his eyes, and his neck rose and fell with each gulp as the cold milk ran down his throat. When he finished, the hairs on his upper lip teemed with milk.

'Kiss me goodnight now.' Reilly smiled.

The small boy's eyes squinted with effort. He seemed infinitely aged, his small naked legs shrouded away in the milky darkness. His rounded head seemed almost grotesque. The boy's face did not acquiesce. Other fathers were driving new cars and dressing in white starched shirts and never cursing. The boy's question was a simple indictment, uttered mutely to himself with the utmost reserve. He spoke to his father, 'Why does God hate us, Da? Why did he send the priests to kill ya?'

Oh, sweet Jasus. How gorgeous. Reilly had to admit it was a major blow against the Christian Brothers and Catholic education at large, to have a fledgling agnostic in the making. Blaming God – that was a kind of rare 'dirty play'. Not that the battle was won, but it was a sweet moment in Reilly's bloody existence.

'Your first mistake there is blaming God!' Reilly quipped.

'Do you believe in God, Da?'

Reilly's eyes gleamed in his head, his gob closed, the rest of his face remaining unseen beneath the shrouded gauze. 'Would ya go to bed before ya get a kick in the arse!'

'Da, do you believe in God?'

Reilly put another cigarette to his lips and began smoking. 'Do you believe in God?'

The boy came closer to his father. His small head was shaking in the stillness. 'I believe in the priests, Da.'

Reilly grumbled to himself. He was getting agitated.

The boy put his lips to his father's forehead. 'I believe in you and Ma, Da.'

Reilly remained quiet, looking toward the benign immensity of the night filled with slow-moving clouds outside. This must have been the kind of blather they were teaching the buggers at school. Reilly thought there was nothing like a belt across the face to keep a family together. The danger was in talking to the buggers.

Reilly looked outside through the window. The cursed rain would be coming soon. He could hear the labouring diesel buses in the distance, returning to the garages for the night. The pubs were empty now. The air was damp and cold. This was the mating hour. Darkness prevailed with the whispered language of moans. Reilly could imagine those bloody neighbours of his rocking that headboard against his wall. Thanks be to Jasus that he was down here now. He could hear them whispering on those nights, going at it after a sup of warm milk and a cheese sandwich. And the shame of the thing hurt Reilly. Poor Mrs Nolan was dying of cancer. She'd never live to see her babies grow up.

Everything was freezing in the dewy blackness outside. March was a bastard. It turned the milk at the doorsteps to an opaque iciness in the early morning. Sometimes it burst bottles. It was all freezing out there and in the huddled houses, all except his oasis of vegetation growing, silently, sweating away in the steamy hothouse womb of his mahogany box.

A smell of mildew rose from the wood rotting around the window-frame. Reilly was aware of those useless hours which turned into days and weeks attending to rotting window-sills. Reilly closed his eyes, the aura of nostalgia and the present filling him with a sudden giddiness. All that time wasted for lack of money, all that life ruined with the sudden paroxysms of passion in the dead of night. He was a man cursed with being born before insulated windows. And that wasn't the half of it. He could have traced disaster to particular moments in his life, or so he liked to tell himself. If he ever got round, as he so wittily used to say, to writing his wrong, he would have chapters and passages in big block letters with red print, 'BOYS, BEWARE!' He firmly believed in the power of education. But for now he was in hell. Those children had it wrong. First comes baby, then comes marriage, and then, God only fuckin knows. For an instant he saw the coffin of Mrs Nolan carried by tiny-fingered infants.

'I'm goin to bed now . . .' The boy's breath had a sourness to it from the milk. 'Okay?'

In the sitting room the night burned in the florid light.

Reilly's kiss was gentle. He had his eyes fixed on nothing, just breathing into his son's ear.

'Do you want me to rub your back, Da?'

Reilly smiled. The child was a bugger, but he came through in a crunch. There were still hidden pleasures in the most awful circumstances. A good scratch had that kind of cross-species appeal undermining all pretension of culture. Dog and man alike must have met and diverged from that happy crotch somewhere on the tree of evolution.

The boy took a flat wooden ruler from the table, and Reilly leaned forward at an angle, almost kissing the table. The boy pulled his father's shirt up to his shoulder blades, tucking the excess material into a loose knot into the shoulder harness of the metal contraption. He slowly edged the ruler between the leathery straps of the harness, running the ruler from the nape of the neck to the hips.

Reilly purred with satisfaction, giving soft commands, 'There, oh, yes, yes, that's it, now.' He had his eyes closed, his face invisible.

Reilly's back was typical enough, one of those fleshy

slopes of whiteness that saw sunlight for a swim once a year.
It was slightly blotched by a small rash from the buckles on
the harness and the two blunt bars that held the head
immobile. The bruising discolouration had faded away. His
back was still spotted here and there with the vague imprint of
iodine on healing wounds. A few slashed zipper-like stitches
ran at various angles on his arms and lower back.

The boy scratched earnestly. He was still at that age when
he didn't deliberate much upon things.

'That's fine, son. Right there . . . Oh yes, glory be to Jasus.'
Reilly smiled vaguely to himself. His face remained hidden
under the cool gauze. He remembered the doctors telling him
he had skin that healed well. His eyes were squinted with
effort and attention.

'You're a great fella,' Reilly whispered.

Maybe he'd been wrong about this business of children.
Calling his son 'Original Sin' seemed extreme in view of
circumstances now. But that was the way with this sort of
bugger, though. In five minutes he'd be mitred again with the
bugger's blathering. Poor, poor boy. Reilly was firmly con-
vinced there was a hidden tragedy in being the offspring of a
middle-class family. He actually thought of it as a curse.
Where was the romance in having a father who owned a Black
and Decker? Nostalgia was coming to an end slowly but
surely with this breed of middle-class buggers. Reilly nodded
his head to the rhythmic scratching. He was one of the last of a
dying breed. He really did think of himself in those terms.
When he read in the paper a death of his own kind, that is to
say the tormented few, he spoke in terms of extinction. Ah
yes, the poor ol family going to rack and ruin for want of a
plain hammer and a kick in the arse. In his most sentient
moments, Reilly thought there was nothing as good as a dose
of madness in a family to educate a mind.

The boy struggled to help his father rise and sit motionless
again.

'Jasus, that was some scratch.' Reilly was all plumass for a few brief moments. Instinct seemed to get the better of him. He fished about in his pocket for a few coppers. He put them in the hot palm of his boy. 'Buy yerself somethin nice, okay? Say yer prayers for yer Ma and me. It'll settle ya down.' Reilly pulled the web of gauze away from his mouth. He put a soft kiss against the boy's forehead. 'You go to bed now, son. Say yer prayers till ya fall asleep.'

The boy's feet moved quietly away by the rising heat of the sitting room carpet. The lino was aglow. The boy felt the tiny hair on his arms tingling in the lushness of the warm darkness. Everything had a sweetness for that one instant, and then the cold starkness of the house enveloped him again as he climbed the stairway.

'Da?'

Reilly winced. 'What?'

'I already said my prayers.'

'Well count sheep or somethin.' Reilly's voice died with a soft, 'Jasus.'

There was really nothing for it now. Reilly could not brood like this all through the night. Upstairs his wife and son were waiting with eyes wide open, staring into the darkness. It was hard to keep this defiance up in the face of those above him. His boy had a communion prayer-book and a savings account at the local post office for all his agnosticism. He'd learnt his catechism too well. He would come around one of these days to the formal religiosity of his betters. He was going to confessions now. That would be the end of it all. No more secrets with a spy in the house. Oh lamentable . . . And what with school and teachers' meetings and psychologists sending the buggers home to draw pictures of their mas and das. Things never changed. It was all spying of one sort or another. Making children confess this and that in the most underhand manner. What was psychology anyway? The same ol balderdash, a mere shifted perspective of geometry, turning a confessional box on its side, installing a couch.

Reilly could hear the boy urinating in the darkness, and then the door to a bedroom opened. He listened, wincing as the boy crept upon his mother's bed. The springs creaked. There were whispered words. A light on the landing went on, and the boy and his mother went into the boy's room. He was crying gently. Then the light went dead. He heard his wife going 'shoo . . .' He thought of his wife tucking the boy into his bed, pressing the cold sheets around his tiny body.

She would be wanting rashers and pudding anytime now, and a cup of tea with just a little milk, but not too much, and not a lot of sugar, and poison the whole bloody thing, and the rashers aren't crispy, and there's tea on the toast . . . Bloody soppy toast that nobody could eat. Can ya do anythin right? Do ya want me to lose this child as well? It's your fault, two children dead because you won't boil an egg for me without settin the place on fire . . . Reilly was a better man than to raise a hand to his wife. Fuckin preserve us! He thought of those big legs giving her a gravity unto herself. Things orbited her, the boy, himself, the cat, all harassed satellites. She was definitely a true goddess, resting seven days a week on the vast whiteness of her bed. Reilly thought of that bed as a sort of launching-pad into limbo for those two babies. It was a sad grave. Only one of her children had ever crawled into the world. But it wasn't his fault. There was something wrong with her insides when it was all said and done.

In the heat of the living room Reilly stood tracing an ancient, ghostly imprint on the carpet that left cryptic clues to what it once represented. Things were slowly becoming meaningless within the confines of his own home. Only the sheer geometry of the house remained intact. Everything else was fading, losing its colour, its definition. What he needed was to remove himself from the fixity of the architecture within the home. It was too subversive, this unconscious knowledge of relative distances between objects and rooms. Life had this logical relationship within his home which was nothing more than a mistaken sense of order. If he could only find the essential arbitrariness of how he had come to live in his house, on this street, in this city, in this country ... The hell with it all! He knew it wasn't the house at all. It was them upstairs, looking into the darkness, expecting him to do something. Oh Jasus, philosophy was no substitute for finances.

He crouched over a tray of plants. The leaves were soft and withered as he ran his fingers along the stems, counting the leaves. He turned on a weak light. A lattice of mesh wire contained a network of dripping taps which intermittently rained a fine mist on the crop. The room was a cocoon of damp heat. Reilly began to feel his armpits sweating in fat droplets. He was shaking. This was the last crop. He had promised his wife. They would not suspect him now. He had spent days pleading with her. 'No ... No. They believe I have stopped. Oh please ... They never found out about this. They just found me selling it. That's not growing it. Don't you see the difference, stupid woman? One more crop. We will go away when this is done, to America or England. Just a little more money ... You understand ... You want the bleeding to stop, don't you? You want that baby to live?'

Memory burned vividly within the dying colours of the hated geometry of his home. There was no escaping those images. They were fleeting but recurrent, usurping themselves in moments of sobriety, rearing up in the mundane activities of his life. It was like losing one's step on a stairs that had been traversed for a lifetime, and suddenly the missed step, as though the engine of monotony died for a brief moment, the horror of what is beyond knowing blazing for an instant.

Reilly gauged right from wrong by the amount of justification it took to convince himself of things, not that this knowledge was of any worth. He understood that knowledge had a vacuity not unlike ignorance. What was the point of knowledge when there were no real ends to things?

At the end of the day his wife was too scared to say no to his will. She was a baffling woman. Reilly's physical presence still commanded respect from his wife. He had that much solace in the undercurrent of animalism still ingrained within humanity. He was a man, and she was a woman. That was the one deciding principle in their relationship. That could never be challenged. He knew that his wife understood she was implicated in creating the dreariness of their life. A certain latitude for physical agitation had to be allowed. The child and child-to-be were diversions instilling meaning for a few months of gestation. He had to acknowledge the difference between her and him, between the sexes. She lived in the confines of her bedroom. That was her duty. She was making a baby. God bless the beast. Yes, yes. He would make the tea, boil the egg, butter the toast, bring her sups of warm milk, rub her swollen ankles. He wasn't cruel.

One night, when he was rubbing oil on the raw stretch marks on her breasts, she began crying. She said something about not wanting any babies. She blamed him, then she blamed herself. Then she just cried, and Reilly was left staring at her belly gleaming in the softness of the moonlight, shaking his head. It looked, for all the world, like a big egg. The neighbours must have heard it all. She stopped crying and wanted to know how one does not get pregnant in a dressing-gown. It was a good question; even Reilly had to admit that one.

Even in his desperate state, it was Reilly who did the shopping, the cooking. He watched her at the top of the stairs, her belly deformed with child under the powder blue of her dressing-gown. At some juncture of his life, both he and his wife had given up a yearning to know for a yearning to make. It was primitive, but god-like. Meaning did seem to be an afterthought of creation. He felt there was a dubious philosophy in all matters of meaning. Wasn't the city bus timetable one of the greatest books of fiction ever created?

That always made the grannies laugh on the buses on a cold winter morning. That's what the audience was for his most sober observations, ol ones with curlers and nets in their hair, smelling of menthol liniments.

Reilly replaced a few burnt-out blackish bulbs in his glorious midnight sun. The stems of his plants were still thin greenish veins, almost translucent under the weak disk of light that hung from the ceiling. Outside, he heard Murphy, the baker, spitting and leaving in his van. Reilly stopped for a moment and then continued. Beyond the tray of cannabis were other crops in various stages of development. The entire crop sloped on an incline. The new seedlings still embedded in the black earth had not broken the soil yet. Reilly drew his body out of the womb of warmth and lumbered ineptly into the kitchen and filled a canister of water which he found he could not lift due to his neck injury. He cursed through four trips to the kitchen to get less than two gallons of water. From the cupboards he took down a sachet of powdery chemicals and stirred the contents into a soft bladder sack which looked for all the world like a bagpipe with its series of pipes emanating from the centre. Some of the powder burned the raw crevice of his finger. He cleaned the cut under the cold running tap-water, then dabbed his finger dry with an old cloth rag. He took a small box from another cupboard, and counted out ten cotton bags. He kept letting his eyes drift from his task to the window, seeing the still flame of the candle burning on the table. Some of the cannabis was none too bad, not great, but customer satisfaction was not his game now. One last crop and he'd do the bunk and get the hell out of this damned place. Slowly Reilly attended to the irrigation pipes. A small leak had developed in one of the lines. Reilly had tied an old sock around the pipe. He had been transporting water to the garden for days now, and the crops were growing more slowly than he'd expected. Reilly was at two minds if he should give the thing a go again.

*

It was an unmitigated disaster how the thing had turned into such a ballocks. Of course there was no keeping secrets from the local clergy. The KGB and the CIA had taken lessons from that bastard, Fr Frank Tierney, and his associates. Caped Crusader of Eden Street, he had his spies. He could hit you with a crucifix at forty paces. He held his rosary beads like knuckledusters, carried holy water to wash blood off his hands. Words defied him. Acts he lived by alone. They caught Reilly down by Baggot Street. He'd been followed for sure. The fuck-up had been the boy buying stuff off that Mick Badger in his little shop. He kept a list of what people were eating and gave it to the priests. Reilly was, well, he was caught living the life of Reilly while the city was caught in the grips of a general strike. He would have been more careful but the wife was the one who kept sending the boy to get currant buns with icing and big pork roasts with cabbage, Brussels sprouts and garden peas behind his back. She kept the hoard under the bed. Reilly knew nothing for weeks. Not that Badger didn't keep his bloody booty going for as long as he could ... It was when Reilly found a box of biscuits, a pack of sausages, three issues of the *Beano*, two women's magazines, a pot of marmalade and a box of plastic toy soldiers under the bed that he saw the disaster. Holy mother of Jasus! He knew he was done for. Reilly wasn't a man to cut hairs.

Ah yes, they got him good. The enigma now, however, was whether they thought he was dealing or cultivating the bloody stuff himself. That was the line between cracked vertebrae and death. Hadn't Tierney asked about his lighting bill? Jasus Christ! How are ya? Reilly felt the tenseness in his shoulders. His neck shook violently. He held his screams in the chasm of his head. Oh sweet Jasus. He resorted to walking backward with tentative steps, scanning the darkness with his feet, understanding everything to come by what had gone past him. There was a terrible inevitability in this vision. The injury was a ballocks, for all the novelty of experience. The doctors said he might limp at the end of it all. Only time would tell. Maybe he should have cooperated there and then with the clergy. They wanted the real story. He gave three accounts – less than it took the apostles to tell their story in the Bible. That was a good one. Tierney broke a bone in his neck. Ah yes, great priests who learned all the right things from the crucifixion's sticky mess, four holy men kicking a curled body, praying with soft grunting voices, with hands clasped together, raised to Jesus . . . 'Oh, yes, St Augustine saw nothing wrong with violence, brother.' They all felt the slightest resistance through their shining cowhide boots, with yours truly below feeling the coarse white hairy legs of that religious spider pumping away, so imperturbably calm, discussing religion to politics. 'Tell me this. Do ya think Cork could beat the Dubs at Croke Park?'

Reilly was unnerved. He filled a series of bags with the intricate weed of cannabis, measuring each bag on a squeaky scale he bought from a tinker. For an instant he heard the faint slapping sound of footsteps. He averted his eyes upward, listening intently. He turned himself about in a cumbersome waltzing step. Jasus! He could have sworn he saw the shadow of heads at the window. And then they were gone. Reilly felt the dryness in his throat. His oesophagus clamped up. He found himself choking under the constrictive pressure of the metal braces. He fought the stifling heat, heaving fitful breaths of the cold hallway. It seemed that his mind was up to its old tricks again. He saw nobody at the window. He opened the door and strained to lean his torso out to no avail. Slowly he moved backward, moving his stiff body into the street. He pivoted his body from one end of the street to the other. The black road gleamed in a glare of icy frost. The narrow streetlights glowed in a string of pearly eggs above his head. Reilly felt the refreshing smells of iciness and detergent in the stinging air. There were still sheets and sundry clothes dripping from the network of overhanging clothes-lines. A few posters fluttered in the wind with the drenched picture of the strike leader standing on the head of some fat capitalist with fists full of money in both hands. Reilly blinked with all the sublimity of animal ignorance. Jasus, there were hundreds of families living out that strike committee's socialistic dream. Not that the leaders were starving . . . Far from it with their afternoon teas and business lunches, arbitrating on this and that point with sugary cups of tea in their soft buttery hands.

Reilly moved backward, stepping up over the lip of the doorway, locking himself away from the silvery deadness of the March frost. He gave a sudden shuddering exudation of that coldness. Inside, he felt a vague triumph. He had the better of the priests, those strike leaders, that fat capitalist. He was making something of himself. He was saving money. He was rebelling in his own humble manner, doing what had to be done. He was working away earnestly in the dead of night on his garden. He had a small hoard of opium to complement the numbing effect of his cannabis. It was something for nothing, which was bloody well hard to come by in this day and age. He felt sorry for the people he met out there at night. He was selling cheap escape to forgotten bellies, to fathers and mothers, adolescent boys and girls. They needed him. They called him the medicine man. That thrilled the life out of Reilly. A title and money. Who could ask for more? He was surviving. He whispered that in his most sentient moments. There were those who died and those who lived. It was something beyond one's own power. Either the mind rebelled of its own accord, or it let the famine eat its cells until madness and dementia set in with death. He was a chosen one. He felt his body, servant to the mad scheming of his mind. It had a life unto itself. It had been subordinate for all these years, and now in the midst of the strike, the latent animalism of survival shook off tradition. It crawled out of the bondage of dockyards. It crawled in some sophisticated ignorance to the library. He could do nothing else. His arse sat on the bus, along for the journey, his face eating sweets. He occupied his

hands with cigarettes. What else could he do? The mind had
made its mind up. There was no other way to say it. It sought
out the dark continents of other worlds. He roamed the
disquieting library, climbing shelves, reaching for secrets,
hiding away in corners, feeling the giddiness of his mind. It
had within its primitive past the history of humanity. It
sought out the numbing drugs of an esoteric past where
madness and death were endured with a languid submission.
The fuck with Fr Tierney and his lot, selling a nation of
starving people for a principle. They endured nothing except
the disquieting smell of hunger. Oh yes, starving people have
a terrible smell.

Those bastards, Tierney and his lot. Reilly remembered
them coming to poor Mrs Nolan, telling her after she had her
cancer and bits of her body cut out of her that she must not
stop having her babies. He heard that on the street from the
lips of Tierney himself. Babies pleased God. He had Mrs
Nolan standing there beside him with her small babies staring
blankly into the sky. He swore that she wouldn't get the
sacrament of the sick if she wasn't going to have more babies.
He screamed that life was subordinate to the glory of God!

The priests called themselves one with the people, spoke
with the same drawling tongues. But that was an easy trick.
And what were those bastards doing? Sleeping off another
slap-up teatime of chips and liver. Reilly proceeded about his
business with an easy smile. What was Tierney's kick-up
anyway? Reilly worked patiently in the circle of light again,
fingering each stem, crumbling the cannabis into the small
cotton bags. He'd have to let the stuff dry out for awhile. He
kept listening for the sounds of his wife and boy upstairs. She
should have taken him into bed with her. But it was always
the same moaning and groaning and so, well, if the boy got to
know too much, God help that boy from . . . Reilly didn't like
to think who would be responsible for what might inevitably
happen. There was a raging cruelty skulking in the dark
frosted nights. Just because there was nobody there now, it

didn't mean that there would be nobody there eventually. They knew about Reilly now, and he knew about them, or at least he thought he knew. If he got out of this with a few thousand quid and a limp, well what the hell. He heard the bedroom door open again upstairs. No, thank God, it was next door.

Reilly's soil was one of the things he was most proud of. It was a rich black dirt, very crumbly, mixed with peat moss and some horse manure. And horse manure wasn't as common as it used to be, even in his part of the city. He got powdered bone marrow from a local butcher and mixed it into the soil. For months, Reilly had smuggled in dirt with coal from the bunker outside. It was within a two-week period when his wife had gone to see her sisters that he had actually dug the hole in the floor and set up the labyrinth of irrigation pipes, lighting, tracks and all.

'Are you making tea or what down dere?'

Reilly stopped his earnest pruning and moved his head into the cold window of the hall. 'We have no milk.'

'Mix it with butter.'

'I'll be gettin milk and sausages if you'll just wait till mornin.' Reilly went back to his work, placing his bags of cannabis into a sailor's duffel bag. He'd have to sneak that stuff up to the hot press for a few days. He scanned the extent of his garden, peering at the fledgling white stalks of his last crop. There was a giddiness in his every move. The dark organic soil gave off a musky odour. Reilly inhaled the darkness, feeling the fecundity of his garden creeping with microscopic life, seeing the silver trails of hidden worms. He let his fingers work the soil around the maturing plants, bedding the stalks in the rich darkness. Their etiolated stalks were tied to canes, giving them support. Some of the vines were already snaking around the canes, spreading out thread-like tentacles everywhere. Reilly stared in the pale yellow light, feeling the metal braces of his own body holding his broken vertebrae in place. There had grown within him a sedate husbandry and fondling tenderness for this dark verdant patch of garden which he alone created. Sometimes at night, when the darkness was so stifling that he just shook with coldness, he would creep from his wife's bed and sit in the wafting heat of his dining room, stare out at the lights of the city glowing in the sky and then, turning, bury his head in the throbbing warmth and caressing aspect of that mystical garden. He was escaping back on these nights to some lost past, feeling the primordial ease of soothing pleasure. Jasus, he was a better man for it. From dementia and hunger to philosopher, to entrepreneur. Great leaps for an ignorant ol sod. Down at the docks they'd let another hundred men go.

Alone in his garden, he wanted nothing in those moments, feeling tears of sweat on his fingers and forehead. This margin of life, like a corridor to a lost Eden, enveloped him. Here in those solitary moments he did not anguish about the plump flesh of his wife, the cursed bugger of a son, and that new creature germinating in her darkness.

For all of it, it wasn't the money that got to him. He gave half the stuff away for nothing. It was the library.

In retrospect, it had begun as a mere novelty, building a garden to grow things to occupy himself. It was done with the best possible intentions. But then again, what was not done with the best possible intentions? First it was cress, the kind of thing that feeds nobody, counts for nothing, but affirms progress. It grew with little soil and lots of water, that was the key. Then it was a small patch of radishes, a few heads of lettuce. Potatoes were a damned failure; some sort of blight, maybe too little soil. Not that any of that mattered. He wasn't eating anything from the garden.

'Forty pounds a night if he did things judiciously,' he remembered someone saying somewhere, sometime. He had a habit of obliterating time and place when he needed to. The first crop was thrilling. He didn't know exactly when the stuff was ripe or mature. He read earnestly at the library. It was comic. The county council was finally doing something for him, financing his education in narcotics. He understood why maybe book-burning was not such an outrageous proposition after he began his self-initiation. For the first time in years he actually felt as though he was accruing some new knowledge, delving into the cryptic mysticism of dark ritualism. Of course these weren't his own words. That's what it said in the prefaces, but that was fine with him. He didn't mind being told how he would feel. The books came in all shapes and sizes. In the still contemptuous silence of the library he crawled from his weary skin. Reilly marvelled at the multitude of perspectives on narcotics. There were books by doctors, by users, by mothers of users, by children of mothers who were users, by mothers and children whose fathers were users, etc. Reilly looked through books with red-faced Indians smoking pipes in the heart of the Grand Canyon, with names like Walking Bear and Sitting Bull. There were so many occult ceremonies, so many continents of mysterious pilgrims. In one book he stared at a picture of immodest Asian priests with smooth yellow potbellies, slanting eyes and small penises, smoking from serpentine bowls in the company of naked Chinese girls. The book was filled with charcoal sketches of bodies knotted in intricate sexual positions. Reilly was excited beyond belief. All he had wanted was to make a few bob and survive the bloody lay-offs, and now he was becoming enraptured in the hidden life of so many people. Well, be damned if he wasn't becoming educated.

He swelled with the pride of a toad when outside the library. He was beside himself with feelings. He bought himself a new hat for no apparent reason. He spoke to himself, remembering those faces, those Persian tents with the sultans and their harems, the strange ruby-blooded sun casting the shadowy train of twenty brides. Jasus Christ! He cherished the very touch of the dog-eared, browning books, feeling the granular residue of aged glue crumbling as he turned each new page. There seemed to be some correlation between sex and these rituals which intrigued him. Reilly saw these pictures as a pleasurable gymnastics. He was no pervert. Perversion was bringing children into a house without money. Reilly took precautions when he worked away at his business. He always read and stared at these pictures with a copy of the *Daily Independent* spread out between his hands. His eyes were forever scanning the edge of the paper, watching the white woolly heads of nodding old women. On the hour the church bells would ring, not all together but minutes apart, and the distant tolling would bring him back from the long spells of languid sleepiness, lost in the unreal colours of other continents.

Suddenly, there were footsteps again. The profound silence was broken. Reilly set the entire mahogany contraption in motion with his foot, and the box glided silently into the dark-mouthed hole. This time he was sure of it. He heard voices, whispers from somewhere outside the house. Maybe the bastards were on the roof, in the back shed, their heads in the letter-box, who knew? Upstairs his wife was rumbling about. She must have heard something herself. She wasn't the kind of woman who expended useless energy.

'Who's there with ya?' his wife whined.

Reilly turned on his irrigation system. He gave one last check to the sock. Then he took his coat from the back of a chair and laboured into the coldness of the hallway. Instinctively, he raised his hand in a gesture of accommodation.

His wife glared from the landing, the boy clutching at her side with his face buried in her blue nightdress. 'You're not going near that strike, do ya hear me?'

Reilly cursed under his breath. 'I'm goin out for a spell. I'll bring rashers and brown bread back for the mornin.' He didn't wait for a response, struggling with the door as he plodded away down the narrow street.

The night walk was gloomy and cold. Reilly braced his raw face against the cold lick of the salt air. The gauze about his face was already wet with the coldness. He proceeded slow

and sound, his head down. He didn't have to be at the Nest
until two o'clock.

In number 30, Eddie Gallagher's boy was at it again with
the new missus. Jasus, right there in the fuckin living room
with the fire blazing away. Christ! Reilly could see the dark
form of their shifting bodies. And the street in the grips of a
strike and all. Some fuckin ignorant honeymooners. Reilly felt
the disquieting prospect of that new marriage with baby and
all. He wasn't fit to curse. He had that sudden urge to kick the
door down, go in there with a big stick and beat them like he
and the boys used to do when they saw dogs going at it up on
the green.

He walked on silently, feeling the dampness of the night
making the gauze stick to his face. He cleared back the
membrane from his nostrils, tucking the sagging material
away on to his forehead, exposing his eyes. The street was
deserted. Reilly walked with terrible pain, limping slightly.
Mucus formed in his mouth with each step. He averted his
eyes away from everything, staring intently at the path,
feeling the isolation of his own spirit moving in the sleeping
hours of this city. He was alone, struggling with an existence
that only knew itself by the manifestation of pain coursing
through the body. Everywhere, things were desolate. He felt
the insignificance of his form trying desperately to move from
one place to another under the cover of darkness. He was
fighting against the sublimeness of culture with his new ideas
rioting in his broken body. That limp of his and those
bandages gave him away now as something strange. Reilly
had never imagined authority outside of Tierney's gang. The
law had existed for him in the heavy black cloaks of priests
from the time he was a child. Not that he hadn't been so naïve
as to think that there was not something else to replace the
cold chapels, the morning masses, the frightening confessions, the horrible faces of middle-aged priests beating the
bare bottoms of boys in their offices. But Reilly had never seen
the beauty of such strange colours until he had seen those

pictures in the library. It was the splendour of colours that first washed over the slab of his own conscience. Now as he walked through these dark streets, he kept painting the darkness in shades of colours. He imagined some Buddhist priest in number 57, smoking his long pipe, stroking the bandaged feet of some chocolate-coloured girl.

If there was one thing that astounded Reilly, it was the amount of dog shite he encountered on these late-night walks. As he looked down on the ground he could see clots of dark faeces. He was struck by the silent life of other species living within his midst. There were languages in scents and howls which he did not understand. Was it like that in those dark secret worlds he kept in his head? Again, he passed another poster of the strikers, again the language of creatures, men to men, and still things remained unsaid, unheard. The same fat capitalist from the other posters stood stoically before the gates of hell with red eyes and long pointed tail. In the background, shackled creatures laboured around the scorching red heat of a foundry. Reilly walked slowly onward by the old canal. He pulled the lapels of his collar close to his chin. Ahead, he could see the dappled milky phantoms of horses standing under the corrugated shelters of itinerants. There were a few caravans and tents in a cluster around a dead fire. Behind him the tenement houses were set against the eerie blackness of the sky.

Before him the grass was matted in frozen clumps of black muddy tracks. People came to this field to abandon old cars, bicycles, and all sorts of rubbish. A few seagulls littered the night sky above Reilly's head.

The itinerants lived in these open fields between housing estates. The air was filled with a smell of smoky meat and burning rubber. Reilly stopped and breathed puffs of hot air into the night. He was feeling the coldness of the frost tingling his fingers and face. He shut his eyes, remembering the warmth of the summer evenings years ago, coming here with girls and bottles of stout. The grass was long and golden then. He used to pick mushrooms in the autumn and strawberries too, kissing girls with that sweet red juice on his lips. And he remembered coming here on the warm summer nights with the boys, paying tuppence to see the itinerants killing animals. It was a strange field, a place where a boy came to learn of love and death.

The itinerants had an old horse and cart which went around the city collecting stray dogs. On his street, when Granny Ryan died and left her house empty, her dog howled terribly into the night. He could be seen by the empty fireplace through the window at night. He ate nothing. Nobody dared remove the animal out of superstition. It was the itinerants who came and took the dog away in their cart. They usually took the dogs away alive to their fields to kill them and bury them, but they didn't that evening. They dragged the dog into the street and beat him to death with sticks and kicks. People came out from their teas to see what was happening. They stood in clusters, not daring to interfere. Some of the children were crying. The women closed their eyes. The men looked from one to another saying nothing. The dog howled horribly, limping toward the crowd. Everyone went inside and locked their doors. Somehow, in that instant, the people on the street had glimpsed into the secret horror of what happens to a man's heritage when he dies. The itinerants threw the carcass on to their cart, taking away furniture and brass ornaments as well from the granny's home.

Reilly moved slowly in the darkness. He was walking in a queer side-shuffle, jerking his body in fits of pain. He was too far from home now to go back.

A face looked at him through a broken window in a caravan. 'Cold ol night . . .'

Reilly tried to hide his face. His body was riddled with the jabbing pain of the cracked vertebrae. Each breath was a laboured attempt to remain conscious. The straps seemed to sink deeper into his back as apprehension filled his body. His chest sweated profusely. Trembling, he saluted with a tip of his hat.

A recumbent figure glared at him. Other unseen faces whispered, 'Jasus! Look at dat face, dere. Do ya see it? Is he drunk? Watch im boys. Look at his face. A fuckin mummy!'

Reilly's face convulsed in a series of horrible twitches under the draped web of gauze. He forced his body forward.

'Get out of it.' The itinerants thought he was drunk. They were laughing in an instant, retiring to their slumber again.

Reilly blessed his luck. These itinerants existed on the periphery of civilization. He saw them as alien creatures who had forsaken the amenities of life for the coldness of rootless wandering. They had heritages that traced them back to Babylon. They moved with a legacy of history within their midst, unwilling to forget, to relinquish anything, artefact or story, to the present. They existed in the company of animals, unkempt, unwashed, in sprawling families, always embracing an ever-growing world. They scoured out an existence in nomadic tribes, feeding on the refuge of civilization. That was the enigma. Rootless, yet unwilling to recede from society. They remained friendless. They did not need the sanction of civilization to exist. They existed despite civic authority. There was this pervasive sense that their ubiquitous existence could not be crushed. Banishment would not suffice. They were not people to be cajoled, harassed. They were nationless, without allegiance. They existed in one place, not because of necessity, but because of a freedom that haunted politicians and capitalists. Yet, in the scope of Reilly's glancing eyes, they covered all this sophistication in filth.

These itinerants had horses and cars and every mobile contraption in between. They had broken-down washing machines and rusting fridges. They cannibalized the discarded belongings of even the most miserable humans living in homes. Even in the worst of times, they always had hundreds of pounds in their pockets. For all their filth, they possessed a religious sagacity for money and electronic gadgets. Reilly remembered that they were the first to have televisions in the city, even before the shops and the managers at the docks. They'd gotten them from England or Japan, or God knows where. In Reilly's estimation, they held within themselves the past, the present, and the future.

Reilly moved by the shrunken horses. They were old and swaybacked with huge underbellies like boilers. The itinerants rode them bareback like cowboys through the city streets. They used them to drag carts, old clothing, scrap metal, anything that could be salvaged and sold. The horses were starving slowly. Reilly dabbed his face. The creatures laboured in the darkness, breathing and snorting through their huge nostrils. A warm smoke covered him like a veil. In the background the canal purled under the soft grassy bank. The horses' stomping hoofs echoed in the dark arc under the canal bridge. Reilly could feel their hot breaths steaming in the cold air as he passed their bodies. He felt the disconcerting glances of those huge heads. He resisted an urge to touch the horses' bodies. He could see there were mongrel dogs curled up sleeping on old blankets. A few greyhounds, too old for racing, slinked through the debris of old prams and twisted bicycles, stalking unfathomable things. They nosed his leg and then retired again into the darkness.

A dark oblong doorway led up a creaking flight of stairs. A vague light emanated in intermittent flashes. Reilly could hear the clink of glasses, the murmuring of people. Jasus! He sighed with a terrible relief. On the landing, faces loomed in black profile, then disappeared. Reilly mustered a breath, working his lean fingers between his harness and his chest. He drew fitful breaths, like a diver about to submerge into water for too long. Ahead, the stairs were half lit with the erratic light of opening and closing doors. Everything came in splattering cataracts as an unseen glass chandelier exploded in colour each time a door opened. Reilly gripped the railings with a mustered fervour and in a series of slow stooping motions counted the stairs in his head, one, two, three, four . . . He averted his head upward, feeling the throb of life becoming more real as he ventured forward. His legs began to buckle almost immediately. There was no oxygen going to his extremities. His lame leg seemed to wag in the darkness, utterly useless. He found himself grabbing it with his free hand, punching pain into it. His invisible face was livid with fear. Some figure loomed before him and then disappeared. Reilly's mouth was a dark orifice sucking in futile breaths of air through the loosely wrapped veil of gauze. His round eyes burned in his face and his mind kept counting stairs, fourteen, fifteen, sixteen . . . His lips moved imperceptibly.

He felt himself collapse with the word 'twenty-three' lost somewhere in his throat. He lay quietly on the landing, his body burning, the terrible restraint of his braces pressing against his heart. His breaths were shallow, reaching only his throat. His chest was on fire. His legs burned with fatigue. The boot on his lame leg tapped the floor. The dark walls reeked with the smell of fornication. He felt his arm shake, and he could do nothing, watching it as though it were some alien thing. A face lowered itself to meet his. He could see only the darkness of a shadow and then the pain of some force in his side, and then a gash of light suddenly exploding in the darkness.

He awoke with the frightful smell of salts passing back and forth under his nose. He gave a sudden jerk. Baptiste held him by the shoulders. 'Easy now.' His voice had that candour of intimacy. He patted Reilly on the head as though he was some sort of obedient dog. 'A drink when you're ready, Reilly.'

Reilly let his eyes adjust to the dim funnel of faces moving before him. Slowly he felt his body reviving itself. A painted face looked straight at him with an unabashed scorn, inflexible. 'He can't stay here.'

Baptiste was wearing a coarse three-piece suit. His hair receded in a dignified yet unnatural shock of black. His hand produced some silver coins. 'Bring another two brandies.'

Baptiste made some half-visible gesture to Reilly which Reilly acknowledged with a smile. Someone had removed the gauze from his face. He could feel the ebb of warmth on the skin. 'Banjaxed,' he whispered, drawing himself forward in a slow movement.

Baptiste applied a soft pressure to Reilly's shoulder. He surveyed the small room, watching sunken heads huddled away in groups playing cards. A series of doors ran along one of the walls, opening and closing intermittently, blinding Reilly.

'I'm okay now.' Reilly took the drink from Baptiste's hand, touching it inadvertently. He supped at the sweetness, letting the hotness rush down his throat. His face was imbued with blood. He smiled in a splutter, coughing up some of the brandy.

Baptiste removed the glass, softly patting Reilly on the back.

'I'm okay. I swear to God now, just let me catch me breath.' Reilly suddenly reached for the pocket of his coat.

Baptiste wagged the money in front of Reilly. 'I have it, Reilly.'

Reilly gave one of his vacuous stares. He eyed the brandy again. Baptiste snapped his fingers, and two more were set before Reilly. He tilted his head and swallowed one glass after another. 'Ah.' Reilly had a ruby smudge of brandy on his chin when he smiled. The cold metal braces had been damaged by the fall. The left brace was slightly warped, forcing Reilly to tilt his head in a pronounced manner. Everything in the room took on a slanted perspective.

Baptiste shook his head. 'The priests.' His words were more a statement than a question.

Reilly nodded. He found the sudden giddiness of the brandy easing his pains. He breathed easier. He looked straight at Baptiste outfitted in his modest tweed suit, his eyes nested in dignified wrinkles, looking straight ahead with an unflinching intent. He was a man of small stature with a fat little belly and a rounded backside. Not that he was a comic figure. Rather, he seemed self-contained in a reserved Western attitude. He had the eyes of knowledge. He demanded attention without words. His face was lightly bronzed from years of sea storms, breezes, tropics. A frost of silver on his sideburns accentuated the golden quality of his skin. He had lived in the tropic of Capricorn for years. He had been involved in some commercial ventures.

Reilly found him a curious hybrid of Western assiduity and tropical extravagance. There was something in his gestures which for all his polish was slightly raw. He was a creature with a beginning but no origin. Reilly could not figure Baptiste as something other than what he was now. He did not speak of birth, of parents, of a youth, of a love, nothing that would have placed him in some town, in some country, at some time in the past. His beginnings must have been in Europe somewhere, that much Reilly felt sure about. And then again, he had this novel theory of Baptiste as some kind of alien creature born to some raped jungle savage, rearing himself alone, a Tarzan boy of sorts, but with the unfathomable history of his father's native tongue in his throat, diverging, not converging, with the savageness of his surroundings, innately knowing of Europe.

Reilly moved forward, staring at the heads of others. He returned his glance to Baptiste. Baptiste had an amiable face that always drew nods of respect, and yet its regal quality was not without malice. Somehow, just as he had stared into the jungle, it had stared back into him, and that was what Reilly found mystical in Baptiste. He moved with an ubiquitous title, among different classes of men, on different continents, and all the while his face had that character of not limiting but hinting at infinite possibility. At bottom he could have been anything. He did not need words with that face of his.

Reilly turned his eyes away. He loved and resented the domineering force of Baptiste's immobile face.

Again, Baptiste asked quietly, 'The priests?'

Reilly nodded with the tilted side of his head.

'I hate violence,' Baptiste whispered. He said it with such tenderness. 'Very unsophisticated.'

Reilly began to say something. Baptiste nodded his head. Reilly persisted with his thoughts. He looked at the dishevelled faces of mirthless men drinking in small clusters, nodding their heads intently to everything. They had become serious with the drink. Reilly could see the women moving among them in their shining stockinged legs, the slow swagger of their hips gyrating with conspicuous intent. He glanced at one young girl, her skin caked in a white powder, accentuating the natural pinkness of lips. She seemed strangely tropical in the company of strange unknown creatures. Her neck was aplomb with a soft train of feathers which snaked to her slender waist. Her eyes were of a deep inchoate brown, almost chocolate. Each time she blinked he could see a soft filmy gloss on each pupil reflecting the faces of men staring at her.

Reilly looked toward Baptiste. He remained with his head aloof, running a white rag across his forehead, ruminating behind the blank stare of his own eyes. Reilly pressed him for a sign.

Baptiste did not avert his eyes. He had principles. He did not let things acknowledge him; he acknowledged things when he wanted.

Reilly set his eyes on the girl again. She had a love spot pencilled in below her right eye. Reilly nearly mistook it for a tear. Her eyelids opened and closed with the simple mechanics of a camera lens, yet her face revealed cracked lines of effort. Reilly had lost that pervasive cynicism of his earlier hours at home. He understood that cynicism was a luxury, a self-indulgence born out of security. Here, the weight of human frailty daunted him. He saw his own weakness in the beautiful legs of the girl before him, imagining the silky shoosh of her scissor legs. He felt a shiver of excitement and rage for her. She elicited not love, just a sense of futility, but not total abandonment. She was dragging others down with her. Reilly clenched his hands against his knees. He was breathing fitfully. She was lost, and yet she had risen for this night and picked out that dress and those stockings and sat before her mirror in the seedy yellowness of some dressing room, playing the part to perfection. Did she draw that tear under her eye for a joke, to fool men, some surreptitious self-delusion to make her believe she was something other than a corpse?

Again, Reilly moved his torso away from her soft feathery body. Baptiste was still inattentive, his black-haired head brooding behind the reserved poise of his immobile face. Suddenly, he raised his finger from his glass and pointed to the girl's foot, shaking his head.

Reilly followed his finger, setting his eyes on a series of exposed, blackened toenails. He felt a sudden shuddering effect.

Baptiste was laughing, his eyes glistening. He had acknowledged the girl now, and she could see him pointing at her. There was a sudden infusion of muffled voices. The room seemed to quiver, and in an instant Reilly could smell her cheap rose perfume mixed with smoke and gin. He put his drink to his lips and closed his eyes, his body trembling. In his head, he could hear the animal whine of the girl running away.

'Never believe in a whore,' Baptiste whispered. 'They are disturbing. You offer so much more. Every man who comes to you has forsaken something else, and he acknowledges his isolation. He has left behind a faith in his priests, in his fellow workers, in his company, in his family. He has come to you to indulge his own weakness. But those whores who have nothing relinquish nothing. They pretend to struggle. Their eyes ask you to do something to help them change.'

'But she . . .' Reilly felt the small eyes of Baptiste fixed on him like needle points.

'This business we are in is not about money. It is about revolution, about death. There are no secrets with dead men, they express everything with a sullen sincerity.' Baptiste let his breath ease outward in a curling blue smokiness.

Reilly could see Baptiste's eyes glistening in the stillness of the warm air. 'I am going away after this time,' he whispered. He moved his head in a gentle rocking motion. Another brandy was placed before him. He drank quietly. 'I am saving money. I never touched that opium. Don't ya see, I have nothing to hold me.'

Baptiste took Reilly's hands into his own flaccid palms. He could see the crescent moons of dirt under each of Reilly's nails. His face looked stoic. 'How is that garden of yours?'

Reilly lowered his eyes.

Baptiste pressed Reilly's wrists, smiling. 'Do you sit at home at night in the darkness thinking of those strange lands, knowing that there are men like me out there, men in tweed suits in the hottest deserts, among savages, in the Himalayas, living and observing alien lives?'

Reilly said nothing. Baptiste remained supremely unnatural. Reilly looked into the round void of Baptiste's face. It seemed to resemble some strange force sucking everything that dared look upon it into it. That was the terror. Pure thoughts passed unmediated from Baptiste's face when he wanted someone to understand. It was a form of telepathy, without words. He remained unchallenged. Reilly saw Baptiste was not human. He was strangely formed in the flesh of man, yet he did not feel pain or love. He was something that had moved through life, through continents, gathering knowledge, documenting facts, dates, like some organic encyclopedia. And what was so terrible was the self-consciousness of this Baptiste. He knew what he was doing all the while. He spoke of himself in the third person, always speaking of that man in the tweed suit. And yet in all his years he had never quivered with the knowledge of what he had in his head. He let it all remain unprocessed by the heart. Only the mind acknowledged his life, forming crude statements.

Reilly felt the ringing sensation of his brandy affecting his head. By God he was Irish, but this stuff was murder on him. Was he acting the part of the fool to facilitate Baptiste? This drinking was not his game, and yet in the company of Baptiste, that self-professed emissary of freedom, he found he could do nothing except accept some preconceived notion Baptiste seemed to attribute to him and his kind. Reilly put his hand to his head with an abject resolve. He touched Baptiste's hand. Maybe there was emotion in the physical contact of two bodies, some brief synapsis of human understanding. Reilly saw the hand was strangely feminine, hairless, with an almost marble smoothness. They were hands that had done no work in years.

Baptiste looked straight into Reilly's face.

Reilly would not return the stare. That would have been veritable suicide.

'You think you are normal, Reilly, but I tell you that solitude is a form of rebellion.' Baptiste slowly began that engine of monotony. His teeth glistened in his head. 'That garden of yours has slowly drawn you into yourself. It begins with a sense of loss, a conscious futility. That strike of your workers and your priests, religion and politics and commerce fighting it out with your wage packet ... You understand nothing at first. There are promises among workers, alliances. People speak in garbled sentiments about victory. Your blood boils. Maybe some industrious wife makes a flag. Someone invariably does. It is all very cosy for a time. Tea canteen and bread for the proud men. But it doesn't last long. Starvation has its own bleak course. It does not take sides in man's struggles. It inflicts suffering and death with a shocking democracy. And then you see that nobody is looking at you dying. You are truly alone. You will not die, of course. Only the infirm will fall into oblivion. But then that is not so much the workings of revolution as of nature. Oh yes, you will persist, starving, yet not dying. This is a Christian country, so you will suffer and pray and gain nothing. And then you begin to understand that what you are fighting is something that has always anticipated this time of reckoning. You and your kind have been fools to think you could have won. So what do you do?' Baptiste let his teeth glisten.

He moved his torso closer to Reilly.

A few faces looked at Reilly. His mouth was half open, languid in the wooing intoxication of the brandy. Baptiste spoke with a voice just shy of dispassion. His words ebbed from his mouth, rehearsed from the subconsciousness of his mind. He was processing some observation that his mind had noted in some country that he could not remember now. Nothing came from the heart. What he knew of life he had gained through an unnatural perspective of omnipotence. He had travelled the globe as some intellectual imperialist, colonizing everything in his tweed suit. And the damnedest spectacle for Reilly was the impervious face of Baptiste, his cold fingers reaching out for an instant to fool other humans with a tender touch. Baptiste knew nothing of guilt. He was a thing created out of the guilt of a thousand, no, a hundred thousand lost souls on some exploration. They created him for the guilt they felt for their crimes, their rapes, their whiteness, trying to salvage that supreme confidence that had brought them out of their homes in Newcastle and Manchester, in Dorchester and Wigan to educate the world. They had lived in the great myth of English lore. A history, a blazing history of Britannia Rules! God Save the King, God Save the Queen, Jolly Good Show; all this set against the drabness of their town lives, the useless words, the same monotony, pub after pub, church after church, the cool English rain making mold on walls, the long lonesome walks of men with dogs who went by names given to dogs long dead. It made life and death something relative, something unreal, the pace of death differing from one species to another, and yet the dogs were replaced with new dogs, and it began again, this droning monotony of English life.

Reilly felt the sentient awareness of this history weighing upon Baptiste. He stood against the drabness of these English lives. He was what all men could have been if they had really wanted to be. A history of conquest was latent, but there nonetheless. And they kept believing that, whilst alone, tinkering about in their tool-sheds with old mowers, nodding reverently to a picture of Queen Victoria that was won on a seaside holiday years ago. They were always fighting for dignity, trying to put on the serenity of masters while looking like fools, smoking pipes on town walls, talking about the weather and a red sky at night being a shepherd's delight, and is your missus taking part in Reverend Green's Jamboree and Punch and Judy piece again this year? And in the air of a Monday, mutton and spuds, Tuesday's side of beef with carrots and a little rhubarb pie, Wednesday's air a lovely curling steam rising from a shepherd's pie with whipped potato and Yorkshire pudding, and four and twenty blackbirds baked in a crumbling apple pie ...

'I am going away after this.' Reilly pointed in some vague gesture to the darkness outside.

Baptiste dismissed him with a soft 'shoo'. Then he proceeded. 'When you have travelled, you see that there is no other place. There is only the mind. All continents and faces blur into one great darkness. You see the Negro and Chinaman, the Irishman, Europeans, sultans in the Far East, all creatures dealing with the same stifling oppression of masters and servants. For you and for them there is that terrible struggle for words to express the horrible fear of knowing that there is nothing to look forward to. And you understand that it is not just you now. There is that wife, those confounded children. Those are the trappings of Christianity. The family is a rare Venus fly-trap. There is nothing to match its deadliness. It is something more dreadful than anything nature has conjured.'

'Could I have another brandy?' Reilly let a faint smile pass across his face.

'You're a true Irishman, Reilly.' Baptiste raised his hand. 'Don't you understand? They remain ignorant. You call them names at night. They did this to you. You punch the darkness with your fists. And then you understand that wives are created by you and your kind. You have made them what they are as much as they have made you what you are. If you could only have had sense back then before all this and left others out of it. But that is not the nature the priests and the capitalists have given you. Don't implicate nature in your sordid mating. Even animals will desist in the propagation of life if there is hopelessness among the beasts. Religion is unnatural, Reilly.'

Reilly put his hot hand on Baptiste's arm. 'Please. They want to kill me.'

Baptiste let his thoughts trail into the murmuring backdrop of sound.

Reilly was shivering again. His face had cooled with his touch of Baptiste's cold hands. The air had a viscous quality, suspending words, faces. He could see the slow animation of Baptiste's face absorbing everything. Reilly could see the emotions registering on the cold immutable face of that English explorer. Not that they could elicit sympathy or hatred. Baptiste was that perfect guiltless artefact created by guilty men. He was wholly unaware of irony. It was only the people who came into contact with him who were left asking questions, deciding to follow or attack. Not that it was as simple as that. There was a simplicity in his voice and integrity in his person which confounded and demanded respect. He was a personification of pure dogma. Once people set their eyes upon him there was some mystical transaction, no, rather a deposit of Baptiste's vision into the other soul. With that came guilt and terror, or blind faith. The myth of Baptiste either exposed guilt or became the foundation for idolatry, religion. As for Baptiste, he remained unchallenged out of ignorance or sophistication; Reilly could not make out which in the blankness of Baptiste's face now. Baptiste was an ultimate form of destruction, a force that held within it so much of history that it moved with a slothfulness, a corpulence of concentric circles which touched the mouths of hungry skeletons who came to eat from myths and nostalgia. Baptiste was some monstrous creation, an intellectual tumour that not only regenerated itself, but grew more sodden and weighty, more grotesque and carbuncular, digesting the lives of those who came to live and eat at its body.

Reilly felt the burden of Baptiste's voice. He understood the priests had their communion, and Baptiste had his. Baptiste was whispering about religion.

Reilly nodded his head, acquiescing to the voice. 'They are going to kill me.' He found himself almost smiling.

Baptiste had that power to make men feel embarrassed about pleading for their own lives, as though to beg and plead was an extravagance, or indulgence in one's own sense of worth. Baptiste stretched his arms over his stomach. He seemed to say, 'There are billions of men alive on this planet, and you dare to speak to me of your fears.' Slowly he opened his mouth. 'There are worse things than death, Reilly.'

Reilly let his eyes drift in his head. The round table was one of those rickety contraptions that rocked with each shift of an arm or an elbow. It was scarified with deep knife slashes of hearts and initials. There was something faintly gloomy and yet romantic in these crude scars. Maybe some sailor had carved a heart for some lost love. He may have been dead now himself, with only this table bearing testimony to some lost emotion.

Reilly saw the young girl again. He felt like calling to her, and then a lean-faced creature followed behind her, smoking. For an instant it seemed as though she was burning below the deep colours of her feathers. And then he saw the nakedness of her long legs, shed of the silken stockings. From her toes to her thighs he was conscious of hair, yes, a dark black hair growing like needles through the black pores of her skin.

Baptiste let his eyes rest upon her for an instant, confirming the cryptic word, 'whore'. He could see an agitation on Reilly's face. 'The opium is already in your pocket, Reilly.'

Reilly removed his eyes from the hairiness of the legs, instinctively touched his pockets, feeling the soft pouch of opium. He swallowed spit in his mouth. 'They are goin to kill me,' he said in a soft tone, almost matter-of-fact.

A crowd of men came through the bar, falling about the place. Reilly hid his swollen face, turning it downward, staring into Baptiste's chest. The men spoke a foreign tongue. Reilly could hear them laughing and whistling to some of the prostitutes.

'There are worse things than death,' Baptiste whispered. The marble tips of his left hand touched Reilly. The other hand remained in a loose fist close to his chest as though he were professing some oath.

Reilly looked into the weak blue eyes 'I . . . I . . .'

Baptiste's face became cold, losing its bronzed look, almost illuminated in the dead light of the bar. He let his eyes move from Reilly to his own hand clutched against his chest. 'An attitude toward death governs a man's way of life.'

Reilly did not understand. His eyes narrowed in two slits.

Baptiste shook his head. 'You must have others acknowledge that you have no fear of death, that you covet something more precious than life, an ultimate freedom.' Baptiste moved his hand away from his chest, exposing a small pneumatic rubber ball.

Reilly looked intently at the small blackness. His eyes were almost closed. The object reminded him of the body of some legless black widow spider.

Baptiste's eyes were shining in the dark. He moved perceptibly closer to Reilly's head. His mouth opened. 'Nitroglycerine.' His eyebrows rippled upon his forehead.

'Suicide,' Reilly whispered. He found himself drawing back from Baptiste's steady palm. The black rubber ball seemed to grow like some shadowy stigma on Baptiste's palm.

Baptiste shook his head, 'Call it extroverted suicide.' Baptiste let his eyebrows settle on his forehead. 'Suicide is something that is done alone with one principle of self-dejection. But it hurts nobody. It is no defence against life. It is committed upon oneself. It treats itself as the enemy. But this . . .' Again, Baptiste was set with that dispassionate face, the hole of his mouth opening and closing, drawing air mechanically like all living creatures, curling words with his unseen tongue. 'You must be ready to die at all times. That is what gives you the freedom to live among men. Do not whisper to me that "they want to kill you". Make them understand that you are living only so you can find the opportunity to be among them and kill everything. You are living by a principle of annihilation, total annihilation.'

Reilly could feel, no, almost see the slow metamorphosis of Baptiste's hunched body raising itself into some indomitable force other than flesh. If a principle could have meat on its substance, Reilly acknowledged it now.

Baptiste kept the sombre blackness of his hand close to his body with the palm opened.

To Reilly, the fingers for an instant looked like legs of that black widow-like ball within Baptiste's hand. 'The myth of these secret explosives has rippled through continents. As with all disease, myth begins with but one's contact with another. Its complexity is so sublime and so damned simple. It has that supreme economy. One contact! That is the essence of true philosophy. It should but name something, and then the passion of humanity should unconsciously believe. There cannot be dialogue with truth. Discourse must remain as a series of incantations, prayers.' Baptiste let his breath pour from his mouth. He took a brandy to his mouth, letting the contents disappear. His throat did not even move up and down, the brandy somehow evaporated into that mysterious darkness of his mouth.

'You want me to kill myself,' Reilly whispered.

'Reilly!' Baptiste raised his voice. 'You are a stupid man. You are not going to die. You will be living with the most beautiful freedom a man has ever had. Others will attribute things to your physiognomy. They will tell of how all within a twenty-, thirty-, forty-yard circumference of you will . . .'

'Die?' Reilly whispered.

'Not die, but experience the mysticism of your presence. People will not talk of death so openly. You will become something that death cannot touch. Ordinary men enter and exit rooms, streets, and when they leave they cease to exist. They die and are resurrected a million times in a lifetime. When they enter a shop that they frequent daily, they are resurrected by the mind of the shopkeeper as some material object with wants and needs, and, when that day's transactions are finished, they leave, and another replaces them.'

Reilly could feel the strain from the braces digging into his back. The numbing effects of the brandy were dying off in the sombre mood of the bar. Even the new group of men were already drinking in secluded corners, saying nothing above a soft murmur. Reilly could see little hope for himself now. Was he to adopt the madness of Baptiste's glistening eyes? He did not want to die. He remained stoic, looking at Baptiste. 'But these are priests,' he found himself whispering.

Baptiste almost scowled, but shook his head. 'No. They still think you are, as you Irish say, "a God-fearing man", so they will not understand your defiance. Their anger will turn to fear. Christianity knows only of martyrs or sinners, men willing to lie down and die for faith. But you will be something other. Reilly, you will not be fearing the Devil, you will be embracing him. His very horns will grow from your head in those priests' minds. They will not dare come near you, because for all their faith they do not really know if they believe in God and heaven. Remember that martyrdom is a public spectacle. It is the profession of hostages and lunatics. It is the power of weakness triumphing over strength. In this fact alone you will be safe, for you are one, and they are many.'

Baptiste clutched Reilly's arm. 'When you die, make sure it is in some darkness away from people except this enemy that has mistakenly come too close. That will be your mission: to measure life in feet and yards, trying to draw the enemy into some obscurity where you can turn and obliterate everything. And that will be what you will want. Total annihilation, a genocide of both good and evil. Leave nothing to interpretation, nothing to conjecture. The key is to have enough of the damned explosive, and to draw those priests close enough so that there will be nothing left to identify. That will be your glory, the darkness of oblivion, the silence of mystery. There will be no words. That is what you must do, Reilly.'

Reilly's mouth was half agape.

'If every generation had only the courage to live and then to annihilate itself completely – leaving nothing to posterity, no books, no religion, no buildings – that would be the greatest gift to humanity. Do not be like God; kill yourself, not your son. God created his Garden of Eden, and he failed, and he would not accept failure, and so he killed his son as some schizophrenic need for sacrifice and deliverance, crime and punishment. He should have killed himself, Reilly. The imperfections of this world are the doings of your forefathers. You have inherited a legacy of lies, a religion predicated on a father butchering his son, the religion of a God with three persons in one body. Where is freedom in that scapegoatism you call Christianity?'

'You do want me to kill myself . . .' Reilly whispered.

Baptiste shook his head. His face was sweating, the indefatigable wall of stolidity faltered, cracking in furrowed lines of weak skin.

Reilly could see the harrowed face staring blankly through the soft light.

Baptiste's sleeve had risen up to his forearm. Reilly saw a vague serpentine tattoo showing against the pale whiteness of the skin.

Baptiste was speaking softly, and then he stopped, his body jerking with agitation, roasting in the grey tweed of his three-piece suit.

'Are you the saviour?' Reilly asked, feeling the strained silence. He wanted to get away from Baptiste.

'There can be no saviour without a prophet first,' Baptiste whispered. The rim of Baptiste's shirt was dripping with moisture. His thin neck teemed with shining beads of perspiration.

It was Reilly who was looking at Baptiste now. He could envision Baptiste travelling through his continents with only that confounded knit bag of his at his side, dressed in that same suit with that reserved pose of some alien interloper, explorer, who had come only to confirm what he already believed. He was supremely independent, everything contained in that bag of his, everything buttoned up in the starched whiteness of his shirts. He had his own watch on a looping chain of gold in his breast pocket which kept a secret ticktocking time owing nothing to the places in which he stopped.

Reilly tensed his jaw, the pain of his spine creeping back into his body from its drunkenness.

Baptiste drew his hand away. He could see Reilly staring at the magenta head of a strange tattooed creature writhing on his arm.

Reilly kept staring at Baptiste, for now he could see the tattoo growing about the saturated collar of Baptiste's neck in a gorgeous fringe of colours. Reilly's eyes glared, he kept imagining the tattoo unravelling itself through Baptiste's body, each face and image from some place he sneered at on his rootless journeys, the painted cartography of his soul bleeding images into his very skin. Reilly shook with a terrible realization that this thing, and that is how Reilly had come to think of Baptiste, was not as supremely isolated from the distant beating history of its past. He was forever scarified by the faces that dared to look into his eyes. For all the pretence of his tweed suit, he was corrupted. Soon those tattoos would be creeping to his chin, along the cold marble of his fingers, each verdant colour of the tropics meandering in the dignified wrinkles of his face. The very quicks of his nails, his teeth, the whites of his eyes would be woven in the yellow Asian dreams of opium lovers exploring continents with their pink tongues, the sexual fantasies of turban-headed sultans in silk tents pouring frankincense into a bride's navel.

And still Reilly could not help but think of those big-nostrilled creatures Baptiste had touched in foreign lands walking in the dank heat of the tropics, greeting and parting from one another with a, 'Tally Ho, Old Chap. We'll have to get you over for tea soon.'

Reilly retreated in a series of abortive genuflections, seeing Baptiste recovering himself, slowly buttoning his collar once more, smoothing the bunched sleeve of his shirt and jacket.

Reilly stood rigid before the doorway to the stairs, waiting to catch his breath. There were more shadows coming up the stairs. Pain stabbed invisibly within his back.

Baptiste seemed to have lost Reilly in his attention to his own appearance. He was now smoothing the unnatural blackness of his hair across his forehead with the flat of his left palm. The loose fist of his right hand was against his heart. He ordered another two drinks from a passing girl. A man came and moved toward Baptiste. He passed Reilly. He was limping severely. His foot made a scratching noise on the floorboards.

Reilly could see Baptiste with the two drinks before him.

The man dropped his body into the chair that Reilly had left a few minutes earlier.

Baptiste rose and applied a soft pressure to the man's back. He watched sunken heads huddled away in groups playing cards.

'I'm okay now.' The man took the drink from Baptiste's hand, touching it inadvertently. 'I'm okay. I swear to God now, just let me catch me breath.' The man suddenly reached for his pocket in his coat.

Baptiste wagged the money in front of the man. 'I have it, Newman.'

Newman shook his head. 'The priests.' His words were more a statement than a question.

'I hate violence, Newman,' Baptiste whispered. He said it with such tenderness. 'Very unsophisticated.'

The sky outside was turning bright in the distant buzz of the streetlamps. Reilly hugged his collar against his sweating body, shivering from the coldness of the icy night air. The river's edge slapped quietly against the banks of the docks. Reilly stood still for a moment, staring at the silvery waterway to other worlds. He was shivering, feeling the suck of the cold dewiness of the early morning air. A lone boat moved silently up the estuary like a beetle. Reilly moved closer to the quay, removing the bag of opium from his pocket. The ship gave a hoot into the immensity of the city. Reilly gave a start, his shoulder harness squeezing his chest. He kept his eyes fixed on the cold lapping waters below him. Slowly, he emptied the bag and shut his eyes.

Reilly walked the streets. He could feel the early dew on the hairs of his arm. He walked down by the itinerants' old field, stopping at the canal bridge. Below him, the cold water ran in a glittering quicksilver. He moved onward. In the desolation of the field he could see all the broken fridges and bicycles as strange as prehistoric creatures still shadowy in the dark blueness of the early morning. The dogs were sniffing about, watching Reilly, shepherding him away from their sleeping masters.

Reilly felt the slow cessation of thought for the first time in months. He was no longer thinking of Baptiste and that dark room in the sky. His body was already healing itself. He could feel his bones healing their hairline cracks. Ahead of him, tendrils of smoke rose from the sloping estate of redbrick houses. The milkmen were already planting bottles of milk and cartons of eggs on front porches.

Reilly tipped his hat to a young girl who worked for the telephone company. She was waiting for her employer to give her a lift. The men on the street used to put bets on how long it would be before she was up the pole.

'Nice mornin.' Reilly smiled faintly, with the dignity and serenity that mornings bring to human contact. He pointed toward the sky and kept walking. His hat was further back on his head, exposing the paleness of his forehead.

An electric milk van glided eerily through the street, the bottles jittering in the coldness. Reilly winked and proceeded slowly, dragging his left leg.

The girl brushed her long hair out of her face, stepping from foot to foot. Reilly could hear the gentle clip-clop of her high-heeled shoes as he left her behind.

In the sky, the chimneys percolated a rich smokiness. The smell of eggs and liver drifted on to the teeming dew. The sun wavered in the coldness on the horizon, rising into the hot coal smoke.

Before Reilly reached his doorway, he could see the water spilling into the street. The weak yellow husk of the sun was already breaking through the low clouds. He had to push through a flood of water when he opened the door. The small hall table was floating in the early morning light. Shoes bobbed to and fro like small boats in the kitchen. A chair had drifted into a corner of the hall, silently butting the coatrack. Reilly turned and faced the cold lake of the dining room. The heaters were dead, the grey bars extinguished by the running water.

Reilly could hear his wife calling him from upstairs. The coldness of the running water sopped his feet and ankles. He proceeded in a series of squelching steps, tracing a light-green eel of hose writhing against the legs of the dining room table. The sock floated like a dead whiting on the surface. Reilly turned the main tap off in the kitchen. The cat meowed plaintively on the table, marooned. Reilly put it out the back window. It disappeared over the back wall.

'What's happened down dere?' Reilly's wife cried out. She was on the landing stairs.

Reilly could see her reflection in the cold lake of water in the hallway.

He went into the dining room. He had not laid the carpet down when he had left that night. The mahogany box had risen on the gentle tide of the flood waters. The dark soil was slowly sifting to the floor, the knotted weeds of cannabis floating toward the hall doorway, running into the street.

When Reilly turned about he could see his wife in her pale blue nightdress, her belly distended with the near birth of her child.

'I think it is time.' Her voice was sweet.

Reilly could see the smooth outline of her white legs.

Reilly's boy held her hand and looked at the silent furniture floating in the yellow light of the morning sun. His eyes blinked mechanically and he smirked with his head cast downward.

Reilly smiled too, feeling the tender soreness of his own face. The mahogany box was adrift in the sucking iciness of the water like a coffin. He reached into the box. Then he raised his body upward. He extended his trembling hands. The metal in his back cut into his flesh. Still, he kept his eyes open defiantly, holding the dripping petals of a red rose toward his wife's plump body.

NORTHERN SUMMERS

FINNEGAN STARED VACANTLY at the blue ocean, enduring yet another holiday by the sea. 'It's good for yer lungs,' his father, Mr White, always said, sniffing the air of the city with disgust as he pulled the car off with a jerk from the curbed road and Victorian redbricked homes. Finnegan was directed to call his father 'Mr White'. It was a rule in the house. Mr White called his wife 'Mrs White', and she in turn called her husband 'Mr White'. But it still didn't seem right to Finnegan that he should have to call his father 'Mr White' instead of 'Father'.

His father had a stock of phrases for the holidays. Finnegan wondered if he stored them with the tattered beach towels, the buckets and spades, and the old flask for tea on the journey. 'It's good for yer lungs,' his father said every year, making the same face every year, although Finnegan began to see there was more and more face and less and less hair in the rear-view mirror every year. And there was grey hair in his ears and nostrils. Poor Mr White, Finnegan thought to himself. For now it was another summer in Donegal with its myths and legends, holidaying near the Giant's Causeway. Wasn't it Finn Mac Cumhaill who tore a hole in the land to create Lough Neagh, throwing an island into the Irish Sea? 'Present day Isle of Man!' his father used to say, year in and year out. And Manx cats? Cats swung by their tails by this giant. Sailing through the air, skimming the Irish Sea, they landed dazed and tailless. How glorious! Strange isle of mystical creatures . . .

Finnegan wiped his saturated neck. The summers lasted an eternity. He twitched his nose. Children carried buckets of water to and from the water's edge. And what of the summer of '44 and the bombers coming over from America? Not just a beach, it was a gateway to World Wars. His father had told him about that. How strange for the gunners to see holiday throngs in myriads of colours with London Town burning to the ground. 'Blitzkrieg!' he thought he heard on the wind. What of the beaches of Normandy then? Only Vikings and Norsemen had landed here on this small island. How different and yet the same. Men with different names – the same hearts, though – plundering, always plundering, bleeding the colours of beach towels, wounded heads the colours of beach balls ... 'Wars come, and wars go,' his father used to say. Finnegan said he understood.

Now, in the heat of another summer's day, he fixed all his emotions on the bleak aspect of the craggy cliff-heads cloistering the bay in its horseshoe aspect, hiding it from enemies with its monstrous cliffs. Finnegan stared on, seeing the worn snaking arteries of sheep trails meandering off into the distance. Everything was in giant scale. He did believe in giants, even now. If he had shortened his name, it would have been Finn. Another giant of Irish lore ... That would have been a great thing, to be called after a giant, to have a heritage like that. Eight-hundred-foot sheer cliffs stretched out before him, each a mere ledge for a giant to rest his head! It made Finnegan's head swoon. He was so small in the midst of all this colossal land and ocean. Eight-hundred-foot sheer cliffs ... From heaven to hell in the step of a foot ... That was where life ended and the precipice to death began, the lip of the universe, a land slowly eaten away by both the indefatigable sea and sheep banished to grow their coats long and their bellies fat. Finnegan could see their white fleeces blotched in stigmas of red and blue. Did they grow that way? Questions ... Always questions ...

In these summer months the sea was less formidable, the

sun glowing for eighteen hours of the day and the yawning bay inviting thousands to idle in serenity, the small towns by the coast washed in a riviera of colour, the flamingo pinks and sky blues, canary yellows and plum purples. And yet, inside, men drank black sombre stout. Why? Why? Questions ... Always questions ... Finnegan took a deap breath, still watching the gulls nesting in these sheered cliffs, staring with a certain fixity of expression at the slow black dribble of people moving up toward the cliff-head. 'It's good for yer lungs.' His father was always pointing. 'Isn't it rude to point?' his sister whispered. She'd get her ears boxed, he thought to himself, before the day was through.

People would not have climbed this cliff-head in autumn or winter. There were stories of sheep seen sailing over the cliff during storms. 'Flyin sheep, me arse! Jasus Christ.' Mr White was a vulgar man. He doubted everything except himself. He could do anything.

Summer in these small towns was a curious time, a transition, a fluxing giddiness rising in all the hearts of those who rose from their meagre lives to stand like Grecian gods, touching the sun with their bare hands for just a brief moment. Sublimeness rang in cash-register drawers. 'Till we meet again!' Always the foolish simpering humour, the cash piling high in the back rooms ... A country that knew only feast or famine ... New shoes for the baby, a new coat for himself, toys for the children, maybe a skirt and stockings for herself, a little perfume ... Summer came, and it went so quickly. 'Like youth,' Finnegan whispered to himself. How many men had climbed that cliff-head? How many men, like apes in the time of giants with names like Finn and Cuchulain, men like sticks in the famine, fat men like his father now, bankers who christened their sons with names from litera-ture? How pompous! His father was a great fan of James Joyce. 'He never read a word of him,' Finnegan had once told his teacher, promptly receiving a pinched ear for being 'cheeky'. Oh yes! Literature can live by word of mouth. Myths persist always. 'Balls,' he smiled to himself, still remembering that stinging ear. Finnegan would have been more comfortable with a proper name.

'Do you want a sandwich?' a voice whispered.

Finnegan shrugged his shoulders. He longed to leave the beach and follow those pilgrims of ecstasy up toward the heavens. 'To touch the sun for a moment,' he whispered.

'It's where shamrocks grow,' his father had said with a keen satisfaction one evening, goading his son.

'Shamrocks, my arse,' Finnegan thought to himself. He kept looking off into the distance. 'To touch the sun for a moment,' he whispered again.

Mrs White made a face. She didn't want thinkers in the family.

Finnegan averted his eyes, though, and could see the beach running for miles in a strip of glimmering yellow, mottled with bodies, all pink and hot. Mrs White nudged him. 'A sandwich pet?'

He smiled.

'No thinking.' She pronounced the 'g'.

He was at that age when his mother felt it still her duty to rub ointment into his nose and ears in the sun, and his little sister could not be dissuaded from burying his body in sand. He had and had always been a brother and a son. He wished he could have been more in these latter years. Humility was waning in his spirit. There was a turgid longing pent up in the depths of his body. Yes! Humility was waning, but he wasn't the kind of fellow who would hurt his mother.

In the distance people touched the sun and held it like a golden coin, and he shut his eyes. 'Money makes the world go round, the world go round.' No more gods and giants, phantoms of a bygone age . . . Fat industrial tycoons ruled without ceremony now, in barren markets with gridiron shelving and fluorescent lights. He sat with his legs encased in a tomb of warm sand, knowing these things and yet saying nothing. Finnegan was a boy on his holidays.

'There ya are now, Finnegan. And some tea with the sandwich?'

Finnegan nodded obediently, saying, 'Thank ya, Ma.'

'Mary! Get away with dat bucket and spade! And if ya hit that beach ball over on me again, God take pity on ya. Now go on down and ask Mr White if he wants tea with his sandwiches.'

'Mr White, Mrs White, Jesus Christ!' Finnegan took a bite of his sandwich, the egg filled with shell, and yet he said nothing. Good sons ate their egg sandwiches. He was a good boy.

'Ask Mr White . . . ' Mrs White insisted.

'I will! I will. But tell Finnegan, don't move out of da sand. Tell him, tell him!'

'She's like a feckin seal with that ball bouncin here and dere.'

Finnegan watched his sister scurrying off toward the water. He didn't think she looked like a seal at all. Seals couldn't move the way she moved.

Mrs White pursed her face and stared into his eyes. Finnegan turned his eyes down to the sand.

Mr White was sitting in a rented banana-shaped chair, wiggling his toes in the cool water. He always bore an edifying grin on his face, like a cat who had eaten a canary. He was sly and yet simple, cautious to the point of absurdity. He wore black braces over his naked back so that they would cover his nipples, a small timepiece pinned to the braces for good measure. 'Cancer's the kind of fella who sneaks up on ya,' he used to say severely to passers-by who snickered at him wearing black braces. 'The nipple is like a rose. It wilts quickly,' he used to grin to twenty-year-old girls. And yet, Mr White was simple more than sly, or so Finnegan had always thought as a boy. But now Finnegan was maturing. He had matured already, a slow painful birth alone in his house, without friendship and love. Not that he was a recluse . . . He had friends. 'Great friends,' Mrs White called them. She had no friends. Finnegan felt sorry for her. Now he was seeing new life with old eyes, with a palpitating awareness of all things. Some emotions were new, and some, vague memories. He recoiled at times into himself, looking for answers. Vague memories flirted in his mind, memories like the faltering self-denial of his first wet dream, where everything was wet and then dry in the morning, and he kept lying to himself, shaking his head, but there it was on the sheet, the creamy grey stain. Did emotions really produce that warmth in his bed?

'We'll have no thinking,' he heard his mother whispering crossly in his dream. She pronounced the 'g', just like in real life.

Finnegan wondered if she knew that Ireland had the highest incidence of insanity in the world. He wondered why they had told him that at school. Did people need to know that fact? Did you have to be aware of madness, or was it just a Christian Brother's way of warping adolescence?

'A good meal is all I ever wanted,' Mr White used to say constantly. Finnegan still believed that. Finnegan looked at his father who was yet again commencing in ludicrous fashion with one of his assorted bathing rituals, saluting his fellow humans with a wink of his eye and then very carefully proceeding to ladle water about his fat jiggling belly and hairy little legs. 'John the fuckin Baptist,' Finnegan shouted.

Mrs White turned, as was appropriate, white.

Finnegan continued watching shamefully as his father sat right back down and sorted himself out, snapping the braces with his thumbs, repinning his timepiece to his braces, then shifting his languid penis in his shorts. Who could have missed it? And how he winked at the young women walking by his dripping body. Finnegan had only known of this peculiarity since this holiday. He tried not to look, but he saw his father in his mind at night, doing that horrible act with a certain smugness, as though he knew he was now in his son's dream. His father had hated him from the moment he had been born. Mr White was a self-professed simple man, and yet that was what made him a vicious man. 'Simple men are the most complicated,' a priest once told Finnegan at confession. Finnegan remembered seeing the priest's head nodding behind the mesh grid, and then he knew it was true. And still he wondered why he had to say Hail Marys for hating his father. When his father had his mind made up, 'it was like shutting a vault and throwing away the key'. Those were Mr White's words. Not having to talk to his wife for a fortnight was his paradise realized. 'It's what keeps me alive,' he used to say when the time was coming near, lest anyone forget that he wanted no talking. Before every holiday, for the two weeks preceding the holiday, he would keep saying, 'I'm leavin me tongue on the mantelpiece, so say it now, or hold your tongue.' He thought he was clever.

Finnegan watched, even as a boy, how his mother, the dubbed Mrs White, kept her distance and how his father, the patriarchal tumescent ulcer, Mr White, kept his distance on these holidays. Finnegan watched his father patrolling the beach in the late afternoons with his eyes, following lovers moving away toward the steep cliffs. Finnegan used to wonder if his father had ever been in love, or if his mother, Mrs White, had ever been in love with his father, Mr White. He never asked them, though. He thought they might have pencilled down the acts beforehand, to keep it clean and honest. He'd seen his mother making shopping lists. It wasn't that far-fetched to Finnegan. What was far-fetched was how he had ever been born.

On these holidays Finnegan understood why people like his parents had children. There was always a certain economy of language and life in his Catholic family. You didn't speak unless spoken to. It was the rule. Catholics lived by rules: no meat on a Friday, confession on a Saturday, staying off sweets for Lent. 'Christmas must have been a mistake,' Finnegan had said in class one day. He could still feel the sting in his ear. On these holidays, his sister acted as a courier of sorts, bringing messages and food from Mrs White to Mr White and vice versa. If Mr White was unhappy, he would send back the plate empty and turn, twisting his face into all sorts of shapes, and then benevolently feed screeching gulls about his chair with Mrs White's sandwiches. His daughter would then have to return, amidst the frenzy of birds, with another array of sandwiches or a salad and a bit of liver.

'I don't know why ya keep servin him hand over foot. It's your holiday as well as his,' Finnegan grumbled, biting into a sandwich of cheese and egg and eggshell.

'Leave him be, for the love of Jesus. Could ya imagine if he was up here with us? "Too hot, too cold, too windy ... Sunburn here and sunburn there ... " We're better up here, away from all that badgerin. And tell me anyway, how's that sandwich? Enough cheese? More butter?'

'No! It's fine, Ma, just fine.'

Finnegan watched his sister scampering across the sand once more with the plate untouched. 'He says there's shell in the egg.'

'Shell in the egg, my arse. Sure he hasn't even tasted the bloody things,' Finnegan shouted, and Mr White turned and put on one of his infamous beet-red heart attack-feigning faces for everyone to see that he was a man troubled by a belligerent family. There were always other sympathetic fathers about, nodding their heads and pointing.

'Why didn't ya feed it to the birds?' Finnegan shouted to Mr White, breaching the silence so fastidiously imposed by Mr White.

'Birds don't eat eggs, you stupid bastard,' Mr White whispered later on, when he came up with his chair in hand, forecasting a phantom storm that mysteriously crept back out to sea. It was always the same. There were no storms. Mr White just had to complain about something.

Finnegan sat quietly in the hot air, as he did every day, in the same place, resigned to watching the morning pass to noon, then to evening. Mrs White punctuated her day with three events: breakfast, dinner, and tea. Finnegan smiled idly by her side and nodded his head yet again when Mr White returned from the water's edge with his chair in hand and his small radio tucked under his other arm, telling everyone that he'd heard that in India they had exploded their own atomic bomb. 'It won't be long before there's nothin out there but dead fish and a red sea.' He said that gently, as though he meant to tell them something genuine, and Finnegan turned his head away as he saw Mrs White smile at Mr White. Yes, there were those moments, even Finnegan had to admit.

Finnegan accepted all these things with a certain solipsism as he grew older, grinning hopelessly most of the time, buried in sand from the waist down, his sister constantly vigilant to his every move, patting down any eruption of sand. One exposed big toe and she went wild with fabulous excitement. 'Will ya cut out the messin! Yer legs are supposed to be walls to keep the water from gettin to the castles and the princess!'

If there was one thing that could be said of Finnegan, it was that he had 'the patience of a saint'. Father O'Brien said those words once when Finnegan said that 'all good things come to those who wait'. People were always putting things into Father O'Brien's mouth, mostly words and food. And people were always putting things into Father O'Brien's hand, mostly money. Finnegan figured religion out over-night. What Finnegan said of himself was that there was nothing that could be said of himself when he used to lie in his bed at night, crestfallen, watching the painted moon move across his wall. Science had spoiled most things. There was no man on the moon; it wasn't made of cheese. No giant in the Giant's Causeway ... Continental drifts and ice ages, these were the ignominious giants. No glamour ... 'Continental drifts ... ' Sounded like music, though, Finnegan had to admit. An emotion even ... Look up continental drift in the dictionary. 'One who looks out to sea and dreams of distant lands.' It wouldn't be there. There were illusory things that only existed in one's own mind.

Now, in these long painful days, Finnegan sat and tipped his neck forward at noon and got ointment on his neck and cream massaged into his scalp for good measure. He was becoming one of those doleful dreamers, a boy slowly slipping into manhood, lubricated from within by seeping emotions, sweating now as his mother's greased hands kneaded his head and back with her rubbery fingers. He felt the salt in his eyes. The wind licked with sand and salt, polishing his body to a shiny mahogany. He took deep breaths, the pressure of his temples raised in grooved arteries of flowing blood. 'All things will come to pass,' it said in the Bible. He was at that age where he looked back to a collage of faces and expressions. He was in among families of fat mothers, watching skeletal grandfathers, their wizened phlegmatic faces being led to the beach for one last dip, baptized for death, their bones rattling with excitement, black crows hopping about in morbid ceremony. Was it really like that, or was he making it up? No! These things did happen. People did die.

Finnegan had a brain that painted pictures. He saw his brain, hunched and frowning in the dim cavern of his cranium at times. He was beginning to use bad language in his dreams, in his thinking, monologues of sinful words and pearly enchantment. The stains grew shamefully obvious. Maybe he could have used a sock. He took a hot sticky breath, odour rising from his body. He was changing ever so slowly. All about, he felt himself moving with the adages of his parents, the same simpering jokes passing through one ear and passing out his mouth. He'd heard it all before, before. All things echoing, echoing in his imprisoned head, faintly, faintly through his buried body, sting, stinging his useless legs ... He slept many hours on the beach, always buried below the waist, hearing the constant coughs and wheezes of rotten lungs set out to dry in the salt air. He whispered softly, 'Lungs like ragged crossbone flags ... ' He used to dream of his family while lying on the beach, feeling them pressing about his exposed body, their hands running across his face, his mother spitting into handkerchiefs, dabbing his dirty face with her sticky spit, his sister laughing, burrowing furiously into the sand, shouting, shouting, 'Don't move those legs, they are the walls to keep the water out.' And he used to say, 'Yes, yes, yes,' and take another sandwich in his hand and pack his intestines with egg and butter and jam and cheese. And he could hear the drawling voice of his father's impatience, 'That child put sand in the sandwiches.' There was always life and death on a beach for a boy like him, he could smell the decaying fish, the garlands of seaweed baking in the sun. Finnegan kept staring, at other times, at the monstrous cliff-head, the sloped head like a mammoth whale, the etched basalt pylons like blackened teeth. This was a place of giants. Science was wrong! He kept wanting to move his toes, to disobey, to be one of those Grecian gods, to stand upright with a billowing toga for just a brief moment and touch the sun with his bare hands. But he sat very still and said nothing.

The sun was becoming so very hot, his mother's hands now like flat metal ironing his back. He wanted something different. He wanted his family to fade away. But they wouldn't. He was a son and brother, a friend in need, a statue on the mantelpiece, his father's shame, his own agony, his worst and best friend, a boyfriend once.

He took short breaths. He kept screaming inside his mind, and yet his mother just kept smiling. So many layers of life wrapped him into a cocoon of isolation. He was the onion boy, the white boy with jellied flesh, buried in sand. He kept pulling at the skins, the bandaged gauze of his dreams sticking in his fingernails, the soft-fleeced cotton wool like the candy floss they sold in the canteen shops, the wool like the beard of God. But he didn't want religion. That was for mothers and old men who were afraid of death. He had a heritage: giants lurking in this paradise. He could feel their ghosts, but all that could wait. He needed to move forward now, to creep, slinking in an idealized swoon into the smoke-filled bars of manhood where women sweated like he sweated, a place of animal whines and swishing tails, where tongues moved with the glistening spittle of anticipation, a universe of groping, with eyes half-closed, a heaven with sin. He kept nodding his head, yes, yes, yes, to feel once more that bloody fruit of his origin, to become once more that squint-faced foetus wrapped in the soft insides of another being . . .

'Would you like a cheese sandwich?' his mother whispered, still rubbing his neck.

He shook his head. Time had passed. He looked at his mother. She had rubbed his back for so many years, soothing the pain, easing the knots.

A man in a red and white striped coat and a straw hat came by with a tray of melting ice creams. He never seemed to look at the parents, just the children, letting droplets of ice cream drip-drop on their heads. He knew the meaning of anticipation.

'Ask me nothin. I'm covered in this cream,' Mrs White growled, trying to make eye contact with the ice cream man. But he just kept turning back and forth in a swirl of red and white, surveying the beach for other prospects, for other children, the dubbed 'Child Catcher'.

Finnegan eyed the ice cream with a strained uneasiness and then blushed. His mother shook her head severely. She knew her son too well. This was the kind of thing that the Christian Brothers were supposed to be vigilant to prevent.

The tepid cream ran down the man's fingers. 'But there are always some fish who slip through the net,' was Father O'Brien's stock phrase. People were always putting things into Father O'Brien's mouth, mostly excuses. This religion would endure with a nod and a wink and a strap, if need be. There was a shop in town that made straps to leather young boys. Finnegan shook his head imperceptibly.

'Don't move, Finnegan!' his little sister whined, scampering away to get money from her father.

Finnegan watched her elastic body bending. He felt the grease seeping into his back. He kept staring at these girls, fascinated by their long, hairless, reddened legs, the pinched red triangular burn between their soft breasts, the hard nuggeted nipples, the gentle ooze of their buttocks as they proceeded slowly, like creatures in a dream, passing him by. The sun was beginning to burn fiercely when he shut his eyes and felt the cool droplets of creamy ice falling on his chest.

'Get back away, you fool!' shouted Mrs White.

Finnegan sat with his eyes closed and felt the sun warming the creamy splotch.

By evening more sandwiches were being prepared. Mrs White's daughter was sent to one of the local guest-houses to get a pot of piping hot tea and buttered scones. Mr White continued to sit in his banana chair, sifting sand through his curled shrimp-like toes.

What a sight, thought Finnegan to himself, his father's polished black shoes waiting obediently by his chair.

'He'll go in for a splash before long now, to wash it off,' Mrs White said to a lady sitting near her who was also making jam sandwiches and egg sandwiches and cheese sandwiches. Even in her suit the lady looked uncouth, her children running around the beach with their underwear wedged up their bottoms, her two babies trotting around naked with their spotty bottoms covered in sand. Mrs White would not have spoken to a woman like this in the city. A week ago, one of her children had said that they kept a hen in the car so that they wouldn't have to buy eggs. Mr White had laughed and asked if they had brought a cow for the cheese the next day. He was the kind of man who said what he pleased even if it pleased nobody else.

Mr White told only two jokes. He'd been perfecting them for an eternity. One was for the city, and the other, for the holidays. He got people to buy him drinks with his two jokes. Although Mr White was unaccustomed to speaking to his son, he did always insist that his son should accompany him to the pubs at night. Mr White was simple and sly, and more sly sometimes than simple. The holidays were his to be spent as he wished them to be spent. 'Time is not free,' he used to say, as he checked the timepiece pinned to his braces. Finnegan shut his eyes with the flawless mechanics of a camera lens. He could see everything in his own mind: the cruelty, and the passion, the stupid love, the acrid vomit of his father on the landing carpet after another night of telling that same joke. Even in his dreams Finnegan could hear his father at that joke, shaking everyone's hand at arm's length, as though he were pulling the arm of a slot machine. It began as always, 'Dere was dis fellow . . . '

'Dere was dis fellow from da mainland who was crippled with an ailment of arthritis ta beat da band. I suppose ye have heard of da crooked man who walked da crooked mile. Well dat was yer man to a tee. Well, doesn't he get so bad dat he has ta stop in bed until noon before his legs are oiled at all. "Dere's only one thing dat's for you," says the doctor. "Go to da sea and get yerself a few barrels of sea-water to bathe in. It's da only cure for a fella like you are."

'Well, off goes yer man with much effort and curses dat would have da Devil blush. Neither love nor hay would get da donkey out da road ta Galway, it buckin and stampin away. Two days later, with the tide full in, our man arrives like a crooked stick. Says I ta him, "A Longford man, I'm presumin." "I am indeed," he replied. "Tell us, sir, but do ya know da proprietor of dis ocean so I could be allowed to fill up me barrels?" "I'm yer man," I said. "One pound will fill three!" I said. He wouldn't pay four shillins, he told me, and so he bade me good day. Night was fallen when who did I see but himself, wrestlin with da most cantankerous mangy donkey I ever had da misfortune to lay eyes on. He gets to me, though, and he says with a gasp, "Jasus! Ya do a roarin trade." I looked over me shoulder, and dere, to me own knowledge, was the tide out beyond where the eye could see.

188

"Da price is two pound, now," I said quite softly, shruggin me shoulders, pullin on me pipe like I couldn't care less about him and his knackered legs. He paid me gladly, and dat was da last I ever saw tell of him again, God rest his soul . . . '

Finnegan always awoke in a cold sweat. He could hear the laughter ringing in his ears. What was there about that joke that hurt him? What depravity brought tears to his eyes in bars, in his bed on those lonesome nights? Was it his father's feigned crippled walk as he proceeded with his coveted joke? 'Stupid joke,' Finnegan choked to himself. Through the years it seemed that his father had perfected that awful crooked walk with such a judicious credulity. It was the moment when people thought that the joke might not be that funny. And Mr White knew that. He seemed to be begging for pity more than laughs for that one tense moment. It could have gone either way, tears or laughs, tears of laughter. Emotions were delicate objects. They were ethereal at times, mystifying. 'Tears of laughter,' Finnegan whispered to himself. It depended, in these bars, on who had seen the boy walk in with his father.

Tears and laughter . . .

The evening seemed to yawn in the bay, the sky streaked in orange and red coloured light, the sheep migrating to the other side of the cliff-head, following the dying sun. Finnegan could see the glint of metal zippers and binoculars on the cliff-head. People were descending slowly. He could barely see the last stray sheep, imagining their plaintively childlike baa-baaing on the cooling breeze. They would see those sheep faces again from windows, in sawdusted shops, from kitchen tables where all meals began, 'In the name of the Father and of the Son'.

'Will you come up with us, Finnegan?' Mrs White said when the tea had been drunk and the family of tinkers, with the alleged hen in the back of their car, had left the beach.

'I'm okay, Ma!' Finnegan said with a sigh, staring as always into the distance. It was always into the distance that he liked to stare. He had to envision the vagueness of something new, to perfect the blotched light and greyness of the horizon.

Mr White stood before his wife, his body dripping with salt water. She dried his massive back with strong pink hands. He had a back like a ledger, white with the red veined lines of the braces marks and the red protrusion of his spine. Finnegan looked at his mother, Mrs White, if you please, draping her body over this man, her husband, Mr White, if you will, the man who insisted on no talking on his holidays. 'Leave yer tongue on the mantelpiece,' he said time and time again. His nipples were small and blood-red, too small, Finnegan thought, for such a massive back and fat belly. It seemed almost comical. It made Finnegan grin to himself.

'You're goin to da pub later with me, okay?' his father said, turning, readjusting his jiggling belly. He had a monstrous hairy bellybutton, too. It made the small childish nipples even more absurd.

'I will,' Finnegan said softly. He wasn't for causing trouble.

The beach was emptying quietly. The sun had taken its toll. He could hear the occasional sobbing child, complaining about glass in his foot, or a burn on her back, or sand in his shoes.

It never ceased, this slow ebb and flow of human life, families and lovers draped in foolish coloured towels of yellow and orange and blue and green. All this from people who only wore black in the city . . .

'Are ya sure ya won't come up with us now?' Mrs White said again and again, snapping blankets of sand and crisps and bread crumbs. There were gulls screeching in excitement. Things survived: memories, hopes, illusions, foolish creatures.

'I'm okay,' Finnegan shouted, cracking the patted sand about his legs in agitated relief. He wouldn't do it tomorrow, he wouldn't let his legs be encased for another eight hours to appease his sister's whims. These legs of his were not pillars;

they would never be pillars. Why pretend? What would his legs be against the roaring sea? Look what the sea had done to the mysterious sloped cliff. Millions of years of slow attrition, the jagged cliffs crumbling into the whispering surf . . . He'd tried to be what he wasn't. 'No more,' he said bitterly.

Mrs White looked at Mr White. Who was to blame? They both stared at their feet. They were more distant than ever in moments like this.

Finnegan watched his sister and his parents depart in a huge ceremony of colour and curses. Everyone was a 'stupid bastard'. The holiday was being 'spoiled by those ungrateful pups'. Mr White was never content when he wasn't complaining.

There were only a few remaining people about as the sun sank, bleeding a pink sunset, casting grey shadows upon the land. People would be wearing black again tonight. He thought of a girl he once knew, of a past holiday on this beach . . .

In the bars there was life and women and all the things he told himself he needed. And friends . . . Hundreds of people singing and dancing and drinking, the music throbbing in his legs . . . He sat with his friends at a table, eyeing girls, murdering pints. He'd met a girl. He could do that. There was nothing wrong with the way he looked. A head like a Titan . . . 'A face like a sheep,' his father screamed once. He was a liar. Night after night, the same girls sitting with him and his friends . . . He drank pint after pint, pouring the black stout into his belly. He wanted to be drunk, staggering to the bar, to the toilet. 'She noticed nothing!' Everyone said so. He nodded his head in the morning hours. The pain, his kidneys like bloated sponges . . . Tomorrow would do. Procrastination! It went on and on, the white froth of Guinness on his upper lip an adolescent moustache. Bandito . . . 'Looks like a Mexican gunfighter!' Nobody mentioned the IRA. It was all hilarious, five friends riding shotgun in a small town.

But they kept whispering to him, 'Tell her, tell her.'

'And why should he tell her anything,' he kept laughing, drunk with love and pain, his urine splashing in a steady sanguine stream. 'It was on the good ship *Venus* . . . ' Tell what to her? A girl he'd met on his holidays, he whispered to himself. A girl who'd loved other boys, who'd love other boys again . . . Tell her what? 'You mean confess?' he shouted, staggering all the way home. 'Apologize! Apologize,' he said in his sleep. The night came to murmur and mutter his secret. He tossed in his bed, to and fro, the stout sloshing in his belly. The days were long and the nights short. Thank God!

The night came to tell. Drunk beyond all measure . . . 'Swam in a brewery before teatime . . . False courage . . . ' He needed what he could get. 'When a ship's goin down, you grab at anything,' he shouted. 'Another round over here!' He wore the same juvenile moustache with each gulp. His head was wet and his hair matted in curls. She came in high heels and a black tight dress. This wasn't the beach. The towels were tucked away in hot presses, draped like exotic zebra skin over the ribbed hissing heaters. 'Tunnel vision,' is what he called it afterward. 'Just sitting there and everything is funnelled in one spiralling direction.' He remembered smashing a glass, everyone laughing out loud. 'Tell her, tell her.' She stood before . . . before him, with the whiff of her rose-scented perfume mingling with the billowing smoke. He felt the nudges. 'So what's the big secret?' 'He's only got one ball!' A spray of stout stained his shirt like a shrapnel wound. He felt himself faltering. The girl was snickering, her red lips so soft and supple. 'One ball,' she purred. 'Three!' he shouted, trembling. Everyone laughed and took a gulp of stout. He'd unclasped the metal braces from around his hips earlier. He thought of himself as one of those gunfighters who takes his guns off before he goes to the showdown. Who wanted to kill someone? Who wanted to be killed? The questions came pouring forth. No time for the philosopher now. 'Tell her, tell her.' The tables shaking with banging glasses and stomping feet ... His legs were etiolated and withered from the clenched aspect of what years of wearing those braces had done to him. He stood shaking. Everyone was laughing. Could they have known his pain? Deformity! That's what it was.

He'd stood, like he thought the girl before him must have done so many times in the mirror, running her fingers over her body, smiling at what she had to offer. She was taking stock of what she was; identity was a personal romance in these early years. You had to love yourself, or at least not hate yourself. 'Go on, tell her.' Tears of laughter ... They liked him too much not to laugh or cry. Seventeen-year-old boys with hormones and friendship and condoms. 'Ah yes, a brother who worked in England was a good thing to have,' Murphy grinned. 'Protestant Eucharist,' another winked. Everyone knew what was what. City boys ... Belfast boys cooling off, tenement boys with eyes in the backs of their heads ... Girls like these like jelly babies, soft supple flesh, so white and unformed, small-breasted girls stuffing tissues in their bras ... Two-week romances ... Everyone reeked of cheap after-shave with rugged names like 'The Aran Man' and 'Texas Splash'. Girls like these! A summer of kisses, tasting big tongues and small tongues ... Three months of the year of courtship, boys on fortnight holidays, simple mathematics, six boyfriends, six slurping mouths, six thousand 'no, no, no, yes, yes ... ' Not their first and not their last kiss, but all these loves, all these girls, would become part of an untarnished history for these boys, each juvenile face captured in the minds of young boys for ever. The occasional photograph in the family album ... Only the young boy knew who she was: his secret love. What is she doing now? Forty years later, and still that same feeling of a seventeen-year-old. She lived her life within one hundred miles of you, and you never saw her again. You shared the same news, the same weather, and yet you did not see these girls again. They are dreams now.

'Tell her, tell her.' They were beating their glasses on the tables. He rose from the table, supported by his taut arms, his face stained by tears of effort. He was never a boy for self-pity, but there were tears. For her? For him? 'I wanted to tell you . . . ' He stopped. Did she have to know? Was he telling her, or telling himself that this would be his life? 'Tell me what?' She was giggling. Didn't she know what he was going to say? Hadn't someone told her, or her friends? Did she think he was going to say something stupid like 'Will you be my girlfriend?'

'Go on,' his friends shouted. The door rattled in the pulling wind; the night had finally filled the sky with blackness.

He stared into her face, stepped back, and the place went dead, an occasional snicker from someone who didn't know, and he whispered, 'I'm crippled.' Some girl whined like an animal. His eyes burned. He bit his lips, putting his hands out to touch her. Everyone went silent. 'Shoo, shoo,' the glasses trembled. The girl felt the faces and the breaths upon her. A poor girl of seventeen caught in this . . . A girl who hadn't even touched a 'you-know-what', or she wasn't telling if she had . . . The moment hung like a hang-noose around her neck. This was supposed to be a game of love, not tragedy. She burst out laughing in sudden excitement. Everyone held their breaths. 'Oh, is that all, Finnegan? I thought you were an alcoholic!' A sigh of relief and admiration rippled through the room, followed by an uproar of laughter, and more stout flung into the air in a torrent of rapture, like whales at an orgy out in the black sea. Finnegan fell forward with his arms outstretched. 'I love you,' he shouted above the screaming, to no one in particular, his eyes closed, tears streaming down his face. He was smiling beautifully, as only he could smile. Everyone was whistling and banging glasses. Some fool had torn paper mats into bits and was screaming, 'Confetti.' The girl sidestepped Finnegan's outstretched arms, and he hit his head with a terrible hop on the concrete floor, and then the laughing stopped for the night for him . . .

He'd lived with that moment for two years. People blamed

him, and others blamed his friends for hurting the girl. He'd seen her again in town, stealing kisses from another boy, except she was becoming a woman now. She would live, too, with that moment for the rest of her life. In ten years would he see her with a family on this beach, pretending not to remember him? You don't forget things like that. And twenty years and thirty years and he would forget what she looked like, but she would remember him, remember that crippled walk. Or would she? Wouldn't they all be walking on canes then? He was born an old man, sipping tea and bread and butter in the greenhouse porches covered in glass. And he would live only with that memory of her face, so pale, confronting an invalid who begged for her pity. Did she see him today on the beach in his grave of sand, always a brother, always a son? He'd wanted to be more! To crawl up that sheered cliff-head, to stand and touch the sun like a god . . . But that was only the fantasy! He wanted less than that.

The sea was inching further inland. It was a good thing the Longford man hadn't come this night in his father's infamous joke, to see the ocean swallowing the land and his legs. Oh yes, the blackening ocean was spilling into the bay, bringing seals and mermaids. They didn't have legs either. He was now broaching a silent cynicism, he was deformed, and he slept with that notion. He had not been blown up in a bomb like he told people when he went to Dublin last Christmas. A girl had kissed him when she heard him speaking, right there in the bar. 'Was it painful?' Words like 'rehabilitation' infused the air with hope. No! That was not his story.

He thought often of how he could have cut his legs up, or poured petrol over them, there in a field, soberly watching the hair singe and his flesh blacken. It would have been easy. He felt nothing except a faint tingle in his legs. But it would have been a lie. Was he a moral boy? He shrugged his shoulders. 'Petrol was expensive' in his part of the world. He grinned to himself. He had friends back in Belfast, friends who knew him for what he was. He had a home and pub to go to. What more could a man want? He was beginning to shiver in the cool air. He felt himself slowly becoming enamoured in a pitiful rage in these late evenings, pitting himself against the sea. 'How futile,' he whispered. What was out there in the sea to hate? Nothing. Would he be drowned? There was no fear of drowning. He always thought it hilarious how normal people had it set in their minds that they must introduce a medium with which to reduce both invalid and healthy creatures to inept splashers, to useless buoys set adrift in the name of exercise. No! He would not drown.

The massive sun was pouring its last orange rays into the sea now, turning the ocean to a simmering red colour, quenching yet another day. In India they had exploded an atomic bomb, his father had told them. That would be what his father would be talking about until the wee hours of this morning. Finnegan had seen his face. Mr White was concerned about worldly things, things that were bigger than himself. He'd be dreaming of that billowing mushroom, and the tiny red dots in Indian women's furrowed brows. Other religions, other wars . . . Finnegan looked outward, the cliffs muted, the beach quiet.

Finnegan's mind painted pictures. But it was dull now. The day and the sun were far, far too much; they bled colour terribly. He thought of the night falling, how its grey curtain seemed like the nylon curtains that are drawn in the cinema as films start. There was that palpitating excitement in this evening for him. Everything was an image, an isolated image. He was naming feelings, smelling the sea and the vinegar chips from the mobile canteens. 'Would he go with his father to the pub this evening?' was all he finally fell upon to grapple over. Things were not that bad. Would he go with his father? Maybe he could tell him to think of a new joke, one without crippled men. He hadn't decided if he'd mention it.

In the distance a girl approached in a creamy dress. Finnegan sat alone, with his legs still buried in the patted-down sand. He watched her coming closer and closer, her long legs whiter than he had ever seen. He'd seen her at his boarding-house, peeking out at the visitors with a childish curiosity, wondering whose bed it was that she made every morning. Did she see the stains on his? He blushed. The late-night tea must have passed, otherwise she would have been serving more of that same tea and sandwiches to all the guests, to all the people like him and his parents and the lady with the hen in her car. The girl didn't even seem to notice him, her dress fluttering gently about her body as she passed where he lay stretched out. She was so close to him. He could have touched her creamy dress. The sea had come in around his legs. He could feel that soft tingling. And then she turned when he was just about to turn his head away, and she smiled, and he smiled, and then she continued to move on up the beach before turning once more to see him pulling himself out of the frothing surf, painfully dragging himself clear on two glimmering crutches. She came toward him, her delicate feet so white, her face draped in black shining hair. They moved away together, in one embrace. He needed this feeling, no matter how he got it. He was saying something in a slow drawl, her dress wavering in the cool light. Sweet surrender, the lamentable pleats ... Tomorrow would be a new day. For now he was saying something like 'rat-a-tat-tat', his body arched over, himself clenching one of his crutches as though it were a rifle, the new moon casting his shadow, casting the shadow of a gunman against the stony sea-wall.

THE DEAD

EAMON SAW THE pinkish glow flooding out the slit of the bedroom door. His ruddy face cringed to a crimson colour; his eyes remained sanguine and glossy. Eamon choked back a tear as he continued to labour in a futile effort to steady the tray he carried. Its trembling cutlery and jittering cup grated on his brain. He wanted to throw the tray down the stairs. Where was the miracle for which he had begged? Couldn't Jesus in his infinite wisdom have granted that one petition? He thought of those burning candles, the blackened church walls, the smoke rising to the marbled nostrils of saints nailed to walls. He stopped and inhaled the dampness of the evening into the depths of his lungs, coughing violently as death passed through him. His arms and legs gave under the burden of the heavy-laden tray. He teetered on the edge of the step. He felt himself falling and let go of the tray. He toppled backward down the stairs. The unmerciful crash lasted but a second. And then there was blood, a thick warm exudation of blood.

'Merciful Jesus, how much more can I take?' Eamon's mother screamed. She hobbled on her arthritic legs across the cold lino and fell upon her dazed son.

'Dermot, get into the kitchen and boil some water.'

Listlessly, Dermot fingered his nostril and said nothing. His mother flew into a rage. 'I'll clip the ear off you, Dermot. Get up for the water, now!'

Dermot still slumped in the chair and ignored the torrent

of abuse his mother hurled at him.

Suddenly, she vented her anger on the unconscious Eamon, slapping his sopping bloody face. Dermot heard the resounding crack and felt an amorphous disgust for his mother. Mrs O'Brien roared on and cursed her sons.

'Ye murdered my son, yer own brother! How can ye sit there like a Cheshire cat, mornin to night, talkin lies into small boys' ears about Ireland and the IRA?'

Dermot jumped out of the chair and, with a crazed vengeance, drove toward his mother. He grabbed her by the hair and dragged her from her slumped son.

'Ye whore, ye fuckin whore!'

He hopped her head off the wall.

'Accuse me of the boy's mutilation, will ye! By Christ, ye! Ye bitch, scourgin our wee Sean in his final days with talk of mortal sin and hell!'

Dermot spat in his mother's face. He lunged his own head into her face.

'Don't think I don't hear ye at night, whisperin, "Repent! Repent! Repent!" Oh yes, ye holy fuckin whore, fingerin yer rosary beads at night, danglin them over his invisible face, and him, all alone, feelin yer disease infectin his soul . . . And he can't escape from ye.' He stood rigid in the hallway. He kept hearing those cries of his brother upstairs. All through the nights, through long plaintive nights, when he crept into that dark room to stare at his brother . . . Did his brother ever sleep? His eyes were always wide open, turning slowly. He could feel the pain. Did he know there would be no doctor? All this time, the useless cups of tea, the new sheets placed under his bleeding body . . . Could he have saved him? Dermot kept shaking. Could he? He shut his eyes once more.

The mother lay limp on the cold lino floor. Still, Dermot persisted, and the roar brought the neighbours around in curious amazement.

Nobody dared to venture into the house, except Dominick

O'Malley, the chief whip of the local Sinn Féin. He was the fierce dominator in the community, despite his appearance of a scampering rat about its business. Everyone knew he wore two coats to make himself look bigger, but they would not have said that to his face. Behind his back, the children called him 'Forty Coats'. O'Malley beckoned to a few of his lads to disperse the crowd. Two men followed him inside.

Dermot limped out through the back door, screaming. 'Fuck the IRA ... fuck the whole bloody lot of ye fuckin bastards!'

Sean began crying upstairs, 'Ma ... Ma ... ' The voice roamed through the house, bleating its abject cry.

'Go home now, go on, Mrs Doyle, if ye know what's good for ye.'

O'Malley left the waning light of the street. He entered the bleak grey house. He was appalled by spattered blood dripping down the frayed wallpaper. 'Close the fuckin door quick. Get up there and calm yer man down before he has the bloody street in on us.' He pursed his lips. 'And Frank, ye go on and check for Dermot. He can't be gone far on that leg of his.' O'Malley shook his head. 'I want that cunt, mind that, da ye hear?'

O'Malley leaned over the mother, clumsily rubbing her face with a handkerchief. 'There now, Mam, yer okay. Ye just come this way.' O'Malley gritted his teeth, taking the weight of the mother on his arm. 'That's it, grand.' He let her collapse into a chair by the fire.

'Oh Jasus, it was terrible ... ' The mother gripped O'Malley's coat.

'Please, take it easy now, Mam.' O'Malley rubbed his hands together in agitation, leaving the room. He began to revive Eamon.

'Oh Jasus, me head is split to bits,' Eamon groaned. His eyes focused on O'Malley. 'Christ, what are ye doin here?'

'Hold up there, man.' O'Malley exposed his teeth. 'Where's Dermot gone?'

'I . . . I don't know . . . Listen . . . don't ye start blamin him . . . ' Eamon tried to pull himself up by the banisters but couldn't. He fell back against O'Malley.

'Our Sean needs a hospital.'

'Please, will ye relax for a minute there.' O'Malley began to lift Eamon, but he resisted. 'Don't touch me.'

Sean called out upstairs, 'Ma . . . Ma . . . '

'It's okay, son,' the mother sobbed.

Eamon looked up at the ceiling. 'That's the way it's been for these weeks. Ye can't blame Dermot. He didn't mean whatever he done. It's the strain! The whole bloody place has caved in ever since Sean got mangled. The house is filled with screams. You should see Dermot's face when the howlin starts up. It gets so bad that we're afraid the Brits will cop on. And so we cover Sean's face with a pillow. I swear to God, there's times when I don't want to let go of the pillow. It would be all over then, the pain and the sufferin. I'll feel him wriggle, suffocatin and clutchin the sheets and blankets. I don't know why I haven't done it yet.'

Sean began to cry again. His voice poured through the house.

O'Malley turned his head away. 'Johnny! Will ye stop him, for Jasus sake.'

Eamon continued to swoon in and out of consciousness. He felt the pressure of pain deep in his head.

'Sean has to be taken to the hospital. Merciful Jesus! We can't go on. We're forever changin the sheets. He's always bleedin! There's at least five pair on the line right now.'

'I have him here,' Frank called from the back garden.

O'Malley drew himself up, patting Eamon on the shoulder. 'Listen, I'm goin to personally take care of Sean, ye mark my words.'

Dermot had a lung of smoke when O'Malley came through the shed door. He was in among the old bikes that he and his brothers had outgrown.

'So there ye are, ye wee cunt.' O'Malley shook his head.

He looked sombrely about the old shed. He had been friends with Dermot's father before he died of cancer. Slowly, he looked around at the work bench with the father's jamjars of nails, bolts and washers all lined neatly, untouched since he died. A full set of spanners hung on the one wall in descending order. O'Malley watched the hedge clippers closely. To its left, an old tricolour hung over a boarded-up window.

Dermot let the smoke in his lungs out in a thin trail, his eyes half-squinted with tears. 'I'm sorry,' he whimpered, putting a hand to his face.

Frank began to laugh with disgust.

'Listen on, head-the-ball, shut yer face, right. Ye want to get yer turn in this mess, do ye, Frank? Cause I'm the man who can arrange for it.'

Frank looked at his mate and then at the floor.

'Now, listen up. Ye lads hang on here and see that nobody comes about. I'm off with yer man at ten to the Wolfe Tone, so hold on until about half nine or so.' With that, O'Malley pushed Dermot out of the shed and into the house. 'Ye just stop in there and say nothin if ye know what's good for ye. Da ye here me? Make us a pot of tea. Come on, man, wise up, for Jasus' sake.'

In the sitting room, there were the glowing embers of the smouldering fire to soothe the tension of the decaying day. Dermot calmly returned with two cups of strong tea. He pushed the door closed and sent a cool draught across the room.

'Here ye are, Ma. Drink the tea I brung you. It'll calm yer nerves.'

The mother took the cup. She cradled the cup in her hands and sipped at the tea.

'Eamon, a sup of tea for ye there. How's the old head?' Dermot placed the tea in Eamon's lap and retreated to the dining room table. Eamon said nothing at all. He didn't even raise his head to acknowledge his brother. His blue eyes were entranced as he stared into the throbbing amber embers. Wisps of eddying white smoke billowed and puffed forth, only to dissipate and vanish up the chimney. Eamon could taste the smoke at the back of his throat.

Dermot fidgeted about. He poked the fire and cursed its dying state. He placed his hand into the fireplace and held a stale piece of bread adjacent to the orange embers. The shifting glow bathed his hardened face in moribund shadows. For a moment he was calm. The crackle of browning toast eased his mind. O'Malley coughed and ushered in the looming tension. Young Dermot faltered under the burden of the night as it weighed down on his body. Tears diffracted the soft light of the embers and trickled from Dermot's bloodshot eyes.

'Who's for toast?' he whispered softly.

Nobody uttered a word. Dermot struggled to his feet and turned away into the grey backdrop beyond the fire. He was sweating profusely. His body issued forth a putrid, musty stench. Dermot felt himself on the verge of sickness.

O'Malley sat in the far corner and absorbed all things. He'd unbuttoned his first two coats, exposing a queer purple-coloured blazer. He looked like a bruised plum, smiling away to himself. He had an acute knowledge of all things. O'Malley's entire existence revolved around these stifling tenement nightmares. He sapped the tension, inhaled the stench of fear, and loved it all so much. O'Malley sensed Dermot's strained nerves.

'Our Sean needs a hospital,' Eamon muttered.

O'Malley rose from his chair, taking deep breaths.

The clock on the mantel tick-tocked away. Its incessant rhythmic tick-tock brought the company to the same heavy pulsing heartbeat. Calm was once again restored to the little room. The mother shifted about in her apron and came up with her black rosary beads in hand.

'Jesus, Mary and Joseph, deliver us!' She began to mutter prayers.

She continued with her pleas to the Holy Family, and each prayer saw another bead of the rosary pass through her flaccid fingers.

'Please, get him to a hospital,' Eamon whispered. 'God have mercy on him.'

O'Malley's superior vantage for tyranny was robbed from him. He hated religion, and prayer had some occult mystery which frightened him dreadfully. He didn't need competition. The soldiers were his effigies; the English crown, his crown of thorns.

'We're doin what we can. Do ye think ye can smuggle a man across the border that easy? Everybody is lookin for us to make a run for it with yer Sean. Use reason . . . '

'But . . . ' Eamon held O'Malley's arm.

'Stop!' O'Malley blushed at his own fury.

Dermot dragged his lame leg across the floor, making a grating noise which tore at O'Malley's head. 'Sit down, for Jasus' sake.'

The mother began crying to herself. O'Malley felt the conspiracy of sounds filling him with fear and alienation.

The mother grew more obstreperous and wailed her prayers in a shrill voice.

'Stop!' O'Malley shouted.

'Please!' Eamon implored. 'Why can't Dermot just go to England?'

The mother went on wailing.

'We have money,' Eamon whispered. He looked fitfully at his mother.

The mother turned her eyes from her beads. 'Ye know he had no father to speak of all these years.'

'What?' O'Malley looked at Eamon.

'Money,' Eamon nodded.

'Ye think I'm some sort of Devil or other, right? How can I go against the word of a hundred other men?' O'Malley drank his tea in silence. He grew sombre. He went to the window and called the men over. The sky was dark outside.

He could barely see the two men standing by the shed. He knew they were already tense, waiting to get away home. This house reminded them too much of their own homes. 'Listen on, go off home and I'll take care of this from here on in.' O'Malley waited until he heard their footsteps die out. Then he drew his body away from the window. 'Bring me the money.'

'Will ye let him go then, O'Malley?'

'Let him come with me. I'll do all that I can.'

'It's all we have,' the mother whispered. 'Every penny we have to our names.'

O'Malley paced about the room. 'I'll do what I can, that's all there is to it.'

The tin box felt warm to O'Malley. He reckoned the hot press, concealing a smile.

'God will bless ye, O'Malley. I'll say a decade of the rosary for ye.'

O'Malley looked openly into the mother's face. 'I don't need yer prayers.' He said it so softly, not without malice, but with the pitch of a man who fears Judgement Day. O'Malley shut his eyes, holding the box. She had dragged religion and eternity into this. Suddenly, creeping memories of past headlines and graphic pictures reared in his mind. He struggled to shut the lid on his collage of carnage. He couldn't. There was the picture in Dublin where charred human flesh flapped on rusty iron railings.

He hadn't read the story, but that picture of his work wouldn't stop haunting him. O'Malley's soul had screamed for forgiveness when he had heard some women at a bus-stop talk of the poor little creature of two months who had been blown across the street and embedded into the railings of Trinity College. 'Protestant Mecca,' he whispered in disgust. Wrong religion . . . Was it a war of crucifixes now? Did people kill each other over the rosary? The memories came in torrents of blood. But he wasn't a fool. Morality had no place in his life, in any of these lives – or just maybe at the end, he conceded. A sprinkle of holy water, an act of contrition . . . Catholics could get that kind of forgiveness.

O'Malley wanted to split the mother's face open. He looked to the clock. It was nine o'clock. He held the tin box close to his chest. 'Thank Jasus,' he muttered. 'Get up, Dermot. We're off now.'

'And Sean?' Eamon asked, staring at O'Malley.

'There'll be a doctor here later on. Say nothin about any of this stuff tonight. Do ye understand?'

The man and youth donned their heavy coats and were subsequently spat from the flat redbrick-faced house into the night. The chill made the two figures cringe and shuffle. The entire street was enveloped in a slight fog. A film of silvery iridescent frost made the road sparkle. The night seemed so peaceful and beautiful. O'Malley started at a brisk pace and ignored everything, his coat tails fanning outward. Faster and faster he fled away from the house. His head was a riot of oppressive sin. 'That Holy Mary Whore!' he screamed inside his head. He turned and looked at Dermot limping behind him. He had suffered an injury in the bomb blast with his brother. O'Malley's face was swollen with rage. 'Come on, Jasus!'

Dermot laboured after O'Malley. 'Fuck her and her religion. You hear me, ye cunt? I'm fightin for fuckin justice. That fuckin bitch and ye in there, singin for yer fuckin supper, by fuckin Christ, and us with no jobs, no houses, and those stupid cunts down south with their tricolours, wavin them and winkin away, pretendin they're holdin up a fuckin blackmail list to the fuckin arse of the Queen . . . Fuckin enemies on all sides! And on a Saturday night, when they have nothin else to do down in fuckin Baile Atha Cliath, our compatriots come up for a laugh and cheap butter and petrol . . . Jasus! And what the fuck? The ol bastards do nothin but rob us, talkin about puttin in a few speed bumps to slow the tanks down. For fuck sake! "My Four Green Fields" and "It's a

Long Way to Tipperary" ... It sure must be with a fuckin knackered Hillman Hunter filled with fuckin Pakistani import tellys. I'm tellin ye, ye fuckin bastard, that ye're never goin to see the light of day again, ye cunt.' O'Malley let his tirade fade in his throat as he wiped snot from his nose in agitation.

They passed silently by one of the gabled end houses, glancing at a new mural of King Billy's ethereal white horse etched into the redbrick wall. It still smelt of whitewash in the misty air.

'Must have been yer wee friends, ah, Taig?'

Dermot moved penitently behind.

They moved silently through long winding streets filled with small houses that seemed strangely miniature. People always had a habit of tilting their heads when entering these houses, as if the ceilings were on their backs. But that only enhanced the warmth of the fires and the sizzling rashers and eggs.

Dermot had lived in these places all of his life. He was trying not to cry. He could see O'Malley was still fuming mad. He moved by his old buddy's house, remembering how Chancer Morgan had been the first of them to get a girl up near the graveyard when he was only fourteen. And he was the first to tell them about how he'd been with the lads when they got this fella's kneecaps with a Black and Decker. He disappeared when he was eighteen. Dermot never believed that his friend had moved to Boston.

They kept moving at a slower pace now. O'Malley was panting with effort.

In another street all the houses were again impeccably clean, cramped with children and old grannies and holy statues. There was a solitary orange light over a small sweet shop at the end of that row. Dermot caught the eye of a cat sitting in the mesh curtain of its window.

O'Malley recovered his senses. He had slowed to a dawdle. He turned on to Sean McDermot Street. O'Malley asserted himself, stiffened his jacket collar, and persevered onward. Dermot tagged behind, obscured from the full brunt of a blustering wind.

Suddenly, O'Malley stopped. An armoured car came swinging round a corner. Four soldiers flanked it on all sides, pointing their Armalites at invisible targets.

O'Malley stepped into the sweet shop and bought a pack of Sweet Afton tobacco.

The soldiers had passed when he came out, but he still felt unnerved, smoking in quick drags.

'Fuckin squaddies . . . '

Again, Dermot followed at a three-pace fall-back, saying nothing. He knew that O'Malley hadn't the tin box with him any more. It wasn't jingling.

Finally, O'Malley stopped, and his head turned slowly toward Dermot. His lips cracked a broad smile. He said nothing except for a laconic, 'We're here, cunt.'

And then O'Malley vanished down Pearse Lane, consumed by the blackness. Dermot said nothing and threw himself from the pooling light of the street. He was blind. His strained eyes distinguished nothing at first. Dermot panicked, lifted his hand to his face. He felt a slight tinge of horror as his thick nostrils inhaled the pervasive fetid alchemy of stale vomit and urine. He groped at the cold slimy walls and the clinging moss that suffocated the walls issuing forth pungent black water. Dermot's hand recoiled. Slowly, he edged along under the canopy of darkness, cursing the blackness. A profound surging impotency rose in his body.

'Where's the fuckin door?' O'Malley cursed in a muffled tone.

Dermot keenly listened to O'Malley and became aware of a murmuring conversation beyond him. Still, he could not distinguish the individual words, but he knew the content. Republicans spoke only one language in that lane. How curious the cryptic whispering seemed. It was as though the words existed by themselves, separate from the invisible speaker. Dermot didn't need to see the faces, for they were ingrained in the words themselves. Words! Words haunted the lane and swooned all those who dared to pass through it. The passion and rhythm of words, such sanctity and sanctuary for forlorn shadows cast against backdrops of crumbling grey houses . . . Dermot hated the words. They were a plague on his soul. Memories of murder murmured, rose and rioted in his splitting spilling head.

'Oh Christ!' he cried.

Dermot jumped with shock. A hot breath bathed his stricken face. He snapped from somnambulant consciousness. Dermot exhaled his sins and gained a curious equanimity. He sensed a presence before him. It breathed in his face, and then he heard spittle being turned. O'Malley was there, too, standing saying nothing. He leaned forward and spoke a single word to the figure. The two edged their way down a few steps and entered the crypt-like Wolfe Tone without demur.

As the black door flung open, O'Malley and Dermot cowered from the glare. Dermot winced as the sudden declamatory roar within the place pierced his cocked ears. O'Malley was gone. He had scurried in his rat fashion to the bar where he was downing a double shot of Paddy's. Dermot stood forlorn against the wall. He felt weak. Murdock saw the lad and eyed Riordon who nodded in acknowledgement. The lights were turned off, and the afterglow faded into oblivion. Murdock struck up a match and lit two large candles. Opposed to the charged riot of emotion, Dermot's gaunt face reeled with terror.

'Dermot, old son, step on over here!' Murdock thundered.

Dermot pulled himself from the wall and reluctantly advanced. The milling crowd of murmuring men parted like the Red Sea, leaving an unobstructed avenue to the awaiting Murdock. Dermot moved on. He could hear the hissing and coughing, feel the globs of phlegm spat from thrusting vicious contorted faces.

'Traitor, traitor!'

A boot shot out from the crowd, hitting Dermot in the crotch. He fell to the ground, ridden with goads of pain. Murdock rose from his chair.

'Who kicked the lad?' he demanded.

The crowd shifted. Suddenly Geary was expelled from the crowd which fast retreated, thereafter ceasing to move. Murdock's face was soothed by the naked shifting flame. In a composed manner, he stood apart from the vile brood of bobbing heads. Murdock cleared his voice and spoke in his familiar laconic tone.

'Geary, see Riordon immediately!'

He then directed his attention to the floor.

'Get up, Dermot!'

Murdock extended his arms. Out of his right sleeve popped a deformed stump of crimpled red flesh. Dermot screamed. Memories of his brother rushed into his brain. He choked in terror.

'Come, come!' cried Murdock with his arms outstretched.

Dermot winced, putting out his left hand. Simultaneously Murdock extended the right stumped arm.

Murdock let the sinews of sheer dominance rise in his heart, letting it culminate in a twitch of his stump. 'Give a hand, son, for a man who gave his hand for Ireland.' He gave a wink. That one was for religion. Murdock was judicious to a tee.

Murdock pursed his lips and stood with the proffered stump in mid-air waiting patiently. Dermot clutched the stump with all his might. He felt the callused deformity turning in his hand, and then quickly he retracted his fingers and toppled forward, barely catching himself from collapsing.

'Sit down, lad, here beside me. Did you have any problem getting away tonight?'

'O'Malley came for me.'

Murdock shrugged his shoulders. 'It's a dangerous city out there. Isn't that right?'

'Can I have a wee sip of whiskey?' Dermot asked.

Murdock turned, 'Get him a whiskey.'

'Now, do ye see that, whiskey for the asking. Are we all that bad, Dermot?'

'Me mother's gone mad.' Dermot sipped his whiskey.

Murdock shrugged his shoulders. 'A cigarette, Dermot?'

'Sean needs a hospital!'

'He'll be taken care of right enough.' Murdock moved away.

Dermot began to sob. 'Please, I swear to God I'm sorry. I done nothin wrong. It's not fair what ye done to our wee Sean. We did what ye asked.'

Murdock smiled to the dark faces staring at Dermot. Murdock listened with prescience. He had heard all these things before: the way twenty-year-olds finally lose their minds. Murdock let them talk on, ranting and raving, spilling their sins out as though in the confines of a confessional. But finally they stopped cold. And then there was silence. It was then and only then that Murdock assumed control once more.

Murdock raised his pint with his left hand and called the company to toast Ireland. He pawed Dermot's sunken head with his pulsing stump.

'God bless Ireland and her children!'

All glasses were raised high.

'God damn the traitors!'

All the glasses hit the table hard.

'God damn the traitors!' roared the crowd.

Dermot lowered his head.

Murdock's infamous trenchant voice gathered force, and so he began, 'I hear ye were picked up by the UDR. And now our Blakey is arraigned on rape and murder charges.'

Dermot had been picked up at Ryan's farm, miles from nowhere. He looked blankly at Murdock.

'You grassed on him, didn't ye?' Murdock shouted.

Balor stepped from obscurity into the pooling light. He loomed over Dermot, brandishing a two-foot rubber pipe.

'Remove his shirt!' Murdock ordered.

Balor tied a loose coil of wire around Dermot's neck, attaching the other end to his hooked finger. He jerked his finger and the wire sank in a red circle into Dermot's neck. The white of Dermot's eyes became lost in his head. He began gagging for air. Balor loosened the wire about Dermot's neck. The thin thread of wire dripped with blood. He took a stick and brought it down between Dermot's shoulder-blades. Balor shot the blunt black nose of the pipe beneath the ribcage, driving it up toward the left lung. Balor was after a ruptured lung. He listened for the tell-tale breathing signs.

Dermot coughed violently, spitting and drooling on himself. Balor let his eye search for specks of blood.

'Hold him up,' roared Murdock from beyond the glare of light. 'I don't want this, and ye don't want this, so come out with it now.'

'No more ... No more!' Dermot wailed, raising his hand pitifully into the air.

Balor stuck the hard handle of the hose under Dermot's armpit.

'Ah ... Ah ... ' Dermot screamed, shaking violently. O'Connor put his massive hand over Dermot's mouth, suffocating the screams. Blood from Dermot's mouth poured between O'Connor's fingers.

Balor stopped and winked. He could feel sweat running down his arm.

Murdock nodded in complicity. 'Let him alone.'

'No more,' Dermot spluttered.

'The truth!' Murdock whispered.

Balor waited with his arm cocked like an obedient dog.

'Some water for the boy,' Murdock said softly, motioning Balor.

Someone held a glass to Dermot's trembling lips. Dermot couldn't see the face. 'No more,' he kept whispering. 'I'm sorry! I'm sorry!' His eyes were swollen shut.

'Begin,' Murdock whispered.

'Water,' Dermot cried out.

Murdock ushered the glass away, a thread of blood wavering in the cool water. 'Later.'

He sat very still.

'Begin!'

Dermot felt the sting of a hand on his face.

'It . . . It . . . It were five o'clock when Sean set the bomb. You know?'

'What?' Murdock roared. 'Speak up, for God's sake.'

Dermot nodded. 'Sean tucked the bomb away in a cupboard for storin clothes . . . I kept tellin Blakey to stop fuckin around with this bird that was watchin . . . ah . . . Please.'

'Go on, will ye?'

'He kept givin her the eye. "Diversion," he said. Jasus Christ! He's to blame! I told him to cut it out. He wouldn't listen.' Dermot whined in pain. He could feel the rawness of his lip. A blow landed on his stiff fingers.

'Keep talking!'

'I . . . I . . . I told him to catch himself on. But she was watchin us like a hawk by then. And then she saw Sean comin . . . comin up from under the shelves. She pretended she didn't see what Sean had done . . . ' Dermot let his head loll on his swollen chest, trying to take small breaths. His lung had collapsed. There was a continual flow of blood from his nose. 'Gimme some water, please.'

'Give it to him.' Murdock walked back and forth. There was blood sticking to his shoes. He lit a cigarette. The rest of the crowd were still, not wanting to turn away for fear of someone looking at them crooked.

'She fooled none of us . . . Blakey put a gun into her spine. Jesus! I said, "Let's walk." Sean was goin m . . . ahah, ahah . . . ' Dermot cleared his throat, holding the blood in his mouth. 'I tried to tell Sean. It . . . It wasn't me at all!'

Dermot's swollen hands trembled.

'Wipe his face, for Christ's sake,' Murdock said, grinding his teeth.

Balor dug the pipe into Dermot's face. There was a crack of bone.

'Jasus! Fuckin leave him alone. Do you want him dead?'

Balor withdrew the handle of the rubber pipe, wiping it clean.

Dermot shuffled his lame leg in pain. A glass was put to his mouth. He coughed, swallowing hard.

'A soldier saw somethin was up with us. Sean moved away. He winked to me. He stopped at the sock rack and nicked a pair of socks, stuffin them under his coat.' Dermot tried to smile, but he couldn't. He let his head fall low.

'The soldier took the bait.'

'Speak up,' Murdock roared.

Another blow landed on Dermot's head. He cried woefully. 'I'm tellin you it all. Please stop. I'll die!'

'Keep talking,' Murdock insisted.

'I knew Sean would be taken to the main ... office and would ... get out. Routine shite! Me and him did what we could ... ' Dermot put his hands up imploringly. 'We did ... I went out to the car and there was Blakey on top of the girl. I fuckin went mad. You should have seen him!'

Dermot paused, his voice trailing softly, 'Why? Why? Why?'

Murdock waited pensively. 'Go on, go on.' He kicked the chair in agitation.

Dermot screamed.

'Come on, come on!' Balor said, trembling, the pipe fat and sweating in his hand.

He began slowly. 'The girl didn't budge when he got up. I didn't say a word. He couldn't have been ... Was there someone watching? You know, they put cameras into most of the parkin lots around the place. "Be calm man," he says to me. "I think she's dead." I nearly fuckin died.'

Dermot pointed into the distance. Everyone looked over their shoulders, except Murdock. That was what set him apart. He had a serene confidence in only his own world. He cared little for other lives.

'"Sean's been had by the law, and it's your fuckin fault!" I shouted. He was a bastard! "Get in there and see what's happenin. The bomb will be goin in an hour," I said. He started fumblin around with his trousers. Off he went, that bastard. Her throat was slit. I pulled her knickers to her waist as best I could. The blood just kept comin.'

Faces grimaced in the darkness.

'She had this holy medal hanging around her neck ... '

'Give over with the poetry,' Murdock grumbled.

Dermot pulled the medal from his coat pocket. Even Murdock stopped and took a breath before taking the medal away from Dermot.

'I ran down the way ... It was ten to six. I nearly fuckin died. I went mad. I couldn't believe it. Sean was standin by the shirt rack where the bomb was hid, soldiers askin him questions. There wasn't time. There were only minutes to go. "Four minutes to go! We'll have to run for it," Blakey said.'

There were long moments of silence, pensive faces nodding to one another, swirling their stout meditatively.

Dermot shivered.

'"How much was in that bomb?" "Enough," he said. There was a minute to go ... And then twenty seconds to go ... I was cryin. People were lookin at me. Blakey threw himself under the cash-register ... All them ol ones with curlers in their hair, and them babies and all ... Jesus Christ, have mercy on my soul! I ... I swear ... '

'He's a saint, by God. Give him a drink of holy water.' Murdock turned his eyes to heaven.

'I'm tellin how it was, Murdock! It's the truth.'

'Your truth,' someone shouted.

'I screamed to Sean that there were ten seconds to go. The soldiers dove to the floor. Sean dashed off.' Dermot threw his hands into the air. 'My brother! Oh God, he was done for.'

'Hold his hands behind his back,' Murdock whispered,

motioning for people to be quiet. 'What I want to know is what you said down at the station!'

Dermot felt the hairy roped loops twisting around his wrists.

'He needed a hospital! For Christ's sake! He could ... could have been saved. You didn't send a doctor! Jesus Christ! His leg was hangin off him.'

'You're a traitor!' Murdock shouted.

Dermot kept shaking his head furiously. 'I'm no traitor!'

Balor tied the wire hoop behind the chair. He shot a jab aimed at the heart, his open palm driving the handle straight into the chest cavity. Dermot lunged forward, blood streaming from his nostrils. The wire sliced the throat in a fresh-cut band. Dermot's heart was traumatized from the hit, the chest swelled in a huge convulsion. Balor walloped the kidneys with two sustained blows, and brought his own knee into the kidney. Urine trickled on to the floor. Dermot's chest turned blue and then a huge red mark visibly grew under the swelling skin. A sliver of skin hung off the neck. The pearly Adam's apple pushed through the neck wound. Murdock stepped back in fear that the heart was going to explode before everyone. The nipples swelled on the hairless chest. Dermot's eyes rolled in his head.

'Get that wire off his neck.'

Balor unhooked the wire. Dermot began convulsing on the floor. Three men tried to hold him down. His body kept bucking against them. Balor kicked his boot into Dermot's back. The body expelled a terrible liquid bile. They couldn't get a hold of the body because of the blood and urine all over the floor.

Murdock clenched a fistful of Dermot's sopping hair. 'Ye grassed to the UDR, ye cunt!'

'Take his trousers off.'

Balor beat his pipe all around Dermot's exposed groin, slipping in the urine with uncontrolled swings. He beat the small penis with the stick, crushing the testicles with the handle of the pipe with some erotic madness. The shaft of the penis filled with blood, getting big, the purple head shining. Balor was shouting and cursing, trundling the legs and knees. His face almost touched the penis as he slipped in the sticky blood.

'Leave him alone!' someone shouted. A man vomited and turned away.

'Jasus Christ, stop it, Balor!'

Murdock went silent. He was shivering to himself. 'Who said that?' He cast his small eyes on the shifting mass of faces. Everyone was looking at Dermot. His body heaved on the floor.

'Blakey deserves what he got!' another voice shouted.

'Oh, this is beautiful, isn't it just. Ye fuckin idiots. He told them everything. We'll be lucky if we see the light of to-morrow!' Murdock was spotted with blood. 'Ye know that Blakey isn't goin to take a rape charge. He's already started coughing up down there.'

O'Malley was talking away to a cluster of men. He was a great finger-pointer, always wagging a finger in people's faces. Six whiskey glasses gleamed in the light of a flickering candle. He was stripped of his skins. 'I said we should have killed him that first night.'

Murdock shook his head. 'Get that drunken bastard outta my sight.'

Everyone remained frozen.

Dermot turned his face with a terrible cry, 'Ye killed my brother!' The dying voice hung in the stifling air.

Balor tried to swing at Dermot, but one of the men held him back. He was shaking madly. 'Let me alone, fuckin get away.'

Murdock frowned. 'Get him a drink now.' He turned around. 'Do ye think that ye can all go back to your beds tonight and sleep easy with the likes of yer man here roamin about?'

'Send him off to America or somethin. Jasus, look at the

state of him.'

'Is this the kind of shite I have to listen to from mornin to night? Don't tell me ye don't know what sort of cunt this lad has been for years. He got his chances.' Murdock had his face in Mick Dolan's ear. 'Ye go right ahead there, mister, and we're dead men. We'll be fucked before ye can bat an eyelash. Then we'll see who's right and who's wrong from the bars of fuckin prison. Listen to me, mate, don't fuckin cross me.'

Murdock looked at the crowd of men. 'Am I the only sane man here?' He knew what they were thinking of: the walls of H-Block, years of going on the blanket, faeces smeared on British prison walls. Bullied in prison to be martyrs, bread and water, cameras flashing ... Rumours ... Didn't they feed Sands up for a year before the hunger? Always a fatted calf for the slaughter ... They knew who owned those prisons. Fighting for a cause that was its own worst enemy ... They had to obey or be killed. Why rebel? All because some boy wept over his brother? There were no free men left in Belfast City.

A slow chant rose from the men. The stink of fear grew.

Murdock was beaming. He was smiling a big wide smile like a dubious politician. 'Ye wee cunt!' laughed Murdock.

The latch on the back door swung open slowly, yawning. Dermot was only semi-conscious.

The brood was left to move about in the decaying candle-light.

Murdock sat back and bore an edifying expression. He had strengthened his position as leader, beaten the boy to a spluttered confession.

'There is the dilemma of Sean to be dealt with,' began Murdock in a soft whispering voice. 'He must already be targeted by the Brits. And then there's Eamon. Both lads will have to be seen to, indeed.'

Reilly raised issue with Murdock.

'Eamon is to be a priest. You can't kill him. It would be no less than political suicide. We're not the fuckin UVF, for fuck's sake.'

Murdock was furious. His moment of glory was snatched from him. A slow mounting murmur began.

'Eamon has no part in this. There's none of us here who are goin to touch him.'

The gathering threw up a unanimous, 'Leave him off!'

Murdock rose, his composed languor gone. Fear burned fiercely in Murdock's eyes, although he tried to mask it with a deliberating nod of the head. He riveted his attention on Reilly.

'So be it, Reilly, the priest lives. But ye mark my words that if he talks ye answer for it.' Murdock took mental note of the dissenters.

O'Connor and Scully wheeled about, shut the door behind them, and stepped into the misty chill early-morning air. The orders had been given to break Sean's neck. He was to have a priest administer the last rites before the final crack. Murphy had concocted a plan to get the priest over. Then and only then could the killing proceed. It was Irish custom.

Dermot was tense, shifting about like an animal hearing the rattle of the slaughterhouse, keenly aware of carnage and squeals, frantically grimacing at the smell of stale meat. He was breathing fitfully. His clothes were sopped with blood.

Redden removed the black hood, unveiling Dermot's petrified face. A ray of light from a naked bulb beyond cut Dermot's face in two. Redden shuddered and replaced the hood quickly. He was unnerved by the expression of helplessness. Redden put his hands in his pockets and squirmed them against his thighs. His breath was a heavy mist rising into the unseen sky. The face had flashed before him, Dermot's eyes stark and wide, streaming with tears, the nose massively swollen. Redden shuddered and walked away.

*

The blue Cortina pulled to an abrupt halt opposite the redbrick-faced façade of tumbling tenements. Scully and O'Connor approached the O'Brien household as their feet slapped the wet road and echoed about the place. O'Connor knocked on the door. The two silhouettes waited patiently still. Nobody came. Scully kicked the door. The hall switch flicked on. The hall seemed to shimmer with dancing light. O'Connor shivered in the raw naked aspect of the light. The mother's awkward form twisted in the translucent undulated glass of the front door. The lock clicked. The two figures pushed their way into the hall. The mother turned. Her battered body vanished. Four empty milk bottles stood like stoic sentries in the porch.

Eamon stood on the landing, stiff and frantic. He crept across the creaking floor.

Murdock made haste with his business at the Wolfe Tone. One thing was for sure: Christmas was to be filled with presents. Over twenty bombs had been planned. Murdock gulped back his black stagnant stout. A car patiently purred in the ebony beyond. Murdock rose, donned his cap and subsequently vanished into the night.

Eamon pushed open the door. Streaks of silvery light spilled from under the door and crept across the floor to confront and set the opposite mildew-ridden wall aglow with diffused pinkish light. The tiny bedroom seemed even smaller at dawn. Eamon stood by the edge of the bed, Sean's mangled body so etiolated and white. Sean had not seen sunlight in over two weeks. The curtains had been drawn since he had been banished to decay and death in the dark, dreary back room. Sean's gaunt face bore no malice. A pathos of pity, his sunken eyes, drowned in glossy brimming pools, begged for forgiveness and deliverance. A white film covered the cold cup of tea adjacent to the bed, and a green mold had spread spores on the two stale pieces of bread beside the tea. Sean lifted his frail left arm and extended it toward Eamon. The H-Block inanition had Sean a veritable skeleton. Eamon peeled the sheet from Sean's flesh. He gripped Sean's arm, simultaneously taking a bottle of Knock holy water from his pocket. Sean's hand fell back; he knew death and salvation were at hand.

'In the name of the Father, and the Son, and the Holy Ghost!' began Eamon.

He sprinkled the holy water about Sean's mutilated flesh. Crystal tears poured forth from Sean's bloody eyes. Tears flowed off his face, drenching his black coarse hair. He sobbed passionately on. Eamon cried bitterly as he witnessed his brother confront death. There was poignancy in salvation, but a tragic regret at the end of a spent life. Sean closed his eyes and bit into his swollen purple lower lip. Eamon grabbed at the pillow, propping Sean's head up, jerking it violently. He smothered his brother's head. The rusty bedsprings, ancient and abrasive, sagged and ground a fine ash-brown powder. Sprinkling dust lightly blanketed the floor. Sean's body contorted, stricken and writhing.

The rocking springs heralded Eamon's grave malice to the assassins-in-waiting.

'What's that noise?' queried O'Connor. The mother fumbled her beads all the while and said nothing.

Sean's butchered leg bled profusely. The hot crimson congealed upon the cool, clinical whiteness of the sheets. Eamon pressed his face against the pillow. An amorphous fear infected his soul. The muffled noise, the frantic efforts of a man's futile gasps at forbidden air were horrid. The bed ceased to grate. Sean's body lay limp. There was a profound silence, save for the oozing pool about the stub of grotesque flesh. Eamon removed the pillow. Sean's chest exhaled in one last mechanical motion and sank like a droning accordion. Eamon's face was ashen and flexed. Eamon was crying bitterly in the cold purple silk of his vestments. He envisioned all those doleful marble statues at the parish church, and they were whispering and making the candles flutter, calling another Catholic son to Jesus.

The mother heard the silence above and thanked God for deliverance. The two men, finally aware of what had transpired, darted for the stairs.

'That fuckin bastard.' O'Connor felt a pang of anger. 'He's done it!'

Scully dropped to his knees inside the room, panting and crossing himself.

The room of the dead consumed his soul and then vomited back a profoundly mad, impotent fool left reeling on the damp hardwood floor.

A pervasive fetid air had Redden double over. He threw up chunks of half-digested potato and meat. Saliva dangled from his lips. On a distant tenement wall, there was more graffiti:

ONE FAITH/ONE CROWN
IN GOD OUR TRUST
NO SURRENDER

'Oh Jasus,' he moaned.

He wavered toward the gridiron gate and collapsed. It was nearing three o'clock in the morning. The abattoir was asleep. Hanging chains clinked against steel gates. The wind was cold and damp.

Murdock stepped from the car. 'It's decided that he's not gettin the hood at all. I have some boys comin on up to finish him off.'

Redden nodded his head. 'Okay then.'

Murdock put his hand on Redden's back. 'Ye go on off home.'

The warm body lay forlorn in the middle of the stockyard as the ragged bloody hood fluttered in the sweeping morning air. Murdock held Dermot by the hair. 'A bullet's too good for the likes of ye.'

Two men dragged Dermot into the back of a car. Murdock didn't even look back, just shouted, 'Have done with it quick.'

Dermot had his face buried in the fat man's stomach. He was clawing helplessly at the man's arms. 'Please . . . '

The car jerked away from the slaughterhouse. The fat man stuck a screwdriver into Dermot's bloody leg. Dermot screamed and Norris held his face. 'Go on, will ye.' The fat man's body was jiggling all over. 'Hold him steady.' The screwdriver sunk into the naked leg again, lacerating a vein. Blood squirted against the window. The fat man grunted with effort. His face was sprayed in tiny dots of blood. He felt the screwdriver hit a bone in the leg and left it there. He took a hammer from a box by his side and landed deep thuds into Dermot's head. The forehead split open and dark entrails oozed down the face.

The car turned down another road, moving under a flood of lights. 'What the fuck are ye doin?' Norris shouted. 'Drive it steady.'

'Army checkpoint back there. We'll go on a wee bit. Aren't ye finished yet? And listen on. Don't fuck up that seat, do ye hear.'

The fat man stopped hammering the head for a few moments. He looked at the soft green of the dash panel. The driver was hunched over the wheel listening to the radio, scanning the road. The fat man wiped blood off his face. He could see the streetlamps covering the street in a faint orange glow. The street was lined with murals of soldiers and tanks, littered with stones and broken bottles. The car passed by a line of abandoned bricked-up houses. A girl was walking alone. He could see the wind blowing her hair about the paleness of her face. Suddenly, the fat man snapped his head back and brought the hammer down on the head again.

Norris let the body slump off his legs and stuck a penknife into the throat. The knife gleamed in the passing lights. Norris kept at the throat. The blade broke in the neck on some bony knob. 'Fuckin hell.' He couldn't cut through the last tough muscles. A flap of skin babbled over the trachea, frantic gasps of air spouting bubbles of blood and mucus. The effulgence trickled down into the concave of the throat, pooling in the navel. Norris could feel his fingers in the hot pink meat of the throat. Blood satiated the muscles. His arm burned with effort. He kept at the slick orifice, climbing all over the seat. The serrated knife ground at the bone deep in the throat. The back of the car rocked gently, cradling the three bodies. The windows were teared with a cool rain. The windshield blades squeaked.

The two men could feel the slow turning of the wheels. Glass crackled under the wheels. Cold street railings slashed the car in bars of lights. Norris stared at the fat man. Both their faces were contorted with fatigue. Dermot's head was bloated beyond all recognition, almost twice its size, skin tearing away at the cheeks. The forehead blistered in welts from the hammer. His eyes were tiny in the sockets, shimmering and weeping. A blackish blue colour began to set under the skin.

'Keep it down,' the driver whispered. The car moved silently in the night.

The fat man was grunting away, beating away at hidden organs. A copious amount of faeces flowed out of Dermot's anus. Norris kept stepping in it. 'Let me at it,' the fat man shouted. 'Ye don't know what the fuck yer doin.' He took a chisel and punctured the throat. The chisel stuck in the plastic seat at the nape of the neck. Blood poured out the dark hole of Dermot's mouth. The chisel stabbed into the forehead, cutting the soft grey matter of the brain in a crude lobotomy. He tore away at the lobes of the brain, scraping the chisel back and forth. The entire body twitched with the last impulses of life. Blood poured into the white of the eyes. The fat man farted with excitement, rocking away on the back seat, grinding the chisel further into the brain. Norris began laughing, mimicking the convulsing body. The fat man pulled the chisel out of the head and smeared sticky bits of flesh on old newspaper. The smell of blood and faeces filled the car.

Norris rolled the window down, putting his face to the cold rain. When the car pulled over, the men sat in the dim light, breathing hard. The fat man was wiping his mouth with the back of his sleeve. He was smiling to himself, shaking with thrills of energy. The massive pumpkin head lolled on the half-severed neck by his side. An eye hung out of the head like a wet oyster.

At seven o'clock Conroy darted from the front seat of the coffin car. He dragged Dermot's stiff body to a wooden lamppost. The head was precariously balanced on the shoulders, hanging by a ribbon of red muscle. The fat man had cut the testicles off the body and packed them into the mouth. The bloody balls clotted the mouth with a wisp of pubic hair and shrivelled skin. Conroy tied the body to the post, then scurried back to the car, and was gone in an instant.

Nobody dared to venture outside. Old women peeped between their curtains. They circled their windows with hot sticky palms as they exhaled long warm pensive breaths. A few radios droned. A crow pecked away at the black wound in Dermot's neck. By the time the Army arrived, someone had already stolen the Doc Martins off the corpse's feet.

THE ENEMY

THE SIGN READ: 'Murphy's Pants are Down Again.'

Not even the children laughed. They were moist from the heavy air, their faces pink with the drizzling rain. The young girls' hair smelt of sweet lacquer. The strong cups of tea, cream-cakes, and chicken sandwiches hadn't been enough to fight the outside cold. Now the greyness fell in a mist of cool rain, making the road gleam and the lights refract in shop windows. The snaking mass of faces moved with an array of umbrellas and upturned collars, dripping newspapers above their heads spilling inky words down bent necks. The children imitated the curses of their fathers under their breath, feeling the dampness squelching between their feet. A half-moon was already moving into the sky, huge and languid, as though punctured by the steel spiral of a church. Most of the shops were already closing for the evening. There was talk of the flu going around. Phlegm festered on the paths.

'Filthy night,' a fat-ankled cleaning lady coughed from the small confines of a small room, towelling the rain from her hair, her mottled arms jiggling on her bones. She looked down the long corridor at the shower of sprinkling light in the hanging chandelier.

Three men in stiff blue suits surveyed the milieu of women. 'Hurry on now, ladies. Tea and biscuits in five minutes.'

The cashiers seemed to disregard the men who impercept-

226

ibly rocked themselves in their shoes in smug satisfaction at being paid to pass immodest glances on another sex.

Piles of pound notes were piled on the varnished counters. Parsimonious-faced old ladies watched young girls count and recount and tot up totals again and again before handing the day's takings over.

Mr Moran moved toward the ladies with ascetic reserve, silently raising his long index finger to his purple lips. He possessed the unnatural ability to influence even the inanimate. His eyes transformed not only the women's personalities; he could assign meaning to objects. Things were either good or bad, based upon his moods. It was something beyond words, though it registered on the day's receipts.

Godwin struggled with a mannequin in the window front of the shop. His wrinkled face contrasted with the beige smoothness of the plaster. He wore an aged tweed jacket, with a V-necked pullover underneath. His neck and head seemed an afterthought of his shoulders, pinched into being with a fastidious knot of his black tie. Some of the girls watched him as he waltzed with the stiff creature, ignominiously attempting to pull a pair of tweed pants about the symmetrical buttocks. An arm came off in his hand. Godwin reeled in weakness, compromising the mannequin, leaving it alone with its pants about its knees. He saw people grinning at the mannequin, as though it had done this sort of bravado of its own accord. He felt a vague regret, his flesh drained of blood. They were not looking at him at all. He was some unobtrusive crepuscular creature who came in the night and changed things, insignificant things, and was gone, and nobody ever thought to wonder about him and his kind. He turned from the damp blackness of the outside world, his watery eyes smiling as he stooped forward into the closeness of the shop, nodding with a certain strained congeniality. 'Tomorrow, tomorrow ...' he whispered, raising all three arms in exasperation just to make the young girls smile.

In the depths of his small crypt he had a store of limbless

bodies, decapitated, armless, legless, without eyes, hair, missing fingers, with chipped faces and broken noses, all with rigid brown lips and no navels. There were men and women, more androgynous than not, and small dwarf progeny with tiny plastic fingers and spotty cheeks. Godwin placed the arm among a heap of appendages. He always felt a giddy terror when faced alone with these strewn corpses, the indignant faces eyeing him.

The outer lights were dimmed, and tea was served in three inornate metal jugs. A small sampling of assorted biscuits was set forth in such a manner that each woman had to step from the congregation and choose her biscuit in a rite of sub-servience. The older ladies obliged themselves by going last, thereby ensuring that they would have the pick of the biscuits. In truth, there was no choice in the matter. Each biscuit had already been claimed before it ever left the bakery, indeed before it was even made. Mrs Foxworth was claimed to have once said she'd have preferred 'to eat arsenic than to swallow another shortbread biscuit again', yet she now had risen in rank, commanding that sublime coconut marsh-mallow, the aspiration of six long years of her life. Ironically, she found that she detested the thing, as it was 'like eating fuckin cotton wool'.

The sobering influence of the regiment of 'no sugar please, Ma'am' tea-stirring gentlemen kept conversation to the drab inventory of recounting big sales and the humble respect of being so well cared-for within the established organization. Only the eldest spinsters dared to dip a biscuit into tea. Everyone knew they had weak gums and false teeth. Allow-ances had to be made for age. The younger women drank their tea anxiously, nibbling their biscuits, not wanting to finish before or behind anyone else. Mr Straight circulated like a cold draught among the women. 'You sold that umbrella, then, to that gentleman this afternoon, then?' seemingly abridging a before-mentioned question.

He extended his arms in almost mechanical reverie. 'Ah yes, we'll survive this bad patch all right.' His pale face suffused with blood, and a ripple of flesh ran down his buttery chin. When he had finished, his arms obediently came to his sides once more.

Godwin ascended from the confines of his crypt, bustling his small body with the thrust of his little piston legs. His life was a series of quick entrances and quick exits. He made no impression other than that he was in perpetual motion, a sort of insignificant comet of uselessness. People set their lives, not like a clock by him, but against him. To the younger girls, he was that horrible abortion of what life could be if youth were lost without love.

Godwin suffered all this, yet he never failed to appear for this tea. He stopped and surveyed the tray of biscuits, eyeing the chocolate-covered biscuit, defying anyone to touch it. Godwin sometimes supposed that his biscuit would actually bite if it were touched by some marauding hand. He animated his body with nods of his head to all the ladies. 'Mrs Badger, this tea is excellent. Don't you think so ladies?' He hadn't even touched a drop.

Mr Moran retained a stately indifference through the episode, with his finger hooked in the ear of his cup. He had been in the employment of the shop for over twenty-six years, and as yet he was a man of only thirty-nine years. The primness of his bony face and hooked nose spoke of a long attrition which he had experienced in fighting notions of staleness and slothfulness. He was conscious that his life was not measured in days, weeks or years, but in decades. In his breast pocket he had a watch which, he was proud to say, he had never wound since the day he started with the shop. He lived for death, the death of other senior employees. He kept a secret record at his home of the three principal fellows who could stop his advancement for so many years. He called them the monsters. At Christmas and other inconspicuous occasions, birthdays and such, he was forever giving the monsters lavish continental items wholly impractical for the wetness and briskness of the Dublin Bay. One Christmas he supplied each of the monsters with shaggy Irish wolfhounds, thus forcing the good fellows to brace the snap of winter. With a check of his watch, Mr Moran moved toward the small table and announced, 'the five forty-eight bus for the South Circular Road will be coming in approximately six minutes.' He ushered the ladies along toward the sink, touching their elbows to move the procession quickly.

The women swallowed the dregs of their tea, helping one another into their respective coats with a 'Good night, sir,' here and there, the flash of a smile passing from the younger girls on Peter Timmons who had given a certain 'you know who' a silk scarf from Paris.

The men, Godwin included, stepped back and let the cackling ladies brush and push one another toward the small exit door at the back of the shop.

The walls on either side of the women were lined with an ornate Gothic black wooden shelving, stocked with inventories of non-perishable goods, jumpers and tweeds, caps and gloves, woolly underwear, and corsets, with other shelves stocked with tins of Christmas biscuits and holiday wrapping-paper, with the occasional shelf of toys, tin soldiers, cannon guns, bows and arrows, Indian headdresses. Everything on these shelves was above the reach of the tallest man in the city. Rather an extravagant railway of ladders and pulleys ran on rails all around the shop. This elaborate network of ropes and ladders would have hampered even the most adroit of monkeys. With such a system, none too few women had fallen off these contraptions, sustaining broken legs, dislocated shoulders and hips, concussions, and bruises to the general vicinity of the head and chest. The owner was proud to announce to detractors of his contraption that, in his memory, mouth-to-mouth had never been administered. He was forever professing there were 'deciding principles' at work which only he fully understood. On one occasion, a certain Miss Scallop slipped and hung by her left ankle, exposing the full extent of her glorious ankles and the ample whiteness of her smooth thighs. She had been fully compensated, though, as the middle-aged son of the owner, previously contemplating a life of celibacy, took a fancy to such acrobatics, marrying her forthwith and thus avoiding scandal and legal proceedings. However, on the whole, such freak incidents still amounted to a lesser expense than the maintenance of an inventory within arm's reach.

'Well, that's that then, thank God,' Mr Moran groaned with a certain intended levity. The three men began gathering the cups ringed with the red-lipped imprints of the women. 'Jasus Christ!' The men rolled up their sleeves, Mr Moran swirling the cups in the sudsy water, Mr Straight drying, Peter Timmons putting the cups into a small wooden crate until the morning tea. 'New rule.' Mr Moran grated his teeth. 'No lipstick till the tea is all drunk. Are we agreed?'

'Right-o.' Peter Timmons rolled his eyes. 'You're goin to tell em that? You know, now, you'll have to reorganize the entire closing procedure.'

Mr Straight rejoined. 'Oh yes, Mr Moran. The biscuits will have to be opened now at five twenty-two, with the water goin on the boil at five twenty-five, the cups scalded at five thirty-one . . .'

'Will ya shut yer face!' Mr Moran shook his head, unable to reckon with the repercussions of a single action.

'Please.' Mr Straight proceeded. His inert eyes surveyed Peter Timmons. Mr Straight possessed a resolute equanimity whereby he could condemn a man to death and yet still shake his hand as though it were nothing personal on his side or the man's side. Rather, it was something quite different. He viewed human inadequacy as something innately biological, a function of all living things. It just so happened that he, in his capacity as shop manager, had taken an irreligious responsibility to define good from evil for the benefit of commerce and other less sublime philosophies, such as keeping the peace. 'How much takins today?' he whispered.

'Close on twelve hundred quid,' Mr Moran replied, letting his fingers trail in the cold water.

'Not bad, not bad.' Mr Straight nodded his head. 'It's gettin harder these days to get anyone to part with anythin at all.'

'Isn't it just. This place has it down, though. A balance of youth and wisdom is what a place like this needs. You only get two types of women in this world: Peacocks and Owls.' Mr Moran extended his head forward, the leanness of his jaw coming to an angular point. His life was a series of rehearsed sentences.

'And what about the ones in-between?' Peter Timmons beamed a smile.

'Wives? Jasus. Good-for-nothin hoors.'

'Wait till the wife hears she's a hoor.' Peter Timmons shook his head gravely, suppressing his laughs.

'Ya stupid bastard. Mind yer place, bucko. Don't think we don't know what ya got up to with the Daly trollop.' Mr Moran stopped himself abruptly and left with the cold basin of dirty water. There was a tear in his left eye. He had invested his life on a principle of wilful subordination which he thought others could never mistake for servility as much as for resolute power, a kind of pent-up rage. He was a creature bound to an instinct for self-preservation which would mitigate violence and even worse things if he were so challenged.

'I'll walk with you to the bus, Mr Straight.' Mr Moran came back and moved with slow deliberation, inspecting the glass cabinets for fingerprints, running his fingers along the mahogany shelves, checking for dust.

Godwin still supped his tea. He kept his small mug in his crypt. He never saw the need to wash his own cup. Rather he believed that the residue of sugar in the bottom of the cup was what gave his tea, above all other cups of tea, that distinctive sweetness. Mr Moran approached and gave the kettle to Godwin without exchanging words. He was still shaking, his soft hands withered and red from the coldness of the water.

Godwin received the kettle with a nod of his head. During the late nights he often stopped his solitary work and put the kettle to boil. Immediately he turned his head away and stared toward the shop window at the mannequin with its pants down around its ankles. He knew he would have to remedy that after he'd gone to the docks for the shop's inventory of plaster and wigs for the mannequins.

'I'll leave you to it then, Godwin.' Mr Straight tipped his cap with discriminating intent, not letting his eyes rest on the man he addressed. 'And see to that spectacle before morning.' His long arm cut through the easy gloom of the soft lights, pointing to the display window.

Godwin let this incontrovertible face proceed as it had done for so many years and did what was expected of him, which was nothing, not even the utterance of words. The three men moved off in a slow procession toward the back exit door, the low murmur of the conversation between Mr Straight and Mr Moran severe and on the subject of the rain. Peter Timmons followed without his naïve smile, with his hands buried in his long brown coat.

Godwin locked the door behind the three dark figures as they disappeared into the cold night air. He could feel the tea in his stomach warming his chest and back. He turned and faced the gloomy aspect of the shop, with the small bulbs glowing in the polished wooden-framed display cabinets. The brass running bars gleamed and smelt of a rich potpourri of herbal odour. He was never awed by the plush spectre of the fine silks and linens draped and folded in green velvet-backed cases. He did not care or even pass judgement on the extravagances of this macabre gloom. He was not one to worry about the implications of the distribution of wealth between people. He had clothes on his back. He gave at Mass with modest generosity. He saw nothing implicitly wrong with the conspicuous grandeur of the shop, rather he had a religious understanding that the world consisted of 'haves and have-nots.' And really, when all was said and done, didn't he have a pot of marmalade stashed away in his cupboard at home?

Slowly Godwin moved through the shop. He participated within its mechanism without conviction of its reality. He saw no use in such things as gold-buckled shoes, or white pearly earrings, and umbrellas with sculptured duck heads for handles, or silver monogrammed money clips. He had resigned himself to his nocturnal life many years ago. He'd believed that there were only two chances in life: birth and marriage. He had been unlucky in both ventures. Of course the option of marriage was inextricably tied to the physical manifestation of youthfulness. He had never called himself ugly, yet his youth was a series of unmitigated disasters, not least of which was the ridiculous spectacle of his mere five-foot four-inch height. By the age of twenty-three he knew his fate.

He had spent ten years adumbrating and reconciling himself to a life lived in the company of his mother. Of course that was a great service, no doubt, to serve a mother above one's own interest. It was a pass to the afterlife. The word 'mother' encapsulated all the horror of those early years. 'Yes, mother. No, mother.' He felt the sympathetic breaths of his mother. She would of course have died with dignity all by herself. She was not infirm. That was the initial problem, inflicting age and decrepitude on his mother's body so as to resurrect his own significance at home. He managed the problem with generous intent. The ladies of the street forever saw his face and hands flecked with bits of dough, or his hair whitened with flour. People said he made the best brown bread on the street and could boil you an egg, soft, medium, or hard, without even the aid of a timer. He had an innate maternalism that old ladies envied. He'd mastered that trick of life with simplistic exactness. Leaving windows open at night had been his mother's downfall. A light wheezing sniffle had crept down her throat to her chest where it set up shop. She was told by Catholic and atheistic doctors alike that there was no hope. He'd spared nothing in her final half-hour of need. It rained holy water. He learned that a lot of afflicting agony could be pawned off on the Hand of God. When it was all said and done, the authorities never suspected foul play. Of course, it was all in his head. As they were so fond of saying in Dublin, 'She died of a fever, and no one could save her.' And that was the way it went, when all was said and done. Godwin had been a model son, and his apple tarts were truly magnificent.

Godwin plugged the kettle into the wall and made a small jug of tea, heaping a few teaspoonfuls of tealeaves into the jug. He checked the clock above the entrance door. He had to be down at the docks by half seven. He sipped the tea, moving toward the front window. A silent panorama of forlorn faces moved silently under his eye. He possessed a disdainful curiosity, peeking out into the window of city life. The wind bore a cold stinging rain, but when was it not raining in Dublin? A young boy walked by in the filthy blackness, self-consciously running his fingers through his hair. Across the street, the tall jeweller pulled down his steel shutters with a hooked pole. A plump young girl stood all alone, drenched in the falling rain, waiting for that married boss who would not be coming to see her now. How long was she going to stand there, freezing under the steaming lamplight?

He walked back to his dark crypt of dismembered mannequins. He rinsed the outer rim of brown tea strains from his cup under a cold dribbling tap. There was still forty minutes yet before he had to be down at the docks. The small room was a cold oblong space with a slanting ceiling of creaking boards. Small slits of light pierced the darkness during the day, exposing the thick air filled with falling particles of dust and crumbling wood. Along the walls were a series of rickety shelves filled with mesh artefacts shaped into ovals. The rudimentary heads were in various stages of development. The mesh torsos were built around long slender poles which ran from the floor, through the buttocks, rounding out in semicircles of pliable tin which served to give shape and contour to the mesh heads. Each of the torsos was flecked in a tapestry of cloths collected from poor-boxes. The cloth was wet and stripped around the mesh frame, basted with a granular flesh-coloured substance like putty. The rank smell of the mixture filled the room with a stifling odour akin to sour dough. In numerous jars eyeballs glinted, some open, others with lids closed like polished snails. The scant strips of eyelashes in another container passed for spider legs.

Godwin set himself at his dishevelled desk and surveyed the progress of his three present creations. Two of them remained headless, the third without arms, a head pocked with the unfinished putty, devoid of eyes and a proper mouth. Godwin stared at the dark holes in the head. He thought of working with the cavity of the nostrils. That was where he initiated all cosmetic manipulation. A strong-bridged Roman nose demanded green eyes; sapphire eyes blazed above the gentle exhalation of a petite nose. Quietly he lit a match. A clean blue flame of gas purred gently on the tip of a short metal canister. He held the flame close to the hidden cavities of the mannequin with the rudimentary head. The holes seemed to inhale the light. The pale orange head glowed softly. The applied fleshy paper had dried in stiff clots, the putty mixture flaking to his touch. It needed more time to dry. Godwin extinguished the blue finger of gas. He thought of the menacing face of Mr Moran admonishing him with that wagging finger he was forever pointing at subordinates. He had asked for a heater for the crypt to dry out the mannequins, yet his words had passed unheeded. He had learned to work with a certain economy of expression which fell short of what he expected and what he knew his hands were capable of producing.

Godwin hated the solitude and vacant expressions of

these creatures. He hadn't a hand to shape the nuances of a refined aristocratic brow or the understanding that composition centred not on size and prodigious bulk, but rather lent itself to the subtleties of slight imperfection, the crooked aspect of a finger or the crescent darkness of an anaemic girl. Faces he called faces, hard faces, round faces, but mostly male faces or female faces, child faces ... corpulent bodies, squat bodies, lean bodies like scarecrows ... These were the generic categories he knew and worked with. God forbid he should create a Mona Lisa who would look so bloody ridiculous in a white bauneen sweater. No, he knew that his creatures' forms were subjugated to some principle other than human likeness.

Outside, the long narrow road curved off toward Grafton Street. Godwin waddled through the oily puddles, sidestepping the rushing tributaries of rain carrying the city's rubbish of newspapers and paper bags. A lost glove crept silently in the darkness like an octopus along with sundry other wayward objects funnelling toward slurping drains. There were few people about, as the buses were running less frequently at this hour. Godwin felt the muted lull in the somnambulent hours of this inactivity. Dark ribbons of smoke rose into the unseen sky. The city and its outlying districts had stopped for bodily sustenance. He pictured kitchen tables spread with chipped cups of pale rose and the vacant plates, with the gigantic jugs of milk harassing squat salt and pepper sentries. This ritual had some sentient unconsciousness that sobered these Dubliners like no other people. He understood that food was a fetish for a nation that had known starvation and famine. His mother had lived in the hot steamy eroticism of boiling cabbage and ribs, serving the watchful eyes of her husband and children. There was a sublimated violence in all those smiling Irish eyes, and in the bleeding face of Jesus nailed above the table. And Jesus, all those grinning false teeth of grannies in murky glasses of water, chomping mutely before wide-eyed children. He could see it now, the silver serrated knives, the bent pronged forks, tarnished with age and spit, the soupspoons and teaspoons, the bread knives all there to conquer and manipulate, a sort of culinary armour for sophisticated Catholic minds.

He walked past the ironic cool green Protestant lawns of Trinity College. Who were they fooling? He shuffled across to the meridian in the centre of the street, dwarfed by the grey elephantine pillars of the Bank of Ireland with her bullet marks from the 1916 rising. The rain soaked into his heavy black coat, the rim of his cap ringed in a crown of rain droplets. He stared down at the bleeding coloured chalk murals on the flagstones, still etched with the face of the round-spectacled Joyce and the snug woolly-jumpered Beckett, and the lunatic eyes of Yeats looking up women's skirts.

He let a faint smile pass across his face. A slow cessation of feeling numbed his raw cheeks and exposed hands. He stopped in the sheltered alcove of a shop front, fumbling for a cigarette. He let a match flare in his cupped hands. He gave a sudden jolt of fear when he raised the match to his mouth, a halo of yellow light falling on a myriad of stark alabaster mannequins. He let the flickering match drop from his fingers and proceeded, the dot of red ash tracing its way through the darkness from his waist to his puckered face.

A patchwork of streetlights and solitary bulbs in upper flats came into view as he made progress toward O'Connell Street Bridge. There were a few shops still open, mostly sweet shops with bleached packages of Corn Flakes and Weetabix, with well-wishing cards, and Mass cards yellowed with age, rows of orange-cellophaned bottles of Lucozade covered with dust. Godwin bought the *Evening Press* from a slumbering old maid who nodded her flaccid head to some unfathomable question. He just left the coins jingling on the counter. He stared for a moment at a crude subliminal lottery of the Catholic church, confronting the imploring face of a white saint holding a black infant child on a small collection box. The radiant white saint seemed to beg the Irish conscience to intercede in darkest pagan Africa. There were black rosary beads for sale behind the counter, pink for little girls, pale blue for toffee-mouthed communion boys with cash stuffed in their pleated shorts. And ignominiously vying with cans of Seven-Up and Canada Dry were the figurines of Holy Mary filled with non-carbonated holy water. It was said that you could buy eternal salvation in any sweet shop in Dublin.

He left quietly. The bitter odour of vinegar assaulted his nostrils as he passed the roar of some Italian turning a blistering vat of chips. He stopped for a moment and stared at the steaming steak and kidney pies, then turned away with a raw hunger.

The dark artery of the Liffey flowed silently toward the dockyards of Dublin Bay. Strings of lights flickered and glowed on unseen wires looped between the streetlights. The black waters reflected the cold night lights. Godwin left the aroma of the restaurants and clusters of smoking people. He walked under Tara Street Railway Bridge, hearing the throaty coo of unseen pigeons, smelling the wet excrement and feathers. Further alongside the river, everything smelt of dank grain, the wet effulgence of the air filled with the hazy dust of maize and Indian corn. Images came like apparitions slowly materializing before his eyes. He gave a strong cough, thumping his chest, spitting out a thick glob of spit. His feet made hardly any noise under the softness of the grain bedding. The granite stones of the river wall smelt of musky algae, the dark magical seaweed of Plurabelle's soft hair wavering in the shallow water. He stopped and felt the furred mildew on the rounded wall, breathing in the effulgence of something feminine. The river was low, drained by the unseen sea-water at Howth Head. There were old tyres and bicycles, and the occasional pram caught in the dredged slime of the blackish muddy bottom.

Godwin looked back toward the arched skeleton of the Half Penny Bridge near the Four Courts. It glittered against the dark channel of the river. They'd been planning to build an art museum over the Liffey, there on the bridge, but nothing had come of it. The Liffey portrayed a city life that spoke more keenly to the senses of Dublin souls. Beneath him, the rainbow of oiliness of excrement and commerce moved with slurred speech, telling itself jokes. Godwin knew that Dubliners' lives centred on the efficacy of something else. Dublin was a city of myths and stories, of ruddy-faced poor measuring life by the strength of handshakes, religious zeal by the number of children in a family. The city nourished itself in the small squat pubs filled with drunken men. It created its own life, not in the sophisticated solitary vigils of Parisian Bohemian painters, but in the pissed signatures of bleary-eyed poets on back-street walls. Dublin was the only city in the world where you could get beaten up by a true genius.

Godwin turned his head, aware of the distant cries of babies, hearing the howls of perishing dogs in doorways, with the rumbling murmur of pubs always in his ears. Slowly, he tipped his head to the majesty of the river that had reckoned with the transient civilizations of Vikings, English, and Irish alike through the centuries.

Godwin turned away, the river still flowing quietly onward with ubiquitous intent. As he walked, he sidestepped the slick entrails of fish guts and shining fish heads. There were old crates strewn everywhere. Blanched heads of cabbages and cauliflowers withered in the cold puddles of water. Blackened potatoes decayed in spongy mush. Godwin stopped and stared at old weighing-scales rocking back and forth, measuring some invisible commodity. The tropical fruits from the day's markets were already losing their verdant brilliance, seeding the brown sludge of the swirling drainage waters, the long black tongue of the Liffey curling this feast towards its waters.

He moved by the silos bulging outward in semicircles of cracked plaster and chipped paint. He could see the shadowy fork cranes rearing like prehistoric creatures in the thick air before him. Again, the rain broke out of the skies. He dreaded the descent into this channel of decaying life. It always left him vacant and melancholy, like he was experiencing a conscious suicide. He crossed the glossy cobbled road, hugging close to the grey façades of the storage warehouses. His breath steamed before his face, the wetness of his coat chilling his shoulders, the greasiness of his hair running on to his brow. He could taste the odour of the fried rashers and sausages he'd cooked for breakfast earlier that day.

Ahead of himself he saw a square of ruby-coloured light glowing in one of the small-windowed sheds once employed for storing animals and political prisoners. There were still rusting iron bars on the windows. Jim Larkin had his general strike down on these docks. Godwin braced himself and proceeded. A soft voice whispered to him from the patch of reddish light. 'How are ya, mister?' He saw the long equine expression of the painted face. The prostitute's hair was slung to one side in a redolent rope of shining blackness. The milky whiteness of the neck frightened him. He drew air into his lungs. 'Leave off . . .' A soft white hand touched his face. He felt the coldness of his shoulders suddenly imbued with a warm flush of blood. 'Jasus, leave off.' The prostitute gave a wry coughing laugh. Godwin stepped on to the unsettling cobblestones, driving his short legs away. 'Bitch.' The solitary word echoed in the silence of the dead warehouses.

Godwin was conscious of the pestilence of ferreting rodents feeding near him in the mountains of grain. The dark glassless windows all about him held secrets of fornication and other hidden pleasures and horrors. When he'd been a little boy he'd seen horses being blinded by the knackers on the docks. He'd never heard such screams before, the huge eyes scooped out of the heads like monstrous oysters. Godwin put his small hands to his face. He stood perfectly rigid. Behind him, the prostitute disappeared, closing the rusting corrugated door of her shed. The light still glowed when he turned his head. He heard a faint murmur, 'Don't ya hurt me . . .' The smell of acrid medication and rose-scented perfume still lingered with him.

The steel grey pylons mushroomed on the open dock where he stood facing the *Bismarck*, a huge freighter of twinkling lights. Godwin could hear the hiss of the main chimney stacks, roasting steam in the night. He laboured up the long slick tongue of the gangway, with his eyes intently watching the glittering water beneath him. When he reached the main concourse he was directed by a leathery-faced man who just turned his head slightly without averting his eyes toward Godwin. Godwin proceeded through a corridor of steel, hearing the echo of his steps on the corrugated mesh floors as he descended a level in the ship. He stared at the massive riveted bolts painted a cold glossy white. There was something strangely unseaworthy in the makeshift aspect of such rudimentary soldering. He stepped through another hatch and went down another level. Here he could hear sailors snoring, see heads and arms askew, hanging from bunks. The smell of alcoholic sleep and the oily liniment of the sailors' cotton blankets filled his nostrils. There were empty bottles of beer and cigarette butts strewn about other dormitories as he slowly proceeded. At this level the steel structure teemed with a cold moisture. He could hear the dark water lapping against the sides of the ship. The faint throb of the engine sounded somewhere near him. Godwin felt a creeping nervousness in his journey through the same cold tunnels of steel. There was a certain uniformity in each deck which made him fear that he might become lost in this vessel for ever. There was no life in this depth, only cold faces, and bodies, one on top of another in bunks. Godwin had the feeling that he was watching sardines in those lugubrious oily tins. Finally, he stepped over a blunt steel rim of yet another hatch.

A slim figure with grey fuzzy hair peeking from a black hat

sat rigid before a small table littered with documents. He said nothing, only stretched out his hand. He touched Godwin's hand, taking the requisition slip. The captain ran his finger down a long list of items and names, checking off the inventory with an adept flick of his pen.

Not wanting to look at the man, Godwin cast his glances around the small compartment. It contained a lone bed, with a blanket tucked neatly away in a box under the bed. On the far side of the compartment, there were a series of pictures of the captain. In one he was sitting rigid in military uniform, with a squat woman standing holding on to his arm before a blazing fire. In another he was in the same attire, the rigid pose an exact duplicate of the former, on some Pacific island beach in the company of a dark-skinned woman festooned in shells and colourful beads. The sky was a beautiful tropical blue.

When Godwin turned again and faced the captain, he met the man's eyes. They looked at him with severity and pride. He seemed to challenge Godwin to ask him something. He fanned a series of papers before him, letting the inky seal dry, and then handed them over the table.

Godwin left without turning his head back, thinking of the picture of that woman by the fireside with her face so round and fat, elegant without femininity, and that other face, so bronzed, white teeth, long black hair, with the dark-patch nipples. He felt a thrill of excitement for an instant. Was it possible that such a double-life could have been lived. There sat that captain, as stiff and reserved as a priest on a confessional, and he had been with some naked savage, and here he was today in all his customary severity and assiduous duty, stamping and sealing government documents of import and export with the legacy of his own life and loves watching him . . .

Godwin made his way along, ascending into the cold night air once more. A forlorn guard on duty in a heavy coat was smoking a cigarette, stepping from foot to foot in quiet agitation, making a monotonous slapping sound. He kept spitting defiantly on the deck. Godwin side-stepped the globs of phlegm and jiggled down the ramp to the quay, moving briskly to a large warehouse. Two Alsatians growled in the doorway, impeding his entrance. Godwin called out and a man stood before the dogs with impatient sternness. 'Give it here, man!'

Godwin felt the man's warm fingers running over his own hands, feeling the undulations of his skin and bones, as though reading some cryptic braille. The man wore rounded glasses which magnified and distorted his watery eyes. He left for a few minutes with his dogs slinking after him, returning with a trolley of parcels. He had an arduous face with a long projection of bony chin which he rubbed intently before he spoke. 'Sign here now, sir.'

Godwin's parcels were an assortment of soft brown packets. Each was labelled with its contents. Godwin carefully unwrapped a parcel and ran his fingers through the hair of a few wigs. The hair was exceedingly soft and fragrant.

'Queer stuff.' The man stroked one of his dogs between the ears. The other creature let its long pink tongue pant hot breaths into the cold air.

The woven hair showed no signs of being singed or even glued. Godwin marveled at the workmanship of foreigners. The undersides of the wigs were of a thin almost skin-like rubber. He scribbled his name on a piece of paper and proceeded toward a line of sleeping taxis.

'Good night, sir.'

Godwin placed his parcels in the back seat of the car. 'Stephen's Green.'

The car retraced the solitary pilgrimage of his walk. Within the confines of the warm car he bore a satisfied expression of accomplishment. He wiped the cold perspiration from his face. He felt a vague solace that such things as cars existed. Not that he had not travelled within a car before. But to retrace the horrible fears and trepidations of a previous journey in the womb of safety augured some inexplicable peace. These machines were the supreme triumph over the vicissitude of life and the past. Within the small compartment of the back seat he contemplated nothing other than the warming sensation of his fingers. The profound animalism of fear which stalked his every moment when he moved on foot suddenly became extinct. He did not have to cope with the sustained isolation of self-preservation. He held science and technology as the great liberator of all humanity, short-circuiting the pervasive animalism of damned evolution. A certain magnanimity brightened his sunken eyes as he looked now without prejudice and care to where that prostitute was in the darkness. 'Bitch,' he smirked to himself. He felt the exhilaration of freedom coursing through his tingling toes. In the front seat, the driver went on with some blather about the weather, and Godwin just nodded his head, saying, 'Tis, tis . . . bad night all right.'

He paid the fare and struggled with his parcels, the thrilling aspect of the journey still filling his senses. His small hand fumbled with the key in the lock. 'Come on, come on . . .' His whole body trembled with excitement. The curious animation of his rather large head with its tiny eyes separated by the long-bridged cartilage of nose gave Godwin the odd characteristic of seemingly trying to comprehend two different realities. The eyes floated in his head, each perceiving some part of his euphoria, the strange savageness of the cold city with its marauding populace moving behind him, the visionary incubation of a car occupying the orbit of his other eye.

He shut the door, the parcels strewn out before him. The silence of the shop was broken only by the rhythmic swing of the clock pendulum. Godwin gathered his parcels and went into the weak light of his crypt. The faceless heads stared through their dark cavities. He could see the walls were weeping from the rain outside. Black puddles formed in the cracked undulation of the stone floor. Godwin went up into the filtering greyness of the shop and searched for an electric heater. He found one in Mr Straight's office, the cord frayed and mended with red strips of electric tape.

Down in the crypt he put his hands over the three glowing bars of red heat. His coat steamed on his back as he opened the brown parcels of wigs and creamy sheeted rolls of opaque cloth. There was a small envelope of polished nails tucked into another parcel, along with a glossy catalogue of mannequins and ancillary items. Godwin laid everything out on the stone floor. The blue flame of his gas canister hissed quietly on the table behind him. The gas smelt sweet in the closeness of the oblong room. He was awed by the perfection of the cheesecloth when he unrolled some of the sheet. The three torsos wavered in shadowy ovals against the back of the crypt. He let his fingers run along the moisture of the material. It seemed to have been treated with some sort of applied lubricant. When he let the tension ease, the cloth withered and stuck to his hands and arms like some convoluted web.

Godwin's coat was hot to the touch, the bars of the electric fire burning the stagnant dust particles and paper flesh of dead moths. He took his coat off and threw it on the floor, loosening the knot of his tie, unbuttoning the top two buttons of his shirt. On the table he saw the lurid exclamation mark of the blue flaming gas. Sweat poured down his face. The walls danced in the light. He walked to his dusty shelves and took down the mesh ovals of unformed heads. The necks fanned out at the base so as to accentuate the slenderness of a female neck. He was breathing hard in the stifling claustrophobia. He understood that Mr Moran had been right about banning heaters from this buried temple. The ominous inventory of body parts remained forlorn behind him. In the far corner of the room he stared at the stiff and contorted aspect of creamy bodies all piled on one another. His feet shuffled unconsciously. He saw the ambiguous grimaced smile of some gaunt female face. A child's eye gleamed. He pulled the blue flame away. It danced on severed corpses. He reached into the abyss of limbs and heads, his eyes stark and wide. The earth breathed through the cracked walls, veins of darkish vegetation rotting on the slick surfaces. He felt the shocking cold dampness within the pit of vapid bodies. Some of the bodies looked like embalmed saints with serene eyes. He withdrew his head. The serpentine cracks in the enamelled chalk flesh were something he understood. It was the hallmark of a redundant hand, creating misrepresentations of something human. Yet the faces in the darkish light of this mass grave gave these figures some dignity in death that was always an intended possession. He understood that he did not even understand the richness of his own creations.

Godwin closed his eyes. He slumped his body in a creaking chair, his head thrust back with the light falling on the slick moisture of his neck and dirty shirt collar. The terror of the moment would pass, he kept telling himself. He closed his eyes. He wanted to revel in this moment of unabridged silence. Slowly he opened his eyes and stared at the soft pink metamorphic gauze rolled so neatly by unknown foreign hands. He saw that there was no latitude for interpretation in the uniformity of these things. These artefacts were not conceived of human frailty and longing. He looked at the foreign words of the catalogue, staring at the generic rigidity of the bodies. They were effigies to some cold mechanical process of the mind where originality was sacrificed to a denigrating principle of democracy. Godwin sat quietly thinking of the muted life within the ancient shop above him. There were secrets he knew that nobody else knew about the shop, the curious idiosyncrasies of its patrons and employees. He treasured these memories in his most solitary moments.

He laughed, the duplicity of his own creations still vivid in his mind. The close aspect of the small oblong room impressed itself around him. He thought about making tea, scanning the eerie light for the dented kettle. His eyes stopped on the three hollow torsos. He felt the slow disso-

lution into obscurity. There was a prodigious army of mannequins on foreign shores waiting to invade the sanctuary of his
life. He suppressed the welling wetness in his eyes. An
invisible enemy stabbed at him in the gloom. He felt the
wounds opening on his back. He thought of his Dublin and
his mother Liffey. His people had braced and conquered the
tyranny of oppression with the profundity of Irish faith and
tenacity through the centuries. But what now? These were
hard people, keen to the physical torture of Black and Tans,
but could those schizophrenic poets and scholars fight
phantom warriors of commerce armed with opiates of dull
copper currency?

Godwin watched his hand quiver. He envisioned the
Liffey carrying forth regiments of grey ghosts from Mountjoy
Prison. He traced her origins to the caves of the hermit Saint
Kevin, to the dark waters of Glendalough steeped with the
blood of Celtic druids. His minds moved in unconscious leaps
of faith, his own imagination etching the details of crude and
intricate experience. But what now?

He turned his eyes from the amorphous torsos. They
seemed to blur before his eyes. His fingers were trembling
again. He would not work tonight. Instinctively, he blamed
it on the weather and arthritis. He picked up a small mirror
and looked at his face, fagged with effort, the eyes sunken in
nests of wrinkles. His trembling hands let the mirror fall. He
knew he would be charged for that tomorrow. He bent
over, groping for the shards of glimmering glass. He stopped
for a moment, entranced. In each fragment he saw the full
countenance of his face, just as it had been contained in the
full square of the unbroken mirror. A lone trickle of blood ran
from the palm of his hand on to a sliver of the mirror. He
could feel the throb of the wound. He drew his head away.
'Yes, yes ...' he kept whispering. He saw that enigmatic
image of his face a thousand times reflected in the shards of
the mirror.

An awful fatigue ebbed in his body. He gathered the warm

coil of the electric heater into his hands and turned off the blue purring gaslight. He saw the shadowy length of his arm fade into the darkness. The blood was still dripping from his palm. He took a laboured breath, side-stepping the brown parcels of hair and hoary membrane, struggling from the darkness toward the lambent light of the shop, weeping.

THE MAN WHO DREAMT
OF LOBSTERS

OLD MICKELINE LAY slumped in a chair by the warm glow of the fire. The flickering light of the flames caught his dangling bony hand as it hung limply over the arm of the chair, casting two grey spears against the faint yellow of the hissing oil lamp in the embrasure of the window.

He heard the hunched shadow of his idiot grandson fingering the spokes of the spinning-wheel. He listened intently and placed the grey shadow in the corner of the room. He wanted to speak, but the words would not come, and so he sat as an idiot in the company of an idiot saying nothing as the fury of his mind arrested images. Still no words came. Old Mickeline's head nodded forward, and his eyelids began to dart back and forth under layers of soft wrinkled flesh . . .

And then there was sleep to wash the black slate of nothingness. He rose out of his crippled body and thought of the sleeping mute that lay still there and wished death upon him. The body jerked and cried bitterly into the sombre face of the hissing orange fire. But his thoughts were so delicate, and the soft collapse of burnt coal in the grate and the billowing in a tiny grey cloud of ash obliterated the shadow's thoughts, and the cloud of ash was consumed by the velvet dripping black. Yet, he strove further into the pulsing venous head. Something was left of the thought, a vague image of a crouched greyness labouring over a spinning-wheel. There was something hidden there, soothed and sustained by the dream. Old Mickeline fumbled about in the pulsing pitch-black labyrinth of his mind, but ultimately he was left impotent, and there was only the sound of the unfaltering wheel, incessantly swishing rhythmically against the raw flax fed on to its spools by the labouring idiot . . .

Suddenly, Old Mickeline jolted from slumber. His flat mottled nose twitched, and his tongue slid out from between his moist purple lips as he gasped for air. The room resonated with a mournful groan. Then paroxysms of coughing gripped his chest and threatened to choke him. But he fought hard, and soon the frantic convulsions of his chest subsided, and he sat quite at ease, turning globs of phlegm in his mouth. His ears cocked, and the sound of burning wood filled his head. He listened intently, and the hissing sizzle of oozing sap brought back memories of screaming lobsters as they were dunked into steaming pots. He had at one time been a fisherman. That had been a pleasant sound, he thought, as he vividly conjured up images of dripping lobsters with nippers snapping helplessly at the air. But his maritime memories faded. He thought of the time when he had stared with his own green eyes into the beady ink-black eyes of full-grown female lobsters, and how in that instant boiling lobsters had become an ominous murderous act. He remembered how he had plucked off the eyes from the two short rigid stalks lodged in the lobster's head. The eyes had popped under the pressure of his fingers, and white juice had trickled from them, wetting his fingers. He sought to rid himself of the memory, but it pressed on in his mind. There were lobsters everywhere, flanked by an army of crabs darting sideways, brandishing pinchers in the air. He threw his hands to his ears as the feverish snap, snap, snap picked away at his brain. He let out a horrific scream as one of the hot-tempered lobsters, as big as a man, snapping irascibly, grabbed him with its pair of mammoth pinchers . . .

Two squint eyes peered out from behind the chair in response to the noise. Old Mickeline continued to splutter cries of desperation and pleas of forgiveness before the antagonistic lobster. The eyes blinked and were once more invisible, vanishing into the darkness. All Old Mickeline heard was the grunting of something less than human near to him. He cried out.

'Michael! Where are ya, boy?'

Again there was complete silence. Old Mickeline strained to drag himself from his slouched state, but the lobster began to scream as lobsters tended to do in Old Mickeline's mind. Old Mickeline flailed his arms about. Suddenly, from behind the chair came some pawing thing. It brushed against Old Mickeline's sparse grey hair and moved quickly down to the face, stroking it gently. Old Mickeline screamed as he felt steam filter up his nostrils. He thrashed about in the chair, nearly toppling it. The black pawing thing instantaneously withdrew itself.

'Old Ickeline! I – I – It's me, Ichael,' croaked the voice of the pawing thing.

Old Mickeline heard the stertorous breathing and cried out, 'Michael! Is it yerself? Come here to me, boy!' The form held its breath and moved quietly and swiftly like a liquid cat across the room, away from the pleading demonic creature in the chair. Old Mickeline sensed it was the boy and knew he had fled from the chair. He tilted his head and craned it sideways, listening for a telltale sound in his black world, but he heard nothing. He moved his head again to the fire and once more drew phlegm from his chest. He churned it about with his massive tongue and then, with a thrust of his wizened head, spat the thick glob into the fire. It hissed violently. He began in a raucous, broken voice, enticing the boy to come forward.

'I've got lovely sweeties here for ya, Michael! Lovely yella and orange drops! Come on now, Michael! Sweeties! Sweeties!'

The idiot boy stood perfectly motionless, peering out from between the legs of the kitchen table at worn heavy boots that pensively slapped the grey stone floor.

Old Mickeline heard his own echoing slaps, and he thought how they were like drops of water dripping into brimming metallic buckets by the sides of jostling boats on a wintery day. He even shuddered as he felt the cold rainwater with his hand. Then he remembered it was only an image. Suddenly, there were incomprehensible words smashing in on his cold icy illusion.

'I a— a— ant da eeties!' croaked the voice that owned the peering eyes.

Old Mickeline drew the smoky air into his lungs, and his face was, at that moment, withered like a rotten red apple. He raised his crooked arm, and out slid a deformed hand. It was a flap of purple skin like a sow's ear, and there was just one protrusion of flesh-covered bone that ran parallel to the flap. Old Mickeline frantically tried to flick his fingers to get the boy's attention, but he could not do so. All he could achieve with the hand was a sound that vaguely resembled the faint snapping of lobsters.

'Did I hear a boy cryin for sweeties? Because I've got some lovely sweeties right here,' continued Old Mickeline.

The boy moved hesitantly and stared at the dark snapping figure. He began to sob softly, and tears welled in his red-rimmed eyes. His voice choked under the burden of the suppressed sobs. He dabbed the flowing tears, and his cheek felt wet and flushed.

'Th— Th— Throw eeties to Ichael!' he cried.

So the bait had been taken. Old Mickeline felt a surge of victory. He attempted to conceal his incandescent lust to touch something human again, but something stirred deep within his belly. He furrowed his brow and tried to think as a child would think. He fought hard to draw upon images of youth, sought to resurrect his own fears and joys. He ventured into the consciousness of a child. He remembered lollipops, how their spectre of colour had always enthralled him as a boy. Words of enticement spewed from his muttering lips.

'Lollipops! Red ones, yella ones, blue ones! Dey're all here, me boyo, if ya only come and take dem from me!'

With that he hauntingly began to snap the pinchers in the air. He let his tongue roll out of his mouth and then curled it up again in a lascivious manner. The boy heard the drawn slurping noise, and he wet his lips.

'Lollipops and sweeties! Plenty of lollipops and sweeties!'

In an instant the boy was in front of Old Mickeline, foraging like a gentle bear in Old Mickeline's lap for the lollipops.

'Wh— Wh— Where are lollipops? Ichael ant l— l— lollipops!'

Old Mickeline grunted with pleasure and grabbed at the head of the boy, pushing it into his crotch.

'Dere, dere! Is it a lollipop dat ya want?'

The stricken boy screamed, but his cries were muffled in Old Mickeline's crotch. The fire hissed on, and contorted shadows loomed large about the room, shimmering to and fro.

Old Mickeline pressed the head deeper, and he let out long deep moans. He could still hear his faint squeals. He slapped the boy's buttocks. That reminded him of when he was a boy and how he had slapped slippery pink pigs and had felt the sting in his own hand, and that had made him happy then, as it did now. He continued to slap and groan, and the boy continued to squeal.

Suddenly, the door latch was unhinged. Old Mickeline grabbed a crop of the boy's hair and snapped his head back. The boy fell to the floor like a slain animal. Old Mickeline cringed in horror at the thought that the boy was dead. All he heard was the door being kicked open. He envisioned Moire in the gaping doorway, teetering into the house like a hunchback with the weight of two pails of water under her. He thought how her face was most probably red and drenched with sweat. Moire spoke in spasms.

'Jasus Christ! I don't know at all, but da well seems to be gettin furder away every day, Mickeline.'

Old Mickeline turned his face before the chill rush of air and nodded his head up and down. With each deliberating nod he mumbled away to himself and shuffled his feet about in front of him, softly kicking the slumped body before him, hoping for a miracle. There was a helpless squeal of pain. Old Mickeline withdrew his feet. He had his miracle.

Moire's oval face moved into the drab yellow light of the oil lamp as she continued to labour with the two buckets of water. Old Mickeline heard the scrape of a bucket against the stone and caught the sound of the chopping water lapping against the walls of the buckets.

'Mickeline! Where in God's name in Michael? And for dat matter, is Peggy not around?'

Old Mickeline said nothing and saw nothing. His mind went blank as he raised his arm and plucked away at grey tufts of hairs sprouting from his nose with his pinchers. The boy revived himself and began to crawl behind the chair. Moire caught sight of his hunched crawling body and dropped the bucket of water, letting the water spill over the stones, soaking them. Old Mickeline heard the trickling water and turned his head again to the sombre fire.

'Jasus boy! What happened ta ya?'

Michael cowered away from her probing hands and massive red face.

'Ichael is a ood boy! I d— d— don't do n— n— nothin bold!'

Moire rubbed his head tenderly, running her flaccid fingers through his damp hair. She put her warm face against his convulsing head and kissed him tenderly and spoke soft words into his ear.

'Shoo, me little lamb! Yer ma's here now. What was it dat upset ya?'

The boy continued to grope at his mother's hands and made feeble attempts to free himself of her embrace.

'I t— t— tired, Mommy! I a ood boy!'

Old Mickeline winced as Moire continued coaxing the boy to tell her what happened. But he knew the boy was without the power of words. Old Mickeline smiled and held back his impulse to pinch the boy. He sat forward in his chair and listened on as the boy mumbled away in his mother's arms, and he tilted his head back and laughed gratingly away into the night. Fire burned in the mother's palpitating breast. She set her black eyes on the swathed figure and inhaled the stench of Old Mickeline's urine-drenched trousers.

'Ya did somethin to him! Didn't ya? Jasus! How many times is it I told ya not ta touch any living thing?' The mother was on her knees, rubbing her watery eyes with the hem of her tattered dress.

Old Mickeline blinked, and tiny yellow crusts fell from the corners of his eyes. His breast rose, 'I ne'er let a hand to da boy, til he started grabbin at me trouser leg. And twas then dat I laid him da boot. Mind ya, twas more of a tap dan a kick!'

Moire screamed in horror. She drew back her body, and Michael's face was soft and acquiescent before her trembling fingers.

'How could ya kick him, Mickeline? He's innocent as a fowl,' she sobbed.

Old Mickeline was content now and snapped his pinchers with immense satisfaction. 'Innocence makes a child tender, but innocence in the mind of a lumberin teenage lad is not innocence but raw violence.' Old Mickeline heard the mother sobbing, but now he wasn't content.

His face grew haggard. He gripped tight the lobster-like pincher, wishing to chop it off. He thought again of that crippled old priest in Galway Bay, how he had seemed to have been transformed from a feeble creature to a godly demeanour. He reflected in awe upon the spectre of the old priest as he embraced the world with his white surplice billowed out and mesmerizing all before him. The priest spoke in great drawn sentences at first. Old Mickeline felt as though the priest had addressed him solely. He stared into the glossy eyes of the priest, and he knew he had sinned before men and before God. He felt shamed, and the weight of his lustfulness crept patiently upon his bending spine, stopping and crouching in the marrow of his brittle grey bones. He saw the screwed-up face condemn him, and he shut his eyes and muttered prayers of forgiveness. But the priest was now roaring, and his draconian nostrils breathed fire upon his face, or so he had thought at the time. 'Vile creatures that scurry in here and beg forgiveness . . . If the eyes gaze upon filth, then pluck them out of your head, for it is better to be blind in this world than to spend eternity in the utter blackness of hell. And if the right hand steals, then let it be chopped off with an axe . . .' Old Mickeline gripped his deformed arm and beat the pink flab against the arm of the chair. Surging unequivocal pangs of disgust shot through the vile appendage. He longed to grip an axe firmly and bring it down upon the criminal hand. He longed to hear it fall with a thud on to the stone and twitch in a sticky mess. His voice was husky and his mind fragmented; guilt and vengeance clashed in his brain.

'Moire! Forgive me, please! It was da pains in me spine. Christ, Moire! I'm a broken man in a black world. It was da dream o' da lobsters, Moire! Dey were everywhere. A great female came and tried ta drag me away, and dere was dis pawin at me face. How was I supposed ta know it was himself? God forgive me, da disease dat God has cast upon me is infectin me mind as it stiffened me back not long ago.'

Moire looked at his haggard face, and pity welled in her heart. He looked so innocent, his words doleful and haunting. She wondered why God had struck him down. And she looked to her son's pale face and swore that there was beauty in what she had created, that her flesh and blood was equal to all men in the eyes of God. Still, she wondered why God had cursed her so and dredged her mind for all its filth. But she found nothing to justify her burden. She removed her cardigan and gingerly moved her son's head off her lap, nestling it on the soft cardigan. The boy groaned quietly, and she whispered that she would not leave him.

Suddenly, the latch of the door rattled, and Old Mickeline felt the snap of frosty air on his cheeks. The shrill singing voice told him that it was Peggy. 'Quiet, ya bitch!' he cried in a raw, husky voice. But the girl paid him no attention, for he still heard the rustle of her dress and the continued trot of her feet circling the room. He wished to see her in the dress she wore and longed to stroke her cold ivory hands and place them on his lap.

Moire stood by and fumed with rising madness, and a rush of blood imbued her face. She shuffled out of the shadows frantically. Old Mickeline heard the mother move and waited for a crisp slapping sound and then a howling cry by Peggy. But all he heard was Peggy, laughing on and on and twirling on and on. He jumped when a thud and groan stifled the merriment. In an instant there was a tumbling, rolling sound, as the steel balls belonging to the lobster pots were dislodged from where they hung on the wall. Old Mickeline thought it sounded like a heavy metal cannonball gone astray, rumbling along the drenched wooden gangway of a ship.

'Peggy! Jasus! Where were ya? Dere's been holy uproar while ya were out.' Moire leaned over and shook her fist before Peggy's face. Peggy went white, her voice shrill with terror.

'I was only with Sean, Ma! Ya said I was allowed ta go out for an hour when I had the dishes done, don't ya remember?'

'And ya left when me back was turned,' retorted Moire as she pressed her face forward and smiled wryly into the startled girl's face. Peggy stared back, helpless and despondent. Her vibrant excitement was snuffed as the wry smile turned grim upon her mother's face.

'Where did ya get dat dress from, Peggy?' whispered her

mother. Peggy felt the words blown into her face and smelt the breath of her mother.

'Twas Sean's sister dat gave it ta me!' she mumbled. She looked away and spied Michael shaking in the dim corner behind Old Mickeline's chair. 'What was it dat happened, Ma?' Moire beckoned with a nod of her head for Peggy to go into the back bedroom. Peggy nodded and whispered, 'Sean is outside da door, Ma. Let me tell him ta go on home.'

Moire straightened herself and glanced to the door. 'Sean! Will ya show yerself for God's sake, and don't be gawkin like a scarecrow!' she said caustically. A long face, equine in expression, poked its head through the open door. Moire watched on impatiently. Sean tiptoed into the room and fidgeted bashfully before Moire. He felt her consume his fleeting spirit of gaiety. When she sucked in her lips, he knew she was bitter, and he thought how her infectious hostility blackened his own brow. Then she pressed her tongue against her cheek, and when her lips blossomed again on her face, crinkled and moist, he felt faint.

'Peggy! Put on da kettle, will ya?' She winked at Sean, and he trembled. 'Sure it's great ta have company, isn't it?' Peggy flipped her dangling black hair out of her face and eyed Sean and giggled.

'Ah . . . Yer too generous, Mrs Ryan! I'd love ta stay, but sure I'm needed back at da house. Dere's a sick . . . a sick cow dat needs tendin!' With that he tugged at his mane of scruffy black hair.

Moire joined her hands together and rubbed them slowly and pursed her lips. 'Yer a vet, den, is dat da case, Sean?' Sean extended his chin and his bottom lip and sucked in his upper lip. He bit it hard and continued to scratch his hair. 'Well, ta be honest, I'm not certified or nothin, but I've delivered a fair number of calves in me time.'

'Oh! I'm gettin da picture now! Yer involved in midwifery.' With that, she advanced and dragged Sean by the sleeve of his shirt to where Old Mickeline sat. Old Mickeline smelt the damp odour before him. He tasted the salt in the air, and offered his pincher to Sean. The boy turned and began to neigh. His lips peeled back and his pink gums glistened with spittle. 'Well now, then.' He smiled again in ignorance. 'It's not dat I'm refusin hospitality, but it's more dat duty calls dat I'll have to pass up da feasts of your delight.'

'What's dat stupid bastard at at all?' Moire scoffed. 'Darken da door again, and you'll be skinned alive. "Feasts of your delight," how are ya?'

'I'd love ta stay for tea, but I'll be in fierce trouble if I'm not scatterin.'

Old Mickeline heard Sean tentatively chomp his teeth in anticipation of his departure. But the chomp gave way to a shriek when the rotted door shook with the blow of a fist. 'Hello dere! Is dere a saint or sinner in dere? Tis meself dat's here and the . . .' The voice of the drunkard was punctuated by a pleading call for order, by a voice that mustered feigned authority. Moire rolled her eyes into her head, and her voice whispered, 'Whist now! Jasus! I think it's yer da, and I'd swear it's da voice o' da new schoolmaster dat was carpin away at him.'

Old Mickeline shifted in his chair, and Sean retreated from him, losing himself in the dim corner behind Old Mickeline's chair. Sputtered laughter continued outside the door, and then a howl like a wolf struck madness in Moire's grey eyes. The fire hissed again, and Moire thrust her head forward and waddled awkwardly to the door and swung it open. But her husband at that very moment made a mad dash at the door, and he came careering through, colliding into Moire. He landed on the dazed body. He cursed and groped at the body, trying to roll off Moire, who lay unconscious on the floor. Old Mickeline heard the hollow hop of her head and reflexively tensed his brow.

The idiot boy instinctively sprung out of the darkness and cried horridly as he frantically pounded Franky's face. 'M— M— Mommy! I ant M— M— Mommy! Why ya urt her?'

'What's happenin?' cried Old Mickeline, inquisitively straining to peel back the pink slits of his eyes.

Sean put his face close to Old Mickeline's and relayed the terrible scene. 'Franky's after fallin like a sack o' potatoes on Moire, and he's at present smudderin her, and Michael's nothin other dan a savage dog bitin away at the cuff o' Franky's hand dat's fightin ta keep da lad at bay.'

'Jasus Christ! Franky! Get off!' croaked Old Mickeline in a rasping voice.

The schoolmaster rushed in and, although he detested having contact with anything human, he displayed a false concern for Moire's well-being. The idiot son cried on, 'I w— w— want M— M— M— Mommy!' Peggy came forward and stroked his head gently, and Michael, feeling the cool ivory hand against his forehead, violently jerked and started to lick it tenderly like a young sniffing puppy. Peggy coaxed him back to his corner, and he whimpered after her.

The schoolmaster followed the boy and caught sight of Sean's head strained over the back of Old Mickeline's chair, inches from Old Mickeline's head. The schoolmaster shivered uncontrollably, remembering the smell of the scant lacquered scab-ridden scalp. That thought had him reflexively scratch his own scalp, and he felt something stir there. He scratched again and pulled out a tiny wiggly crab-like creature and crushed it in his fingers. Old Mickeline heard the scratching and the disgust in the voice of the schoolmaster, and thoughts of crabs and lobsters became hauntingly vivid before his eyes. He beat his hand on the edge of the chair and snapped the pinchers incessantly.

'Get over here, Sean!' the schoolmaster snapped laconically. Sean hesitantly stomped his feet and straightened himself up. In one motion he emerged from the dark with an assured equanimity. He felt he could be of assistance and spat into his hands, as though ready to deliver a calf. He pointed his finger toward Peggy and shouted, 'Peggy! Get a sup a water,' and added as an afterthought, 'and a fresh linen cloth would come in handy for the blood.' But there was no blood, thought Peggy puzzled and bemused. She wondered if he was thinking of calving.

The schoolmaster dragged Franky off Moire's chest. Franky wildly swiped his hands about in the air and tried to coax the schoolmaster into a brawl. The schoolmaster's incorruptible face felt Franky's foul liquor breath. He solemnly frowned and further affirmed his hate for human frailty by retracting his hand from Franky's saturated forehead. Franky's ignominious face puffed up.

Sean knelt down before the unconscious body and brushed against the schoolmaster. The schoolmaster felt the touch and recoiled his shoulder in disgust. He wanted to slay the vet where he stood.

Sean rolled each of his sleeves up and, after cracking his knuckles, began. 'Cloth!' Peggy squatted beside him and slapped the wet cloth into his hand. Sean dabbed Moire's head with the cool water and spoke encouraging words into her deaf ear, 'Yer all right now! Da doctor's at hand.' He gave the cloth back to Peggy, and she was enthralled by his bedside manner and wanted to say, 'Is dere anything else ya need, Doctor?' but instead deleted 'Doctor' from her inquiry, fearing that her remark would be taken as an insult. She also didn't want to make a fool of herself, she added as an afterthought.

'I think I'll check da ol ticker ta see if she's still alive.' Peggy nodded in agreement. Sean began to feel about Moire's chest, until he found a soft pumping sensation under her left breast.

The lids of Moire's eyes peeled back, and she screamed as she stared into his pensive face. 'Ah! Ya filthy thing, get dem udder-grabbin fingers away from me! Jasus! I'm a dacent, God-fearin woman!'

Sean let out a scream and tumbled backward, 'Jasus, Mary, and Joseph! Peggy! Tell her I was only renderin her da benefits o' me professional capacity as a medicine man!' Before Peggy could utter a word, Moire was damning Sean and calling down on all the saints to preserve her honour.

'More of a witchdoctor it is ya are! Mother o' Jasus! I'll bate da head off ya, Peggy, for lettin dat idiot go at me.'

The idiot son crept about behind Old Mickeline's chair and sobbed softly. 'M—M—Mommy! I a ood boy! Come an r—r—rub mu ead.'

Old Mickeline reached out with his pinchers and whispered, 'Come here ta me, boy.' But the boy stood perfectly still and watched the searching pinchers snapping before his eyes. Moire's black skirt swished about as she frantically began to fling her arms and legs about in an attempt to turn herself over. Old Mickeline thought of her pink flesh and her wrinkled thighs and then of pink lobster on dripping blocks of wood by the shore, and he heard again the grating roar of the shingles. There were brooding, plotting lobsters everywhere, in the sea, hidden by the mutinous copper waves, on land, in the murky pools and crevasses. He heard them, heard the scrape of their claws on the jagged rocks, saw them darting among the rocks, heard the faint splash of their armoured tails. Now he eavesdropped on their gargled references to heavy nets and bobbing lobster pots.

The mother sat up and began to rub a large lump which had risen on her head. She stared out the greyish white mouth of the doorway. The schoolmaster saw her in the pale light of the harvest moon. He placed her among the beasts of the tropical jungles. Her simian qualities seemed so real. She opened her mouth, and all he heard was the 'Oooh ... oooh ... ah' of some primeval man. He felt privy to the secret of what man's missing link must have looked like. His thoughts were typically English, and he knew that his fellow countrymen must have, at one time or another, thought as he did now. He understood why flogging was the only way to treat these Irish peasants. The schoolmaster came to see himself as a circus trainer. He thought of the big tent and the smell of elephant manure steaming in soft heaps. He heard the crisp crack of the leather whip cutting the hinds of obstreperous beasts. He looked again, and the monkey still squatted in the doorway, and he smiled benevolently. The animal's lips moved up and down saying, 'Oooh ... oooh ... ah,' and he had a sudden urge to crack open peanuts and feed the beast.

A sprinkle of white powder glistened and fell from the mother's head, and he heard her speak as a human. 'Muinteoir! What is it dat brought yerself here ta da house?' She keenly sized him up and down and knew that he hated the word 'Muinteoir'.

He clenched his fist and said, 'If you would be so kind, Mrs Ryan, I would like you to address me by my proper name, "Schoolmaster", and refrain from using the Irish derivative.' With that, he tipped his head back and turned to Peggy. She didn't comprehend the nature of his spurious smile.

'What's wrong with sayin Irish words, Muinteoir?' Moire carped behind his back. 'Isn't dis Ireland, da land where da mother tongue is da Gaelic?' The schoolmaster did not turn, ignoring the question completely, and began to address Peggy. The mother rapped the table with her knuckles. 'Excuse me! How dare ya ignore me! If I ask a question, I'd better get a straight answer! Do ya here me?'

Sean realized his opportunity to gain favour with Moire and rolled back his burly chest and exposed his massive gummy teeth, 'Do ya hear dat, ya ignorant bastard?'

The schoolmaster approached Sean and scoffed at him, referring to his teeth as 'something only a horse would envy'. Sean bobbed and weaved about the room and threw blows to the left and right of the schoolmaster's face, but the school-master never flinched.

Moire's face grew stiff with rage, and she bellowed out, 'For da love a Jasus! Will ya quit da fool actin, Sean?' He stopped suddenly, inches from the schoolmaster's face, and panted madly for air. 'Right! But by God, man, ya got away this time from a batin, but next time dere won't be da womenfolk ta save ya!' He winked at Moire, and she turned up her lips in disgust. Peggy's face went red with shame. Sean went mad, sandwiched between the dour eyes. He once again shot his face into the schoolmaster's face and heckled away, 'Muinteoir! Muinteoir!'

Moire unceremoniously dove at Sean and pushed him into a chair by the table. 'I'll fight me own battles, if it's all the same to ya, Sean! Yer nothin but an ignorant amadawn!' She then pivoted about on the heel of her foot and spat into the face of the schoolmaster. 'God forgive me!' she cried, 'Twas a sneeze dat got away from me, Muinteoir!' The schoolmaster stood motionless, leaning on his furled umbrella. The monkey needed a beating, he thought to himself, as the sticky mucus dripped off his face on to his brown coat. He ran his fingers over the grooves on the handle of the umbrella. He wanted to teach her a good lesson. He longed for the swishing sound of the whipping black tongue as it wrapped about the vile insubordinate creature. He teetered, inebriated by the lust to maim. But he did not strike, and when he opened his mouth, it was to say, 'God bless you.'

Moire was shocked and distraught, but she said, 'Thank ya,' and offered the schoolmaster a seat before the fire, which he obligingly took. Peggy broke out laughing, and even Sean could not refrain from cracking a grin. Moire cast an insidious eye upon Peggy. The black of Moire's eye grew in lustre, and Peggy was afraid of the throbbing thing. Yet, she remained calm and gingerly looked down at the floor. 'Dat's it! Stop gawkin at me, and stick on da kettle for tea dis minute!'

The kettle was filled promptly and suspended over the heart of the fire. Moire leaned over her husband, and his weatherbeaten face was swollen purple in patches. 'How much did Franky consume, Schoolmaster?' The schoolmaster set the spitting matter aside and wallowed in his victory over the beast. He had used intelligence to outwit the spitting ape, he gloated to himself. He strove for his most exaggerated English accent, 'I heard him brag that he drank an amount to the tune of four shillings.'

Moire let her husband's head drop to the floor, and he groaned, 'What da fuck is at ya, man?'

'Jasus! Did ya drink a river dry? Four shillins is more dan two pints o' whiskey!' Franky blinked, and an imperturbable flushing warmth made his head swoon. He didn't fight back, but asked for a hot sup of tea.

'I'll give ya milk instead; it'll coat yer stomach,' retorted Moire.

Franky again raised his head and began to grow fierce. 'But I'm not partial ta milk! Jasus, every time ya make me drink da stuff, I get a rash!'

'Well den, ye'll have nothin at all!' she shouted unrelentingly.

Old Mickeline leaned forward in his chair and stoked the decaying light of the fire. He tapped about with the poker until he felt the heap of turf stacked out of the way of the flames. He took out a sod of the crumbling turf and tossed it into the fire, and a spray of iridescent needles flew up out of the ash, vanishing in an instant. The schoolmaster was burned by one of the needles and jumped back from the fire as Old Mickeline flung another sod into the grate. The schoolmaster inspected his hand and rubbed the red blotch. He looked again, and a black smear ingrained itself into the red. 'Well then,' he began.

Old Mickeline listened to the inflection of the voice and hated the man. He began to snap his claw again as he bent his head down before the schoolmaster. He asked in a menacing manner, 'Sir! Would ya be so kind as to count the scabs on my head?' His laugh was short and hoarse. The schoolmaster wanted to bury an axe in Old Mickeline's skull, but he only withdrew his head and swallowed hard.

'Why did ya come ta Ireland, Schoolmaster?' inquired Moire, as she searched the cupboard for clean cups.

The schoolmaster looked sheepishly at the turf, and he saw himself burning. He cringed in despair as his effigy grew red and then grey in the intense blaze. 'I was once in the camp of the Marxists,' he said without expression. 'I came as a pilgrim, as a banished man in search of paradise'. His head rose. 'I had always felt that a true prophet would never be accepted in his own land, so when they scorned and ridiculed me, I paid them no heed. I was beyond nationalism, beyond paying allegiance to a false idol . . .'

'Here! Here! Up the King's arse!' interrupted Franky as he dragged himself to his feet.

The schoolmaster was oblivious to everything except his burning effigy, throbbing and flaking in decay amid the blazing flames. 'I thought there was hope in your daughter! She listened in class, and her eyes lit up with the mention of paradise! I said, "Comrade," and she said, "Yes, Comrade," and that was beautiful.' All eyes fell upon Peggy. She began to say something as she opened her mouth, but her father cut her off.

'Go on, man!' shouted Franky.

'What a fool I was. A Marxist in a land of saints and scoundrels. Ireland is no place for atheists. I dare say, there's less freedom here than in all the world.'

'Well Jasus, dat's da tyranny o' da English for ya!' snapped Moire.

The schoolmaster turned and looked into her fierce-grimaced face and whispered, 'No, ma'am. The tyranny of England could never approach the tyranny of Rome. If the English had enjoyed that success in Ireland, you peasant Irish would be kissing the King's ring and singing proudly, "Britannia rules".'

Sean sat with his mouth gaping wide, and his eyes never flinched. He addressed the back of the schoolmaster, 'Ya say ya were banished from England cause o' yer dealin with Marks's?'

'Those fools! It's the poor that disgust me. Karl Marx said it best. The proletariat lacks "class consciousness".' The schoolmaster threw his hands to his head and shook with the burden of idiocy that strangled his genius.

'Franky! Dere's Marks's livin in da next town, isn't dere?' Sean asked in an unsure tone. 'Jasus! I thought dere was anyway!'

Franky rubbed his chin and tried to think, but his head ached every time he tried to remember. Finally, he shouted an emphatic, 'Yes! Dey're a shower o' rebels if ever dere ever was. A couple o' them wanted ta start a rebellion with a landlord, and what proceeded was a bloody affair. Oh! I remember it well now. Dere were leaflets circulated about the place about them.'

The schoolmaster stopped groaning. 'You mean to say that there is a popular movement of Marxists in the next town?'

He jumped out of his chair, and it fell to the floor, knocking against Old Mickeline's legs. Everyone waited for Old Mickeline to scream, but he didn't. Moire knew that the disease had fully numbed his legs, and she was once more conscious of the pervasive smell of decay and stale urine.

'I don't know about popular, Schoolmaster,' began Franky. 'Dere was a fair squanderin o' lives, and in the end the Marks's were beaten badly by da law.'

The schoolmaster could not believe it. His tongue hung out of his mouth in amazement.

'Is that why your girl called me "Comrade"? This family is involved with the Marxists. I suppose that fellow in the corner is only a spy in the guise of an idiot.'

The idiot peered out from behind the chair at the mention of the word 'idiot'. He had a furry rodent which squealed faintly in his mouth. Old Mickeline jerked his head back and shrieked, 'Da Lobsters! Dey're here, Moire! Save me, for Jasus' sake!'

The idiot boy dropped the rodent and cried. 'I a ood boy! M— M— Mommy! I ant food!'

Moire ran over to her son and slapped his hand, 'Don't play wit dem things again! Do ya hear me, Michael?' The idiot son cried even louder, and Old Mickeline convulsed in his chair. Even Franky saw the dripping custard flowing from his father's eyes and wished for death to fall upon his father. Moire heard her husband's mumblings and so prayed for death, too. She then turned to the schoolmaster and screamed, 'Don't dare refer ta my son as an idiot!'

'The secrets of the movement are safe with me, Comrade,' shouted the schoolmaster as he clapped his hands together. His sentences rambled on and on, 'And to think I was in the hub of a Marxist insurrectionist movement and failed to make contact for so long.' He shook his head in utter disbelief. 'How did you know I was with the Marxists?'

'Jasus Christ! It seems dat da Marks's have gained support in England and are comin ta free Paddy Marks from his state of captivity, he bein secured in a Dublin gaol and all. Christ Almighty! And ta think dat da sheep-rustlin bastard was only livin in the next town!' cried Sean.

The schoolmaster wasn't listening. Tears filled his eyes. 'And to think that I was actually giving up on the Marxists. To think that I sat here only moments ago and witnessed what I thought to be an effigy of myself.' He ran and embraced Sean, crying out, 'Comrade! Working men of the world, unite!'

Sean shrugged off the schoolmaster. 'I'm no friend o' da Marks's. Dem filthy sheep-thievin bastards. As a matter o' fact, if yer such good friends o' dem, tell dem dat I'm holdin dem responsible for da slaughterin o' me best ewe.' With that, he banged his fist on the woodworm-ridden table.

Moire watched as Franky turned to the window and lowered his bruised face. She blinked and then saw her husband's eyes roll back in his head. She stared hard into the eyes, tracing red thread-like strands of blood against the pale glimmering white film of the eyes sunken deep into wet sockets. Moire stared on and on. He was but forty years of age, but he looked more a man of sixty. There was no romance in her heart, rather the figure before her only reminded her of pain and suffering now. But she could not hate him, just as she could not hate herself. To hate would have been a luxury. To live at the edge of the mutinous foaming beast was to know no such luxury. There was only honour and respect for the unknown, and, when the hoary mist crept upon the land and froze all living things, husband and wife nestled together by the crackling fire, and they bathed each other in the warmth of their own foul breath. And the smell of their warm fish-breath was not so disgusting, but pleasant in the wake of the white world beyond.

The outside world was real and murderous to her, its description etched perfectly in her mind. Suddenly, she shuddered and saw the lone pulverized tree with its shimmering crusts of ice . . .

And as she stared on and on at her husband, the bruised face grew placid, and the pink lids were slowly drawn down like heavy falling curtains at the end of the act. From somewhere beyond, a voice echoed faintly, impinging on her cold universe.

Old Mickeline heard the trenchant voice of the schoolmaster. It was a sharp voice, keen and precise, and he thought how the schoolmaster used it like tweezers to pick at the hearts of the confounded. Old Mickeline seemed to feel the pinching tweezers pluck away at the rotten quivering jelly of his infected brain. Again, his pincher began to snap frantically, and he moaned and spat up pieces of his lungs with extreme agony.

'I gave her German books! I wanted to deconstruct her pristine mind. The innocent white dress had to be soiled, the body had to be pummelled by the desperate kicking boots of the working men,' shouted the schoolmaster. The inflections of his voice were low and drawn. Old Mickeline knew the schoolmaster's sanity had snapped at that instant. He snapped his pincher, and he howled out again, 'Muinteoir! Please! Please come pick da crab lice out o' me brain, for I'm forever hearin da snap, snap o' deir pinchers.'

The schoolmaster turned and raised his quivering arm

before Peggy. 'Comrade! God is dead, and the New Word will be made flesh in the birth of the Marxist state.'

'Here! Dere'll be no talkin o' God in a Christian household!' roared Franky. He tensed his face and struggled to say what he meant. 'I mean . . .' Old Mickeline heard Franky bang his fist on the edge of his chair in complete madness. 'Jasus! Well anyway!' Franky regained composure, and Old Mickeline sensed him draw in a long slow breath of air. 'What's dis about Peggy readin Germanish books? Sure she can't understand the Germanish language,' he said in an irreverent mocking tone. Old Mickeline marvelled at his son's tenacity and now longed for the schoolmaster to leave them be with their own language and friendship.

The schoolmaster smiled at the seemingly calculating figure of the father. He wondered if all the Marxists were so conniving and secretive and so apt to play the town idiot before strangers.

Sean broke into a contemplative vein and addressed Franky. 'Regardin yer question concernin Peggy's knowledge o' da Germanish, I feels as though I can be an enlightenin source, seein dat I completed sixth class. It's not dat Peggy is in command o' da Germanish, rather, it's dat da book is a translaughterin from da Germanish.'

Old Mickeline laughed to himself and let his tongue hang out like a panting old dog. He shook his head violently, and another stream of greenish vomit erupted from his open mouth. 'Jasus! Get a cloth,' cried Moire frantically. The gargled sound of the spewing half-digested food reminded him of the plotting lobsters . . . Now the gargled whispers of the lobsters were filled with cryptic allusions to 'the bourgeoisie' and 'the proletariat', and he even heard mention of a faction of 'red army crabs' that had pinched and plucked their way to victory over a 'bourgeoisie emperor crab'. Old Mickeline hid all the while, behind a jagged rock washed with a hoary veil, and thought about ambushing the lobsters. He heard the fierce communion of the lobsters' sensibilities as they snapped their pinchers in unison. He, too, kept time with the lobsters and stroked the inside of his thigh. The incessant snap, snap, snap soothed his hatred, and soon he was wanting to fall before the prodigious female lobsters, wanting to kiss their cold, shiny pinchers, begging them to accept him as one of their own . . .

And then Old Mickeline felt a wet smelly cloth being dabbed about his mouth. There was the drone of Franky mumbling to himself. Old Mickeline listened on and envisioned his son gingerly scratching the cleft of his chin in an intense display of idiocy. Again, Old Mickeline coughed up phlegm and was content with his ruminative thoughts dwelling on the image of acquiescent lobsters greeting him with open pinchers and calling him 'Comrade!'

'"Translaughterin" seems a strange word, Sean. What does it mean in da precise meaning?' queried Franky.

Sean understood that Franky was thoroughly bewildered by the domineering presence of the schoolmaster. He grinned with immense satisfaction and eyed Franky. 'Well, translaughterin is da kind o' goin-ons dat da philosophizin sort do be engaged in. Only, da problem does be dat dey do be gettin da old words all wrong as dey write dem inta da other language. Usually, translaughterin is concerned with some o' da Greekish philosophizers. Dere does be hundreds o' da books in da English about da Greekish fella by da name a Paddy O'Something-or-other.'

'Plato is the name of the philosopher, Comrade!' interrupted the schoolmaster. The schoolmaster sat by the fire nodding his head, all the while in disbelief at the sheer secrecy and bravado of his fellow Marxists. He felt unsettled and thought they were consciously testing him. He in turn thought of ways to win the favour of his allies.

Old Mickeline heard the schoolmaster clearing his throat and waited for the tweezer-like selection of precise words. But it was Franky's demonstrative voice that fought to reaffirm itself as the voice of authority and action. Old Mickeline tried to swallow the phlegm in his mouth, but it was blocked from sliding down his throat by a swollen flap of flesh. He coughed violently. He heard a glass shatter and then the grumble of Moire. The idiot son screamed in terror and cowered in the corner like a frantic animal.

Old Mickeline heard him cry out, 'I d—d—don't ant a l—l—lollipop, Old M—M—Mickeline!' But he could not respond to the idiot. Old Mickeline roared, and the lodged phlegm was spat up into his mouth. Then he sat still and tasted a faint sweetness in the phlegm. He knew it was blood.

Franky began again. 'Peggy! Gimme da book dat da Muinteoir gave ya!' The schoolmaster didn't flinch and winked at Franky with uncanny affection. 'Muinteoir it is, Comrade!'

Peggy came out of the back bedroom with the book dangling between her fingers. Franky watched her approach him, and looked into her green eyes. He nodded his head and said, 'Thank ya, Comrade!' in an exaggerated tone.

Old Mickeline smelt the scent of Peggy's damp body and rubbed the inside of his leg with his pinchers. The idiot boy was also drawn by the sweet scent of his sister's body. He stopped pawing at the squirming furry brood of wet black baby rats and crept slowly forward into the yellow light. Old Mickeline heard the sniffling snoutish nose and, in one sweeping motion, swung his pincher into the blunt face. The idiot fell over and cried in a broken, sobbing voice, 'Ah! I h—h—hurt! H—h—help me, Mommy! Tell Old M—M—Mickeline, I d—d—don't ant l—l—lollipop!' Old Mickeline let his head fall back, and a trenchant howling issued forth from his gaping face. It struck terror in those about him. Old Mickeline's pincher pulsed from the sting of the blow, and he squeezed it with his other hand.

The idiot continued to scream on and on, 'I d—d—don't ant l—l—lollipop, Old M—M—Mickeline!' Peggy fell to her knees and embraced the idiot and whispered soothing words into his ears, 'Yer okay, Michael! Dere is no harm dat will come to ya!' But the idiot heard the howling laugh of Old Mickeline and squirmed away from Peggy in terror.

'Lollipops! Lollipops! I've got lollipops for me great ol laddy, Michael!' Old Mickeline's succulent tongue rolled out of his mouth. He wanted to pinch the nape of the idiot's neck and then laugh madly as the idiot croaked away incomprehensibly. 'Come to me, lollipop!' he cried in a shrill tone once more.

Franky sat motionless, gripped in appalled muteness. Somehow he couldn't bear to look at his idiot son reeling in the arms of Peggy. But the hair on the back of his flaccid hands stood erect, and he tried to open his mouth. He could hardly breathe, suffocated by the tyranny of his father's ominous presence.

The horrors lingered in the schoolmaster's brain, and the laughing old man wouldn't stop. He stared into the horrible contorted face seeping yellow custard puss from squint eyes. He shut his own eyes tightly and rubbed them. He felt as though he were being infected by the primeval roar of an inhuman beast. These were no Marxists, he cried to himself. They were too base and vile, too animalistic even to ponder the words 'restraint' and 'revolution'. The schoolmaster wanted to move, to run from the claustrophobic house and curl up snug in his own house. He longed for the solitary sanctuary of his thoughts. 'Let the bitch be with those who worship bovine gods,' he screamed out as he suddenly rose, looming over Franky.

Moire's face was pallid, and her massive chin sagged as she lowered her head to the sight of her idiot son gently stroking a squealing wet rat once more. She said nothing and caught sight of the schoolmaster fleeing the house like a grey phantom. In an instant, the black night absorbed him into nothingness, and it was as though he had never existed. But what did exist, and what had existed for an eternity, was the mournful wailing of Old Mickeline. That cry had assaulted her in her waking and sleeping hours. That scab-ridden face had smiled and placed wet lewd kisses on her trembling lips when she slept in the arms of her husband.

'M—M—Mommy! M—M—Mommy! I don't ant l—l—lollipop!' cried the idiot in terror, as he heard Old Mickeline beat his pincher against the arm of the chair.

Moire stared at the incarnation of sin, and winced her massive face as the image of an idiot with a wet black rat in its mouth congealed in her brain. And although she turned her eyes to the grey floor, she could not stop the image. Worse still, the idiot seemed to grow more severely deformed as the image persisted. Now his harelip was a grotesque cleft of scar tissue, bleeding green liquid. 'Was it me sins, Lord?' she whispered in the droning manner of a tortured soul that would have welcomed death as a gentle bearer of a sweet destruction.

Franky was not drunk now. Rather, he was sober and melancholy, and tears streamed down his face, as though he were staring into the centre of the sun, staring into a fierce light that revealed absolutely nothing but pain and blindness. He cried helplessly, peering out of watery eyes into the beguiled face of his wife. He wanted to drive his fist into her face. He shot his eyes to the wall where a hanging cross cast a shadow upon his wife's back. Yet, there was no consolation in the effigy of a half-naked bastard who bled to death all those years ago in a foreign land. Where was the loving father when the son felt the nails pierce the blue blood of his royal veins? Violence was the final expression of love. There were to be no words, only blood. With the image of blood congealing upon all things, Franky jumped out of his chair and ran out of the open door, screaming.

Old Mickeline bit frantically into the pincher, and the blood tasted hot and sweet. He heard his son's screams fade into oblivion, and now he was only conscious of Moire's false teeth clattering violently.

'Jasus! I'm goin after him!' Then the door slammed closed and Old Mickeline felt another snap of frost against his puffed cheeks.

All that remained in Old Mickeline's brain was the sound of Moire's clattering teeth, and that brought back memories of the lobsters as they crept out from under shifting shingles and crevasses along the jagged coasts.

'Where's dere a stick so I can light da lamp, Old Mickeline?' Peggy blurted in terror, as she fumbled about in front of the faint orange face of the fire.

Old Mickeline listened closely and didn't hear the hiss of the oil lamp. Her pasty trembling voice told him of her presentiments. He moaned quietly and reached for the poker. He felt the cold iron rod and rolled it back and forth in his pincher. He opened his mouth and extended his face out before the orange glow. 'Come here and I'll give it ta ya,' he said in a soft coaxing voice. He sniffed the air, and the redolent smell of her hair brought back memories of young girls. A goad of pain shot through his pincher, and he heard the clang of the poker as it fell against the cold stone floor.

Peggy shrieked in astonishment and threw herself away from the grasping pincher that beat the arm of the chair. 'Stop it, Mickeline!' she pleaded helplessly.

Then there was silence, save for the snapping pincher. Old Mickeline still smelt the fragrant hair, and he reflexively buried his pincher between his thighs.

. . . It was a dripping day. Sweat dripped off the foreheads of shuffling women. Plum-faced children capered about purple ankles. The lane drip, drip, drip, dripped. Rippling shallow pools were blinding. He needed cool relief for his thick congealing blood. A man's lips moved, and he wondered who he was speaking to, and then he felt the pain, and the drips of blood dripped and dripped down his chin and dotted the granite path. The girl was lost, and the tears dripped, dropped down her face. He pressed a stiff finger to his face, and that made her smile, and there were no more tears to drip, drop. He moved quickly away. She trotted beside him. Her lips moved, too, and he moaned. He said there were lollipops for her, and the lustre of her red lips glistened in the heat. He saw her reflection in the pool and the reflection of a yellow ball amid a slate-blue background. She liked red ones the best. He had a big red one. She said she would cry. That wasn't a lollipop! She didn't like him. Her little face was a crumpling ball of paper. There was a hole that opened wide on the face. He heard the crack. She lay quite still, limp in his hand. She could not cry. He shivered and moaned. He opened his coat, and her face vanished. He moaned, she groaned. There was a sharp pain. The clump of black hair felt like velvet. It smelled like mink oil. The slapping sound was crisp. There was a stinging feeling in his hand. The face was swollen and purple. He didn't like the face. He heard the hopping sound of the head, like the hollow echo of a woodpecker at work. It resonated, hopping from between the dripping grey walls. The face wasn't a face any more. The lane dripped and dripped red. He was in the street, blind. The glimmer of sun oppressively bright . . .

The air dripped red and stained the outer world. Hostile faces pressed through a sea of lapping sanguine cringing faces. Rattle, tattle went the evening, and a horse trotted by and shook music from its harness. The bells distorted his face. Now the horse was gone, but the elephantine face remained. Tolling bells . . . The priest remained in the pulpit. Swish, swish went the ashen surplice. Swish, swish went the stick. 'Peel the flesh; flay the moist bloody pink flesh.' 'And if the hand offends, then chop it off; if the eyes see what they should not, then pluck them out.' He sat below. A cataract of spraying spit fell like a mist upon his head. A baptism, redemption . . .

Chop, chop went the butcher's cleaver. Meat fell with a thud. Flies swarmed in the dripping pools of blood. He tasted the wet sawdust in the air. A little girl sucked a lollipop. He screamed. Everyone stared. The girl ran. A trail of sawdust followed her out of the butcher's. She was stuffed with sawdust. He scooped sawdust up in his palm. He wanted to go to the dripping lane and stuff the sawdust into the rag doll with the bloody ... But she had no face. He wiped the sawdust off his hands.

He was by the sea. The creeping beetles were dripping, and the canvas boats melted in the sun. His hands were black, red and sticky. The tar tasted black and granular. He spat wildly. 'Cut it off!' The wizened face of the priest reared up before him, the face embedded in a lobster's shiny shell. The face stared into his green eyes, demanding justice.

He fumbled in his trousers. Young girls shrieked. The lollipop man stood erect and laughed madly before the mutinous copper sea. The hands were sticky, and he stopped moaning. He was limp. The sea breeze sent a tingling sensation through his spine. His exposed penis hung and dripped and dripped in the cool breeze.

Snap, snap, went the lobster's pinchers. The cleaver felt wet in his hand. He tasted the salt in the air. He looked into the condemning lobsters' black liquid eyes. One of them advanced and brandished its pincher, admonishing him, lecturing him. He pinched the beady black balls. The lobster clawed and snapped aimlessly, profoundly blind and maimed. He flung it into the sea, and it sank into the depths of the chill blackness. Another lobster pinched him. He turned about. 'If the hand offends, then cut it off!' it gargled furiously.

The cleaver came down with a thud on the black and bloody hand. Sea gulls squawked in alarm, and lobsters frantically clawed their way from the pooling blood.

He fell and lay still. Someone shouted, miles away, 'Don't touch him, look at the scabs on his legs!' He could not move. His eyes were stung by brimming pools of frigid saltwater.

'We didn't want the lollipops,' cried little girls. He smelt them and moaned dolefully. They ran, and he saw their pigtails bob up and down as they vanished into the purple horizon.

A lobster clawed its way to where his face lay. 'Glory be to

God! It is done!' it said in a forgiving voice that curiously wallowed in the thought of the dripping bloody fingers and loved the violence infinitely more than the cure . . .

The idiot boy rocked back and forth in a mesmerized state. He crept out into the waning light of the sombre fire. Old Mickeline lowered his head, and a languid smile eased the tension of guilt.

'Eggy! Come ere, Eggy! I g—g—got lollipops! Red lollipops,' called out the idiot in a faltering mimic of Old Mickeline's voice.

Old Mickeline waited for the infinite terror of Peggy's shrill screams. Impatiently, he plucked away at the blotched wattle of red and purple flesh hanging from his neck. Then he heard the idiot prowling forward, like a black cat. 'L—l—lollipops! C—C—Comrade!' the idiot said in a low purring voice.

Old Mickeline reached out with his pincher and stroked the idiot's jet-black hair. 'Give her da lollipop, lad!' he said in a droll tone.

Peggy screamed and Old Mickeline heard the pitter-patter of her feet. But the idiot boy was far too quick. Old Mickeline thrust his pincher between his legs again and howled maddeningly on. Snap! Snap! He was at ease, and the brutal tranquillity of his world was ink-black. He nodded his head up and down and felt the sticky corruption oozing forth as he whispered to the idiot boy, 'Lollipops! Lollipops! There's a girl that loves lollipops!'